A PLUM

KATE VEITCH is a journalist a. ... Melbourne, Australia. Currently, she divid ... between San Francisco and New South Wales, Australia.

Praise for Kate Veitch's *Without a Backward Glance*

'A compelling drama with a lot of heart and humanity, impossible to put down.' —*Australian Women's Weekly*

'Similar to Anne Tyler in her wry affection for her characters and to Anita Shreve in her aptitude for crafting compulsively readable plotlines, Kate Veitch delivers a remarkably assured debut.' —*Booklist*

'A self-assured, moving, hopeful story about the frailties of one – all – families, and the capacity to rage and to forgive.' —*The Age*

'A powerful read . . . Veitch writes with sharp insight into the dynamics of families and the clusters of vulnerabilities, longing and tenderness which define them.' —*Adelaide Advertiser*

'A vivid dissection of a fractured family. Veitch has created an enthralling tale of the private sphere.' —*Australian Book Review*

Trust

kate
veitch

A PLUME BOOK

PLUME
Published by Penguin Group
Penguin Group (USA) Inc., 375 Hudson Street, New York, New York 10014, U.S.A. •
Penguin Group (Canada), 90 Eglinton Avenue East, Suite 700, Toronto, Ontario, Canada M4P 2Y3
(a division of Pearson Penguin Canada Inc.) • Penguin Books Ltd., 80 Strand, London WC2R 0RL,
England • Penguin Ireland, 25 St. Stephen's Green, Dublin 2, Ireland
(a division of Penguin Books Ltd.) • Penguin Group (Australia), 250 Camberwell Road,
Camberwell, Victoria 3124, Australia (a division of Pearson Australia Group Pty. Ltd.) •
Penguin Books India Pvt. Ltd., 11 Community Centre, Panchsheel Park, New Delhi – 110 017,
India • Penguin Books (NZ), 67 Apollo Drive, Rosedale, North Shore 0632, New Zealand
(a division of Pearson New Zealand Ltd.) • Penguin Books (South Africa) (Pty.) Ltd.,
24 Sturdee Avenue, Rosebank, Johannesburg 2196, South Africa

Penguin Books Ltd., Registered Offices: 80 Strand, London WC2R 0RL, England

Published by Plume, a member of Penguin Group (USA) Inc. Previously published in a Viking
Australia edition.

First American Printing, July 2010
10 9 8 7 6 5 4 3 2 1

Copyright © Kate Veitch, 2010
All rights reserved

Ⓟ REGISTERED TRADEMARK—MARCA REGISTRADA

LIBRARY OF CONGRESS CATALOGING-IN-PUBLICATION DATA
Veitch, Kate.
  Trust / Kate Veitch.
    p.   cm.
  ISBN 978-0-452-29635-0
  1. College teachers—Fiction.   2. Women art teachers—Fiction.   3. Accidents—Fiction.
4. Life change events—Fiction.   5. Self-actualization (Psychology)—Fiction.
6. Australia—Fiction.   I. Title.
  PR9619.4.V45T78   2010
  823'.92—dc22   2010011200

Printed in the United States of America
Set in Bembo

All truths wait in all things,
They neither hasten their own delivery nor resist it,
They do not need the obstetric forceps of the surgeon.
The insignificant is as big to me as any.
What is less or more than a touch?

from Walt Whitman's 'Song of Myself',
found underlined among Clarice Beckett's papers

BEFORE

ONE

Knees bent, racquet poised, Susanna waited tensely at the net for Gerry, behind her, to bounce the ball his ritual three times. There: *tok! tok! tok!* Yet, for all that she'd steeled herself, still she flinched as the yellow blur whizzed past her right ear. The week before, her husband's erratic killer serve had thudded into her lower back at top speed; the bruise was still there. No matter if this was just their local club's B-grade mixed doubles match, Gerry always believed in playing hard.

Joe, receiving, barely reached it in time. His soft return should have been an easy shot for Susanna, but instead she froze, then swiped her racquet ineffectually through the air. Gerry let out an anguished yelp and lunged forward – too late.

'For god's sake, Suze,' he cried. 'Blind Freddy could've got that!'

'Sorry,' she said, grimacing. 'I thought you —'

'That was *yours*. You've got to kill it!'

She frowned at the handle of her racquet and shifted her grip. At least the sun wasn't in her eyes any more, its light filtered now through the trees that bordered the courts, on the edge of a large park. They switched sides and she crouched at the ready again, trying to look like a serious player.

They lost that game, and Susanna heard her husband suck

exasperated breath in sharply through his teeth. Joe's partner, Wendy, gave her an encouraging smile as they changed ends, and Susanna made a grateful passing comment about the trees, how thin the spring leaf cover was this year. 'The drought,' said Wendy succinctly.

Susanna nodded sadly, wondering if the verdant Melbourne she'd grown up in was gone forever. 'Remember how we always used to moan about the rain?' But Wendy, ready to play on, didn't answer.

As Joe prepared to serve, Gerry hissed at Susanna, 'Remember, he hits topspin, so you've got to cut it.' *Cut it?* she wanted to ask. *Remind me how you do that?* Then Joe's serve came, and seemed manageable, but her return sailed way over the baseline. Instantly her ears were pinned back, alert for Gerry's admonition.

'What'd I say? Cut it, cut it!'

'Not a Grand Slam y'know, Gerry,' called Wendy across the court. 'Go easy.'

'Not to worry, Wen,' he said, an easy grin in his voice. 'Susanna likes to get a bit of advice, don't you Suze?'

'Absolutely.' She gave Wendy an airy wave across the net.

As they played on Susanna managed several decent, practical serves, even holding her own in a couple of rallies, but she felt besieged. Joe and Wendy were not just stronger but also more strategic players than her, which as she understood was why their blasting returns were always aimed at her rather than Gerry, who'd taken a step down from A-grade to play doubles with her this year. *Strategy's just not my strong suit.* Susanna knew that, but it had never been a problem in the years when she'd played with her mother and their friends. They'd laughed a lot; sometimes they lost track of the score, and didn't even care.

Just do your best, she told herself. *It'll be over soon, and then you can relax.* Immediately, a voice in her mind shot back: *No you can't! Remember? The exhibition. The article.* Susanna cringed. Belinda, the head of her department, had been incredibly patient, but she was going to have to come up with the goods. Her job, Belinda had made clear, depended on it, but without a single idea to offer she —

'Suze!' Gerry yelled, and she snapped to attention just in time, thankfully, to make a passable shot.

Finally the match ended, and as they walked off the court together Wendy made a point of saying 'Well done, Susanna.' Susanna smiled her thanks. She found Wendy a bit intimidating. Nominally, they both taught at the same university, but Wendy was a professor of law with a big office in the heart of the main campus, while Susanna had pottered along for almost fifteen years at an outer-suburban annexe of the visual arts department. Very much the poor cousin.

There were no facilities at these courts, so they'd all left their bags on a bench in the shade. 'Glass of wine?' Gerry asked, unzipping the natty black cooler they'd brought. Susanna handed round acrylic glasses while he unscrewed the cap from the bottle, and poured. 'To the victors,' he said sportingly, raising his glass in a toast.

'Cheers!' Wendy and Joe responded; all took that first welcome sip. The wine was a New Zealand sauvignon blanc, greener than grass, and after the first mouthful Susanna realised that what she needed first was water. Placing her glass carefully at her feet, she glugged half the contents of her refillable water bottle. '*Rraah!*' cawed a nearby raven hoarsely, as though its throat was parched too. She looked up at the big glossy bird, watching her with a beady interrogative eye from his perch on a nearby branch. The tree, like so many in the park, looked like it was on its last gasp.

Joe was raising his glass to Gerry. 'Well, and here's to the famous architect. Heard you being interviewed on Radio National the other day. You won some competition in the States, right?'

'Design for an art gallery extension in Kansas City,' said Gerry.

'Yeah, that was it. Fantastic, Gerry!' Joe clapped him on the shoulder.

'It's a pretty big goal for us to kick, all right.' Gerry flicked back his thick, still-blonde forelock a couple of times with the splayed fingers of one hand, wearing that sweetly serious look that always made Susanna think of Robert Redford. His eyes were just like Redford's too: the blue of old denim, and twinkling, and irresistible. 'We're hoping this'll really put Visser Kanaley on the map.'

'As if you're not already!' said Joe. 'What did the bloke on that show call you? Australia's most innovative architect?'

'One of,' Gerry said, with a small self-deprecating gesture. '*One of* Australia's most innovative architectural firms.'

'Not just Australia,' said Susanna, taking a half step forward; he rested an arm along the top of her shoulders. 'Gerry's concept of interstitial development is getting serious attention in Europe, too, as well as —'

'Connective interstitial envelopment,' he corrected, and gave a modest shrug. 'My little niche.'

'Connective interstitial envelopment,' repeated Wendy, slowly, as though weighing each syllable. 'What exactly does that *mean*?'

'Briefly? Utilising existing buildings and the spaces between and adjacent to them to extend their use and function,' said Gerry helpfully, and Susanna saw him smile as the expression on Wendy's face changed. 'Development, in other words, designed to minimise demolition and disruption to services, while maximising existing infrastructure. Cost-effective, and a vast reduction in consumption of resources, and space.'

'Ah,' said Wendy.

'World'll be beating a path to your door,' said Joe, and took a swallow of wine. 'Mark my words.'

'Actually, I've just been asked to deliver a paper on it at a conference in New York, next February.'

'There you go! Congrats, Gerry.' Again, Joe raised his glass to him. 'Love New York.'

Wendy asked, 'Will you go too, Susanna? Still on holidays in February.'

Susanna shook her head, about to explain that Gerry *worked* at conferences and therefore preferred to attend them, if not with his business partner Marcus, then by himself, but her husband interjected. 'No holiday for our Suze this summer. She'll be flat out producing paintings for the solo exhibition she's got coming up.'

Susanna cast a startled glance up at him, but his height – or her lack of it – made it hard to read his face from this close angle.

'A solo exhibition! That's great news, Susanna,' said Wendy. 'Where's it going to be held?'

'It's just —' Susanna began.

'At Booradalla Council's new civic centre,' Gerry said. 'Award-winning building. Quite a buzz about it.'

'Oh, yes. That's out near your college, then?' Wendy asked Susanna, who nodded. 'Marvellous, Susanna. You'll be sure to send us an invitation, won't you? I don't think I've ever seen your work.'

No one has, Susanna thought. *Because I haven't got any.* 'Oh, it's not till mid next year. And – well, it's not exactly New York,' she said with a laugh.

'Boy, what I wouldn't give to be in the States for the election in a few weeks,' Joe said, and, as they sipped their wine, the conversation turned to Obama's chances.

'If America had compulsory voting like us, he'd be home and hosed,' said Gerry, to a general murmur of agreement. Privately, Susanna was tired of hearing about the American election, but she wasn't about to say that. It would just make her sound provincial. Glancing down, she noticed that her T-shirt was clinging unflatteringly to her puddingy tum; she pulled it surreptitiously away, hoping the others, all taller and leaner than her, hadn't noticed. She often found herself feeling like the little teapot, short and stout, but how much could she do about that? It was just her build, like all of the Greenfield women; that, and middle age. Yet Gerry, eight years her senior at fifty-three, seemed barely to have aged since she'd met him.

Looking at him, laughing now at some joke of Joe's, she saw that he'd got over the grumpiness of losing their match; his handsome face looked smooth, at ease. Pleased, Susanna smiled as she poured the last dribble of wine into his glass.

'We'd better get going, eh, Suze?' he said, tipping it down. 'Time to break up the kids' pot party!' Everyone chuckled: it was well known that the Visser teenagers, Seb and Stella-Jean, were a credit to their proud father.

The previous Thursday, it had already been dark when they were driving home from their match, but now the clocks had gone forward to summer time. 'Isn't it lovely having this extra hour of daylight?' she said to Gerry, behind the wheel. He didn't comment. 'Should I call the kids?' she wondered aloud. 'I could ask if they've —'

'You know,' said Gerry suddenly, 'in all the years since we set up Visser Kanaley, there's just one thing Marcus and I have never seen eye-to-eye on: entering competitions. Waste of time and money, he reckons. This Kansas City thing: he thought we had Buckley's of winning. But I was right, and already the feedback's been phenomenal. One international win raises your profile exponentially.' He glanced at her. 'Right, Suze?'

'Right,' she said, nodding as she gazed absently at the little pink-lit clouds daubed in rows on the pale evening sky. Cockleshell sky, her father used to call it. It occurred to her that clouds would make a good subject for her students. *Oh, I could paint some for the exhibition! Maybe I could do a whole show of cloudscapes?* She was clutching at straws, she knew. 'Honey, why did you tell Joe and Wendy about the exhibition?' she asked. 'Remember I said I didn't want to talk to people about it yet?'

'Because that woman gets up my nose sometimes, that's why. "What exactly does that *mean*?"' he said, putting on a sour face. 'Princess Smartypants!'

'I s'pose she can be a bit —'

'And I can't stand the way she looks down on you, Suze. You can tell.'

You can? Susanna frowned, nibbling doubtfully at a rough fingernail. 'I don't . . . I don't think Wendy looks down on me . . .' she said. 'Although after she comes to my exhibition, she might. God, I feel so – I don't know. I wish it wasn't happening.'

'Poor pidge,' he said, using his pet name for her. 'You worry too much. Listen, everybody's impressed when they hear "solo exhibition", but will they actually trek all the way to the outer 'burbs to see it? Not likely!'

'I guess not.'

'This show's only happening so the university can tick that particular box on your performance activity blah blah, you've told me that. All you have to do is whip up a few tasteful nudes and bung 'em in some nice frames. Done! Who's going to care?'

I care, she thought, her stomach clenching with anxiety. *It has to be good.* Belinda had put herself on the line for this, securing the booking at Booradalla Art Gallery. Again Susanna's mind started casting about for possible themes, something that might get her started. Not only for the exhibition: the article, too. She had to get something published, something major. Belinda had promised to help with magazine and journal contacts. *I've just got to write it first.* Problem was, she'd written nothing in fifteen years, since her monograph on Clarice Beckett, whose moodily atmospheric paintings of the Melbourne suburbs had been ignored for decades after her death in the 1930s. That monograph, surprisingly well received, had not only helped revive interest in Beckett's work but had boosted Susanna up the career ladder, from high school teaching to the university. But times were very different now, and if she didn't fulfil the current requirements, she'd be a prime target for redundancy in the inevitable next round of cuts. There'd been rumours —

'Suze?' Gerry tapped her arm. 'Don't you reckon that's what you need?'

'What?' she asked, trying to look as though she'd been paying attention.

'Some proper coaching, to improve your game. I'll shout you a few lessons with a professional. Christmas present.'

Susanna opened her mouth, intending to say, *What a good idea. Thank you, darling.* But that wasn't what came out. 'Gerry, I can't do the tennis any more. I've got too much on my plate. You'll have to find a new doubles partner.' She closed her mouth abruptly, shocked. 'I'm sorry, darling,' she added, bracing herself for his reproaches.

'Hmm . . .' he said thoughtfully. Daring a sideways glance, she saw that he wasn't looking pissed off after all. 'Well, if that's what you want, Suze.'

'Maybe next year, after my —'

'You know, honey,' he said genially, taking a hand from the steering wheel to pat her thigh. 'I probably shouldn't say this, but you haven't really got the instincts to play tennis.'

She nodded slowly.

'Not *good* tennis.'

'I know, Gerry,' she said shortly.

'Hey,' he protested, sounding wounded. 'No need to get upset!'

'I'm not upset,' she said. He glanced at her suspiciously, and she gave him her most reassuring smile. 'Really! Not at all.'

'Okay then,' he said, mollified, turning into their street.

In an inner-city suburb whose streets were shoulder-to-shoulder iron-laced Victorian terraces or bijou weatherboard Edwardians, their house was the anomaly: the seventies brown-brick eyesore. They'd bought it for a song fifteen years ago, their intention, of course, from the moment they'd moved in with toddler and new baby in tow, being to renovate and turn it into a modernist showpiece. In that time, while all their neighbours reblocked, replumbed, extended, put in new kitchens and bathrooms and second storeys tucked back from the heritage streetscape, Gerry had drawn up a score of plans. But somehow, their house remained just the same lumpish ugly duckling.

Gerry turned in at the gate and parked. Lights were on already inside the house. 'Ah good, the kids are home,' he said, and gave a warm sigh of satisfaction. He patted Susanna's thigh again affectionately, and she softened.

You love every bit of this, don't you? she thought. *Your home, your kids. Me. Renovated or not.* She picked his hand up and gave the middle knuckle a quick kiss. *I'm a lucky woman.* They got out of the car, and began to unload the tennis gear.

TWO

Another weekend was slipping all too rapidly away, and once again Susanna had achieved nothing of substance. It hadn't even been her turn to take Stella-Jean and her friend Tessa to the Sunday market, where the two girls had a thriving clothing stall; instead, she'd gone walking with her mother around the lake near the retirement village. How had that, even with all their talking, managed to take up half the day? And faffing around the house, followed by hours – hours! – in the supermarket, the other half.

She turned a corner and the couple of bottles that had escaped from one of the shopping bags (probably of the sparkling mineral water Gerry liked) clanked irritatingly against each other. *Almost home.* Parking as close to the front door as possible, she took just a couple of bags inside.

Susanna no longer really saw the interior of her home; familiarity had bred a kind of domestic blindness. When they'd first moved in, she'd painted every room with an unusually flat paint more often used on theatre sets, the intense, saturated colours – vermillion, indigo, deep plum – reflecting her excitement at owning their first family home. But the paint had proved a poor choice, fading badly, while its lack of sheen showed up every one of the many marks which had appeared over the years. Walls, furniture, decor: all awaited the swan-like transformation that Gerry insisted would one day occur.

The front door opened into a scruffy living room, and past that the open-plan kitchen, with its original orange tiles, and the dining area dominated by a large window looking into the backyard. Susanna dumped the shopping bags on the floor near the fridge and walked rapidly down the long hallway which barrelled off at an angle, passing half-closed doors to bedrooms and bathroom. The hallway terminated in a barn-like space known as the games room. Once, long ago, it had been Susanna's studio, but even she could hardly remember that era.

She could hear the rapid-fire popping of a fast and furious ping-pong game. That would be Seb, 'winding down' with his doubles partner Clarence Chong from their Sunday tennis match. They'd had an extraordinary couple of years, playing now at the highest level for their age. A shoo-in, both Gerry and their tennis coach declared, to win the junior championship in a month's time. *What a pity*, Susanna thought, *that they're not likely to be playing in the adult competition next year after all.*

'Hi guys!' she called. 'Hi Stella-Jean!' From her jealously guarded half of the room, her daughter lifted a hand momentarily, busily feeding fabric through a whirring sewing machine. A dividing line of thick red tape ran the length of the floor, right down the middle, in an attempt to alleviate bloody border disputes. On Seb's side was a riotous jumble of everything to do with games and sports, including an open cabinet overflowing with trophies. On fifteen-year-old Stella-Jean's, order and industry: neat shelves and stacked boxes of fabric and accessories, the sewing machine, a cutting table, and at the far end, a rack of finished clothes and other equipment for the market stall.

'Hey, Ma!' yelled Seb, spinning around to flash Susanna a winning smile that was uncannily like his father's. His friend Clarence smiled and ducked his head in greeting while the ping-pong ball snapped from paddle to table to paddle in a ceaseless white blur.

'How are we all?' Susanna asked. 'Any news about your uncle, Clarence?'

'Not really. No change, Dad says,' Clarence said, coolly whipping a tricky shot down the table with a flick of his wrist. 'The doctors aren't – you know. They don't think he's going to recover.'

'Oh dear. I really am very sorry to hear that.' A large ginger cat leapt from the arm of a sagging couch and sashayed over to Susanna, tail waving, to arch his back against her calf. 'Yes, Tigger, hello to you too,' Susanna murmured as she bent to stroke him.

'When's dinner, Ma? I'm *starving*.'

'You're always starving. There's a car full of shopping that needs to be unpacked; the sooner that's done, the sooner I can start cooking. Clarence, you're welcome to stay for dinner, you know.'

'Thanks,' he said, 'but I've got to get home.'

'Mum!' said Stella-Jean crossly, tossing the fabric she'd been sewing into a waiting basket. 'Seb's been whacking me with ping-pong balls for, like, *hours*.'

'That's *crap*,' cried Seb. 'The occasional mis-serve!'

'On purpose!'

Susanna kept her face a practised blank. 'Come on, guys. There's ice-cream melting in the car,' she said, and turned away.

In the kitchen, chopping meat and vegetables, Susanna ignored her children as they contrived to collide with each other and wrangle at every turn while putting the shopping away. Pointless trying to stop their arguing: they'd been at it from the day her daughter was born, or at least from the day she could raise a chubby fist to whack her brother. To Susanna, who, far from fighting with her younger sister, had been ever the peacemaker between Angie and their mother Jean, it was a source of utter bafflement.

She turned from the stove and saw out of the corner of her eye that the kids were about to slink off back to their own pursuits.

'Not so fast!' Susanna said. 'Feed Tigger, please, Seb, before you disappear.' On cue, the ginger cat, standing over his bowl, miaowed commandingly. 'And Stella-Jean, if you could set the table, thank you. Set places for Auntie Angie and Finn, too.'

'We're not going to wait for them before we eat, though, are we?' asked Seb, looking anxious. 'Angie's *always* late.'

'Depends if they come straight after church,' Susanna said. 'If they're really late, we can start without them.'

'Yeah, just don't guts everything before they get here,' sniped Stella-Jean, to which Seb responded by reaching out one astonishingly long arm and knocking the lime-green and turquoise crocheted cap off her head. She snarled at him and scooped it from the floor.

'I haven't seen you wearing that cap before, have I, sweetie?' Susanna asked. Her head tilted to one side as she peered at it curiously. 'Um . . . is it actually a tea-cosy?'

'Correct!' said Stella-Jean proudly, pulling loops of her soft brown hair out through the holes where spout and handle should be. 'Cute, huh? This Filipino lady at the market makes them.'

'It's . . . eye-catching.'

'It's looney,' said Seb.

'G'day, troops,' said Gerry, home from wherever he'd been. A client meeting? Marcus's? Susanna couldn't remember. 'Mm, smells great,' he said, lifting the lid on the pot of curry now bubbling on the stove. 'When's dinner? I'm starving.'

'I think that's Seb's line, darling,' she said, turning the gas down under the pot. 'Half an hour, or when Angie and Finn get here, whichever's sooner.'

'Just time for me to catch the news, then,' Gerry said, and sauntered off to the living room. The kids, she saw when she looked around, had vanished.

Forty minutes later, with a salad made but no sign of her sister, she called them all to the table. Gerry, a bottle of wine in one hand and glasses in the other, took his favourite seat facing the window. 'Here you go, chef,' he said, passing her a glass of wine. 'Your mother is a terrific cook,' he told the kids as the aromatic smell of basmati rice and the rich scents of curry filled the air. Susanna sent him an air kiss; she loved the fact that no matter how simple the meal, Gerry seldom failed to make an appreciative comment.

'Excellent dinner, Mum,' added Seb dutifully.

'*Enak sekali*,' put in Stella-Jean. *Very tasty* in Indonesian. Not only had she been studying Indonesian at school, but they'd holidayed in Bali almost every year of her life. Since she was five Stella-Jean had been declaring that she was going to live in Bali one day, and lately had taken to adding 'and run a business there'. 'Just finish school before you take over the world, okay?' was her father's usual rejoinder.

'So, Sebastiano, you and Clarence won again today,' Gerry said, once the first rush of appetite had been satisfied and everyone was slowing down. 'Not that I expected any different, but thanks for the text. Quarterfinal next week, eh? Then, roll on the junior championship!'

'Have to make it to through to the finals first,' said Seb rather sullenly.

'Of course you'll make it to the finals,' Gerry said. 'Don't be ridiculous.'

'Depends if Claz's *family* say he has to go to Hong Kong before then. 'Cause of his uncle and his massive stroke.'

'No way is young Clarence going back to Hong Kong till after you guys have won that trophy, uncle or no uncle.'

'And then that's *it*,' Seb continued gloomily. 'Because he has to go and help run their business. Forget about next year.'

'Then next year, we'll just have to find you a new doubles partner,' said Gerry with considerable energy. 'If his family *do* insist on him leaving. Personally – I probably shouldn't say this, but I think Clarence would do a lot better by staying here. You two are right on the verge of making it. You could be a world-class doubles team. You could be the next Woodies.'

'Could've been,' Seb said, poking at his food.

'Lucky Clarence, I say,' said Stella-Jean. 'I'd *much* rather be managing a clothing business in Hong Kong than bashing a stupid ball around.'

Seb glared at her. 'Who cares what you say? You're just *weird*.'

'Kids, please, not at the dinner table,' said Susanna. 'Now Seb, I know you're disappointed, but please remember that this is a very stressful time for Clarence's family. They have to make their decision, and it's not for us to criticise.'

'Fuck 'em!' Seb muttered.

'Sebastian!' Susanna was shocked. 'Don't *ever* disrespect someone else's family like that.' There was a fraught silence around the table. Susanna took a deep breath. 'Now, *I* think what needs to happen next year is that you concentrate on your study. You've got Year Twelve coming up, the most important year of your school life. We don't want *anything* getting in the way of that.'

'Well,' Gerry said, after a diplomatic pause, 'in further tennis news, you may be interested to know I'm going to be playing A-grade again. Starting next week.'

'Really?' said Susanna. 'How did you —'

'Bob Cummings called me earlier.' Bob was their club president. 'He's got it all sorted. I'm filling a vacancy on the A-grade team, and he's got another couple for the B. You're off the hook, Suze.'

Susanna stared at him. *He knew there was a vacancy. That's why he wasn't cross when I told him I didn't want to play any more.* The realisation made her feel stupid, somehow.

Gerry gave an abbreviated air-pump. 'A-grade singles – *yes*.'

'Go, Pops,' said Seb. 'But do you reckon you're up to it? I mean, at your age . . .'

'Watch yourself, you cheeky pup,' said Gerry, grinning as he took a mock swipe at his son across the table.

As the two launched into an involved discussion about assessment and rankings, Susanna turned to her daughter, still ploughing her way through the meal.

'How's your day been, Stella-Jean?' she asked. 'Did you and Tessa do well on the stall?'

Stella-Jean swallowed and nodded. 'Two hundred and eighty-three dollars, after the rent. I sold *heaps* of my new singlets, and Tessa sold lots of her felt dolls, too, but there's way more profit in the singlets. For an outlay of . . .'

She rattled off numbers and percentages; her mother nodded, not even trying to follow. A decade-old memory waylaid her. Shopping with the kids in the local supermarket – five-year-old Stella-Jean dressed in her primary school uniform, brand-new and much too big for her – Susanna had been dithering over some product when Stella-Jean took a break from scrapping with her brother to pipe up, 'Get the big box, Mummy, it works out nearly two dollars cheaper.' And she was right. It was almost uncanny. Gerry had started calling her the Pocket Calculator. On their holidays in Bali they'd all come to rely on Stella-Jean to calculate the exchange rate from rupiah to dollars, and get a fair price. Not the *cheapest* price; she always stopped bargaining at a certain point and the Balinese sellers always agreed: fair.

Stella-Jean had stopped her profit-and-loss summary now and was looking at her mother expectantly.

'That's terrific, sweetie,' Susanna said, scrambling to catch up. 'You're, ah, doing very well, then.'

'You weren't *listening* to me, were you? I said, how soon after Christmas are we going to Bali? You have booked, Mum, haven't you?'

This was not a moment Susanna had been looking forward to. 'I, ah ... I don't know that we'll be going to Bali at all this summer, I'm afraid. I've got to focus on work for this exhibition next year. And the article I have to write.' What Susanna didn't say was that, apart from these demands, she was also hatching a secret plan for a trip to Europe with her mother, after the dreaded exhbition was over. Europe was expensive, but if she put aside what she'd have spent on the family going to Bali, she'd be able to save enough. And Jean, who couldn't cope with tropical humidity, had always longed to visit Italy. 'I'm sorry, sweetheart.'

'Mu-*um*!' wailed Stella-Jean. 'We *have* to go to Bali. I have to talk to Putu, about *business*.' Seb sniggered loudly and she turned on him, suddenly furious. 'What are *you* laughing at?'

'*Biz-ness,*' he mocked, putting air quotes around the word. 'Look at you, you're wearing a flipping tea-cosy on your head! What business is it again? Nutbar Enterprises?'

'Shu*t up*,' she shrieked.

'Okay you two, that is enough!' shouted Gerry. He thrust his almost-empty dinner plate away; it hit the cast-iron pot with a *clang* as loud as the bell at the start of a boxing round. Everybody jumped, and Tigger leapt from a chair where he'd been snoozing unnoticed and streaked for the backyard, the cat flap slapping behind him. In the sudden startled silence, the scrape of the screen door at the front of the house sounded very loud.

A woman's voice called, 'Hello-o-oh? Anybody ho-ome?'

'Oh, great,' said Gerry, rolling his eyes. 'It's the God Squad.'

Susanna hissed, 'Can we all just pretend to be civilised, please?', shooting a fierce look around the table as she jumped to her feet. 'Come in, Angie, come in! Have you eaten?'

'I'll fire up the Gaggia.' Gerry headed over to his pride and joy, the gleaming coffee machine on the bench. Almost the only thing he and his sister-in-law had in common was their love of good coffee.

Susanna's younger sister, her figure set off by a vintage dress with a cinched waist and darted bodice, chattered nonstop all the way from the front door, while eight-year old Finn bobbed in her wake whining, 'I'm *ti*red! Where's *Stell*-a?' He made a beeline for his cousin, pushing his chair up next to hers. Susanna was used to seeing big dark circles under Finn's eyes, but tonight he looked almost too exhausted to eat. Stella-Jean, however, had already spooned a sizeable portion of curry and rice onto his plate, and Finn started wolfing it down. Where did that skinny little body fit it all?

'Nice dress, Auntie Ange,' said Stella-Jean. 'Gotta love a sweetheart neckline.' Her aunt made a little playful curtsey, hands tipped toward her sculptural collarbones.

'So, how's god today?' said Gerry. 'Omnipotent as always?'

'And full of eternal love, even for you, Gerry,' Angie answered gaily, lifting her wavy dark-blonde hair up and back with both hands. 'Ready to receive you, any time.'

'Good for him. Tell him not to hold his breath, though, eh?'

Susanna asked deftly whether there'd been something special this evening at Faith Rise.

'Oh, *yes*, we had the most *wonderful* visitor this evening,' Angie said, raising her voice over the throaty roar of the coffee machine. 'Pastor Tim invited a marvellous musician to visit us. Gabriel. He writes the most *beautiful* songs – and his voice! And the way he gets *everybody* to sing! Finnie, wasn't the music man fabulous?'

Angie's glowing smile, her dancing eyes, made Susanna smile too. From the day her peaches-and-cream baby sister had been brought home from hospital, Susanna had adored her – to the surprise of many, who'd expected the older sister, stocky and plain, to be jealous. Instead she had always been Angie's staunchest defender. Looking at her now, Susanna thought she was as radiant as a film star. *No one would ever guess what she's been through.*

'Everybody at Faith Rise just loves him! Helen told me – you know, Pastor Tim's wife – she told me he might stay here and become our musical director. Pray God, he will.'

'Musical director,' Gerry mused, returning to the table with a frothy cappuccino for his sister-in-law and an espresso for himself. 'I see. So, your outfit's going to be Melbourne's answer to Hillsong, eh? The happy-clappy mega-evangelists.'

Don't bait her, Susanna begged him silently. *Please.*

'No, Gerry, not at all,' said Angie, smiling as she spooned in sugar. 'For one thing, we are *not* Assemblies of God. I don't expect you to understand this, but Faith Rise is a very different church to Hillsong.'

'Really? So why the name change? What was wrong with St John the Boring?'

'Nothing was wrong with St John of the Cross, but Pastor Tim wants people to know we're not the same old church: we're young, we're informal, we're *engaged* with today's community. Our faith rises up to meet the challenges of the modern world.' Angie lifted both cupped hands, face glowing.

Gerry leaned toward her. 'Branding, Ange,' he said in an instructive tone. 'Tell me, why is a McDonald's quarter pounder better than a traditional Aussie hamburger, with real meat and a slice of beetroot and a pineapple ring if you want it? Well, guess what – it isn't. *But it's a Macca's!* Golden arches; Faith Rise.'

Angie looked at him with pity. 'Gerry, this is what I know: that God loves me, and my saviour died for me that I might have eternal life. Nothing to do with hamburgers.'

'Wow, that's very cool, Ange,' interjected Seb politely. 'Mum, I'll get the ice-cream out, yeah?'

'You adored Gabriel too, didn't you?' Angie said to Finn. She started singing, rollicking from side to side in her chair. *'Put your* hand, *in his* hand, *I'm with Jesus, he's mah man* . . . All the kids were singing along. Weren't you, sweetie?'

'I was not singing,' Finn said, looking stern. 'I don't like people who makes you sing.'

Angie laughed and leaned across the table to caress her son's face. 'Of course you liked him,' she said. 'And no one ever *makes* us sing, sweetie, we just *do* it, because we love singing. Make a joyful noise unto the Lord!'

Finn pulled his mother's hand away from his cheek; he was focused on the ice-cream Seb was scooping into bowls. 'Se-eb? What's that one? Not the chocolate – the other one?'

'Hokey-pokey,' Stella-Jean told him. 'It's good, you'll like it. Give Finn some of the hokey-pokey too, Seb, don't guts it all yourself.'

Angie bowed her head for a moment, and then cast a radiant smile around the table. 'How blessed we are,' she said, 'to share this time together.'

'Blessed,' repeated Gerry, with impeccable irony.

Susanna steered the conversation away into neutral territory, and for some minutes, at least, calm prevailed. Finn, whose ice-cream had disappeared so fast he might have inhaled it, suddenly deflated, slumping against Stella-Jean's shoulder. 'I'm *tired*.' His thumb slid into his mouth.

'Why don't you —' Angie began, and Susanna knew what she was about to suggest: that Finn go to sleep on the couch. Then the two sisters would have a long talk as they cleaned up the kitchen together, while Gerry either watched TV or worked on his laptop, and the kids skulked off to their rooms to do whatever teenagers did therein. *The whole weekend gone,* thought Susanna a little desperately, *and I haven't done a single sketch or had one worthwhile idea.*

'School and work tomorrow,' said Gerry firmly, standing up. 'How about I carry the little fella out to the car for you, Ange? And, kids, here's the good news: you get to clean up the kitchen tonight.'

Seb and Stella-Jean made glum faces, resigned to their fate. Angie was looking crestfallen, and Susanna remembered that her sister's most recent tenants had moved out. Her poor sister, who did not like solitude or silence, would be going home to exactly those things. *But Gerry's right.*

'Good night, Angie,' she said, bending to hug her sister, who turned sideways in her chair toward her. 'I'll call you during the week, okay?'

Angie kissed her cheek and nodded dolefully. Gerry hoisted Finn's angular body lightly to his shoulder. The child looked down at Stella-Jean, his small face blank with exhaustion.

'Will you be at school tomorrow, Stella?' he asked scratchily. 'Will you come and get me tomorrow?'

'Aren't I always there on Monday, Finnster?' she said, patting his bare calf. 'Mondays and Thursdays – aren't I always there?'

The little boy nodded solemnly as Gerry toted him toward the front door, Angie trailing behind. Finn raised one grubby hand in a farewell salute, and Stella-Jean raised her own in return.

THREE

She's just like Mum, Angie thought, as the principal of Finn's school went on and on, lecturing her. *Always criticising, always trying to make you feel small.* And Finn's teacher, who'd seemed so nice at the beginning of the year, just kept nodding nonstop at everything the dry old stick of a principal said. As if Finn being late to school sometimes was some sort of crime!

'Unsettled . . . disruptive to . . .' Blah, blah, blah.

'You don't understand,' Angie said. 'I'm a working single mum, I'm doing my best. Trying to make ends meet and pay a mortgage. I *try* to get Finn here on time.' Her bottom lip began to quiver. 'When I got the message to come straight away for an urgent meeting, I thought this was something really serious. But if I'm not at work, I don't get paid.'

The other two exchanged a quick look. 'We appreciate you coming in so promptly, of course,' said the principal. 'And there *is* something more serious than punctuality at issue, Angie. Finn has been fighting.'

'In fact,' his teacher put in, 'he's *attacked* another child.'

Angie flinched from the word. 'He just gets upset sometimes, he —'

The principal leaned forward 'He tried to strangle another boy.'

'*What?* No!'

'Yes. A soloist in the school choir, very nice boy. If the lad's friends hadn't been so quick, Finn might have really —'

'No, he didn't *mean* to.'

'Finn admits that he attacked him,' said the principal grimly. 'And why? Because Lucas was *singing*.'

Angie drove home in shocked silence, Finn in the back seat with his arms crossed tight and face scrunched down toward his chest, refusing to say a word. He stomped straight into his room and didn't emerge till she called him – begged him – to come and have dinner.

She cleared plate-sized spaces amid the drifts of detritus covering the kitchen table and put down their fish fingers and mashed potatoes. The two of them, alone again, like forlorn survivors of a shipwreck, in this big house. *How am I going to pay the mortgage this month?* Over a fortnight since the latest sharers (as Angie preferred to call her succession of tenants) had left. And those latest children, too, had fought with Finn.

Watching TV afterward, sitting side by side on the shabby old couch with its many stains and old burn holes hidden under throws, Angie's mind turned uneasily toward a truly sinister possibility. *The enemy within*, she thought. At Faith Rise they didn't talk about 'the Devil': Pastor Tim referred to him as *the enemy*. The enemy we must be prepared to do battle with at any moment. The enemy who could insinuate his way into your life, your mind, yes, into your *soul*.

No, no! Surely simple jealousy could explain what Finn had done. In a way, she hoped so, because otherwise . . .

Is the enemy within my son? Angie asked herself, gazing at him as he sat solemnly sucking his thumb and watching what was supposed to be a comedy, judging by the raucous canned laughter, though he never cracked a smile. *Is he there now, inside my own darling little boy?*

As though sensing her scrutiny, Finn darted a swift sideways glance at her and jerked his thumb from his mouth, tucking it tight inside his folded hand as though it might get away.

'Finnie, *why* did you try to hurt that boy?' she burst out. 'Please tell me, sweetie.'

Finn shook his head fiercely. 'No!'

'Is it because he has such a nice voice? Do you wish you could sing like that too?'

'No, I don't!' Finn shouted, his face contorted. He clapped both hands over his ears. 'I don't don't *don't!*'

Angie tried to hug him. 'Finn, *please!* Let Mummy —'

Finn hit her arms away. 'Nobody! No!' he yelled. Throwing the rug aside, he ran from the room and while Angie was still getting to her feet his bedroom door slammed so hard the house shook. His wild defiant shouts: was this the enemy, flaunting his power over her boy? Frightened by the thought, she hurried down the cluttered hallway and pushed the door open, to see Finn kneeling amid the usual muddle of clothes and toys in his room. For a fleeting moment she saw a picture of utter innocence, the little boy in his pyjamas praying, but then with a lurch of dismay, she saw that he was pulling apart one of his most treasured toys: Robo-Boy, a fearsome-looking plastic warrior who stood guard by his bedside every night. What could make a child destroy his own beloved toy? Even as she came toward him, he succeeded in wrenching one arm off and threw it at the wall, then flung himself forward in a passion on to his unmade bed.

Angie tried to pull his flailing body onto her lap; he kicked and struggled but she persisted. 'Jesus *loves* you, Finnie,' she cried above his yells. 'He loves you and he loves Mummy too and he will never stop loving us, never ever.' *Please, dear Lord*, she prayed, *help me, guide me. I don't know what to do, I'm so alone.*

Gradually Finn's struggles ceased, and he quieted. She drew him closer. 'I know you didn't mean to, baby,' she murmured.

'If my daddy was here,' he said, so faintly she could hardly hear him, 'he would fix things.'

Her throat tightened. 'I know, my darling,' she said. 'He would.

But Daddy's in heaven now with Jesus, isn't he? He's helping God to watch over us and keep us safe.'

Finn gave a huge exhausted yawn. The storm had passed. 'Tell me about Daddy,' he said, and she lay down next to him. With her son curled into the curve of her body, Angie looked up toward the ceiling. The fluorescent stick-on stars she'd put up there had lost most of their glow, but still lent a dim intimation of night sky. 'Your daddy was born in a beautiful green country called Ireland,' she began, as she always did, and stroked Finn's hair back from his sweaty forehead. 'He came from far away on the other side of the world because God wanted him to be here and meet your mummy.'

Finn's hand rested on the inside of her shoulder, his fingertips patting a gentle rhythm on her collarbone as, in a soft and dreamy voice, she told the story of his daddy, Davey O'Reilly. Finn had no real memory of the father who'd died before he was two years old, and Angie found an unassailable solace in the romantic vision she'd created. No longer the awkward young guy she'd met, the self-taught handyman-carpenter who could recite reams of Irish poetry but struggled to read a newspaper, who worked hard but smoked way too much dope, Davey O'Reilly had become an heroic figure who could do anything, 'the best man in the whole world'.

'And he looked just like me, didn't he?' asked Finn.

'That's right. Your daddy had beautiful brown hair, just like you, and he had a lovely big smile like you do too. All the time when he was busy working on this house, making it nice, he was always smiling. 'Cause he was waiting for somebody special, wasn't he?' she prompted.

'His princess!' said Finn. 'And then one day, he saw her, walking down the street.'

She told again the beautiful fairytale of their meeting, of love at first sight. And it was true. Angie had never felt really loved till she met Davey, not in all those jangled years of drifting around Australia, Asia, Europe, trying to fill the emptiness inside her with drugs and lovers, and then more drugs, and more lovers. All those restless adventures;

all those men she'd slept with, trading her body for a hit of smack, a bed for the night, a lift across a border – but most of all, for a few hours' relief from the dreadful loneliness that was her most faithful companion.

She was nearing the end of the story now. 'And he said, "Angie, my princess, let's get married" . . . and she said . . .' She paused, to let Finn deliver the punchline.

'*Yes!* And then they had a bay-bee!'

'That's right!' She cuddled him close. 'And *you* were that baby, our own darling Finnie-boy.' Her voice was sweet and warm. 'And we were so happy, Mummy and Daddy and our little baby boy.'

Finn sighed contentedly, and soon his breath acquired the level rhythms of sleep. Still Angie lay there looking up at the dim fluorescent constellation overhead, thinking about how the fairy story had ended. She'd thought she could stay clean forever, but she had fallen back – 'Just a taste!' – and dragged her Davey down too.

She had heard Finn say to others what she'd taught him: *My daddy died in a accident; he got elec-ta-cuted*. Finn didn't know that was a lie, so he wasn't sinning. God knew the truth, God had *always* known the truth, but he'd forgiven her because she had come to him and opened her heart, accepting Jesus as her saviour. Almighty God, who kept watch over every fallen sparrow, had been watching over her, too, and waiting.

Easing herself up from Finn's bed, Angie kissed his sleeping cheek and drew the blanket up to cover him. The night had cooled. She wandered slowly down the hallway of the rambling, run-down house.

In the lounge room, she turned the TV off and sorted through a pile of scratched CDs till she found one of Davey's favourites: *Harp of Erin*. Looking at the picture of him on the wall, the dear little pencil sketch Susanna had made back when everything was hopeful, she saw it was hanging crooked, and the glass covered in dust. She took it down, wiped it tenderly with the sleeve of her cardigan, and hung it straight again. She and Davey had been so happy here; she would never give this place up.

Settling on the couch, feet tucked up to one side, Angie gave herself to the yearning music. She'd thought she would never feel lonely again, once she found God and love at Faith Rise; yet, like a rat in winter creeping into a hole, the loneliness was creeping back, and it frightened her. Tears filled her eyes. *Why doesn't anyone want to stay here? To share this beautiful old house?* All she wanted was to make it into a haven for other single mothers. They were always so pleased to move in, the tired, stressed women struggling to get by on the pension or crummy part-time jobs, with their one or two or sometimes three kids, needy and clinging, or watchful and tough. And then, they always moved on.

She wiped the tears away, gazing despondently at the cardboard boxes stacked in a corner, left by the latest sharer to depart. Would their owner really come and pick them up, as she had promised? Probably not. They hardly ever did.

The harp music ended in a plangent swoon of notes. Angie knew she should get up; she should do the dishes, or the washing, or her overdue taxes, but she felt too weighed down to move. She rested her head on the arm of the couch and let herself be swept away on the current of sorrow.

Were those footsteps on the verandah? She sat up quickly. Most likely the woman who had just moved out. A knock at the front door. Angie snatched up a couple of tissues, blew her nose hard and blotted her eyes. Would her visitor know she'd been crying? *Too bad. No one cares anyway.*

But when Angie opened the front door, she saw not her former tenant, but a slim man in a checked cowboy shirt with pearled press studs, holding an acoustic guitar in his right hand and smiling politely. 'Gabriel!' she said, astonished.

He brushed a long curl shyly back from his face, not moving closer. 'Hello, Angie – I'm glad to find you at home.' His smile intensified.

'Pastor Tim's wife gave me your address, but it was the Lord who told me I should come here tonight.'

'Oh! I'm — I —' She was gesturing him in with a sweep of her hand. 'Please!'

His eyes were such an unusual colour, a lovely pale green that made Angie think of water and glass and other cool things, and also reminded her that her own eyes were hot and probably swollen from crying. She stole a quick look in the mirror: her eyes weren't too bad, but her hair – like a bird's nest! Embarrassed, she tugged her fingers quickly though it.

'Can I get you something?' she asked. 'Coffee, tea? Herbal?'

'I have a song for you, Angie,' Gabriel said. 'Something our saviour wants you to hear.' He was already tuning his guitar, one foot on the rung of a wooden chair, and Angie noticed for the first time that one of his boots was built up much higher than the other. From an accident, she wondered, or had he been born with one leg shorter than the other? She felt a rush of pity.

'Here you are,' he said, as though offering her a gift. 'This is called "Hold On To You".' His voice, beautiful, rich with feeling, rose and flowed into every corner of the room.

'I thought I'd been left alone
Thought I'd no one to call my own
Thought they were just my footprints
Lonely in the sand . . .'

Angie's hands clutched each other, fingers intertwined before her breastbone, as she listened so hard the delicate whorls of her inner ears seemed to be tingling. *He knows just what I was thinking. He knows me so well!*

Gabriel sang verse, chorus, another verse. Angie felt the words flowing straight into her heart. His eyes were closed; his face wore an expression of rapt absorption she'd only seen before on the faces of men while they were having sex. Or praying, she amended hastily.

His eyes opened and held hers. 'Sing with me, Angie,' he said.

She gasped. 'Oh! I can't!'

'Yes, you can. I heard you singing at Faith Rise; God has blessed you with a wonderful voice. A gift.'

The words thrilled and won her. Line by line, he led her through the chorus:

'I will hold on to you
And to your soul, it's true
Hold, on, to you.
You'll sit right by my throne
You'll never be alone
Because I'll . . . hold on . . . to-oo you . . .'

Tears sat ripely in Angie's eyes, but these were not the sorrowing tears she'd shed earlier: these were tears of joy.

Gabriel put the guitar aside. 'I feel the presence of the Lord Jesus, right now, here in this room,' he declared. Raising his right arm high, palm up, he closed his eyes. 'Precious Lord . . .' Angie bowed her head as he thanked God for his abundant blessings, and asked for his continued guidance. 'Help us to know and serve your will, guide us on the path that takes us ever closer to you. We praise you, dear Lord, with every note we sing. Amen.'

'Amen,' said Angie fervently. Oh, to be filled again with the certain knowledge of divine love! What joy! 'Jesus, saviour, thank you!'

Gabriel sat with her, drinking the coffee she made, answering her questions with such openness. He talked of how he'd grown up in a strict Lutheran family in outback Queensland, of being called by the Lord to evangelise, and about his adventures (so different to hers!) with his guitar and his gift of song, spreading the Good News all the way from the Gold Coast up to the Torres Strait Islands. He'd been intending only to visit Faith Rise, he told her, at Pastor Tim's invitation, on his way to Perth where a much bigger church had asked him to be their musical director. But, he mused, if God had another plan . . .

'Might you – stay?' Angie asked, and held her breath.

'It's in his hands,' Gabriel smiled. Then he leaned confidingly toward her. 'Angie . . .' A lock of his long hair swung forward; she had a momentary urge to touch it, lift it from his face. 'Tonight, I think I saw the path God wants me to follow.'

She felt a tremor, deep inside. 'You did?'

'When you sang with me before, I had a kind of – vision. A new band, playing and singing with me. Musicians burning to praise the Lord with song, and two girls, or maybe three, singing with us. Girls just like you, alive with the joy of Christ, blessed with lovely voices like yours —'

Angie listened, eyes wide, lips parted. 'The Faith Rise Band,' she cried excitedly. 'Gabriel and the Faith Rise Band!'

'Gabriel and the Faith Rise Band!' he repeated softly, and gave a delighted laugh. 'You're amazing!'

'It just sounds *right*,' she said, blushing with pleasure. 'Oh, if you were to stay – how *wonderful*! For Faith Rise,' she added.

'But Angie . . . the church in Perth has a place for me, to live and to work,' he said, suddenly serious. 'I'm here with just my guitar, you see. Pastor Tim and his family have been putting me up, God bless their kindness, but if I were to stay, here in Melbourne – I'd have to find a place to live. Somewhere I'd have peace and quiet to write my songs, maybe with a space big enough for the band to practise . . .'

'How big?' she asked eagerly. 'This room: would this be big enough?'

'This room?' He looked around thoughtfully, and she saw it through his eyes: the worn-out furniture, the dust and clutter, the cobwebs hanging in the corners.

'I'm going to get rid of all this junk.' She swept her hand dismissively as though it was all gone already. 'I've been wanting to, for ages. And it's big, isn't it?'

'It is,' he agreed. He got up and walked around the room; Angie noticed now how he limped, and felt pity for him again, and admiration. 'Yes,' he said. 'A band could set up in here.'

She drew a deep breath, sparkling with hope. 'Because, Gabriel, the thing is – I've got two spare bedrooms here! In this house! You could have one for yourself, and one to compose in.' Her hands were clutching at each other again. 'And it's quiet here, I'm at work most days. I've got just the one little boy, and he's at school, and he's very quiet too.'

Gabriel cocked his head toward the ceiling, as though listening, and then gave her a slow, building, beautiful smile. 'They say the Lord works in mysterious ways,' he said. 'But you know, Angie, sometimes he makes the path he wants us to follow very, very clear.'

Lying on the floor of his room, Finn walked Robo-Boy toward him, right up to his face. See how big he was? And strong? Robo-Boy had torn his own arm off and didn't even *cry*. That was his way of showing Finn how he could be strong too. It didn't matter what people said about you, or if they laughed at you, or sang mean songs about you. None of that mattered because on the inside you were *strong*.

Finn, I'm gonna help you, said Robo-Boy in his strange metallic voice. *Lucas Beal and his gang won't ever get you again.*

And I'm never going to suck my thumb again, Finn thought, *because Robo-Boy's helping me not to.* 'Thanks, Robo-Boy,' he said.

That's okay, Finn.

His mum came in, light and skippy like she was dancing. Finn looked up curiously. She wasn't usually like this in the mornings. And she wasn't in her dressing-gown, she was in her proper clothes already.

'Finnie!' she said. 'Finnbar Finn, my special little guy! Isn't this a *beautiful* morning?' She swooped down and gave him a kiss. Finn held up Robo-Boy so he could say hello, not that Mum could hear him. 'Oh, look at poor Robo-Boy!' she said. 'We need someone who can fix his poor arm.'

Finn shook his head. 'He doesn't need to be fixed.'

'You know what, sweetie? I bet our *new sharer* will be able to fix him.'

Finn didn't much like the way she was looking at him. 'What new sharer?' he asked.

His mum's laugh was like fizzy drink spilling over the top of a glass. 'You'll never guess, Finnie! You know the wonderful man who did the special music and singing at Faith Rise?'

'No,' he said, sitting up straight and shaking his head from side to side. 'I *don't* know him.' He held Robo-Boy in front of him, and Robo-Boy raised his one big strong arm high in the air.

'Of *course* you do, Finnie! It's *Gabriel*. He'll be the most wonderful sharer we ever had.' She dipped in to kiss him again, on the top of his head. Just then the phone started ringing in the kitchen and she jumped up. 'You get dressed now, honey, and we'll have brekky and get you to school before the early bell. Your teacher's going to be so happy with us!'

Finn tried to keep talking with Robo-Boy but it was hard to hear him now. 'Oh, Helen, you are so cheeky!' he heard his mum say, in a voice that was either teasing, or else she was being teased. Helen: that was Grace and Lily's mum. Grace and Lily were the two meanest kids at church; all the other kids sucked up to them because Pastor Tim was their dad, but Finn didn't, so they hated him, and he hated them back.

But then his mum's voice went quieter, and when she came back into the room he could tell that something had happened to make her feel heavy again instead of fizzy. *It's something bad about the music man*, Finn thought hopefully.

'That man walks funny,' he said.

'No, he doesn't, honey,' Angie said, too quickly. 'Hey, we want to get you to school *early*, remember?' She began to pick through the jumble of clothes on top of his chest of drawers for clean ones, trying to get her head around what Helen had just said.

Whenever the phrase 'give a blessing' was used at Faith Rise, it signified a donation to the church. Helen, after teasing her about how all the other single girls were going to be *so* jealous about Gabriel moving in, had told her how thrilled Pastor Tim was that Angie was 'giving this blessing' to the church. In that moment Angie understood they assumed she was offering the rooms to Gabriel rent-free. Angie felt sick with embarrassment. *The mortgage . . . I need that money.* But of course she couldn't say that. And it was *she* who was blessed, of course, to be able to offer this. What Faith Rise had given *her* was more than she could ever repay, and she was honoured to offer this wonderful man a home, and a haven for his music.

She nodded, twice, confirming something to herself, and turned to Finn, who was sitting hunched on the side of his bed. 'Come on, honey,' she said, holding out the clothes she'd chosen.

'I don't want him for a sharer.' He was trying to remember the word he'd heard Grace and Lily say last Sunday when they were laughing and whispering with the other kids. In a loud voice, he said, 'Gabriel's a *cripple.*'

His mother dropped to her knees beside him, her face stricken. 'Finnie, no! That's a *terrible* thing to say! Jesus would be *so* unhappy to hear you say that.' She folded his hands together, and hers around his, bowing her head over them. 'Forgive us, dear Jesus, for the unkind things we say. We don't mean to hurt people, it's just the – the —' She stopped suddenly. 'Lord, keep the enemy away from us, and from those we love. Far, far away. In Jesus' name we pray. Amen.'

'Amen,' said Finn mechanically.

'Now then!' Angie popped her bright smile back in place. 'How about I help you get dressed?' Finn gave his mother a doleful look and slowly raised his arms.

As she peeled off his pyjama top and pulled a clean T-shirt over his head, Angie had a sudden, vivid memory of Susanna doing exactly this for her. She could see herself, sitting on the edge of her own bed, just as Finn was now, but she'd been a year or two younger; six, maybe. Her older sister was crouching before her, pulling her singlet on. As her head popped free, Angie had seen their mother standing watching in the doorway, arms crossed, mouth thin. 'Don't do everything for her, Susie. You're not her servant, you know.'

'Yes, Mum,' her sister had replied over her shoulder – but she had given Angie a secret smile. Angie saw again the way Susu's eyes had crinkled up reassuringly. Just as Angie was smiling back, Mum said, 'Little princess.' Not the way Daddy called her that, with a cuddle in his voice: the way Mum said it was like she was putting rubbish in the bin. Ashamed, Angie had watched from the corner of her eye as her mother moved away, leaving the doorway empty.

And then Susanna had leaned in close, and planted a little kiss on Angie's forehead. Now, all these decades later, Angie raised her fingertips to the spot. She could feel that little kiss there still.

She leaned in and gave her son a kiss there, in the middle of his forehead. 'Stand up, Finnie,' she said softly. 'Let's get these pants on, hey?'

Resigned, Finn stood.

FOUR

Susanna had been standing in front of the mirror in the en-suite bathroom for a good few minutes (rather than her usual thirty seconds), leaning in close, peering hard at her hair as she lifted one section after another. *I had no idea I'd gone so grey*. She twisted around to try and see if it was the same in the back. *I wonder if I should get it coloured?*

'Susie,' a familiar voice called. 'Are you home?'

'Mum!' Susanna turned away from the mirror with relief and trotted down the hallway. 'How lovely to see you.' Her mother had put her bag on the kitchen bench; they hugged, holding each other's forearms for a moment, smiling. 'Have you been at the museum?'

'Yes. Miriam from the book group dropped in, which reminded me that I've been carrying this month's book around in the car to give to you.' Jean tapped the cover of the paperback lying beside her bag. 'It's an easy read, it won't take you long.'

'Thanks, Mum, that's great. If it wasn't for book group, I don't think I'd get around to reading a thing these days. How is Miriam?'

'Bored, she says,' said Jean. She'd begun automatically tidying the bench, putting things away. She and Susanna were as familiar with each other's kitchens as their own. 'Wishing she'd kept up a couple of days a week at the medical clinic instead of retiring completely.

I told her she should do some volunteering. I get so much out of my two afternoons at the museum.'

'I know. And the museum's lucky to have you.' Looking at her mother, Susanna thought, was eerily like looking at herself: an older, slimmer, more neatly dressed version of herself. 'Mum, when did you stop colouring your hair?'

'Oh, the minute I retired. I don't care if it makes me look older, I only ever dyed it because I had to. Grey-haired secretaries were definitely not in vogue.'

'I like your hair grey. You look better every year.' Susanna plucked at the flesh around her middle. 'I wish *I* had a waist like yours. I just can't seem to lose this spare tyre, lately.'

'It's the menopause, I'm afraid, creeping up on you,' said Jean briskly. 'I had the same problem from my mid-forties, for about ten years. Keep up the exercise, that's the critical thing. I do wish you hadn't given up the tennis, Susie. If my knees were still up to it . . .'

'Next year, maybe,' Susanna murmured.

'And you must have regular check-ups. Heart, especially.'

'Because of Dad? But I thought Dad's heart problems were caused by rheumatic fever when he was a child. Weren't they?'

'Check-ups can't hurt. Well, look at all these drawings!' Jean was standing by the table, where Susanna had gathered every sketch she'd made over the past few months, however rough or incomplete. 'You *have* been busy.'

'It's just bits and pieces,' said Susanna. 'I've got a meeting with my boss tomorrow, but still no real ideas for the exhibition. Or this piece I've got to write.'

'Never mind; you'll come up with something.'

Susanna sighed. 'I don't know, Mum, I think I've really —' she shook her head.

Distracted by movement in the backyard, both turned to the large window and saw Seb lugging the big container of grey water to be bucketed on to thirsty plants, and Stella-Jean heading for the rotary clothes line with a laundry basket.

'I do like the way your children help without having to be asked,' said Jean approvingly. 'Just as you did.'

Privately, Susanna suspected their father's urging was behind this burst of helpful activity, and sure enough, a moment later Gerry appeared, secateurs in hand, and started cutting back a purple-flowering vine that had launched itself from the side fence and was trying to take over the lemon tree. Jean tapped on the glass, waving; Gerry looked around and grinned as he waved back at her. It was one of the many nourishing pleasures of Susanna's life that, from the start, Gerry and her mother had got on so well.

Stella-Jean, arms above her head at the washing line, looked sideways toward the house. 'Hiya, Jeejee,' she called, flapping an unpegged tea towel as a flag of greeting.

'Darling girl,' said Jean fondly. 'She's going to have a bit of a struggle with those sheets; I'll just go and give her a hand.'

Susanna watched them – two peas from the Greenfield pod of short, curvy females – first stretching to unpeg a sheet, then holding it wide between them and coming to and fro in the folding. An image from one of Helen Garner's early novels came into Susanna's mind: two women, here in the inner suburbs of Melbourne, performing a kind of courtly dance as they too folded a sheet together beside a backyard clothes line. Such a graceful, telling little scene.

Show me, whispered a voice in her head, and on impulse she turned over one of the sketches on the table, picked up a pencil, and began to draw. The young woman and the old together, the sheet between them, their faces serene and open. A peaceful scene; a simple, necessary chore. *Domestic work; women's work*, she thought. *That used to be depicted, often, in art, but one never sees it any more. Why not?*

A lightbulb went on in her brain. *This* could be the topic of her article: the way a subject that had for centuries depicted women in action, absorbed in their work – and clothed, rather than as aesthetically or sexually appealing nudes – had disappeared. Was it because of the changing nature of women's employment? The continued devaluation of such tasks in a society increasingly dependent on both technology and outsourcing? Rich material to consider.

Excited, she began to scribble down ideas, and had just got her initial thoughts down when her mother came back in, carrying the basket of neatly folded washing, chatting with Gerry who was right behind her.

'Your mum's staying for dinner,' Gerry announced. 'Right, Jean?'

'Oh, are you cooking?' asked Jean archly.

'Do, Mum,' Susanna urged. 'I'd love you to.'

'That's very kind of you both, but I'll say no, thank you. It would mean driving home after dark and I've been finding night driving hard on my eyes lately.' Jean patted her daughter's hand. 'That's one of the pleasures of going to book group, Susie, having you as my chauffeur.'

'But book group's not till next week. I'll see you before then, won't I?'

'We usually manage to, don't we?' Jean said. 'No matter how busy you are.'

'We do,' Susanna agreed. They kissed goodbye, and Gerry saw Jean out to her car. Susanna could hear her mother's distant laughter, and Gerry's joining in, and smiled to herself as she looked again at her quick drawing of the women folding the sheet. Dancing; yes, they did look as though they were dancing.

'Whatever those things are, do you have to drop 'em on the floor like that? It's like a bloody brick landing, every time,' said Gerry, frowning at her. They were sitting up in bed together, pillows stacked behind them against the slatted wooden bedhead.

'Sorry,' Susanna said, reaching for the next one in the stack of large black spiral-bound notebooks. 'They're my second-year students' art journals. I have to finish marking them.'

'Their journals get marked? I would've thought they were just for their own use.'

'Oh, everything gets marked these days. These are worth twenty per cent of their overall mark, not that you'd guess that from looking at most of them,' she said, turning pages rapidly. 'Most of these kids seem to think it's enough to just slap in a few pictures they've torn out of magazines, and scribble down a list of websites. Sad, really. When I think of the care we lavished on our journals when I was at art school. We drew and wrote and took photos and poured all our dreams and ideas into them ...'

'Kids are way too cool for that now, Suze,' Gerry said, turning back to the MacBook Pro propped on his angled knees.

Susanna sneaked a look at him. She liked being able to watch him like this, while he was so focused on the screen; liked the way the soft light from the bedside lamp gilded his hair and the stubble on his chin. She thought of the Happy Prince, in Oscar Wilde's story – but Wilde's golden prince had stood immobile on his pillar, while her handsome husband was alive and warm, right here beside her. She stroked his arm dreamily below the pale blue sleeve of his T-shirt. 'What are you working on?' she asked.

He pivoted his knees obligingly, swinging the big laptop toward her. 'Remember we were talking about design competitions, and how important they are? Well, this is what young Alberto's come up with as Visser Kanaley's entry for a new visitors' centre in the High Plains National Park.'

Susanna stared at the maze of lines on the screen. Gerry clicked through, saying tersely 'North elevation' and so on. None of it made any sense to her, but she nodded, murmuring, 'Uh-huh, uh-huh.'

'As you can see, it's yet another take on the Murcutt-style pavilion,' Gerry said. 'Completely inappropriate for this site. This would require complete demolition of the existing building, which admittedly is butt-ugly but it's structurally sound and it's *there*. Trucking every brick of that out to landfill, then trucking in every single nail of this new structure.' He shook his head impatiently as he swung the laptop back toward himself. 'For fuck's sake. I don't know why we employ some of these kids. Do they actually get what I'm saying about connective interstitial envelopment, or are they just sitting there watching me flap my lips? Then they trot off and reiterate exactly what got rammed down their throats at uni.'

Susanna made some noises to indicate intelligent concern and, seeing that he was engrossed again, turned back to her students' journals. She had her own quandaries about the young people she was dealing with: how could she help them to see what a useful tool an art journal could be? And beautiful, too. Because on the evidence before her, they didn't get it.

'Phew! I'm finished, for tonight anyway,' she said at last. 'You nearly ready for lights out?'

'Just about,' he said distractedly, and kept tapping. 'There.' She heard the little zooming sound his computer made when an email was sent. He looked at her over the top of the glasses he had to wear these days for reading; it was amazing how he could even make glasses look like the most desirable fashion accessory. 'Just putting a rocket under Seb's coach, telling him he'd better get cracking and find Seb a new doubles partner – a really good one.' He took the glasses off and rubbed hard at his face. 'I still cannot *believe* they lost their quarterfinal. It was appalling.'

Just remembering the raised voices, slammed doors, and dark silences from both Seb and his father when they had arrived home from that recent match made Susanna's chest tighten. 'I think – I think we were all disappointed.'

'Disappointed!' Gerry snorted. 'A bit more than disa-bloody-pointed, I can tell you. They were playing like they *wanted* to lose.'

That had been the accusation he'd hurled at Seb, and she knew how the thought outraged him. 'Well, that's great that you're getting on to Seb's coach,' she soothed. 'The sooner we find him a new partner, the better.' She leaned over to kiss his cheek. 'I'm just going to brush my teeth.'

While she was flossing and brushing, a thought that had been niggling at her rose again, something she'd been meaning to put to Gerry all week. Sitting on the edge of the bed beside him she asked, 'Darling, do you think Seb has a girlfriend? Could that be distracting him? Worrying him?'

'Nope. I'd know about it if he had,' Gerry said with confident authority. 'He's been too sports-mad to get serious about girls.'

'You're probably right; they've both been late bloomers that way, like I was. For which,' she added, 'I'm not ungrateful.'

'Not much longer, is my guess. Young Sebastian . . . There'll be girls lining up at the door any minute, you watch.' Gerry smiled, aware both that his good-looking son was the spitting image of himself and that he, at fifty-three, still turned the heads of women of all ages. He always noticed.

Susanna frowned, flicking a fingernail between her teeth. 'Gerry, you have talked to him about, you know, safe sex and so on?'

'Yeah, a couple of times. Or tried to. He assures me in no uncertain terms that he knows *all* about it.'

'I suppose he does. They know everything, kids these days.' She leaned closer toward him. 'More than I ever did, that's for sure.'

'Oh, you knew enough, I seem to recall,' he responded, raising a suggestive eyebrow. His hands reached to caress Susanna's breasts, cupping each and hefting gently through the thin cotton of her nightie. 'Little pigeon.'

'Shweeet-heart,' she purred in response. She slid one hand to his crotch, and stroked. Under the light bedcovers, she felt his penis swell. *Mmm, in the mood . . . A little more of this and that . . . And if I lifted up my nightie and climbed aboard, I'd probably come, too.* That's what she should do – but that position, despite being more fun, was also more effort, and she was tired. Okay: lazy. Susanna went back round to her side of the bed, shedding her nightie in one quick movement as she slid under the covers, beside Gerry.

'Not much of a striptease, pidge,' he said, drawing her close. She nestled her head into his shoulder, her cheek resting on the smooth flat part of his upper chest, and lightly tickled his nipples, pinker than her own, just to watch them crinkle up, then raised her head a little and grinned at him.

Sometimes she still saw him just as he'd been the night they first met. A pub in South Yarra; a Friday night, crowded and noisy. She'd noticed him the minute he walked in, but they were no match – she a plain and unremarkable newly graduated teacher, he the confident, good-looking, going-places architect – so she'd stood back and watched her girlfriends flutter round him, like parrots round a bird-feeder. At the end of the evening, when Gerry followed her outside and asked her for a date, she'd been so sure he was kidding she'd almost been offended. But no: he'd really wanted her. Wanted to take her out, talk to her; wanted to kiss and make love. To *her*! He still did, even now when her body was becoming middle-aged, whereas his had hardly changed at all.

Gerry made a growly noise and folded his other arm around her; she snuggled deeper. She loved feeling his arms around her: his size and muscularity made her feel womanly and safe. As he kissed her he slid one hand to her thigh, moved it slowly over the ripe contours, trailing his fingers over her vulva. She lifted, stroking his leg with her instep, arching her body toward him. With an appreciative 'Mmm . . .' he kissed her again, and she pressed her mouth to his.

Yes. She loved saying yes.

Gerry shifted his mouth to one of her breasts, then the other; kissing and licking, he began to follow the well-charted course down her body. She stroked his hair; its thick silky softness such a luxuriant pleasure. He was licking between her legs now; she didn't actually get off on that, but had never objected, or even hinted so. Soon he moved up again, and slid into her. Sex, it occurred to her, was not dissimilar to playing tennis: strokes, returns, and volleys, all pleasantly familiar, practised, and enjoyable – more enjoyable than their tennis partnership had been. She moved willingly with and against him, and after a suitable length of time she clenched the muscles of her thighs and pelvic floor and made the sounds of orgasm, to be rewarded by Gerry's habitual throaty noise of appreciation, acknowledging that he could move now into those final thrusts which brought them to conclusion.

They rested together for another minute or two, a closeness she always found gratifying. 'Mmm, honey,' he murmured as he withdrew, 'that was good.'

'Was it, darling?' she teased affectionately. 'I mean, when you could be playing A-grade?'

Unexpectedly, he went still. 'We're married, Suze,' he said reprovingly. 'There are no gradings.'

'I'm sorry,' she apologised. 'That was a silly thing to say.'

'S'okay,' he said, reassuring her with a last cuddle before turning over and falling immediately and soundly asleep. Susanna slipped out of bed again to go the toilet; a wet spot, apart from being unpleasant to sleep on, would just mean she had to change the sheets earlier. Lying in bed again, with one hand resting on his broad warm back, she thought about his comment – *There are no gradings*. Such a masculine way to put it – so Gerry! – but what he was expressing, she realised, was the essence of his commitment: to her, to their marriage, to their family. He was saying, simply, there was nothing with which their life together could compare. *It's perfect.* She gave a contented sigh, and finally, gratefully, allowed her muscles, her nerves, her whole body and mind, to relax.

FIVE

Seb woke in the middle of the night with his bedside light still on and his laptop, lid ajar, pressing into his side. He stared at it woozily then fell back against the pillow with a grunt. Checking out porn sites, that's what he'd been doing: trying to get off on images of girls giving blow jobs, being fucked here, there and everywhere. He must have fallen asleep. What kind of guy falls *asleep* looking at that stuff? Cum spurting over their tits, their faces. *You're meant to get turned on, not zoned out!*

And then, with a hot gout of shame, what wasn't fantasy came crashing in on him: the insistent, intrusive memory of the fight he'd had with Clarence before their quarterfinals match. It wouldn't let him go: the stupid things he'd never meant to say, the cringe-making memory of his high-pitched cry: 'You don't care! You don't care about *us*.' Tears, god, *tears* had brimmed from his eyes, and Clarence had seen them. Seb rolled his head back in agony, only to find himself looking up at the poster of Rafael Nadal above his bed: his awesome biceps and lion-like gaze. Rafa would never crack up like that, no fucking way!

They had gone out then and played so unbelievably badly, worse than if they'd never been on a court together before. Visser and Chong, the doubles team who'd always shared an instinct for how each other would move, almost like they were the same person in two bodies: down in straight sets.

And now Clarence was gone. Gone for good, gone for ever, and there was not a single freaking thing that Seb could do about it.

He lay on his side with the laptop propped against a pillow, and went to Facebook. No, Clarence hadn't updated his status, not since the day before the doomed match. Seb updated his own: *pondering icebergs.* Cool and deep, that was the idea. And icebergs too were mostly hidden, below the surface. So did that make them great big fakers, just like him? He roamed from one friend's page to another, commenting on a photo here, posting on a wall there. He checked out Sylvia Albanese's page: shit, she had close to five hundred friends! What the hell was going on with Sylvia Albanese? Did she really want him to be her date for the senior school social? Year Twelve chicks, especially ones like Sylvia, *never* wanted Year Eleven guys to take them to the social. And yet Sylvia and a couple of the other girls like her all seemed to be angling for the same thing. *Weird.*

You didn't *have* to go to the social with a date. In fact, the school discouraged it. Until last week, Seb had assumed he and Clarence would cruise in together, cool and casual, dance a bit and just hang, having a good time with *all* their friends, male and female. Whereas a male–female couple who went to the social together was likely to spend a good part of the evening making out. Was that what Sylvia expected? And the other glamour girls?

The mobile phone on his bedside table thrummed. Rolling over to look at the message, he saw it was from his sister, just on the other side of the plasterboard wall. *U awake?* Okay, damn it, any distraction was a good one right now! He rolled back to the other side of the bed and rapped twice on the wall. Two knocks came quickly in return.

'Whassup, face-ache?' he said quietly, sticking his head round the edge of her door.

Stella-Jean beckoned him in. 'Can't sleep.'

'Nah, me either.' With a single long step, Seb crossed the narrow

45

room whose pink walls were barely detectable behind the chock-a-block shelves, the pinboards, photos, stuff from Bali, and fancy dresses on satin-covered hangers displayed like they were in some museum. With some difficulty, he found himself a perch on her similarly cluttered bed. His sister was sitting up cross-legged in her PJs; busy making something, as usual, working some kind of green ribbon around the top of that thing that looked like a kid's toy. Knitting Nancy: dumb name. He pointed to the lengthening tube spooling from the bottom of the little wooden figure. 'Old Nancy looks like she's having a big green poop.'

'Charming.' Stella-Jean gave the tube a quick, efficient tug and kept twisting the ribbon in and out round the metal hooks atop Nancy's head. 'Like that disgusting old sloth-cloth you're wearing. You do realise it's more hole than fabric?'

'Wouldn't be a sloth-cloth if it wasn't full of holes.' Seb looked down proudly at the T-shirt in question as he settled back against the wall, his long arms around his knees and super-size feet sticking up like paddles in front of him. 'Why haven't you got anywhere comfortable to sit in here?'

'Maybe I would have, if this room was bigger than an iPod.'

'Oh, poor diddums.' The door, which he hadn't quite closed, widened with an eerie creak; they both watched as Tigger insinuated himself through the gap and sprang onto the bed with a soft miaow of greeting. Seb rubbed the big orange cat's ears. 'Look, after this place gets done up,' he said more kindly, 'you'll have all the space you want.'

Stella-Jean shook her head gloomily. 'We'll be dead before that happens. Dad's never going to renovate this dump.'

'Yeah, he will. One day. Ouch!' He lifted the cat's front paws from his bare thigh. 'No claws, Tigs.'

'Don't you think it's weird? Our dad's this, like, world-famous architect, but we live in a daggy old shoebox. All he ever does for here is draw up plans.'

'That's because he *is* this world-famous architect. You don't get it, Stinker: he keeps changing 'em because he wants our place to be the best. He just doesn't want to let us down, that's all.'

'You think so?' She snorted derisively. 'Anyway. How come we're both awake but him and Mum are dead to the world? We're the teenagers; *they* should be awake, lying there worrying about us.'

'You want 'em to worry? Then get a bong at least, for chrissake.' Seb jerked his chin at the shelves opposite, stacked with containers of Stella-Jean's jewellery-making materials. 'Look at all this kindie crap! It's like being inside the freaking useful box on *Playschool*.'

'Me and Tess are doing very nicely with our so-called kindie crap, thank you very much.'

'You and Tess, you and Tess. Anyone'd think you were, like, twins, joined at the hip or something. Except you look like a duck and she looks a, I dunno, a heron.'

'Shut up.' Stella-Jean said automatically, but her flying fingers had paused. 'You know, I was thinking . . . If Tessa's family took *her* off to go and live overseas somewhere, I'd be a basket case.'

Seb shot her a lightning glance, but she was looking carefully down at Knitting Nancy. 'I'm not a basket case,' he said, then leaned forward to pick at his big toe.

'I didn't say you were,' she said tartly. 'I just said *I* would be. Anyway. What me and Tess want to know is, who are you going to the social with?'

Seb's head jerked up. 'What?'

'She bet me a king-size Kit Kat it'll be Princess Sylvia.'

'How do you know anything about the school social? You're in Year *Nine*, you should be invisible.' Fat chance. His sister had never been invisible.

'Me and Tess accessorise half the girls in senior school – not that *you'd* know. And we have it on good authority that Sylvia Albanese *and* Georgie Patrakis *and* Chelsea Trumper all want you to be their date. Everyone is like, wow! That dumb jock? That dumb *Year Eleven* jock?'

'But I don't want to go with any of them,' Seb muttered.

'Crap on,' scoffed Stella-Jean. 'What, scared you'll get torn apart?' She mimed a tug-of-war with both hands.

'No, I just don't wanna . . . you know . . . give anybody the wrong idea.' Still fiddling with his toes, he could feel his sister's eyes boring into him.

'What wrong idea, exactly?'

'Meh,' he shrugged, trying to sound careless and casual. 'Like I'm, you know, committed to one of 'em.'

She giggled. 'They're not asking to *marry* you, you know!'

Seb ignored her, watching from the corner of his eye as she started working the ribbon on Knitting Nancy again. Suddenly she dropped it into her lap.

'Oh! *I've* got an idea.' Stella-Jean beckoned him closer; he inclined toward her, further, further, until finally he toppled onto her. She pushed him back to upright and Tigger, who'd got slightly squashed, gave them both an offended look.

'No, listen. This would really mess with people's minds,' Stella-Jean said, gleefully. 'You should ask *Rory* to go to the social with you.'

'Rory?' He leaned back against the wall, gobsmacked. 'But . . . Ror's been my buddy since we were in kinder. We used to have sleepovers, for god's sake. Like, little kid sleepovers.'

'So? She can be your buddy and still be your date. Plus she's stunning-looking.'

Seb looked startled. 'Is she?'

'Don't tell me you hadn't *noticed*.' Stella-Jean clicked her tongue slowly, several times. 'You are hopeless.'

He pictured walking in to the social with Aurora Feng: her ballet dancer's body, slender and strong, in some slinky dress instead of school uniform, her long black hair *not* in a ponytail for once. Yes, when you actually thought about it, she *was* nice-looking.

'It'd be so *cool* to go with her. It'd really piss those princesses off,' said Stella-Jean with relish. 'They still haven't forgiven her for having that big scene last year with, you know, that Year Twelve guy who looked like Johnny Depp.'

'You mean Rob de Clario?' said Seb, his brain popping up an instant picture of the guy in question. He'd known Rob and Rory were an item, but only vaguely. Too focused on the tennis. 'The girls paid out on her for that?'

'Oh yeah, big-time. He was s'posed to be out of bounds to her, she was only in Year Ten. She's been getting the big freeze all year — it would be too cool for her to turn up at the social with *next* year's Rob de Clario. Ha ha!'

Seb gave her a questioning look.

'*You*, you moron!' she said. 'Sheesh! You think Sylvia and Co. are after you for tennis tips? Look in the mirror sometime.'

Seb pulled his knees in closer to his chest and tried to look blasé. 'So . . . how do you know Rory hasn't got a date already?'

'I have my sources. Go on, Seb, ask her. Hey, I'll ask her for you, if you want.'

'You stay out of it, face-ache!' He stared at her shelves, thinking. If Rory was his date . . . all the questions were answered. Yeah! Good old Rory: she was . . . *safe*. He unwrapped his arms from round his legs and sat back, inhaling breezy relief. Except — 'Let's be clear: you don't tell *any* of the girls this was your idea. Understood?'

'Wouldn't dream of it,' said Stella-Jean smartly. She dusted her palms together as at a job well done. 'And now,' she said, 'nick off. I'm ready to go to sleep.'

'I'm almost scared to touch you,' said Seb, but he knuckled her upper arm hard anyway, and leapt off the bed as she yelped and swung at him. 'Horrible *dree*-eams,' he wished her in a syrupy voice as he closed the door.

'Same to you, fuckhead,' said Stella-Jean, smiling as she switched off her bedside light.

SIX

'See you,' said Susanna, releasing one hand momentarily from her precariously clutched load of bags and books in order to give Gerry, still halfway through his breakfast, a quick wave.

'You're off early.'

'Meeting with Belinda before my first class. Oh, honey, it's your brother's birthday today. Don't forget to call him.'

'Yeah, yeah,' said Gerry, forking up egg and tomato. His brother Ed ran a swimming pool supply shop and still lived in the same Perth suburb where he and Gerry had grown up. They had absolutely nothing in common and would probably never have made contact again after their parents died, if it weren't for their wives sending Christmas cards and the like. *Why do they bother?* Gerry wondered. He had Susanna and the kids, he didn't need any more family than that. 'Have a good one, Suze.'

Ten minutes later, about to head off on the six-kilometre run to the office, he just about tripped over Seb, curled lankily in a patch of sunlight on the living room floor, still in his boxer shorts and a raggy outsize T-shirt. He was nose to nose with Tigger, who was accepting his attentions with slit-eyed graciousness. Nostalgia stopped Gerry in his tracks. How vividly he could recall Seb as a plump toddler, and as an older child, lying on the floor just like this, communing with some earlier feline in the succession they'd owned over the years. He knelt down beside his son, fiddling with the laces on his running shoes, feeling a real pang of loss for that physical closeness he'd enjoyed with the kids when they were little: the small, sweet bodies sitting in his lap while they ate, riding on his shoulders, demanding to be swung around till they were dizzy, or thrown whooping into the air. '*Again!*' they'd shriek. '*Daddy! Again!*'

'What's on at school today, Sebbie?' he asked.

'Just the usual stuff.' Seb was making patterns in the fur of Tigger's flank with his fingertips.

'Morning's moving along, mate.' Gerry flexed one foot, testing the tightness of the laces. 'You planning on getting dressed any time soon?'

'Plenty of time,' Seb said, but rolled over to his knees, and then stood. 'Uh . . . Dad?'

'Yeah?' He glanced up. From this angle Seb positively loomed. He wondered if he was now shorter than his son.

'Do you . . . ah . . . I just . . .' Seb started picking at a paint bubble on the wall.

Gerry rose, noting with relief that he was still the taller, though not by much. 'What's up?' he said, giving Seb's shoulder a friendly squeeze.

'I was just, um, wondering. How old you were you when . . . ah, when you had your first girlfriend?'

'Hmm . . .' Gerry rubbed thoughtfully at his freshly shaved jaw, taking his time to answer. *So, he is starting to think about girls. I'll bet some of his mates are way ahead of him; he feels self-conscious.* He liked that his son had come to him for reassurance. 'Well, you know, growing up back in Perth, I guess it'd be fair to say I was pretty sport-obsessed. I was a serious cricketer, remember. Plus the tennis. And the swimming. Kind of didn't wake up to girls till —' Gerry threw him a questioning glance. 'When you say girlfriend, you mean my first, uh, *real* girlfriend? Sex, we're talking about?'

Seb grimaced but nodded emphatically.

'To tell the truth, Sebbie, that didn't start happening till I came over here for uni.'

'Really?' said Seb eagerly. 'So, how old were you then? Eighteen?'

'Let's see . . . No, nineteen, I guess.' Gerry chuckled. 'Yeah. I guess I was a bit of a late developer.'

'Nineteen,' Seb repeated. His face had cleared. 'I won't even be *eighteen* till March.'

'That's right. No rush. You've got plenty of time to get your heart broken, don't you worry. And break a few yourself.' He put a hand up to ruffle his son's hair. 'Well, I better get a move on. Off to the pickle factory.'

'Cool. See ya, Dad.' Unexpectedly, Seb took a half-step forward and gave Gerry a quick hug.

Gerry closed his eyes for a moment, feeling immeasurably satisfied with every decision about fatherhood he'd ever made, from having kids in the first place to the story he'd just told his son. 'Have a good day, mate,' he said tenderly, stepping back and opening the screen door.

'You too. C'mon, Tigs.' Seb set off jauntily toward the kitchen and the cat leapt up, pretending alarm, and bounded after him.

Gerry did his usual warm-up stretches against the gate post of the low brick fence out the front. The 'not till uni' story had been spontaneous, but, he thought, just right: the truth would've made Seb feel even more self-conscious, inadequate. *Late developer!* Gerry laughed to himself. In fact, he'd just turned fifteen the summer he started fucking. Eileen, a smart, unconventional twenty-year-old, visiting Perth for the holidays; they'd met on the beach. She'd taken one look at the well-built adolescent and scooped him up. He'd barely had his cock out of her all summer. The following year he'd taken up with a teacher at his school, an adventure not as perilous as it would be these days, but still with the addictive frisson of danger, and by the end of high school he'd had it off with three or four women teachers. Some married, some not; all scrupulously secret liaisons. He had never boasted to his mates, never even wanted to. He'd learned back then that possessing such secrets gave him a potent sense of having one over on everybody else, which was far more exciting than mere boasting.

As Gerry finished his stretches and filled his chest with deep preparatory breaths, he took some of those earliest trophies from the cupboard of memory and polished their gleam. Miss Adams, the apple-cheeked history teacher with her pale pink, incredibly sensitive nipples; Mrs Bertram, geography, the first woman who'd let him know she wanted him to spank her. He could recall with perfect clarity the sharp report of his hand on her quivering white buttocks, the magically precise mark appearing redly on her flesh, her thrilled whimpering gasps. These were right up there, amongst the hottest memories of his life.

Satisfied, he popped the iPod buds into his ears and set off with Bob Marley's rich triumphant voice pouring straight into his brain. Perfect! Music, and the smooth untiring rhythm of feet, legs, breath. It was akin to sex, the blissful absorption of his morning run. He *needed* this; it was when ideas and inspiration came to him, without which he wouldn't be the architect he was, and Visser Kanaley would be just another boring little firm.

He certainly needed inspiration now, if he was going to produce a worthwhile design for the High Plains visitors' centre in time for this competition. He'd only been to the site once, but thanks to all the photographs and topographical information online, he knew it well. In his mind, Gerry traversed the ground again, then lifted off for an aerial survey, seeing the access road through the mountains, the jagged ridges, the sheltered bowl in which sat the squat concrete box that was the existing visitors' centre, plonked artlessly amid enormous boulders. Physically he was grounded, running steadily down familiar urban streets, but his inner eye was scanning the High Plains National Park, flying over the site like a bird seeking the place to build his nest —

His nest. That was *it*! A bird's nest, enclosing the boxy existing building – which could become the required administrative offices – in a rounded, rising form, sculpted yet natural. The winds would flow around it. Within the nest's walls, there'd be a walkway – its timbers sourced from within the park itself – winding up, with strategically placed asymmetric windows offering enticing views, drawing people up, up. The upper level would utilise the solid foundation of the box below. He could not only see it, he was there, stepping it out. Information displays, a cafe, a viewing deck from which the drama of mountains and bush was spread out at last before the visitors: their reward.

Yes! Gerry lengthened his pace, bounding along now. He had a winner here, he could feel it in his bones.

Sweating, breathing from down deep, he turned in at the gate to the converted Richmond factory that was Visser Kanaley's office, fished his key out of his pocket and into the lock of the artfully rusted steel door. *Huh?* Already unlocked! Yet he was always the first one to arrive. Dreading a break-in, Gerry wrenched the door open and took two huge strides through the vestibule and into the office proper. All good: the score of desks untouched, messy or neat just as their occupants had left them last night, and all the handsome white Macs sitting there, silent and waiting.

At the far end of the enormous open space, from behind the glass wall of the partners' twinned fishbowl offices, one light was on, one screen softly glowing. Marcus Kanaley, sitting in front of it, raised his arm in greeting.

'Marco!' Gerry sang out, and loped up there. 'G'day, mate,' he said, wiping the sweat from his face and neck with his T-shirt. 'You're in early.'

'Somebody has to try and keep this place afloat,' said Marcus dourly. 'And having been awake since four, I thought I might as well stagger in.'

'Yeah? Going by the look of you, I'm amazed to hear you had any sleep at all.'

'Oh, great. Do I really look that bad?' As Marcus stood and looked toward the mirror hanging on the wall opposite, Gerry noticed how his podgy belly strained at the lower buttons of his shirt. Marcus groaned and frisked his fingers anxiously at his dark, thinning hair. 'God, what a horror show. Fat, fifty, and balding. I can't bear it.'

'Fifty-two, if I'm not mistaken.' Gerry dropped onto the black leather couch and stretched his long muscular legs out in front of him. 'Don't tell me: you had a visit from John.' John was the married man with whom Marcus had been having a clandestine affair for years. Too many years. Right now they were trying to break it off, again, as one or the other periodically tried to do; agonising attempts, which never lasted.

'No,' said Marcus testily, plopping back into his Aero chair. 'I did *not* have a visit from John.'

'Ah. In that case, you were lying there all night *wishing* you'd had a visit from John. Honestly, Marco. I probably shouldn't say this, but don't you think it's time you just —' he made a slicing motion with one bladed hand '— killed it? Moved on?'

'What the hell do you think I'm doing?' Marcus said. 'Or *trying* to do.' He glared unhappily at Gerry, and then his eyes welled and he swung around abruptly to dash the tears away, snatching a tissue from the box on his desk. 'Fuck it,' he muttered.

'Oh, mate. Shit,' said Gerry softly. Face creased with sympathy, he watched Marcus break a large piece from the muffin sitting on the desk and stuff it in his mouth. 'Seriously. Wouldn't you be better off with someone who's properly gay? This bi crap . . . If John can't even make up his mind which team he's batting for, what chance have you got?'

'*Thank you* for that helpful comment, Gerald,' said Marcus. 'Can we not talk about this right now? I'm going to make a coffee.'

'Good-oh. Make me one too.' Gerry stood up, stretching his arms, elbows leading, far above his head, then ducked his nose toward his right armpit, sniffing. 'Woof! I'm having a shower. Then I'll fill you in on my latest stroke of genius: how we're going to win the competition for the High Plains visitors' centre.'

'I'd rather you filled me in on how we're going to pay the bloody wages bill next month. *That's* what this outfit needs, not another dog-and-pony show.'

Poor old Marco, he really is blue, Gerry thought as he soaped himself up in the shower at the rear of the office, next to the kitchenette. *And his looks are definitely going.* He ran his hand over his own flat belly, smug in the knowledge that *his* body was in as good shape as ever. Not an ounce of flab. Stronger than he'd been at twenty; erections like a stud bull's. He stood with his legs apart and reached behind to wash between the cheeks of his arse; lifted his balls, a gratifyingly large handful, to wash beneath them; rolled back the foreskin of his uncut penis, rolling the head around with the pad of his thumb under the stream of water. Gerry liked his genitals. Plenty of admiring comments his tackle had earned.

'*I can feel it, coming in the air tonight,*' he sang as he dried off. Terrific song. One of his favourites. Humming the rest of the chorus under his breath, he tucked a periwinkle-blue shirt in to fresh jeans. He took his time combing his hair, using just enough product to hold it but still allow a boyish flop, and when it was right he spun 360 degrees before the mirror on the ball of one foot and gave his reflection a snappy wink.

Visser Kanaley's dozen or so employees were now filing into the office. A cup of coffee sat fragrantly steaming on Gerry's desk; he turned to Marcus, on the other side of the glass wall, to give him a thumbs up of thanks. Marcus nodded and held up his super-size calculator to show that he was preoccupied with budgets.

Gerry waved acknowledgement. All right, so Marcus didn't want to hear about the High Plains project right now. No problem. He called Alberto in to his office and explained, not unkindly, the total concept change for the visitors' centre. Firing off one rapid sketch after another, Gerry took him through the new vision and its iteration of the principles of interstitial envelopment. 'High Plains Eyrie, we'll call it,' he said, and was well pleased by the way Alberto nodded eagerly. Gerry liked this mentoring aspect of his work. Watching Alberto walking quickly back to his desk, he thought, *This little project's going to punch well above its weight, I just know it.*

Visser Kanaley would weather the economic downturn. Marco would crunch numbers endlessly – look at him, the big old teddy bear, stabbing away at his calculator, all frazzled concentration – while Gerry had the vision. Theirs was the best of partnerships; it *worked*, it always had and it always would.

With this swelling sense of wellbeing and optimisim, so pleasantly familiar, Gerry turned to his computer and opened his email. Well, look at this: the organisers of the New York conference had sent the schedule through. He ran his eye quickly down the list of speakers: excellent, none of the big names who'd been touted as attending had dropped out. And *Gerald Visser* was up there with 'em.

As was *Marianne Zavos*. Gerry's attention snapped back to that name. He smiled. He hadn't seen the lovely and talented Ms Zavos since Prague – what, two years ago? Three? So, her career must be moving right along, if she too was to be a speaker at this conference. Maybe he'd send her a brief email: light, congratulatory – with the subtlest hint of anticipation.

Gerry's eyes slid to the drawer of the small filing cabinet, with its locked upper drawer, that stood tucked in under his desk. He liked anticipation; it was part of the pleasure. But only part.

SEVEN

'It's an interesting idea, in its way,' Belinda said, flicking the pages of Susanna's proposal with her thumbnail. The kindness of her tone, along with the qualifier, made Susanna's heart sink. 'But I don't think it's worth pursuing for publication. For one thing, it seems to me that the relative lack of images of women at work in contemporary art simply reflects the decline of figurative representation in general. And for another, I'm afraid these issues are perceived, rightly or wrongly, to have been addressed back in the seventies.' Belinda leaned forward and said gently but firmly, 'No one's hungry for this topic. It's not sexy.'

'Oh,' said Susanna faintly. She liked her boss, a hard-working woman in her mid-thirties who struggled tirelessly to maintain staff numbers and conditions in an area that the university increasingly regarded as peripheral. She trusted Belinda's judgement. 'It was just a passing thought,' she said, embarrassed, reaching across the desk to retrieve her failure. 'Sorry.'

'Wait up,' Belinda said. She held the proposal higher, like evidence. 'It also strikes me that this could make an excellent theme for your exhibition next year. All sorts of rich allusions. Consider Vermeer, for a start. Visually, I think this could really work.'

'You do?' said Susanna, lifting her head, attentive and hopeful as a dog whose owner has just picked up the lead.

'Certainly. Especially in a conservative venue like the Booradalla gallery. Our annual staff and student exhibition is probably the most radical thing they mount each year, and you know how careful we are not to put in anything too challenging. Drawings and paintings of women engaged in domestic activities would be perfect for them.'

'I see,' said Susanna.

'So, my advice is, use your idea for that. Voila — you've got a theme. Great!' Belinda handed the proposal back, and Susanna understood that their meeting was over. *This is a life raft; why do I feel disappointed?* She was at the door when Belinda said, 'Oh, did I see you carrying an armload of jacaranda blossom in from your car? It looked beautiful.'

Susanna nodded. 'For my second-years. I want to get them thinking about recording seasonal ephemera: tie it in with cherry blossom viewing and Japanese woodblocks, for instance, and Monet's waterlilies.' *I'm blathering.* 'It's about seeing their journals as more than a place to stick pictures out of magazines.'

'Wonderful,' said Belinda warmly. 'This is why students love this course, Susanna. You're a terrific teacher, you really are.'

Susanna smiled wanly, and left.

If I was a terrific teacher, these kids' journals would have reflected that, she thought as she walked around the room, dropping a sprig of jacaranda before each student's place. *I'm not. I'm dull. A fraud, a failure.* The students had collected their journals from her table at the front and were flipping through them, some just checking the mark she'd given them, a few also reading her comments.

She launched into her planned speech about the seasons and their fleeting moments, about tapping into a sensibility shared both with other people experiencing that seasonal moment, and with a whole art tradition. 'Smell it, feel it, imagine it,' she urged, but was aware that her voice lacked the spark of inspiration she'd felt this morning, when she'd seen the branches of jacaranda hanging over the fence from their neighbour's tree, dripping blossom, and had this idea. 'Above all, draw it!'

Some polite nods, as they eyed the mauve bells cautiously.

She talked about Monet: one flower, one artist, and a series of sublime paintings that had enriched art lovers around the world, and about how even the Impressionists, for all their radical espousal of painting *en plein air*, had treasured getting permission to copy the work of the great masters in the Louvre. Artists had spent months and years in there, just drawing.

What am I squawking about? Her stream of words slowed down, and then dried up. She sat at the front leaning her elbows on the table, her chin in her hands. What was really occupying these young people's minds? Not her rabbitting on, that was plain. *I might as well walk out of this room right now.*

'Are you okay, Susanna?' asked hijab-wearing Noor.

'Yeah,' said Angelo. 'Whassup, miss?'

'I'm just wondering what the point of all this is,' she said.

Her students looked sideways at each other. 'The point?' asked one boldly. 'Of – of the journals?'

Susanna agreed, lifting her shoulders. *Yes, why not the journals?* 'I feel like we're just not on the same page here, so to speak.'

A little silence. 'You said it, miss,' said Angelo. '*Page.*'

'Page?' She raised her head from the support of her hands, frowning.

'As in, paper,' said Bianca, cool and acerbic. 'We don't really *do* paper.' She stood up, raising her right hand, and Susanna noticed that she'd capped each fingertip with the bell of a jacaranda blossom. It looked magical. 'Pre-digital,' Bianca said, pointing at Susanna, then, turning, drew a big circle in the air around her classmates. 'Post-digital.' She sat down.

'That's right,' said Tom, a photography major, not unkindly. He leaned over and tugged his laptop from his bag, on the floor beside him. Holding it one-handed above his head, he said, 'See: these are our journals.'

'And our art galleries, for that matter,' said Bianca.

'Like deviantArt,' said Emily, a pre-Raphaelite swan of a girl. 'DeviantArt is *huge*.'

'A bit emo, in my opinion,' Bianca said, adding, in a conciliatory tone, 'but there's plenty who like it.'

'Susanna, we're all posting images online, all the time,' said Noor. 'If you're not online, you're nowhere.'

'Plus what's coming up, what's on. Reviews, opinions,' said Angelo. 'In between Flickr and Twitter and the blogosphere, a journal – like, an actual *book* – it's kind of . . . history.'

There was a room-wide murmur of agreement. More students were pulling out their laptops, others holding up their mobile phones; not mere mobiles, Susanna presumed, but iPhones and BlackBerries. She couldn't tell the difference; she hadn't even got the hang of using predictive text.

'I've looked at Facebook,' she ventured. 'I've seen photo albums on Facebook.' She didn't want to say she wasn't a member. Were they even called 'members'?

'People who are kind of serious about photography don't use Facebook,' Tom told her, bringing his laptop to her table at the front of the room. 'The resolution is too limited, there's no way for people to see the detail of your work.'

'Oh.'

Emily joined them with her own laptop open to the deviantArt website, clicking through it rapidly. Thickets of images flashed on the screen, a vast array that was apparently just the '*favourite deviations submitted in the last eight hours*'. Susanna ran her eye down the sidebar menu: traditional art, digital art, designs and interfaces, artisan crafts, manga/anime, community projects . . .

'I put *heaps* of web addresses in my journal,' Bianca was saying, and other students called out that they had too. Susanna looked up and Bianca fixed her with an interrogator's gaze. 'Didn't you look at them?'

Susanna hadn't. But she spent her lunch hour glued to the computer in the shared art department staff's office, looking through the sites they'd emailed to her, fascinated and impressed. It was simultaneously very exciting and the most humbling experience of her teaching career. *I have been a snob*, she realised. *A sanctimonious, hopelessly outdated snob.* She saw again Bianca's accusing, jacaranda-clad gesture: *pre-digital; post-digital.*

I bet I'm not the only art teacher who's floundering with this, she thought, and *ping!* Her brain lit up. *This isn't a seventies issue. It's topical, and pertinent, and sexy.* This *can be my piece for publication!*

She felt a nervous inward shiver. Was she being ridiculous? So soon after the disappointing conversation with Belinda, could she actually have stumbled on another idea? One that might really work? And even if this topic was good, how could she, so spectacularly ignorant, write about it? *My ignorance is part of the story,* she realised. *I write that in: confess it.* Oh, and consider this: her students had already done half the research for her! She was reaching for a pen – how deliciously apt that she would instinctively reach for such a pre-digital tool to get her ideas down, on the despised *page* – when her mobile, on the desk beside her, leapt and buzzed twice, like a huge dying blowfly. Susanna jumped. *New message*, the screen said.

She picked the phone up and pressed the button. *OK with you if Leonard joins us for dinner tonight before book group? X M*

Susanna texted back a single word: *Lovely.* She liked her mother's friend Leonard. She'd had a notion that over this evening's dinner, she might talk to Jean about her idea of a trip to Europe together next year, but that could wait.

I'll bet Mum knows how to use predictive text, she thought. *Probably even those face thingies: emoticons.* She gave a small chuckle as it occurred to her that she was actually going to *enjoy* writing this piece. What an extraordinary prospect!

Jean flipped her phone shut, pleased to have got Susanna's quick response, then sat back in her chair, arms folded and lips thoughtfully pursed, regarding the picture she'd just hung on the wall. She had replaced one of her late husband's watercolour landscapes with a portrait he'd made of their two daughters, aged perhaps eleven and six. It was not a great painting, but that was not the reason it had been sitting in a cupboard since she'd moved here to the retirement village. Despite the stiffness, the unconvincing hands, Neville had captured rather more of the sisters' relationship than Jean liked: Susanna in the background, looking not out at the viewer but, with a proud smile, toward her younger sister, while Angie's winsome blonde curls and bright eyes lit up the picture. *Always stealing the limelight.* Jean caught that thought, and mentally slapped herself on the wrist. *Stop that! It never bothered Susie, so why am I still letting it bother me?*

Jean rose with a sigh and walked through to the kitchen of her neat, pretty unit. *Susie is truly a good person. A better person than I am.* She took the teapot outside and emptied the leaves on the meticulously tilled soil around one of the espaliered camellias in her courtyard. A few flowers on the gardenia bush had already opened; Jean leaned down to them and inhaled, but without really taking in the pleasure of their sweet fragrance. Her mind was elsewhere, wrestling with a problem more difficult than those brain-teasers her friend Leonard Styles enjoyed solving. It was Leonard, tactful and persuasive, who'd suggested she might put some pictures of her younger daughter up amongst the others on her wall; he who was encouraging her to tackle this most taxing of problems: forgiveness.

Forgiveness. A concept that had always seemed as facile to Jean as a greeting card. Now she was trying to grasp its essence, what it might mean for her, and she was finding it very, very difficult. *It's like learning another language. And I'm too old.*

But that was merely an excuse, even though she was indeed seventy-three. Jean knew that forgiveness had never been her strong suit. She had resisted it all her life, and especially since Angie proved to be so ... impossible.

Where had it begun? Where had things started to go wrong for her younger daughter? No – Jean corrected herself – *between* her younger daughter and herself?

She put the teapot down and started twisting the small furry bud-like seeds from the branches of the camellia. Helping a plant to direct its energy, its growth, that was easy. Just so with Susie: she'd been an easy child, a joy, always so open to guidance and advice. And look at her now: a good career, a solid marriage, two nice, capable children.

But with Angie, the problems had been there from the start, and the way people responded to her looks certainly hadn't helped. *What a pretty baby!* That's what Neville had said the minute she was born, and everyone – *everyone!* – had agreed. She was indeed a pretty little thing, like apple blossom, all white and pink, but Jean felt instinctively that it was a mistake to go on and on about it. Was she the only one who even noticed Susie, plain and brown as a nut, standing by as her little sister was cooed at and exclaimed over? Valiant little Susie, ignored but never complaining, never protesting, never resentful of the new star who'd stolen all her light.

Why could no one else see how *unfair* it was to make such a fuss of one child, especially for something as frivolous and unearned as prettiness? Fairness had always been a guiding principle in Jean's life, and she had been a fair mother. Scrupulously so. Neville should have had more sense, but he was besotted. Father and older sister, both were Angie's willing servants, as the demanding baby became a temperamental child, then a blindly wilful teenager.

Only Jean had treated Angie with the firm hand she needed. The things everyone else let her get away with! Even when she finally got expelled from school, Neville had been reluctant to chastise her. It was always, *She means well. She does her best. She's highly strung. She'll grow out of it* – to which Jean had snorted, 'I doubt it!' And she'd been proved right, alas, as Angie went from folly to disaster to tragedy.

Jean stood now by the espaliered camellias, face grim and shoulders rigid as the ghastly events of those years of Angie's drug addiction beat at her again: the lying, the stealing, the police knocking time

and again on their door, searching their house – the thousand and
one betrayals both small and large. The tremulous hope Neville held
out every time Angie swore she was giving it up, going into rehab,
turning her life around. Time and again, the dashing of that hope.

It was what Angie did to Neville, that's what Jean couldn't forgive.
The apple of her father's eye; he'd had no defences against any of it.
He always had a weak heart, and she broke it: that's what killed him. And
then Angie's own husband, that poor foolish boy. He'd never touched
heroin till he met her. *She killed him, too.*

Forgiving Angie would mean that she'd got away with it all: the
years of unremitting selfishness. The deaths. Let her take up with
these fundamentalists and their born-again mumbo-jumbo; let *them*
forgive her, if that's what they were so keen on. Not Jean Greenfield.
She had more steel in her spine than that.

But Leonard had put forward another proposition: that forgiveness
might be the stronger, the more courageous thing to do. Jean respected
him too much to dismiss this idea, much as she'd have liked to. Leonard
was a former magistrate, a tough-minded, admirably fair and balanced
man, a rationalist and atheist like herself. Therefore Jean had forced
herself to listen, even though the very word *forgiveness* made her so
angry she wanted to evict it from her mind. Even allowing it to sit
there quietly was a challenge that at times felt downright dangerous.

And how does one forgive, precisely? Jean had no idea. If there were
a pattern, a recipe, a form, then she might be able to follow it, but
there was none. After considerable hesitation she'd taken up Leonard's suggestion about putting the portrait up, but look: here she was
turning herself inside out, again, over this girl who'd always received
far more attention than she deserved.

Jean clicked her tongue and bestirred herself, picking up the teapot
from the white patio table. Make a cup of tea – that, at least, was a
straightforward and pleasant thing to do. She went inside, closing the
glass door behind her, only to pause and open it again. The air was
warm, and sweetly perfumed. Why not let it in?

EIGHT

Stella-Jean had taken hold of Finn's arm to tow him through the stream of kids surging out of the yard of the local primary school when she suddenly felt his skinny body go tense, like one of those antelopes on a wildlife program when it sees the lion creeping up. He stopped dead and the kid behind bumped into him, setting up a chain reaction of bumps and shoves. Swiftly Stella-Jean scanned the crowd for the source of her twitchy cousin's alarm.

There: that clutch of boys up ahead, idling just outside the gate, sneaking glances in their direction. The one in front, with the show-off looks: she'd seen him before. They were waiting for Finn, and not with friendly intent.

She prodded his shoulder. 'Come on, Finnster; stick with me,' she said, and walked straight toward the gate at a fast clip. She fixed the boys with a tough look as she approached, but they had eyes only for their prey. Four of them had formed a semicircle around the good-looking kid, and all five now raised their right hands, each making a kind of microphone of his fist but with the thumb poking out stiffly toward his mouth. The leader counted them in, tapping his foot – *one, two, three* – and his followers drew a deep breath, eyes alight with excitement.

'*Thumb, thumb, thumb, suck-a thumb, thumb, thumb,*' they sang in perfect harmony. '*Suck-a thumb, thumb, thumb, suck-a thuuuumb . . .*'

She recognised this little outfit now: they'd been the stars of the school's concert a couple of weeks ago. She'd come with Mum and Auntie Ange; Finn had failed to bang his tambourine in the back row of his class's contribution.

Pretty Boy tossed his head back and opened his mouth wide. His big voice powered out. *'You suck your thu-ah-hum, 'cos you're so du-ah-hum.'* The gang of four kept their chorus going, their faces vivid and eager, waiting for their victim to crack. Other kids were nudging each other, stopping, watching. Any moment now Finn would explode and go for them, and then he wouldn't stand a chance. And they'd say it was all his fault.

'Stay cool,' Stella-Jean told him tersely out of the corner of her mouth. She got between him and the group. Almost up to them now. Pretty Boy's sneer was hardly endurable: she felt an insane urge to turn, grab him, slam him up against the wire fence. Another step, almost past – oh, but he was so *close*.

She spun around, and Finn turned with her. The group dropped their fist microphones, grinning avidly.

'You've got a really great voice,' she told the leader, her voice dripping admiration. The boy smirked. 'You know, my dad's friends with one of the judges on *Australian Idol*. I could arrange for him to hear you.' The backup group gasped and crowded closer. 'What's your name?' she asked the leader, but his hard eyes said he'd already picked her for a phony. *Smart kid.*

'His name's Lucas!' volunteered one of his little buddies, thrilled.

'Lucas what?'

The star of the show looked away.

'Lucas Beal,' said Finn, and his tone confirmed that he and Lucas had a history – not a pleasant one.

'And we're the Breeze,' said the sidekick eagerly. 'Lucas and the Breeze!'

'Lucas and the Breeze. Wow.' In a fluid motion Stella-Jean flipped out her phone and held it up toward them. 'How about you guys do that song again. I'll shoot a little clip and show my dad tonight. Stick it up on YouTube.' The other boys were just about jumping out of their skins with excitement; only Lucas, sullen-faced, had got it. 'I'll make sure everyone sees it,' she promised. 'The teachers. The principal. All your parents. Everyone can listen to that great little song. 'Cause it was *so* clever, wasn't it, Lucas?'

Lucas picked up his bag. Show time over.

'Yeah, come on, let's sing it again,' urged his chatty pal.

'Shut up,' snarled Lucas. He pushed past them, heading in the opposite direction, leaving his puzzled subordinates to straggle after him. The onlookers eddied like leaves and began to drift away.

'Any time you want an agent, Lucas,' Stella-Jean called after him. 'I'm watching your career, you know. Every move.' She could tell by the way his shoulders hunched, shrinking his neck, that he had heard and understood.

'Come on,' she said to Finn, nudging his arm in the direction of the park. Once they had crossed the road and were well away she said drily, 'What a nice boy.'

'No, he's not!' Finn protested. 'He is *not* nice!'

'I know, Finnster. I was being sarcastic.' She saw that he didn't get it. If Finn was a kid who felt okay about asking questions, he'd've asked one now; she answered it anyway. 'Sarcastic's when you . . . when you say something as though you mean it, but you don't really mean it. Kind of.'

'But,' he said hesitantly, 'when you say something you don't mean – that's a lie. Isn't it, Stella?'

'No, a lie's when you say something that isn't true.'

'But it *isn't* true that Lucas is a nice boy!'

See? People said Finn was dumb, or didn't pay attention, but the thing was, he just didn't get things the same way other people got them. 'Being sarcastic's not telling a lie,' she said. 'It's more like . . . a joke. A joke that you say as though you're not saying a joke. Sort of a reverse joke.'

'Oh, I get it,' Finn said, but she knew her cousin was just being polite. Yet most people said he had bad manners, he was rude. *Most people are idiots.* They were well in to the park now. Finn looked around to check the coast was clear, then slipped his hard, grubby little hand in hers and gave it a squeeze. 'Thanks, Stella,' he said. She squeezed his back and then they discreetly let their hands part.

'Half an hour on the play equipment,' she said.

'I know,' he nodded. 'Did you bring the snack?'

'Yep.'

'Is it yummy?'

'No, it's horrible. There!' She snapped her fingers. '*That's* sarcasm.'

He grinned and took off, hooting noisily, across the long stretch of grass beneath the canopy of tall, parched elms. *Crazy little monkey!* she thought as she watched him bounding away toward the playground on the far side of the park. *She* could call him 'monkey'; nobody else.

No one ever said good things about Finn. *D-words,* she had told her mother once, *I'm so sick of hearing D-words about Finn,* and when Susanna asked her what she meant she listed them on her fingers. *Dumbo, dodo, dopey, der-brain:* he copped those from other kids all the time. Adults said he was *difficult,* and *demanding,* and *ADD,* which stood for attention deficit disorder, and she hated the smarmy know-all way they said it. *Dyslexic,* too – oh, and the latest she'd heard mutterings about: *defiant disorder.* Oh puh-*lease!*

Why couldn't they just shut up and figure out what was going on inside Finn's wacky little head? It wasn't that hard, really, to see what would set him off, and how to wriggle him around it. Instead, most adults were oblivious till he started to lose it, and then handled things so wrong that Finn ended up flipping out completely. *I can handle him, though.* It was a pretty bizarre thing to be proud of, but she was.

When she arrived at the fenced playground, Finn was on one of the swings, legs flailing as he propelled it higher and higher. Stella-Jean sat at the nearby picnic table and pulled out her Australian History text, getting stuck into the homework essay on federation while the lesson they'd just had on this less than riveting subject was still fresh in her brain.

She glanced up from time to time, checking. There were a few other kids in the playground but Finn was always by himself. *The only place I've ever seen him really playing with other kids was in Bali.* The couple of times he and Auntie Ange had come with them on holiday there, he'd hung out all day with the local kids in the village they stayed in, playing complicated games with little stones for markers, climbing trees and kicking balls and spending hours in the rice fields capturing slimy critters. Even though the local kids didn't speak much English, they were nice to him. So were the adults. Balinese people never yelled at kids, never got crabby. It was the only time she'd really seen Finn *happy*, day after day, his face smiling and opened up. Not the way he often looked here, like he was stuck in a cage and somebody might start poking sticks at him any minute.

By the time Stella-Jean finished the essay, more than half an hour had passed, yet Finn, she realised, hadn't hassled her for his snack. She stood, scanning the playground, and spotted him hunkered down in the far corner with his back turned, tight as a turtle. Finn was tossing little dusty puffs of tan bark up in the air, first over one shoulder, then the other, in a rhythm, and then she saw him smack his forehead with the heel of his hand. *Uh-oh.* She knew this smack would have come after a certain number of tosses, but didn't wait and count till the next one. Burrowing in her backpack, she found the bag with the cinnamon bun and hurried over, ripping the paper away from where it had stuck to the thick white cap of icing.

'Mmm,' she murmured invitingly, squatting in front of him. '*This* looks yummy.'

Finn ignored her. A small clump of tan bark sailed up over his right shoulder.

'Guess I'll have to eat this big fat yummy bun all by myself. Or maybe I'll go find that nice boy Lucas Beal and give it to him.'

Finn's head shot up. 'Oh, Stella!' he cried, wounded.

'Just kidding, Finnster, I'm just kidding. Come over here and eat this before you whack yourself unconscious.'

He thrust his lower jaw forward, signalling refusal, but she waved the glistening bun before him like a snake-charmer with his flute. 'Chocolate milk too,' she crooned, walking backward, and he followed her as though entranced to the bench beside the picnic table. When she handed the bun over he tore into it as though he hadn't eaten for a week.

'I saw a film of a shark attacking a surfboard the other day. It made me think of you.' Stella-Jean bared her teeth and shook her face at him, making savage growly noises. 'I wonder what'd happen if my hand accidentally got between your mouth and that bun?'

Finn grinned. 'I wouldn't *bite* you!'

'Nah. Not without icing, anyway.'

He ripped open the carton of chocolate milk and drained it in big noisy gulps, wiped off his milk moustache with the back of his hand, and gave a burp so huge and explosive it seemed to deflate him. 'Charming,' said Stella-Jean as he slumped back, as relaxed now as he'd been taut before.

'Hey Stella, guess what? Did you know me and you have got the same middle name?'

'We do? So what's *your* name?'

'Finnbar *Greenfield* O'Reilly.'

'Oh wow, yeah! That's just like mine, which is – um . . . uhh . . .' She frowned, looking to him for help.

'You *know*. Stella-Jean *Greenfield* Visser!' her cousin cried, delighted.

'That's it! D'oh!'

Grinning, he leaned his head on the back of the seat, looking up into the canopy of elm leaves. 'It's nice here,' he said peaceably.

'It is. But pretty soon we got to go home to my place. You remember what we do there?'

'The schedule,' Finn nodded earnestly, ticking off its points on his

71

fingers. 'First, homework, and after *that* I can watch *Cities of Gold*. Yay! Then I read you my book, then I can do drawing, then we have spaghetti bonayase, and *then* you read me a chapter from a long book. Or maybe two chapters if I try and read some too.' He exhaled loudly. 'And then my mum comes and I go home.'

'You got it!' Stella-Jean lifted a hand to high-five him, but Finn had suddenly slumped again. 'What?' she asked.

'We got a new sharer moving in,' he said, gloomy as Eeyore. 'Today, I think.'

'You do? Have you met the kids?' Poor Finnster, always having to cope with new people coming and going. 'Are they nice?'

He shook his head. 'There's no kids. It's a *man*, and I don't want him!' Finn crossed his arms tightly and hunched over them. Why was his mum changing everything around? Their lounge room didn't even feel like the same place any more. A few days ago, a truck had brought a huge metal bin and left it out the front. Every time he looked, his mum had thrown more stuff into it. This had never happened for any of the other sharers. 'And he *sings*,' he said, his voice spiky with suspicion.

Like Lucas Beal, thought Stella-Jean. 'Hey, not everybody who sings is bad, you know,' she said gently.

Finn looked at her as if she should know better. 'Why does everybody think if someone's got a nice voice it means they're a nice person?'

'You don't think that, Finnster?'

'No! I think they're just trickers!' said Finn, his jaw thrust forward again. He stared at the ground for a few moments and suddenly burst out, 'Stella, you know *what*? I am *never* gonna suck my thumb again!' He jerked one hand free of his armpit and smacked himself on the forehead, hard.

Stella-Jean flinched and grabbed his arm. 'Whoa, buddy, whoa! No whacking yourself!'

'I've got to get it through my thick head,' he explained darkly.

Who had urged Finn to get things through his thick head? *Just about everybody.* Stella-Jean stood and started loading up their bags.

'Okay, cuz, let's move it on out,' she said in a hokey cowboy accent. 'City o' Gold's a-waitin'.'

With his backpack slung over one shoulder, Finn followed her moochily from the park, thinking about what was happening at his house, and wishing it wasn't. At least Robo-Boy was watching out for him; Robo-Boy and Stella-Jean, between them, had stopped Lucas and his gang today. Finn raised his arm, slowly, stiffly, the way Robo-Boy did when he was summoning his powers to keep everything safe.

So, this is the music dude from Faith Rise. As Auntie Ange – who'd arrived late, well after she and Finn had eaten their spaghetti bolognaise – introduced him, Stella-Jean thought, *Yeah, he kinda looks like a musician.* It was the long curly hair, mostly: a bit hippie-ish, and definitely way cooler than any of Angie's other friends from Faith Rise.

Finn, who'd leapt for the front door yelling 'Mum!' when he heard her arrive, fell back when he saw who was with her, and was soon slumped on the couch again watching *The Incredibles* for the four hundredth time.

Angie relieved Gabriel of the bulging plastic garbage bag he'd lugged in and dumped it in front of Stella-Jean. 'Ooh, just wait till you see what's in *here*,' she said. The excitement in her voice was a dead giveaway. Stella-Jean dropped to her knees, tore open the bag and started pawing through the contents like a terrier. 'Oh. My. God,' she said with awed fervour as a riot of fabric spilled across the floor. 'This is *fabulous*! Wow, look at this jacket! Where did *this* come from?'

'The emerald velvet? Flea market, Barcelona,' said Angie, watching with a two hundred-watt smile. Stella-Jean held a flowered crepe dress up toward her. 'And I got *that* when I was about your age, in an opportunity shop in, um, Hawthorn, I think. Oh, Stella, the op shops back then!'

'Wowie ka-*zow*-ie!' crowed Stella-Jean. She jumped up and hugged her aunt ecstatically before throwing herself back into the treasure trove. 'But you've never even *shown* me this stuff. Where's it all *been*?'

'I've kept finding things all week, stuffed in cupboards, out in the shed. Anything that was worth keeping I put aside for you. But you wouldn't believe the *tons* of rubbish I've got rid of! By the time they picked up the skip today it was completely chock-a-block. And now the whole house is cleared out.' Angie turned her glowing face toward Gabriel, who smiled back at her. 'Every single room is ready now.'

'*Thank you*, Ange! This stuff is so cool!'

'I knew you'd be thrilled, sweetie. Oh, I've got some things for your mum too. Is she here?'

Stella-Jean shook her head. 'Book group.'

'Mum! *Mum!*' said Finn, pulling urgently at Angie's arm.

'Finnie darling!' Angie bent to hug him. 'My special little guy! I haven't even said hello to you properly!'

'But Mum, what about *my* room?' he said urgently. 'You didn't throw away any of *my* stuff, did you?'

'Oh, honey, wait till you see. Your room is so beautiful now: the bed's fixed, I've got rid of all those clothes that were too small, all the broken old stuff is —'

The skin around Finn's mouth and the sides of his nose went white and taut. *Uh-oh,* thought Stella-Jean. 'Not Robo-Boy,' he said. 'You didn't throw *him* away?'

Angie hesitated, then cast her eyes toward Gabriel. 'It was *broken*, Finnie,' she said.

Instantly, Stella-Jean knew what had happened to Robo-Boy, and so did Finn. And he knew who was to blame. Letting go of his mother's arm, he rounded on Gabriel. 'You threw him *away*? In the r*ubbish*?'

'You heard what your mum said, didn't you, Finn?' Gabriel said. 'That thing was broken.' He had a smooth, gliding kind of voice, Stella-Jean thought, like his sentences were lines in songs, just sliding away. 'We don't want broken things around, now, do we?'

Finn gave a horrible, wordless yell and flung himself at Gabriel; Angie cried out '*Finn!*' in a panic and the boy stopped short, quivering.

'*You're* broken,' he shouted, jabbing his finger again and again in the direction of Gabriel's feet, at the two-inch sole of his built-up shoe. 'We should throw *you* away! You're a *cripple*.'

'Finn!' said Angie again, her hands flying to her cheeks. 'Gabriel, he doesn't mean it. I'm sorry, I'm sorry.'

'You tricker,' Finn was screaming, 'go away! We don't want you sharing our house!'

Oh boy, Stella-Jean thought, getting to her feet, cross with herself for not being quick enough to stop this one, or even see it coming. 'I think you should all just leave the —' she began to say, but both Angie and Gabriel were moving toward Finn and she stepped forward too, protectively. Gabriel was the closest and in a second he had Finn's left arm, just above the elbow, in a pincer grip. With a shriek of surprise and pain, the child crumpled sideways.

Angie, her hands clasped imploringly, cried, 'Finnie, tell Gabriel you're sorry. Please, I *know* you didn't mean that!' She looked beseechingly to Gabriel, 'I'm *so sorry*.'

The look on the man's face made Stella-Jean go cold inside. Despite the rage and anguish roiling around him, Gabriel's face was still and smooth, like a mask, his green eyes like chips of glass. *Is he feeling anything, at all?* Impossible to tell.

'You see, Angie? The children of disobedience,' he said, and his even, gliding tone was horribly at odds with what was happening. 'Just as I warned. No, he must learn. He *will* learn.'

He shook Finn's arm, still gripping it tightly, and commenced to haul him, struggling, toward the front door. 'Time for us to go, my little friend,' he said. Finn's face was twisted up in pain and fear.

'Stop!' cried Stella-Jean. 'You're *hurting* him! Angie, stop him!'

Angie threw her an agonised look and scuttled after them. By now Gabriel had Finn almost out of the room, out of the house. 'How *could* he?' she said over her shoulder, but Stella-Jean understood, with a clutching of horror, that Angie meant, *How could Finn do this to Gabriel?*, not the other way around.

Reaching the front door, she saw her dad standing on the path, panting, in his running gear. He had one hand half-raised toward the stranger who was towing the gasping Finn past him, Angie hurrying behind.

'Angie? What the hell is happening?' Gerry asked, baffled but clearly ready for action. 'Are you —'

'I'm fine, it's okay,' said Angie breathlessly. 'We're just going!' Then they were past him, out the gate and heading toward a van that was parked at the kerb.

As Stella-Jean hurtled after them, Gerry grabbed her wrist, pulling her up short. 'Wait up Stella, wait up. What's going on?'

'Dad, I —' she said, trying to tug away.

'Stay! Here!' he barked, holding her. 'Tell me what's happening. Who is that bloke?'

Stella-Jean gulped in air, trying to find words. 'That's, uh – Gabriel, from the church, he's moving in to Angie's house and I – uh – Finn chucked a wobbly and went for him and then Gabriel —' she made a helpless gesture toward her own elbow '— and now he — Look, he's just carting him away! *Da-ad!*'

The others were in the cabin of the van now, and the engine started up; they were about to drive away.

'Let them go,' said Gerry firmly. 'I don't want you getting involved. Let her sort out her own bloody problems.'

'But, Dad, what about *Finn*?' Her father had released Stella-Jean's wrist now but there was no use running after them, the van had already pulled away from the kerb.

'Maybe it's time somebody took a firm hand with that kid. Maybe somebody's finally going to set some boundaries.'

'*I* take a firm hand with him! *I* set boundaries!' Stella-Jean cried.

'I know you try to, Stell,' her father said, 'but it's not your job.' He flung a sweaty arm over her shoulders, turning her back toward the house. She twisted around, looking at the van as it drove away down the street. As it turned the corner she thought she could see Finn's small pale face at the window, staring back at her.

She raised her arm to him, forlorn and desperate, but tonight her cousin did not – or could not – return the salute.

NINE

'You just sit there and relax, darling,' Jean said. 'Leonard'll help me; he knows where everything is.' And indeed he did, as Susanna realised watching her mother's friend get out the mustard, or the colander, as needed, with quiet efficiency. *My friend Leonard Styles*: that was how Mum always referred to the tall, courteous man who'd moved into the retirement village a year or so ago – but surely they were more than just friends? Susanna hoped so; she thought him a very suitable companion: active, intelligent, a good conversationalist. *Would Mum actually get married again?* Susanna felt a tingle of presentiment that an announcement, a significant announcement, was going to be made this evening.

Not wanting to hover, she went across to the living room and looked around, trying to figure out what it was that had vaguely registered as being different when she'd arrived. Not the flowers, not the furniture . . . It was — *oh!* The pictures, on the wall! Susanna froze for a moment, then went closer to make sure. *Yes.*

'Mum! You've put up Dad's painting of me and – Angie'. Her voice dropped as she said her sister's name. Jean hadn't had even a snapshot of Angie on display, not since the day Susanna's father died.

'Yes, dear. A bit of a change,' said her mother in a neutral voice. Amazed, Susanna gazed across the room at her and saw her mother

glance swiftly at Leonard, who was assiduously picking over a bowlful of lettuce leaves. 'Actually,' Jean said, 'Leonard suggested that
it . . . might be a nice idea.'

Ah, did he now? Susanna's respect for Leonard Styles ratcheted up
several more notches. She went over and leaned against the bench.
'Thank you, Leonard,' she said quietly, and he inclined his head in
acknowledgement.

'Now, Susie, look at this,' Jean said, in a tone that declared Change
of Subject. She handed her daughter a newspaper clipping. 'Aren't
these paintings lovely? When I saw this article I thought, these are
the sorts of paintings Susanna could do for her exhibition.'

'Oh, Mum, I'm flattered! But this is so far out of my league. Cressida
Campbell is one of our finest artists.'

'I'm sure you could do things just as good as these,' said Jean.

'No, Mum, really!' Susanna protested. 'I play a bit of tennis, but
I don't kid myself I'm up there with Serena Williams.'

'Well, *I* think you are,' Jean said stoutly. Their eyes held each other,
then they both laughed. 'Now then. Dinner's ready. Let's sit at the
table in the courtyard, shall we? It's still light enough.'

'Might I ask, Susanna,' said Leonard, as he put some grilled fish
on her plate, 'what sort of pictures you're planning to have in your
exhibition? I'm not very knowledgeable about art, forgive me, but
I am interested.'

She told them, rather hesitantly, about the 'Women's Work' idea,
and found herself buoyed up by their enthusiasm. Maybe it *was* a
good idea after all. Their simple dinner was soon finished, and Jean
apologised to Leonard for the lack of dessert. 'One of our book
group members has a patisserie, so Susie and I always save ourselves
for whatever wicked indulgence Jo brings.'

'Of course, my dear,' said Leonard.

'I'll put the kettle on,' said Susanna, half rising, but Jean held up a
hand to stay her. 'Wait, Susie.' She and Leonard exchanged a meaningful look. 'There's something we wanted to tell you.'

Susanna's heart did a little skip. 'I thought there might be.'

'We've decided, Leonard and I, that we're going to take a trip overseas next year. A big one: ten weeks. We're going to visit all those places in Europe I've always wanted to see.'

'Your mother's never been to Venice,' said Leonard. 'A situation which must be remedied.'

Susanna couldn't, mustn't, let her face fall. This was exactly what she had hoped to do with her mother next year.

They outlined their itinerary: Italy, Spain, France, Germany. 'It'll be the trip of a lifetime,' Jean said, and Leonard took her hand and held it. 'A Grand Tour.'

This is *like announcing their engagement*, Susanna realised, and let go of her own unvoiced plans, and her disappointment. 'The kind of trip well-heeled young couples used to make, when they were on their honeymoon,' she said, raising one eyebrow cheekily.

Her mother giggled, and Leonard raised her hand and brushed the back of it, with its ropy veins and its age spots, with his lips. Susanna, watching, felt her heart open to their clear and abundant happiness.

Tonight, the members of the book group had gathered in the comfortable Eltham home of Denise, a primary school teacher, whose attractive adolescent daughters had wafted through several times collecting iPods and homework and compliments from the visitors before being told by their mother affectionately to clear off. On the long wooden table amid the water and wine glasses, the nibbles and dips, sat copies of that month's book, *Without a Backward Glance*, a novel about a troubled family where the mother had walked out on her husband and four young children in 1967 and not been seen again for forty years.

'Well now, what did you all think of my choice?' asked Denise, displaying her copy in what Susanna recognised as a teacherly gesture. *Show and tell.*

'Well, it was certainly easy to read,' Susanna offered. 'I gobbled it down in a couple of nights.'

'Same here,' said the youngest of their group, Amy, who was doing an MA in Australian Literature. 'A page-turner. Pretty lightweight.'

'But does "easy to read" necessarily mean lightweight?' Denise asked with a smile. 'I think this novel deals with some quite *heavy* issues.'

'Maybe, but the characters were absolutely *awful*,' said Jo, the patisserie owner, who always brought strong opinions to their meetings as well as her delicious cakes. 'The mother!' She shuddered with revulsion. 'I hated her right from the beginning. How could any mother just walk out like that on four little children?'

'Are you *kidding*?' cried Andrea, a potter struggling to restart her career now her kids were in school. She'd had an exhibition a few months ago; Susanna and Jean had attended and each loyally bought a piece. 'How could she *stay*? She was suffocating! All through that opening scene I was thinking, run, girl! *Run*.'

'How can you possibly say that, Andrea? Run off and destroy her own children's lives? She was a monster, incapable of love.'

Voices were becoming heated. Susanna and Jean, sitting across the table from each other, exchanged a careful look.

'But *did* she destroy them?' asked Denise, in a tone encouraging rational discussion and civilised debate. 'What would they have turned out like if the mother had stayed, do we think, given that she was so miserable?'

'They each already had certain character traits, that's made clear,' said Miriam, Jean's recently retired doctor friend.

'That's right. Life isn't all black or white, Jo,' said Andrea. 'Nor are people. Every character in this book has flaws; that's what I like about them. They're flawed people, but they're not *bad*.'

'Abandoning your own children isn't *bad*?'

'What should she have done, then? Just let herself be stifled, because she was a mother?'

'No one *made* her have four kids, did they! And besides, she didn't have to stay at home. Why didn't she just go out and get a job if she wanted one? That's what *we've* done,' Jo said, with a confirming glance around the table.

'You think she could have done that so simply?' asked Jean.

'I doubt she would've had many opportunities,' Miriam said thoughtfully. 'Not in the sixties.'

'In 1967, women in Australia had to resign from the public service when they got married. *Had* to. Did you know that?' Jean said. Puzzled heads were shaken. 'Contraception was still something you only talked about in whispers, and virtually impossible to get unless you were married. And terribly expensive. If you were pregnant and desperate enough, you risked your life to have a backyard abortion. No government assistance for single mothers.' Some of the younger women were looking startled, but Jean went on. 'Women couldn't get loans on their own, not without a male guarantor, not even to buy a fridge, let alone to buy a house or start a business.'

'Really? That sounds . . . unbelievable,' said Amy, the MA student.

'Nevertheless, it's true,' Miriam confirmed. 'A lot's changed. You know, the only reason I was able to study medicine was because the Whitlam government abolished university fees in the early seventies. My family would never have paid for a *girl* to go to uni.'

There was a stunned silence. Jean looked around at the quietened faces. 'I'm sorry, I didn't mean to lecture. I just thought I could add to the context. Of the novel, I mean.'

'So, you agree that she was right, Jean?' said Andrea confidently. 'The mother was right to leave.'

Jean frowned. 'No – not at all. Duty trumps pleasure, especially when it comes to family. She was selfish and immature. She had no stickability.'

'But creative self-fulfillment isn't just pleasure! It's hard work,' said Andrea, with anguish in her voice, and Susanna thought of her handsome pots and what was required to make them, the time and energy squirreled away from the endless duties of domestic life.

'But no one suffers if you don't express your creativity, whereas if you neglect your family, they *do* suffer,' said Jean firmly.

No one but Susanna seemed to hear Andrea mutter, 'But if you can't be creative, *you* suffer. Or doesn't that count?'

'That's what I believe, at any rate,' concluded Jean.

'I agree!' said Jo. 'That woman was so selfish, my god! And at the end, the way all her kids just forgave her — it made me want to throw the book across the room. She didn't deserve one *shred* of forgiveness.'

'Ah,' said Jean. 'Forgiveness.'

'And what do we all think of forgiveness, as an issue?' asked Denise in that bright teacher's voice.

There was a silence.

'Well, it's a good thing, of course, isn't it?' said Amy. 'It's what you're supposed to do.'

'It's healthy,' said Andrea.

'Yes, not forgiving people gives you cancer,' said Fiona, who'd been quiet, as she often was, all evening. 'Or is it stress that does that?'

'But in the book, they made it out to be so *easy*,' Jo griped. 'I don't see how those kids could possibly have forgiven their mother so easily, not after all that.'

'What do you think, Mum?' asked Susanna curiously.

Jean took a sip from her glass, and put it down. 'I'm afraid I don't know much about forgiveness,' she said quietly.

Jean was so quiet in the car on the way home that Susanna wondered if she might have fallen asleep. About halfway back to the retirement village, however, her mother said suddenly, 'Actually, the marriage bar for female public servants was lifted a year earlier, in 1966. I'm afraid I misled you all, for dramatic effect.'

'Uh-huh,' said Susanna, amused at this confession. 'I think that's permissible, under the circumstances.'

'You know, when I first I got a prescription for the pill, our local chemist wouldn't fill it unless Neville came in and said I had his permission.'

'Good heavens!' Susanna shook her head. 'Mum, I'm ashamed to say I didn't know half of what you told us. It makes me think, if *my* generation doesn't know about how things really were for women, and so recently, then what about the next one? It's scary. A lot of my students think feminism's a dirty word, or at least hopelessly old-fashioned.'

'Except for Miriam, those women tonight have all grown up being able to *assume* their right to an education, a career.'

'Yes. None of my students, girls or boys —'

'They couldn't even *imagine* what it was like!' Jean interrupted her, the vehemence and hurt in her voice shocking Susanna. 'Having to watch both my brothers – and neither of them *half* as bright as me – go off to university. While I had to go to secretarial school, and learn shorthand and typing.'

Susanna glanced quickly at her mother's familiar profile, backlit intermittently by the streetlights. 'I know, Mum. That's part of what's changed,' she said cautiously.

'*I* should have been a lawyer!' cried Jean. 'Not a legal secretary. I would've been twice the lawyer Bob was!' Bob was her older brother, dead now, in whose law firm she'd worked for more than forty years. 'Do you know, Susie, even Bob thought I shouldn't keep working after I got married. And especially after you and Angela were born. It was only because of your father's health, and that we were so short of money.'

'Mum, that's not the only reason,' said Susanna firmly. 'It's because you were a really *good* legal secretary. The best! You know that, and Uncle Bob knew that too.'

'Oh yes,' her mother conceded. 'A good secretary.' She crossed her arms and sighed. 'Fat lot Bob's partners cared: once I turned forty they started pressuring him to hire some pretty young girl, like they had. But Bob wouldn't. He trusted my opinion on a lot of things more than theirs.'

'I'll bet. And with good reason.'

'This is why I wanted you to have a proper career, Susanna,' said her mother, placing a hand briefly on her forearm. 'To have security, and not be dependent on favours. And to be given a bit more respect, for heaven's sake, than a secretary.'

'And all those paid holidays, don't forget,' said Susanna, attempting to cheer her mother up with a bit of flippancy.

'*And* all the holidays!' Jean agreed. Some lightness returned to her voice. Complaining was not, after all, something she approved of. 'You wouldn't have got any paid holidays as an artist, darling, would you?'

'Oh Mum, I would never have made it as an artist, it was just a teenage fantasy. You knew that. You got me to see what good sense it made to be a teacher, otherwise I could've just drifted off into —'

'*You* would never have drifted,' said Jean sharply. Angie; Angie was the one who'd drifted. 'The artist's life wouldn't have suited you; you were always too responsible.'

And now I only know how to be a teacher; I've completely forgotten how to be an artist. That awful clutch of panic started to wring Susanna's insides. Her breath came shallowly. *I'm responsible for this exhibition and I just have the one idea, and I still don't how to get started.*

'Oh, Susie, I had another thought,' Jean said, turning toward her. 'About your exhibition. This might sound odd, but what if you were to attend a life drawing class? It would give you impetus, don't you think? And . . . confidence.'

Instantly, Susanna's tension ebbed. It was uncanny how well her mother knew her. *Better than anyone else.*

'I think you're right,' she said. 'Maybe I need to *not* be a teacher for a few hours a week, at least. Focus on *my* creative flow.' She drove in through the pillared entrance of the retirement village, past the quiet rows of units with their tailored gardens, and swung smoothly into the parking space beside Jean's small car. 'Mum?'

'Yes, dear?'

'Thank you. For everything.'

They looked at each other, not needing to smile.

'You're more than welcome,' said Jean softly. 'I always enjoy my evenings with you, Susie.'

'Me too,' Susanna said as her mother opened the door of the car. 'Because I'm with my best friend.'

Jean turned back to her. 'What a lovely thing to say! A very big compliment.'

'I mean it.'

They kissed each other's cheek. 'Bye-bye,' they told each other. Once Jean had unlocked the door of her unit, she gave a little last wave, and only then did Susanna reverse the car and drive slowly away.

TEN

Standing up there in front of the congregation in his usual fawn pants and chirpy-chirp smile, Pastor Tim seemed today about as charismatic as a sparrow. Every eye was on the man beside him, with his cowboy shirt and long wavy hair and sea-green eyes, guitar resting beside him. Angie barely heard the pastor's cheeping about auditions for the band, she was transfixed by Gabriel. *He shines*, she thought, *like the beam of a lighthouse. If I'm ever lost again I need only look for him.*

It occurred to her, daringly, that this is how it must have been when Jesus walked among us. *The way people were so drawn to him.* And just as she was thinking this, those amazing eyes turned to *her*. Gabriel was beckoning her to come up to the stage, to join him! People were turning to look, they were nudging each other. Angie put a surprised hand to her throat. She almost tripped over someone's feet. Helen, standing at the side of the stage, caught her hand as she went past and flashed her an encouraging smile.

Pastor Tim gave her shoulders a squeeze. 'Girls, ladies: our own dear Angie will show you that you needn't be nervous. Come and audition next weekend, join your voice with hers, singing with the Faith Rise Band!' and then he was stepping to the side as Gabriel played the first few bars of 'Hold On to You'. Gabriel's lovely eyes held hers, like he was reaching out and steadying her, and he was smiling at her as he sang. She came in at just the right moment, she hit and held every note, and everyone was listening, everyone was watching her.

After the service, Helen said – loud and clear, making sure everyone standing nearby heard too – 'Pastor Tim wants to start a new coffee-and-Christ chat club for our young mums, Angie, and we'd like you to lead it.' She took Angie's hand, smiling, and swung it a couple of times. 'With me, of course. You're just the girl we need!'

I'm the girl they need! A leader! Angie was floating on a glorious, shining cloud. All because Gabriel had seen something in her, something special. *He sees that I am worthy*, she thought with a soaring heart, *and now everyone else does too*.

Finn would have liked to go to Stella-Jean's place after church, have dinner there like they often did – or used to do. Now that Gabriel was their sharer, they went home, and they ate sitting up straight at the neatly set table. Tonight, Mum was so happy, it was like bits of light were zinging off her, and it was kind of hard for Finn to look at her, and her voice was too shiny too.

Angie always did the dishes straight after dinner now, and Finn had to help.

'There!' she said as she put the last dish in the rack. 'You just dry that one Finnie, and then – it's our story time!' Finn glanced at her suspiciously as she said to Gabriel, 'Before Finn goes to bed, we like to sit together on the couch and read a Bible story.'

No, we don't. We like to sit together on the couch and watch TV. But Finn wasn't going to tell Gabriel that. He wasn't going to tell Gabriel anything.

'Beautiful,' said Gabriel. 'I'll come and join you, if I may.'

Angie gave Gabriel a big dimply smile. 'Of *course*. This is your *home*.'

Finn sat on the couch with his mum and Gabriel sat in a chair close by, holding his guitar, watching them. Finn couldn't relax with him watching them. He made sure never to look in the man's eyes; they reminded him of ice cubes, and one time Finn had touched an ice cube that was so freezing cold his fingers got stuck to it. He didn't want to get stuck to those eyes.

'You love this special Children's Bible, don't you, Finnie?' Finn nodded; this was true. It was a grand book, with big colour pictures that had a layer of special paper over them you could sort of see through. Angie told Gabriel, 'It was his daddy's. Finn's grandmother sent it from Ireland when he was just a little baby.' Finn scowled. *Don't tell him private things like that, about my Daddy.* 'What story shall we read tonight, Finnie?' she asked, cuddling close beside him.

He shrugged. His thumb wanted to be in his mouth so much, he was scared it was just going to leap in there, but he trapped it under his thigh. *Stay there.*

'You should choose the story, Angie,' Gabriel said. 'Read the story of Mary and Martha.'

'Oh, the two sisters,' Angie exclaimed brightly. 'Yes, of course.'

Gabriel strummed his guitar very softly as she read about the two sisters Jesus came to visit, one who worked hard to make Jesus comfortable and cook the meal, the other who sat by his feet listening. And when the hard-working one complained, Jesus told her that what she chose to do was good, but what her sister had chosen was better still.

'For she has made the better choice, and it shall not be taken from her,' Gabriel repeated when Angie had finished reading. Still strumming, he said to Finn, 'You understand what that story is teaching us?'

Finn nodded, and went to slip off the couch, but Gabriel said, 'Wait until you're given permission to go,' and Angie quickly put a soft hand on Finn's arm and said, 'Wait', too.

'Let's make sure you *do* understand, Finn,' said Gabriel in his smooth voice. 'It's about making choices, isn't it? Let's see if you can pick the right choice to make. Let's say there's a boy named . . . well, we'll give him your name. Finn. And this boy Finn has a bad temper, and he calls his friend a bad, hurtful name. His uncle hears him and tells him to say that he's sorry. Finn grits his teeth,' Gabriel laid his hand flat on the guitar strings and showed what gritted teeth look like, 'and says to his friend very quickly, "I'm sorry!" His uncle says, "Finn, you didn't sound sorry. In fact you sounded very angry. If you can't sincerely apologise for what you did, I'd like you to stop and think about how you caused your friend pain, and pray for God's help to have a heart of apology." Now, Finn has a choice, doesn't he? He can obey and do as he was asked, or he can defy his uncle and walk away, with a bad attitude and a bitter heart.'

Finn sat rigid on the couch, staring at his knees.

'Which choice is the better one to make, Finn?' asked Gabriel, so silky. 'To be obedient and do God's will, or to be defiant, and not care about how much you hurt people?'

Finn could feel his mother silently urging him to say the right thing. *You're a tricker. There is no choice,* he wanted to yell at Gabriel – at both of them. But he couldn't.

'Finnie,' said his mum, nudging him.

'Obedient,' Finn muttered.

'Obedient,' said Gabriel. 'Yes. Pray to God to have a heart of apology. That's what you should do, isn't it, Finn? Because you hurt somebody with your bad words.' He strummed some loud notes that resonated, filling the whole room, then slapped his hand down on the strings and stopped them. In the sudden silence, in that voice that was soft and hard at the same time, hard as steel, Gabriel said, 'Kneel down then, Finn, and pray to be a better boy, and make better choices next time.'

Finn had no choice. He slid from the couch and kneeled down, closing his eyes and lowering his forehead to his clasped hands. What he prayed for, though, was not to have an apologetic heart.

While he knelt there, Gabriel got Angie to sing with him, a new song he was teaching her. He told her he was going to record a CD, and she would sing backup vocals on that. Finn listened and could hear so much in his mother's voice, how she was happy and nervous and proud and . . . and something else. Something Finn hadn't heard before.

When they were finished Gabriel told him to stand up, but as Finn was about to leave the room, he said again, 'Wait.' Finn stopped. 'I spoke to Melissa this afternoon.' That was the Sunday school teacher at Faith Rise – Faith Kids, the group was called. 'Melissa told me that you didn't do drawing with the other kids today.'

'Finnie doesn't like to colour in,' said Angie quickly. 'He likes to do his own drawings. They're very —'

Gabriel raised a hand and stopped her. 'And what's the better choice here, Angie, for you to make?' he asked kindly. 'Should you allow Finn to defy his teacher and his elders, or should you help him learn that he must be obedient? As *we* are obedient, Angie, to our Master's will.'

'Of course,' Angie said fervently. 'You're *right*, Gabriel, of course you're right.'

He's wrong, he's wrong, he's wrong, thought Finn. But he couldn't say anything.

Gabriel had brought home the outline drawing from Faith Kids of grinning children clustered around a grinning bearded man in robes, and Finn was sent off to his room to colour it in. He closed his bedroom door firmly behind him, thankful to be alone in the room which, even though it was so bare these days, with so much of its familiar clutter gone, was still his own. He put the photocopied drawing on his small desk and got out the packet of textas from the top drawer, along with a sheet of heavy white card he had saved from some packaging. On that sheet of card he drew a figure, a mechanical figure, dark and powerful.

You're back, Robo-Boy, Finn said silently as the figure took shape, and Robo-Boy said, *Yes, Finn,* and told him about where he'd been, and his adventures. He was so tough, so fearless. When the drawing was complete, Finn lifted up one corner of his mattress and slid Robo-Boy under it, as far as his arm could reach. *You stay there, Robo-Boy,* he said. *Okay?* Yes, he was okay. Then, quickly, Finn coloured in the Faith Kids' drawing as roughly as he could, deliberately going over the lines.

The door opened behind him. Finn could tell it wasn't his mum. He would not turn around, he would not look. He felt Gabriel standing right behind him, there against the back of his chair.

'That's the best you can do, is it?'

Finn nodded.

Tzung!

'Ow!' Finn's right hand flew to his ear and its sudden burning pain – as though the biggest mosquito in the world had just bitten him – then his wrist was grabbed, hard, and his hand jerked away.

'Don't waste your time getting smart with me, you little shit.' The man's breath, hot on Finn's stinging ear, his voice low and hissing, like a snake. 'You'll be sorry.'

Then Gabriel dropped Finn's wrist, and stepped back. 'Very well. You can go to bed now, Finn.'

Angie lingered in the bathroom after her shower, plucking stray hairs, examining her reflection minutely. *I'm still pretty,* she told herself. *I know I'm forty, but I'm still pretty.*

When she came out, smoothing the front panel of her vintage satin dressing-gown, Gabriel was in the kitchen, leaning against the table, facing toward the bathroom door.

'Oh, I'm so sorry!' Angie exclaimed. She blushed; it was as though he knew what she'd been doing, thinking. 'I didn't realise you were waiting for the bathroom.'

Gabriel made a single movement of his hand, summoning her. Angie came close, damp tendrils of hair still clinging to her forehead.

'I was waiting . . . for you,' he said in a low voice. They looked at each other and she felt breathless all of a sudden. Putting her hand to her chest, she took a couple of deeper breaths. His eyes followed the hand, then rose, slowly, up to her face.

'Your name is perfect,' Gabriel said. 'You are like an angel.'

She gave a quick delighted giggle. 'Oh! That's exactly what my dad used to say. He was the one who called me Angela. My mother wanted to call me something else but Daddy said I looked just like a little angel, and he in*sist*ed.'

Gabriel stood straight, away from the table, and the next moment his arms were around her. The heat from his body – he was holding her so close, Angie thought she might faint. 'He was right,' Gabriel murmured into her hair. 'Angel, shining and pure . . . You want to make the better choice, don't you, Angie? You want to do your Master's will?'

'Yes,' she whispered. 'Oh, yes.'

Tonight. It was so soft; had she misheard him? Imagined the word? She drew her head back, looking uncertainly into his extraordinary eyes. 'To – tonight?'

He placed a forefinger on her lips – 'Shhh . . .' – released her, and Angie watched him turn and limp away. She went to her own bedroom. Without allowing herself to think about what she was doing, she changed her cotton nightdress for another one: silk, with soft antique lace at the bodice. She got into bed, turned out the light and lay there, shivering in anticipation, wondering.

It seemed forever before the door silently opened. Gabriel was outlined there for only a moment, and then all was darkness again. She sensed more than heard his approach, soft as a huge moth. Then he was beside her bed, lifting back the covers. Lying his body down on top of hers.

'Gabriel.' The name floated from her lips in a heartfelt murmur, but he lay his hand across her mouth until she understood: she was not to speak. He lifted his weight fractionally for a moment while he tugged the nightdress up. *Tear it*, she thought. And, as he pushed inside her, *please*.

Gabriel came and went without a word.

In the darkness, once he was gone, she lay there still aflame, and trembling, and triumphant. *Mum always said it was Susanna who was the good one, the one who did the right thing and made the right choices. But it's me, it's me! I'm the one who's chosen now!*

ELEVEN

This is insane, thought Seb, close to panic. *How did I get myself into this?* He'd breezed through the school social with Rory, the exams were over, the school year was almost at an end – so why the hell did he have to go and complicate things now? He wasn't even sure how he and Rory got from strolling out the school gates mid-morning – no particular agenda, just because it was so easy to nick off now – to being here, in his bed, totally *un*relaxed, naked and sweaty and trying to . . . hook up. Do it. Have sex. *Fuck.*

Trying being the operative word, he thought grimly. Holy shit, he was going soft. Oh, *no*, not again. He held the condom on, pushing desperately, trying to find Rory's elusive hole. *Fuck!* he ordered himself fiercely. *Stick it in! This is what guys do!* But his dick did not agree.

'Seb,' said Rory. They'd tried various positions: they were on their sides now, with their bodies angled for what they'd hoped might be better access. 'Seb! Let's take a breather.'

'Okay.' They both flopped onto their backs.

Rory pointed to the poster on the wall above them. 'He's cute. What's his name again?'

'Rafael Nadal. He's a bit more than cute, actually; he's now number one in the world,' Seb said. Discreetly, he reached down and got the poor sad condom off his poor sad cock, letting it drop on the floor, and gave a sigh so big it was virtually a groan. 'Sorry, Rors. I dunno what's . . .' He shrugged helplessly.

'It's cool,' she said. And she really *didn't* sound pissed off, he realised, which was some small relief.

'I keep feeling like I'm doing something *wrong*,' he said. 'I mean, obviously I'm *doing* it wrong, but worse than that, like I'm . . . committing something. Not a crime exactly but . . .'

Rory reached across and patted his arm casually. 'Chill, Visser. This was my idea, remember? It's not like you lured me here and forced yourself upon me. And we're both seventeen: totally legal.'

'Yeah. You're right.' He relaxed a little. 'Sorry,' he said again.

'Have to say, though, I never would've thought you'd be the type to get performance anxiety.'

'Performance anxiety,' Seb repeated in a neutral tone. *Is that what this is? Just first-time nerves?*

'Yeah, I figured that being the big tennis champ, you'd have the pre-match jitters all sorted out. Kind of thing,' said Rory, pushing at his shoulder to free her long black hair from under it.

Seb nodded thoughtfully. 'Oh, yeah. Well. Bit different to playing tennis, actually.'

'True,' she agreed, pulling the sheet up over them. 'Clothes, for one thing.'

'And standing up.'

'And no spectators.'

'Which is just as well!'

They both sniggered, and then Seb couldn't help saying, 'I guess Rob de Clario never had performance anxiety.'

'A lady never discusses her previous gentlemen friends,' said Rory primly. 'Besides, that was so long ago, I can hardly remember. We've both moved on. Well, *he's* moved on, and I'm trying to.'

Seb knew Rob had taken a gap year before going to uni, working, and now backpacking overseas. He'd have liked to ask Rory more about what had happened between them, but was afraid his curiosity would be seen as jealousy, or comparison, or just kind of creepy. Even though he and Rory had been friends for so long, this —

'Friends!' he said suddenly. 'Maybe *that's* it!'

She raised her eyebrows at him. 'Friends?'

'Yeah. Maybe it's because we're *friends*, that's why it's not . . .' he waved his hand in the general direction of their lower bodies, 'you know, not happening.'

'Friends can't get the hots for each other? Oh, that would be *extremely* disappointing!'

'Yeah, no: maybe we just need some time to kind of . . . shift gears. Don't you reckon?' Seb was quite excited by this possibility. 'Because you and me used to, you know – we used to make little plasticine animals together in kinder. Remember?'

'I do,' said Rory. She poked him in the side. 'Your elephant was ridiculous.'

'It was not. It was a great elephant.'

'You wish! Y'know, it's kind of amazing. Who'd have thought the little shrimp you were back then was gonna turn into such a hottie?' She rolled over onto her front, giving him an exaggeratedly come-hither look. 'Even if you do need to get a bit more practice with how to shift that gear stick.'

He laughed, biffing playfully at her cute little nose. *I'm laughing about it*, he realised. Who else but Rory could he possibly do that with?

'Yeah, I was a shrimp, wasn't I?' he said. 'For ages. I still remember seeing you one night in the city a couple of years ago – I think it was the first night of one of the Harry Potter movies or something – and you were all dressed up, with make-up on and stuff, and I realised, shit, she looks like she's twenty, and I look about twelve.'

'Thirteen,' she said. 'You were being hard on yourself.'

'Yeah, well. I can remember back then, I used to look at the guys who were getting hair on their chests and their voices were breaking and stuff, and I used to feel kinda *sorry* for them. I thought it looked . . . gross. And then it started happening to me. I remember we were on holiday in Bali, and I just lay there the whole time on this big carved bed on the verandah feeling totally, comprehensively, blah. My mum was worried I was sick, and my dad was like, "Get up, ya lazy bastard!" And then after two weeks I stood up and I'd grown ten centimetres. Literally. I got all these stretch marks —' he pulled the sheet down and rolled to one side to show her the silvery lines across his hip.

'Wow!' said Rory, putting her glasses on to inspect them. 'Wadda you know, so guys get them, too. There was this one girl at my ballet school, it seemed like overnight she got these huge boobs and these enormous thighs. It was awful. She had to give up ballet. I was *so glad* it didn't happen to me.'

'Yeah,' said Seb. 'I really like your body,' he added, more or less as an aside. 'It's kinda . . . aerodynamic. Like you could fly.'

Rory shot him a pleased look. 'Why, thank you, Mr Visser.' They lay back down side by side on the pillows. It was very pleasant, actually, just lying there with her. He started mucking round with Rory's long dark hair, draping strands of it across his face. It was really soft, and each strand felt so clean and separate.

'And you've got beautiful hair, Miss Feng.'

'Ta,' she said. 'So . . .' There was a pause. 'Would I be right in thinking you're still a virgin?'

Inwardly, Seb cringed. *But what's the point in denying it?* He clasped his hands behind his head, gazing up at the ceiling and whistling ostentatiously.

She laughed. 'That's so sweet,' she said, resting her head on his arm. 'Really.'

'You reckon?' said Seb. *Oh, phew!* 'I think it runs in the family, actually. My dad told me he didn't start hooking up with girls till he was at uni. I was almost thinking it's my biological destiny or something. And my mum's always going, "You're in Year Twelve next year; forget sport, forget girls, you gotta focus on your study."'

'You know what? They're right. I don't want to have a serious relationship again till I've finished Year Twelve. I don't care if it seems like a ridiculous cliché, I *really* want to get into medicine at Melbourne Uni.' Rory drew a deep, determined breath and let it out slowly. 'And that's gonna be *hard*.' She started tapping lightly on Seb's chest with her fingertips, apparently deep in thought.

I wonder what's in the fridge, Seb thought. *Maybe we should get up and eat something.*

'Hey, you know what?' said Rory suddenly, propping herself up on one elbow. 'Seb?'

'What?'

'All the social pressure to be hooked up with someone – what if we let everybody think we're an item? Any parties or stuff where you need a date, we're it for each other. Hang out a bit. See? Then everyone thinks we're taken. The pressure's off.'

'Yeah . . .' said Seb slowly. He could see how that could be a good thing. *It's a jungle out there, but maybe I don't have to enter it.*

'And if we study together too . . . Now, that'd be smart. We're mostly doing the same subjects, right? Biol, Chem, Maths Methods?'

'Yeah,' said Seb. 'But I think I might've made a mistake going for Maths Methods. It gets marked higher but it's definitely not my best subject.'

'But it's *my* best subject, and Chem, you're outstanding. English, we could really help each other there. I reckon we can *ace* it.'

'Riiight . . .' Seb nodded slowly as her plan took shape. 'Yeah. This could work, on a whole lot of levels.' He gave an incredulous chuckle. 'This is the sort of idea my *sister* would come up with! Oh, sorry, Rors, I don't mean you're like my sister.'

Rory laughed; she had a great laugh, surprisingly loud. 'That's cool. Your sister's pretty amazing, you know? One day, you're gonna be going, "Oh yeah, I'm Stella-Jean Visser's brother." Guarantee you.'

Seb looked horrified. 'Promise me you won't tell *her* that.'

'Depends. What'll you offer me to keep my mouth shut?'

It was so great to be lying here, yakking like this. Like when they used to lie on their mats next to each other during nap time and Miss Barnes had to tell them to shush – except that in Miss Barnes's kinder group, they had their clothes on. Rory had shifted so that her hip was hoicked up against his, and now she moved her thigh to rest across his groin. The pressure was pleasant; more and more pleasant.

His dick started to get hard; they both noticed, but just kept talking. She started rocking slightly, and that was even better. She rolled her leg further across, splaying her slender body atop his, still rocking; they were both facing the ceiling, the wing-like back of her shoulder rubbing his chest, while his dick was sandwiched between her bum and his own taut belly, and as his hard-on grew so did the pressure. She reached for his right hand and placed it between her legs, guiding, curling his fingers over. Seb had never really touched a girl's cunt before, certainly not like this. It was moist and hot, with surprisingly wiry fur. It alarmed him. Deftly, he reversed the position of their hands, so that his was on top of hers.

'Show me,' he murmured, and she did. He could feel her fingers working under his, he could feel the glute flexing in her small arse, no meatier than a boy's, he could feel their bodies ramping up the voltage a notch, several notches. He wrapped his other arm around her torso, pressing her tight to him. The system was gonna reach overload, any second; Rory started making sounds that were not like any he'd heard her make before, and not like the women on the porn sites, and then her fingers were *tugging*, kind of, yes, or was it her whole body, he could feel her pelvis bucking under their stacked hands and she was making harsh, very ungirly noises, grunts really, a total turn-on, and his balls filled and shot white light up through his cock and blew the top of his head off into the sky, the universe, the Milky Way.

Some minutes later, after he had re-entered earth's atmosphere, he managed to say 'Wow!' Unoriginal, but heartfelt.

'Yeah,' Rory murmured. Her thighs were still trembling. And her glasses were still on, which seemed odd and endearing. 'Double wow.'

They lay sweatily entwined, just breathing, coming back to earth. 'Not bad, for your first performance.'

'I didn't have to do a thing,' said Seb sincerely. 'I was in the hands of a master. Mistress. Why doesn't that sound right?'

'Damn sexist language. You know what? I've never come like that before.'

'Nor have I,' he said with fervour, and even though he couldn't see her face he could feel her grinning.

'Eesh, my leg's all icky. Hand me those tissues, Visser.' They disentangled; she wiped the cum off her hip while he mopped his belly.

Rory rose, all dancer's grace, seeming almost to unfold and float from the bed. She plucked his towel from the back of a nearby chair, sniffed it hard a couple of times and wrapped it around herself. 'Okay, I'm going to have a shower now.'

Seb watched her leave the room, then lay back and let himself revel in the fabulous, glowing fact: *I've had sex*. Not the standard format, but definitely sex. *And next time*, he told himself, grinning cheesily, *I'll get the ace in the hole*. This was as good as winning any of those trophies lined up on the shelf. Better! *I've fucked a girl; I have a girlfriend.*

I'm not gay. He heaved a great blissed-out sigh of relief. *I'm not gay!*

TWELVE

Susanna had spent most of the morning preparing the kitchen for the annual Christmas baking, and was now checking that everything was in order, according to the recipes that had been handed down through generations of Greenfield women. In four separate clusters on the island bench she'd assembled all the ingredients for the fruit mince tarts, the Christmas cake, the shortbread, and of course the Christmas pudding, which would be mixed and ceremonially stirred today, then left to sit overnight before boiling.

Stella-Jean, meanwhile, stood by the table at the far end of the room, in perfect but unconscious imitation of her mother's pose, right elbow supported in her cupped left hand as she too ticked off with her index finger what *she* had assembled – the stack of butcher's paper, the textas and pastels and jumbo crayons. Each year, with Finn's help, Stella-Jean produced a great quantity of colourful wrapping paper, and in three weeks time, on Christmas Day, the family would pile their gifts, all wrapped in this bright bounty, under a decorated pine tree in the living room. It gave Susanna great pleasure that her daughter had added a new tradition to the ones she herself so enjoyed maintaining. Yes, there was a lot of organising; yes, there were all the attendant and inevitable frictions – but it was worth it.

'Aren't they a bit late?' Stella-Jean asked.

Susanna glanced at the clock on the wall, and frowned. 'Yes. And Mum's usually here early.'

'This year, if Jeejee and Auntie Ange start fighting with each other, I'm going to fall down on the floor and pretend to faint, okay?' Stella-Jean sounded like she was quite looking forward to the prospect. 'That'll distract 'em.'

'I'm sure that won't be necessary,' her mother said. 'I think just looking at you is distraction enough for anybody.' She raised a hand across her forehead, pretending to shield her eyes from the vision of Stella-Jean in her lime-green leggings and a polished cotton mini-dress with swirling orange and pink paisleys, part of the haul Angie had given her. Bright plastic clips secured her hair in a dozen little bunches.

'It's for inspiration,' said Stella-Jean, gesturing grandly at the paper waiting to be embellished.

Both turned as they heard Angie's three-note 'Hell-o-oh!' at the open front door, and in she came, shepherding Finn before her. Once in the kitchen, Angie gave his shoulder a small meaningful nudge. Finn cast a fleeting glance at Susanna and then said, to his feet, 'Hello Auntie Susanna.'

'Oh! Hello to you, Finn! Nice to see you!' He was already scuttling across to join his cousin at the table.

'Finn's been working on his manners, haven't you Finnie?' said Angie proudly.

Finn said, 'Can we start drawing now, Stella?'

'Go for it, Finnster.'

'What do we say?' his mother prompted.

'Please,' Finn said, after a moment's hesitation, and then climbed right on to the table to gain maximum access to the big sheets of paper. Stella-Jean would have liked to tell him, *You don't have to say please to me*, but maybe he'd hear it the wrong way, as just another piece of criticism. Finn had been so tense lately, jumpy, like Tigger the cat on a windy day.

'Um – Ange: come with me and get some lemons, eh?' said Susanna, beckoning her sister to the back door. As soon as they were outside she said in a low voice, 'Wow, I'm impressed. I'm not used to Finn saying hello like that.'

'You can thank Gabriel,' said Angie happily. 'He's helped me see that the way I was letting Finn behave is not the way God wants *any* of us to behave. Children should respect us, just as we respect God.' She had the slightly smug expression of someone who has mastered an elusive skill. 'It's simple, really, but I needed Gabriel to show me.'

'Well, that's marvellous,' said Susanna, wondering about Stella-Jean's dark mutterings about Gabriel being weird and Finn unhappy. *Could she be a little jealous?* Because even if the "respecting God" line wasn't Susanna's cup of tea, the new tenant was clearly having a positive influence. 'Congratulations, Ange.'

'And Finnie's teacher says he's much quieter now, and hardly ever misbehaves. And Gabriel makes sure I get him there on time, too.'

'That *is* incredible,' said Susanna, grinning as she gave her sister's shoulder a playful bump with her own. The man must be a miracle worker! They each picked a couple of lemons from the tree and walked back up the path together. Through the kitchen window they could see the kids already hard at work.

Finn was hunkered low over the large sheet of butcher's paper, concentrating fiercely. This big red circle in the middle of the page, this was Gabriel's mouth, wide open as he sang, and all the jagged green diamonds around it, spread over every bit of the paper, these were his eyes, watching, watching you all the time. Finn picked up the black crayon and made a grid over the whole thing: these were the prison bars he would put Gabriel behind, one day. Lock him up and never let him out. *There!* He sat back on his heels and regarded his first drawing with a thin smile of satisfaction.

'Here, Stella,' he said. 'This one's finished.'

'Good job, Finnster.' *Who gave you that horrible haircut?* she'd have liked to know. Too short and kind of patchy: it made his ears stick out and his big chin seem even bigger. He looked like one of those refugee kids you saw in documentaries. 'Hey. You want to use the jumbo textas too?' she asked, offering him the packet.

Finn nodded, selecting one with care. As Stella-Jean covered her own paper swiftly in loose swoops of crayon, she watched him out of the corner of her eye. He had always liked to draw geometric patterns – not for Finn the stick-figure family, the wobbly house with peaked roof and two windows – but she had never seen him being quite as precise and intense as this.

From one side of his fresh sheet to the other, Finn drew row after meticulous row of wavy pink lines, then, turning the paper forty-five degrees, he intersected them with purple lines. Pink was his mother's favourite colour, purple was his. This is how it used to be: him and Mum. Now she was with Gabriel all the time; even when she was with Finn, she was *really* with Gabriel. And she was always going *Shh, Finnie, shh*, because Gabriel needed everything to be quiet for his songs. If Finn wasn't quiet Gabriel got angry, striking out quick and hissy like a snake. In the thickest, blackest texta, Finn drew a snake's forked tongue, an angry V here, there and everywhere among the wavy pink and purple lines.

At the island bench, Angie nodded as Susanna listed all the assembled ingredients: the various dried fruits, the different sugars, the treacle and flours and spices and so on. Suddenly Angie gasped and clutched at her sister's arm.

'Oh, Susu, I nearly forgot.' She trotted over to the corner of the kitchen where, on entering, she'd propped a large grey cardboard folder, and carried it back to the bench. 'I meant to give you this *weeks* ago. Come, see.'

Susanna withdrew a sheet of paper at random. 'Oh, will you look at that! It's baby Stella-Jean.'

'Huh?' Stella-Jean swung round, and her mother brought the sketch over to show her. It was in pencil, of a round-cheeked infant with flyaway hair. 'Wow, I was so *cute!*'

'Is that Stella?' asked Finn, rising to a kneeling position and craning to see over Susanna's arm.

'Yes, it is,' said Susanna, lowering her arm obligingly. 'Do you recognise her?' She took more drawings out of the folder: all were of Seb and Stella-Jean, as babies or toddlers or very young children. 'Oh, this is terrific! Where did you find them, Ange? I thought *all* this stuff got chucked out.'

'I saw this folder sitting by the bin one day, ages ago, and —' Angie mimed furtively carrying something away.

'Mum! You chucked them out?' Stella-Jean was mightily affronted. 'Pictures of *me*?'

'I didn't *mean* to, sweetheart. There was a mix-up with — never mind.' She could still remember the row she and Gerry had had; she'd ended up apologising, but still couldn't really see how it was her fault, when he'd been the one who cleared everything out in one ruthless day. 'It was just, there wasn't room to keep everything once I didn't have the studio any more.'

'What studio?'

'The games room used to be my studio, when we first moved in here. I used to draw a lot then.' *Draw and paint*, she remembered. *Somehow, amid all the interruptions.*

'How come it got turned into a stupid games room? An art studio's a much better idea.'

'I agree,' said Angie. 'Your mother's art is *wonderful*. You should've kept using that room, Susu.'

'Oh, but – the kids were getting bigger . . . They needed . . . It just . . .' Susanna shrugged helplessly. How to explain how selfish it had seemed, having that whole huge room to herself, especially when she'd been finding less and less time for her art? A whole family's needs for time, space, attention, to balance against her own increasingly spasmodic and unsatisfactory creative efforts. 'Then I started teaching full-time, at the college . . .'

'Well, you're not going to chuck 'em out this time,' said Stella-Jean firmly.

'I won't, don't worry. Thank you, Ange,' Susanna said, giving her sister a kiss on the cheek. 'I'm so glad you rescued these, way back when.'

Angie glowed. 'And then finding them again, when I was cleaning out my house for Gabriel.' This, and so many other marvellous things – *all because of Gabriel*, she thought, her heart swelling with the love she longed to tell of, to sing, to shout from the rooftops. But this beautiful thing, this love that was growing between them was a secret treasure, still so new and precious it couldn't be spoken of – not yet. Not even to each other. But anyone, surely, who saw them singing together with the Faith Rise Band would see, would know, that *something* special was happening. If Susanna saw, she'd know at once what a wonderful man Gabriel was, how he'd transformed Angie's whole *life*.

Ask her, urged an inner voice, *ask her now!* 'Susanna —' she said, and stopped, clasped her hands in ardent supplication, then went on in a rush: 'Please, come to Faith Rise with us this Christmas!'

Susanna felt a lurch in the pit of her stomach, as though she'd missed a step on a familiar staircase. 'Faith Rise?' she stalled. 'This Christmas?'

'Yes! It's going to be so special this year, with Gabriel's music. If you come on Christmas Eve you could see me singing with the Faith Rise Band. Please! It would mean *so* much to me.'

'Oh, Ange. Another time, I will. But right now I'm just too busy.' *Oh, don't be a coward*, Susanna thought. *Tell her.* 'And darling, after that other time I went, I realised I'm really *not* a churchy sort of person.'

For most of her life, Susanna had barely given religion a thought, taking the atheism she'd grown up with for granted. But when Angie first got involved with Faith Rise she'd gone there with her – once. As well as being appalled by the inanity and conservatism of the pastor's sermon, she'd been baffled by the constant references to sin, and astonished at the young congregation's joy and gratitude at being miraculously rescued from it. *What sin?* she wanted to ask them. We all have our faults, we all do our best; why this big melodrama about *sin*? And in any case, even when you've hurt other people – 'sinned' against them – how could believing in one particular version of god make amends? No, the very thought of sitting through all that again made Susanna feel quite itchy.

'But you *are*,' said Angie with conviction. 'You went to all those churches when you were in Europe. You loved them, you told me you loved them.'

'I loved the *art*,' Susanna said. 'I loved all the statues, and the frescoes and paintings. And the beautiful woodwork and the – the *bells*, I love the way they ring the bells there, in Europe,' she ended, a little desperately, holding her hands up and swinging them to and fro.

'Susu, I'm not trying to convert you, I'm not asking you to accept Jesus as your saviour,' Angie said, and then gave a little nervous giggle. 'Not yet, anyway. I just want you to share the joy!'

'I'll go,' said Stella-Jean.

The sisters' faces both swung toward her, mouths agape. '*You* will?' said her mother, and 'You *will*?' said her aunt, at the same moment. Finn was staring at her too, but said nothing.

'Christmas Eve? Yeah, I'll go.'

Angie clapped her hands. 'That's *wonderful*, Stella!'

Finn dropped his face as quickly as he'd raised it, hunching over the paper again and colouring over the same spot so hard his texta tore a hole in the paper. '*Psst*,' Stella-Jean hissed, wanting to give him a reassuring wink, but he wouldn't look at her.

'And then,' said Susanna, inspired, 'perhaps your friend Gabriel might like to join us here for lunch on Christmas Day.'

Now Stella-Jean looked up, aghast, but before she could protest Angie shook her head. 'That's so sweet of you, but Pastor Tim and Helen have invited him to share Christmas Day with them, after the early service. Otherwise I'm sure he'd love to. But I'm *so* looking forward to you meeting him properly and *really* getting to know him. Once you do . . . oh, you'll see!'

'Yes, lovely,' Susanna smiled, hoping that this awkward and

unexpected discussion had been safely got through. She held her right hand to her ear in the telephone gesture. 'I'll just find out where Mum is,' she said, and walked quickly into the living room.

'Ooh, and I need a bathroom break,' said Angie. She hesitated, then made a little rush toward Stella-Jean and hugged her tightly. 'You are the *dearest* girl,' she said. 'God *bless* you!' and left the room almost skipping.

Finn was drawing again: a grid of purple squares – his room, repeated – and in each one a thick black L ending in a fat round blob. *That's Robo-Boy's arm. And every time Gabriel comes in and says, 'Say you're sorry, Finn,' and, 'Kneel down, Finn, pray to be good,' then Robo-Boy will jump out from under the bed and he'll* roar *so loud and he'll smash Gabriel to bits with his big strong fist.*

'Finnster.' Stella-Jean leaned closer to her cousin, who hunched away from her. 'Hey, Finn. I'm only going to Faith Rise on Christmas Eve so I can check him out. Okay? Not because I wanna hear him sing. It's like I'm an undercover cop checking out the bad guy. You get what I mean?'

After a few long seconds he looked up, very serious. 'You know he *is* the bad guy?' he whispered.

'I know.'

Finn nodded. 'Okay, Stella.'

Angie came back into the room with freshly combed hair framing her bright, eager face in soft waves. Susanna's expression, however, was clouded. 'Mum's been at the doctor's,' she said. 'She says it's nothing important, just took longer than she thought. She's on her way now.'

'Oh, fine then,' said Angie gaily. 'Susanna, I was just remembering the Christmas when you gave me Silver. That was the most *wonderful* Christmas present I ever had!'

'Silver?' Susanna asked as she collected scales and measuring cups and mixing bowls from cupboards and drawers. 'What silver?'

'Silver the pony! Remember?'

Stella-Jean dropped her crayon loudly on the table, gobsmacked. 'Mum gave you a *pony*?' Even Finn stopped drawing to hear about this.

Angie laughed. 'Not a *real* pony, Stella! It was a beautiful little silver horse your mum won at the Royal Show. I loved that little horse so much.'

'You did,' Susanna smiled. She remembered now the shiny little nickel statuette she'd won on some sideshow. 'You adored it.' Night after night, Angie had come in to her room and stroked the pony's die-cast mane, talked to it, kissed it good night. Susanna had been fond of it too, but her younger sister's devotion had been impossible to resist. 'I can still remember your face when you unwrapped it.'

'I couldn't believe you'd *given* it to me. You were always so good to me, Susu. A saint!'

'Oh, don't be silly,' Susanna scoffed gently, touched.

'Have you still got that horsie, Mum?' asked Finn. He'd begun filling a new sheet with groups of three joined circles: purple, pink, orange; purple, pink, orange. Him, Mum and Stella-Jean; him, Mum and Stella-Jean. That's how they'd be after Gabriel was gone. Around each group he drew a yellow sun, shining brightly.

Angie shook her head softly. 'No, I don't know where Silver is now. Maybe off having adventures with some other little girl. Or boy.'

'Hi-ho, Silver!' said Susanna, and they both giggled. 'Okay, come on, Ange. Time to get on with the Christmas baking.'

Consulting from time to time the recipes propped on the bench beside each cluster of ingredients, the two sisters started weighing and measuring. 'This is a great tradition,' Angie enthused as she tipped currants from a cup into a larger bowl. 'You'll have to join in, Stella darling, so you can carry it on.'

'I don't think so,' said Stella-Jean, who didn't actually care for Christmas cake, and found shortbread very disappointing. 'Me and Finn will just do the pudding stir and make our wish. That's all the tradition we need.'

Jean arrived a few minutes later, apologising for her tardiness, and pecking cheeks, as surprised as Susanna had been when Finn, nudged by his mother, said, 'Hello, Jeejee.' She brushed off Susanna's query about the visit to the doctor, while simultaneously admiring the kids' growing stack of coloured wrapping paper and taking the apron that was kept just for her from a drawer. 'Well, well,' she said, tying it at the back of her neat waist as she advanced on the bench. 'I see you two girls have been managing things perfectly well without me.'

'Ah, but *we* still have to check the recipes, Mum,' said Susanna. 'You know them off by heart.'

'Oh dear!' Jean exclaimed. 'We're not letting *Angie* measure the ingredients, are we? Remember the year you thought all the spices were a *table*spoon of each instead of a teaspoon?' She chuckled. 'We had to throw the whole pudding out and start again!'

Instantly, Angie's face changed. 'That was your writing,' she said angrily. 'It *looked* like tablespoon. *Every*body thought it looked like tablespoon.'

'That wasn't *my* writing, dear, it was your great-grandma Evans' writing,' said Jean, all trace of humour evaporated. 'And three generations of women had made that recipe, year after year, without making that mistake.'

Susanna and Stella-Jean exchanged a speedy glance, Stella-Jean rolling her eyes up under the lids and miming a sideways topple.

'I don't know why you bother with this Christmas paraphernalia anyway,' said Angie. 'Puddings and presents! It's so hypocritical, when you don't even believe in God, let alone that it's the birthday of our saviour.'

Susanna made a noise somewhere between a groan and a whimper, but they both ignored her. 'It was a pagan celebration long before the Christians hijacked it, Angie,' said Jean crisply. Her face had become crisper too, somehow, the soft, lined skin lifted by her vigorous application of reason, as if argument was a kind of Botox. 'Solstice feasting goes back a lot further than two thousand years, you know.'

'Yeah, but the *winter* solstice, Jeejee,' said Stella-Jean. Argument had never fazed her, either. 'It's only because it was the British who colonised Australia that we do the pudding and everything, in the middle of summer.'

'But none of that *matters*,' said Angie passionately.

Jean turned toward her, a supercilious comment poised on her lips, and saw that Angie's face, so merry when she'd arrived, so *pretty*, was now furious and sulky and miserable again: an expression with which Jean was all too familiar. *I did that to her*, she realised, one hand flying momentarily to her mouth. *Exactly what I had promised myself not to do. Am I so lacking not just in kindness, but in self-control?*

'Of course,' she said, gathering herself, with a shudder. 'Of course. And Angie, to tell the truth, I found Grandma Evans' writing hard to follow sometimes, too. It's our being here, making these old recipes together, *that's* what matters.'

Angie narrowed her eyes suspiciously. 'Hmph.' She picked up the measuring cup full of sugar she'd set aside when the argument began. 'I wish I'd grown up in a *Christian* family,' she muttered petulantly, as she tipped a stream of white crystals into the mixing bowl.

Susanna looked from one to the other with a wary smile. 'Is everybody okay now?' she asked. 'Can we just make the pudding?'

THIRTEEN

'Suze! Hey, Suze!' Gerry swept like a gale in the front door, through the living room, and on to the far end of the kitchen where Susanna sat at the table, head down to a writing pad and surrounded by books and magazines.

'Hi, darling,' she said, still scribbling as hard as she could go. Gerry stood across from her on the other side of the table, waiting; by the time she looked up, he was standing with fists theatrically balled on his hip bones, and a pouchy mouth. 'Sorry,' she said at once. 'I just had to get that bit down before I lost it. How was your meeting?'

'The meeting,' he said, pulling a chair out from the table and spinning it around to sit, legs akimbo, facing its back, 'was ... in a word ...' She smiled in anticipation, knowing that if he was drawing it out like this, the news must be good. '... fucking fantastic!'

'Hooray!' Susanna clapped, grinning, aware that Visser Kanaley urgently needed some new work to come in. She was vague on numbers, but knew that some clients had put jobs on hold, and others had cancelled outright. At a dinner just last week Marcus, on the second bottle of wine, had confided to her that he was worried – 'worried sick', he'd said, and even Gerry had not rebutted him with his usual confidence. And this morning, ahead of the meeting with a Sydney developer, she'd thought her husband seemed uncharacteristically tense.

'So, tell me!' she said, pushing her pad and books aside to show he had her full attention.

'You're going to love this, Suze,' he said. 'It's all because of that design I whipped up for the High Plains visitors' centre. They haven't even announced the short list yet but this developer's wife is on the board and she's *rapt*. A total convert to the Visser vision, and she's got hubby on side too. The guy's got three private hospitals in Sydney he wants to extend and upgrade, ASAP, preferably without taking them out of action. Like he says, one thing people *haven't* stopped doing is getting sick.' Gerry gave a hoot of triumphant laughter. 'If we can nail this, there's a ton of work in the offing. We're home and hosed.'

'That's fabulous,' said Susanna. 'Oh, Marcus must be so relieved!'

Gerry flexed his fingers, palms out, a couple of times. 'Ah! Our Marco's eating humble pie, let me tell you. Swears he'll never whinge about me wasting time on competition designs again.'

'What a relief,' Susanna repeated. So, Visser Kanaley wouldn't be ending the year in the financial doldrums after all. She'd dreaded having to deal with a Gerry who was on edge and grumpy throughout the long summer holiday. As she went over to his chair to give him a congratulatory kiss, the hard light of the setting sun, streaming in through the big west-facing window, flashed in her eyes, and she stepped across to pull down the blind. End of the day, and later than she'd realised: it was light till so late now. 'Oh, darling, I've been so preoccupied with this article, I'm afraid I haven't made any plans for dinner,' she said apologetically. 'Seb's out with Aurora and Stella-Jean's doing something with Tessa so I —'

'Suze! Focus!' said Gerry, snapping his fingers impatiently toward her. 'Listen! This guy's really keen. He's flying us up to Sydney on Friday to meet his team, then there's some pre-Christmas party Saturday arvo, on the harbour. On his spiffing great private yacht, thanks very much. His wife's going to be there, and I want you to come too. That'd be just the right thing.'

'*This* Friday?' She sagged. 'That's a lovely idea, but I really don't think I can.'

'Sure you can! It's the last week of college, isn't it? You can take an early mark. Or fly up Friday evening, after work. The kids are perfectly capable of looking after themselves for the weekend.'

'Well, I know. But I've organised a couple of interviews, for this article.' She gestured toward the paperwork on the table. 'They're the last things, and then I can finish. And Belinda says she's got a contact at *Praktika* who might be interested in publishing it.'

'Publishing what?' said Gerry. He reached out to pick up the topmost of the scattered books, frowning at the hideously pop-eyed cartoon face on the cover, the title issuing in a speech bubble from its tombstone-toothed mouth: '*Krazy!*' he read aloud. '*The Delirious World of Anime + Comics + Video Games + Art.*' He looked across at her, bemused.

'It's surprisingly interesting, really,' Susanna said, 'much more than —'

'You're writing an article about *comics*?' Slowly shaking his head.

'Not comics exactly. It's about how technophobic old fogeys like me cope with teaching art to students who've never known a world without the internet. Pre-digital; post-digital.'

'Really. Well, this subject's not going be any less fascinating if you have a weekend off. Come on, Suze – live a little! Party on the harbour, flash hotel in the Rocks. I was thinking we could have dinner at the Wharf, maybe go to a play . . .'

'Oh, sweetheart,' Susanna said regretfully, 'I'd love to. But the thing is, I've also got Finn staying here for the weekend. Angie's going to be in Sydney too, isn't that a coincidence? For a wedding.'

Gerry looked thoroughly exasperated now. 'Oh, *great*. It's amazing how your sister manages to inflict herself on us even when she's not around.'

Susanna sank into herself a little. 'She hardly ever has a chance to get away . . .' she murmured.

'Is she taking that fella who's moved in with her?' asked Gerry, with a meaningful lift of one eyebrow.

'I don't know.'

'What do you think of him?'

'I've barely met him,' said Susanna carefully. 'He seems nice . . .'

'Stella didn't think so.'

'Well, he seems to be having a positive effect on Finn's manners, at any rate.' Susanna cast about for some way to restore her husband's good cheer. Her face brightened. 'But, honey, isn't Marcus going to Sydney too? You could —'

'Yes, Marcus is going,' said Gerry flatly. 'But Marcus has his own after-hours plans. He's meeting John up there for a dirty weekend.'

'Oh, *no*. Don't tell me that's on again.' Susanna clapped one hand to her forehead. 'I just don't understand why a lovely person like Marcus keeps going back to this relationship, again and again. It's like an addiction.'

'His choice, Suze. He loves John, and John loves him but he can't leave his wife.'

'How can John say for a *moment* that he loves him, when he's been keeping Marcus dangling all these years?' asked Susanna. 'And his wife supposedly doesn't *know*?'

'Apparently not.' Gerry lifted his hands in a gesture of helplessness. 'What can I say? People's private lives are complicated.'

'Some people's, maybe. Not mine, I'm glad to say.' Susanna shook her head, then came toward him with arms extended, and Gerry rose from his chair to receive her hug. 'Darling,' she murmured, snuggling close. 'We can still have fun without going to Sydney.'

'Yeah? That a promise?' Gerry bent to kiss the back of her neck.

She wriggled, pressing her breasts against his chest. 'It is,' she said. 'Most definitely it is.'

'Nothing like this in Melbourne, now, is there?' said the developer as his yacht glided serenely past the North Shore's lovely coves and sandstone cliffs. 'That bathtub you call a bay!'

'No, Chris, nothing like it,' said Gerry amiably. Coming from Perth, he found the never-ending and occasionally ferocious rivalry between Sydney and Melbourne amusing. Hoping to stir Marcus, who was nearby talking numbers with Chris's right-hand man, he added loudly, 'This has got to be the most beautiful city in the world.' Their host's chest inflated as pridefully as if he'd created the whole magnificent vista himself, but Marcus refused to take the bait, just twisting the corner of one lip at his partner before resuming his conversation.

Terri, the developer's wife, a lively woman whose leathery skin testified to her devotion to the outdoors, offered Gerry another Sydney rock oyster. He'd already slurped down a good dozen, at least; these guys didn't seem to give a toss about the global financial crisis. 'What a pity your wife couldn't come,' she said.

'Sure is. Next time,' Gerry answered with a smile. Susanna really was missing out on a glorious day: the bright blue of the summer sky, speckled with little cotton wool clouds, the deeper blues of the water. On shore, red roofs and white houses and blocks of units almost lost in lush green foliage: frangipanis, palms, tall silky oaks, and angophoras with their twisted peach-coloured limbs. A huge ocean liner, like a floating horizontal skyscraper, moved slowly out toward the Heads, hooting deeply; fleets of sleek racers rounded buoys, their bright spinnakers popping and billowing, while chunky yellow and green ferries bustled dutifully from wharf to wharf.

As their yacht passed a large gaily decorated boat there was an eruption of applause; Gerry glanced across to see a bride and groom embracing, having just, he presumed, exchanged their vows. Everyone on board was cheering, clapping, snapping pictures of the happy couple backgrounded by those fabulous Sydney icons: the Bridge, slicing the azure sky, and the sails of the Opera House arching up, up, like a dazzling pile of ivory.

Had this groom, Gerry wondered, made a choice as sensible as his? A good-hearted, biddable woman like Susanna, so much better suited to marriage than a temperamental show pony like his first love, Justine. But these newlyweds looked to be in their forties, and another thought suddenly lobbed into his brain: *Who would I choose now, if I wasn't planning to have kids?* Instantly, he dismissed it: *irrelevant.*

'Bet they reckon it'll all be plain sailing from here, but they'll soon find out,' Chris commented cheerfully as he steered past the wedding boat. 'Gotta take the rough with the smooth, eh Gerry?' He and Gerry shared a knowing grin: fellow long-termers. The developer and his wife, Gerry thought, seemed to be travelling well: thirty years, three grown-up kids, a successful business in which she clearly had a big say.

Terri beckoned him over to where she was telling a group how she'd been bowled over by Visser Kanaley's proposal for the High Plains centre. 'Describe it for us, Gerry,' she said, and he obliged, embroidering the tale of his struggle to find a design that honoured the unique natural elements of the park, allowing his listeners to get the impression that he'd camped out at the site for weeks, waxing lyrical about how, by assuming the vantage point of an eagle gliding over the landscape, he'd finally been granted that breakthrough vision – the nest.

'What an inspiring story!' said Terri. 'Monica!' She called over a young woman Gerry had noticed earlier. 'You *must* include this in the profile. Monica is our PR genius,' she told Gerry. 'We'll get her to interview you properly while you're here. Listen to this marvellous story, Mon . . .'

After Terri was called away and the knot of guests had dispersed, Monica stayed, chatting to Gerry, and he was pleased to have her to himself. She was a stunner: mid-thirties, tall, with porcelain skin and masses of dark auburn hair. When she went to get them both another drink he checked out her arse: ripe and luscious. He loved an arse that jiggled as its owner walked.

When she came back, he pretended to notice her wedding ring for the first time and inquired, looking around with innocent curiosity at the other guests, whether her husband was there too. Monica shook her head. 'Dan's working in Hong Kong. He's a flight instructor,' she explained. 'He only gets back here once a month.'

Is that so? After their conversation had charted a suitably discursive course through other topics, Gerry suggested casually that she could interview him that evening. 'Over dinner maybe? If you're free . . .'

She was.

Monica ordered a cocktail, a serious one rather than some cream-drenched girly thing. Gerry took this as a good sign, and followed suit with a dirty martini. A serious cocktail made for serious flirting, the whack from that belt of spirits imparting, after just a couple of sips, a delicious frisson to every word and gesture.

They followed up with a glass of champagne each, and some appetisers. The fried baby artichokes with aioli proved a particularly good choice: as well as being delicious, the fact that they were served in a single basket made it unavoidable that his and Monica's fingers would touch, casually, as they reached and dipped.

She's gorgeous, he thought, watching her pop another of the salty morsels into a mouth as marvellously sensuous and greedy as Nigella Lawson's. The champagne ramped the buzz up a notch to a kind of reckless gaiety: they were sparring now, showing off and laughing at each other's jokes. Oh, he relished this stage, the unspoken agreement that each would present their wittiest and most engaging self to the other, back and forth in a sustained and stimulating rally.

Dinner, and with it a bottle of wine. Monica actually got a note-book out, murmuring about press releases and the in-house newsletter, and jotting things down from time to time as their conversation covered Gerry's ideas and achievements. She was a good interviewer, a good questioner, a good listener. Being in the spotlight of this lovely young woman's attention was entirely satisfactory.

From there, it was easy for Gerry to ask some questions of her, and for these questions to become more personal. Both felt the urge to know, to reveal. They were dancing closer and closer to the edge, each enraptured by the other's grace and skill – and their own.

The waiter came, poured the last of the wine, cleared their plates. They accepted dessert menus but Monica soon put hers face down on the table.

'Not for you?' said Gerry, and when she shook her head he lowered his menu too. 'Coffee?'

She shook her head again and unhooked her small leather bag from the back of the chair. 'I'll just . . .' she pointed her chin toward the restrooms. Had something shifted? Gerry couldn't tell. While she was gone he asked for the bill, and paid. What did it mean that she didn't want to linger? *It all depends on what happens in the next few minutes.* He felt in his pocket for the condoms he'd bought before coming to the restaurant. He wanted the opportunity to use them, very much.

Monica returned, dropping her bag on the table as she sat down. Strange: in her absence he'd registered how noisy the restaurant was, but now that she was back it didn't seem so. It was as though they were enveloped in a little bubble of silky quiet, with the bustle of the waiters and the laughter and loud talk of their fellow diners nothing more than background.

This moment. This was it: when the playfulness deepened, when the thrilling gravity of a question still unasked entered the space between two people and hung there. Waiting.

'My sister-in-law's staying with me at the moment,' she said. 'With her two kids. Did I mention that?'

He shook his head slightly, with a noncommittal smile. *So, no going back to her place.*

'You must miss your husband,' he said. *Lay it on the table.* 'I mean – once a month? That's hard.'

She looked at him very directly. 'It is.' Delicately, she brushed a few strands of dark hair away from her mouth, and lowered her gaze to the white linen tablecloth. 'It's really hard because . . . What's really

hard is, to find someone who . . . ah, who knows . . .' Her voice was
sinking, lower and lower. '. . . What you need.'

Gerry exhaled the breath he didn't even know he'd been holding:
ah! 'And what do you need?'

Monica raised her eyes again to meet his. 'A firm hand,' she breathed.
She was leaning toward him, forearms resting on the tablecloth, offering him shadowy cleavage and the pale globes of her breasts. Gerry
reached across and picked up the slender strap of her bag; he draped
the narrow strip of butter-soft leather with unhurried precision over
the top of her wrists. They both looked down now at the black strap
lying across skin that was as pale as milk. In slow motion, she raised
her forearms a few inches.

With infinite delicacy, like a man reaching out to catch a bird, he
wound the soft leather between her raised wrists, looping it around
them. Each could hear the other breathing. He held the strap in
one hand and – tugged. In the moment the strap tightened, pulling
her long-fingered hands toward him, he saw her lips part and the
movement in her long pale throat as she swallowed. His cock leapt
like a colt.

Her eyes had gone dark with desire. He released the strap; she
withdrew her hands, dropped her wrists, let the bag fall into her lap.

'Where are you staying?' she asked, her voice drifting from her
mouth like smoke.

It had been a long and exciting day, fuelled, for most of the wedding guests, by a great deal of champagne. Not for Angie: she'd
had just the one glass to toast the bride and groom, out on the
harbour. Tracy getting married was certainly something worth
celebrating. Tracy even surviving – that was miracle enough! By
rights she should have been dead a hundred times by now, *and so
should I,* Angie thought, but here she was. Here they all were, a dozen
of the old gang, most of whom she hadn't seen since . . . since the

bad old days. She closed her eyes. *Thank you, Lord Jesus, thank you for saving me. Let me never fall again.*

The party was winding down; the other girls were on their last drinks, lolling on the big luxurious sofas in the hotel lounge, their high heels and pretty bags discarded on the floor. In the far corner, a grand piano tinkled, as well-dressed people came and went to the vast reception desk nearby, and trolleys of expensive luggage were wheeled past to the lifts.

'I'm gonna have a wedding just like that,' sighed one of the girls, who'd given herself owl eyes by rubbing her mascara. 'On a great big gorgeous yacht like that. I don't care how much it costs!'

'S'not how much it cos',' slurred another. ''S the *love.*'

The love, thought Angie. There had been plenty of love between her and Davey at their simple ceremony in the registry office in Melbourne, even if they had been so stoned they'd signed the wedding certificate in the wrong places, so his signature was beside her name and vice versa. Didn't matter, they'd just signed it again, giggling like mad.

'When're you gonna get married again, Ange?' asked a woman with a puffy face and rolls of fat bunching round her midriff. Rhonda: she'd been there, Angie was fairly sure, in that registry office ten years ago. 'Must have fellas asking. You've still got your looks, that's for sure – not like me!' she added with a raucous laugh.

'When the time is right, the right man will come,' said Angie, smiling. 'God will bring us together.'

'What, God's already got him picked out, has he?'

'That's what I believe. What I *know*, with all my heart.'

'Yeah? I'd be asking God to speed it up a bit, if it was me!' said Rhonda, tipping the last of another bottle of champagne into her glass.

Angie allowed herself to drift off, dreaming of that beautiful moment – soon, soon! – when she and Gabriel would stand before everyone at Faith Rise, and Pastor Tim would say the words that joined them *in the sight of God*, forever. Gabriel would take her hand; she could almost feel the ring slipping on to her finger . . .

She turned her head to the side, away from her good-natured but unbelieving, tipsy friends, to gaze at the magnificent sparkling chandelier hanging above the hotel foyer, and at her dreams. Only in his songs had Gabriel spoken of love, so far – and that was love divine, not human. But surely the next time he came to her, in the night, in the darkness, he would speak, he would say the words she longed to hear . . .

The muted *ding ding* of the bell at the reception desk drew her eyes downward. A gaggle of Japanese tourists milled around their mountain of luggage, while at the nearer end of the long expanse of polished granite, a tall blond man inclined his head toward the woman beside him as they waited for their room key. Something in his movement, the bend of his neck, caught her attention. *I know that man.* Who? She took in the woman – not familiar – at a glance: a striking redhead whose figure-hugging little black dress was moulded over a large, shapely bottom. But the man was definitely —

'Gerry!' she gasped, sitting bolt upright. She looked wildly to the women with her. 'That's my —' and stopped. The girls weren't listening anyway. *That's my sister's husband!*

No! Maybe it wasn't him? His back was to her, after all. Her eyes were now so acutely focused it seemed they might jump straight out of their sockets. He was the right height, the right hair, the right —

She watched as the man's hand slid down the redhead's back to caress the substantial swell of her buttocks. Was that Gerry's hand? Angie's heart was thumping, *boom, boom, boom,* rocking her whole chest. She saw the man, standing so close beside the young woman, shift his left leg and slide it, smooth and forceful as a tango dancer, between hers, pushing her knees apart. The woman's back arched; Angie drew in her own breath, sharply. And then, just as swiftly, the man withdrew his leg. As though it hadn't happened. The desk clerk handed him the key, they turned and walked toward the elevators.

Angie rose; he could have seen her, if he'd looked that way, but he didn't. As they entered the lift, in that moment as they waited for the doors to close, she had a clear view at last of the man's face. Gerry Visser. The man who had stood in her parents' garden twenty years ago and watched her sister walk toward him on Daddy's frail, proud arm. Who had promised to love and cherish, be true and faithful, to *Susanna*, as radiant and beautiful in that moment as she would ever be.

She watched as Gerry slid his right hand under the woman's long hair, taking hold of the back of her neck. Angie's hand rose involuntarily to clutch her own nape. With a visceral instinct she knew exactly how hard his hand had gripped: not to hurt the girl, but to claim her.

And she saw the face of the young woman as the lift doors closed: ardent, heavy-lidded, ready.

It was a torment to stay in the hotel that night, to lie there knowing she was under the same roof as that . . . that bastard! *Adulterer. Sinner.* All night, Angie burned with rage. And the question burned in her brain: *What should I do?*

Tell her sister? Surely: Susanna must know the truth.

But it will destroy her. She could imagine all too well the agony this betrayal would cause her sister; the thought of it made Angie herself curl up in pain. *How could I possibly do that to her?*

More: from her own bitter experience of having heard too much bad news over the years, Angie understood that the bearer of bad tidings is forever associated with them. If she told Susanna what she had witnessed, she too would be tainted with it, somewhere in her beloved sister's heart and mind.

She tossed the bedclothes off, then on, restlessly rearranged the pillows yet again.

Gabriel. *Gabriel will know what to do for the best.* But then she realised with horrid certainty that the same truth applied to Gabriel: if she told him, he would flinch from her. He would never want to be part of her family; part of her life; part of her.

Gerry's wickedness had caught her in its web, and Angie was stuck there, somewhere between knowledge and complicity. *It's as though I've been poisoned by his sin*, she thought, getting up and pacing the room. *I hate him; I hate him.*

FOURTEEN

Gerry lay with his hands clasped behind his head, staring at the far wall of their bedroom. It needed painting. *The whole place needs painting.* The walls in the hallway still bore marks of the kids' attempts at home decorating, back when they were preschoolers, a million years ago. He heaved a heavy sigh. Here it was Christmas morning, and the house was silent as a tomb. *You know your kids have grown up when they don't come pounding in at sparrow fart on Christmas morning, demanding to open their presents.* The realisation made him feel old, and melancholy.

There were other reasons not to be cheerful. If it hadn't been for Chris, the Sydney developer, coming through with a nice fat cheque, Visser Kanaley wouldn't have been able to pay their December wages bill. The two or three staff who'd left the firm lately would not be replaced any time in the foreseeable future. Every day, it seemed, another client cancelled, and Gerry had a nasty feeling – which he hadn't shared with Marcus – that the Kansas City gallery people were getting cold feet about their planned extension. If he could just keep them on side for another six weeks, till he could meet with them in person after the New York conference . . . *Yes, that meeting's going to be critical. Make or break.*

Susanna, lying on her back beside him, was snoring gently. He shook her shoulder; she murmured, and rolled onto her side. Gerry contemplated her sleeping face. Disappointing, the way she'd been so distracted lately, ridiculously preoccupied with this paper she was writing, and her damn art show. For a moment he found himself envying Chris his marriage to Terri, not only a wife but a savvy business partner. Someone who understood what was going on in the wider world.

Sunlight was seeping in now around the edges of the blinds. Gerry was just thinking of getting up and going for a run, since his family was apparently going to treat this like any other day and sleep in, when he felt a soft stroking on his arm. Susanna had woken and was looking up at him with a drowsy smile. 'Hiya, handsome,' she murmured.

The irritation he'd been stoking faded away. 'Hello, sleepyhead,' he said, smoothing back her tousled hair. She caught his hand and gave the knuckles a little kiss. 'Merry Christmas.'

He was just lowering his head to kiss her when they were interrupted by muffled voices from the hall, and the bedroom door being pushed vigorously open. In came a tray, carried by Seb, with his sister right behind him carrying another. On their heads were those cheap sets of reindeer antlers, bright red, Stella-Jean's festooned with green tinsel.

'Merry Christmas!' they yelled in unison.

'Well, if it isn't Prancer and, um, Blitzen,' said Gerry.

'Hello, kidlets.' Susanna sat up, plucking at the neck of her night-gown, which had slipped somewhat indecorously to one side. 'Merry Christmas. What've you got there?'

'It's the Christmas Day travelling cafe,' said Seb proudly as he put his tray down on the foot of their bed. 'See – cappuccinos all round. I made them!'

'He wouldn't have had a clue if I hadn't showed him,' said Stella-Jean. 'Also on the menu: croissants!'

'With Jeejee's apricot jam,' their mother said, smacking her lips. 'Yum yum.'

Gerry took the cup proffered by Seb, and allowed his daughter to wriggle a Santa Claus hat onto his head. 'And there I was getting all sentimental about the way you guys used to storm in here before dawn, squawking, "Has Santa come? Where's our presents?" This is a vast improvement.'

'Damn straight, Pop,' said Seb. 'Santa's little helpers, that's us.'

Gerry bit into a croissant that had spent rather too long in the oven and shattered now into a shower of flaky crumbs. The kids perched at the end of the bed, munching and chattering. Susanna was laughing. He felt a powerful wish to nail this moment to the wall, capture it for all time. This silly, happy, perfect moment. 'For smart-arsed teenagers,' he said through his mouthful, 'you're not too bad.'

'Sorry I was asleep when you got home last night, sweetie,' Susanna said to Stella-Jean. 'How was your visit to Faith Rise with Auntie Ange?'

'Complete crap,' said Stella-Jean, screwing her face up in disgust. 'They didn't even have proper Christmas carols, it was all "Sing Along with Gabriel".' She dropped her croissant on a plate and raised both hands high above her head, swaying to and fro with a dopey, wide-eyed grin. 'Honestly! I think they're all on some *drug*.'

'They are,' said Gerry. 'It's called "religious fundamentalism". Now you know.'

'Totally nutso. And to think they're doing it all over again this morning. Right now!' Stella-Jean rolled her eyes. 'Poor Finn.'

'Ah well, he's working up an appetite for your mum's roast turkey.'

'Not that there's ever been a problem with Finn's appetite,' Susanna added.

'Mine either,' said Seb, tearing another croissant apart and slathering it with jam.

With the croissants eaten and the coffee drunk, the moment, perfect though it had been, moved on, and the kids with it, to attend to last-minute present-wrapping. Gerry was in the kitchen making himself another coffee, since Seb's effort hadn't actually been that great, and turned the machine off to see his sister-in-law walking through the living room, having let herself in as though she owned the place. Finn, he noticed, was over by the Christmas tree adding more presents to the pile, placing them carefully, one here, one there.

Angie paused in the doorway of the kitchen, looking around, presumably hoping to see her sister since she was avoiding Gerry's eye. She was wearing strappy sandals and a silky pink dress – you had to give the woman one thing, she always dressed well – but the look on her face was grim and decidedly un-Christmassy.

'G'day, Ange,' he said. 'Cheer up: Christ the saviour is born, haven't you heard?'

'Yes, I *have* heard, thank you,' she said, casting him a death-ray glance. 'It's not *me* who needs reminding of the Good News.'

'And good will to all men. And women,' he said, handing her his own just-made espresso. 'Here you go.' She took it with a grudging thanks, peering at the perfect crema as though she suspected him of having poisoned it. 'Have to say, Ange, you sure as shit don't *look* like it's good news.'

'Do you mind not swearing, please?' Angie asked with furious politeness. 'Today, of all days?'

'Come on, swearing's one of this country's great traditions,' Gerry smiled, all amused superiority. 'Along with secularism. Did you know that more people nominate "no religion" in the census here than in any other country? And a *bloody* good thing, too, if you ask me.'

'No one did ask you.' Angie put down her cup, having drunk only a few sips. 'Excuse me.'

I think I will go for that run, Gerry thought, watching her sashay down the hall. *Less time spent around her, the better.* He laced up his running shoes and set off, into the glare of a summer morning that was already heating up, determined to enjoy an hour of exercise and solitude before the rigours of a day which would include one in-law too many and an over-abundance of rich food. *But that's the deal*, he reminded himself. *That's what I signed on for.*

By the time he got back, fabulous smells were emanating from the kitchen, and he panted straight through the living room, past Seb and Stella-Jean haranguing each other about some adjustment to the Christmas tree, to find his mother-in-law standing in the kitchen, a fresh apron around her middle, basting the turkey.

'Jean!' he said, giving her lined cheek a kiss. 'Merry Christmas. You look like an ad for a 1950s housewife. Why didn't I marry you instead of a career woman?'

'I was a career woman too, young man,' she smiled. 'Don't tell me *you* don't take women's careers seriously either? My daughter assured me times have changed!'

''Course I take women's careers seriously.' Jean opened the oven door and he hefted the heavy baking dish back in. 'Just not as seriously as their cooking, that's all.'

Jean picked up a wooden spoon and smacked at him playfully; Gerry pretended to duck. They both knew Gerry had nothing but admiration for his mother-in-law, who'd worked so hard, kept the family going, despite an invalid husband and a younger daughter who — well, the less said, the better. *And maintained her sense of humour,* he thought. *What a trouper.*

Tigger biffed his head against Gerry's shin. 'P'rrow, *p'rrow*!' the cat said urgently. Gerry looked down and saw that strands of green tinsel had been looped around his furry neck.

'Okay, I'm phoning the RSPCA,' he called toward the living room. 'You do know there are laws against decorating companion animals at Christmas, Stella?'

'Leave Tigger's necklace alone, it suits him!' Stella-Jean yelled back. 'Jeejee, don't let Dad take it off.'

Jean gave Gerry a sweetly rueful smile. 'I'm afraid I wouldn't *dare* disobey my granddaughter. Not when it comes to matters of style.'

'Style — is that what you call it? Watch out, Jean, she'll have you in a set of gilded reindeer antlers any minute.' He gave his mother-in-law a second peck on the cheek. 'Well, I'd better get myself freshened up for the day's proceedings, eh?'

Opening of the presents always took place while lunch cooked, with places assigned by long custom. Gerry sat on the couch next to Susanna, who was wearing a pair of dangly red earrings Stella-Jean had made; Jean, divested of apron, was in one armchair and Angie in the other; Seb was on the floor by the tree, poised to begin handing out the parcels in their brightly coloured paper, with Stella-Jean and Finn hovering. Gerry let it all wash over him, genially semaphoring delight at the socks Seb gave him and Stella-Jean's vintage shirt. Susanna's present was a genuine surprise, and a great one too: the tennis racquet he'd had a covetous eye on for months.

'It's perfect, Suze,' he said, standing to heft and twirl it. 'How did you know I was after this one?'

'I got a bit of advice from someone in the know, didn't I, Seb?'

'Welcome back to A-grade, Pop,' said Seb. 'And thanks for these!' He flapped the envelope containing the gift Gerry always bought: tickets for the two of them to the men's semifinals and finals of the Australian Open at the end of January, both the singles and doubles.

'Another few years, you could be playing there yourself,' Gerry told him. Seb rolled his eyes, but he went on, 'No, seriously. Your game's getting better all the time; once you're set up with the right partner, you'll be cooking with gas.'

'Maybe,' said Seb, removing the tinsel from long-suffering Tigger's neck and replacing it with a new black cat collar. Stella-Jean, watching with pursed mouth, nodded her approval.

Finn, after early signs of pending over-excitement, was now engrossed in the geometric puzzle someone had given him. Angie was spraying herself with perfume. Jean made a little speech thanking everyone for following her request and donating to NGOs on her behalf: a goat in Mozambique, a pig in Cambodia, a midwife's equipment in Ethiopia. 'I feel like a very rich woman!' she concluded, and they all clapped, though Gerry wasn't sure what it was they were applauding, exactly. Didn't matter; all in the spirit of the thing.

A whoop of excitement came from the verandah, and Stella-Jean staggered back into the room carrying a sewing machine in its case, having followed a thread, spooling from its miniature parcel under the tree, out to where the machine had been concealed. State-of-the-art, apparently; her grandmother had arranged its purchase from a friend at the retirement village. 'Absolute bargain,' Susanna murmured in Gerry's ear. 'Mum says Betty's eyes just aren't up to sewing any more.' Gerry kept to himself the observation that maybe Betty should have figured that out before she got a brand-new machine.

Seb was now distributing, frisbee-style, Angie's identical presents. She had given each member of the family a CD: *Hold On To You: Four Songs of Praise by Gabriel McHale*, whose soulful photo graced the cover. 'Gabriel composed every song,' Angie announced, beaming. 'And he plays the guitar, of course – and, ah, if you look at the credits, you'll see *my* name. I'm one of the backup singers!'

Susanna, making enthusiastic noises, jumped up from the couch and began pressing one button after another on the CD player she'd never got the hang of. Gerry put his copy aside, not bothering to unwrap it. He saw Stella-Jean catch her brother's eye, then glance meaningfully toward the rubbish bin in the kitchen, flicking her wrist as though to say, *You reckon I could piff it in from here?*

'Very thoughtful, Ange,' said Gerry. 'You've single-handedly quin-tupled the guy's Christmas sales.'

His sister-in-law shot him that death-ray look again. 'This CD is already selling *hundreds* of copies. And *these* ones are all individually signed, if you care to notice.' Susanna got the CD player working and the room was filled with slow guitar chords and a warm tenor voice.

'I thought I'd been left alone
Thought I'd no one to call my own . . .'

Jean said, 'Your friend has a very nice voice, Angela,' and Susanna murmured agreement. The chorus began and Angie sat up very straight, eyes bright with excitement, as the women's voices joined Gabriel's:

'I will hold on to you
And to your soul, it's true . . .'

132

Unable to stomach it, Gerry got up quietly and went out to the kitchen. He lifted a corner of the muslin covering Jean's glazed ham, staring at the thick, cross-hatched skin studded with peppercorns. Or were they cloves? The treacly song continued, dripping infuriatingly note by note into his brain. He moved things around on the bench without any purpose. *How long does this go on for?* Another sappy verse, and then at the second chorus Angie could contain herself no longer and started singing along.

'You'll sit right by my throne
You'll never be alone
Because I'll . . . hold on . . . to-oo you . . .'

Gerry could see her through the opening between the two rooms, and she could see him too, though no one else could. He lifted his face toward the ceiling, throat long, and began to soundlessly imitate a dog baying at the moon. Angie's voice, *ooh-yoooh,* broke off abruptly and he turned away, laughing to himself.

The moment the song finished, Angie turned the CD player off.

'That was really lovely, Ange. I'm so thrilled!' Susanna said.

'Dad! Last presents!' yelled Stella-Jean. It was family tradition that everyone had to be in the room for the unwrapping of each gift. Gerry came back to his seat and watched Finn savaging a piece of the bright paper he had laboured so hard to colour, to get at whatever was within.

Gerry noticed that Angie was still standing by the CD player, with her arms crossed and a face like thunder. Seb, in charge of distribution, picked up a final parcel. 'Here, Ma, lucky last's for you.'

Susanna read the little card, smiled at her mother and carefully unwrapped the rectangular parcel, revealing several sketchbooks of various sizes, along with drawing pens, pencils, and a set of watercolours. She knew at a glance that all these materials were of the highest quality. Jean must have visited a good art supply shop, asked for advice, spent quite a bit of money. 'Thank you so much, Mum,' she said, with a heartfelt smile.

'For your exhibition, Susie,' Jean said. 'The beautiful pictures you're going to make.'

'So, *now* you're recognising Susanna's talent,' said Angie suddenly, her voice hard and penetrating. Everyone jumped.

'What on earth do you mean, Ange?' Susanna asked.

Angie was staring at their mother with angry eyes. 'It was *you* who talked her out of art school,' she said. Jean's face had frozen. 'It was you who made her go into teaching. She could have been a brilliant artist if it wasn't for you!'

'Don't *say* that!' cried Susanna, distressed. 'I never —'

'Let's not get carried away, Ange,' Gerry drawled. '*Brilliant artist.*'

'And you!' Angie rounded on him furiously. 'Did you ever encourage her? No. You'd rather have a *ping-pong* table.'

'That's quite enough,' said Jean in a steely tone.

'Ping-pong!' cried Seb, jumping to his feet. 'What a great idea. Come on, you guys.' He jerked his head at Stella-Jean, who hauled Finn up with her, and the three of them skedaddled down the hallway. The adults were left, vibrating with tension, around the festive tree.

'You're wrong, Angie. I know you mean well but you're wrong,' said Susanna, trying to make her voice firm.

'She's talking complete rubbish, is all,' said Gerry. 'But what else would you expect from someone who thinks Adam and Eve rode around on dinosaurs?'

Very clearly and deliberately, Angie said, 'You don't deserve to be married to my sister, you pig.'

'Stop! Don't *fight*,' Susanna cried, waving desperate hands at both of them. 'It's Christmas.'

'Do you *want* to upset Susanna?' Jean asked her younger daughter forcefully. 'Is that what you want?'

'Hmmm . . . What Angie wants.' Gerry leaned back on the couch, knees wide, arms folded. 'I probably shouldn't say this, but isn't the answer obvious? Anything she can get! You know, Ange,' he said, feigning a conversational tone, 'I'm trying to remember if I've ever known you to do anything but take, take, take. Even when Davey the Leprechaun was alive, you were round here every second day with your hand out.'

'My husband was a better man than you by far!' she said, face vixen-sharp. 'You always despised him, just because he was a carpenter and you're a big-deal architect.'

'No,' said Gerry. 'I despised him because he was a junkie. He didn't last long as a carpenter after you —'

'*Don't!*' Susanna cried.

Suddenly Angie snatched up her bag. 'I know none of you under-stand this, let alone *care*, but I'm going to tell you anyway. My life is guided by the knowledge that Jesus Christ was born this day for all mankind, and that he died for us too, so that we might know eter-nal life. That *I* might have eternal life. And now, I'm going! Because I *can't be* with people who don't share that faith.'

'Angie, darling, don't go!' Susanna made to jump up from the couch but Gerry placed one hand firmly on her shoulder, pressing her back down. 'We're your *family*. Please, stay!'

'Don't fucking plead with her!' said Gerry.

'Gerry!' said Jean sharply. 'Have *neither* of you got any manners?'

Gerry and Angie both ignored her, glaring at each other, eyes hot with a hatred neither had allowed themselves to voice before.

'You know what you are, Gerry Visser? You're a great big bully. You bully everyone around you. But you're not going to bully me!' At the hallway door, Angie turned, snapping, 'God forgive you,' before disappearing with a swirl of pink dress toward the games room.

'Oh, remembered you're a Christian, have you?' Gerry, standing now, flung at her back. Susanna let out a cry of anguish and made to follow her sister but Gerry said, 'No! Let her get the boy and go, if that's what she wants to do. You are *not* going after her.' He towed his wife by the wrist into the kitchen, and kept going out to the backyard.

Jean was left sitting alone and still in her armchair, but in a moment Angie was back, propelling a stricken-looking Finn before her.

Stella-Jean, behind them, cried, 'Wait, wait, let me get his presents!' and scrambled on the floor gathering his books, toys, T-shirts and shoving them into a plastic bag. Angie didn't even slow her stride, passing through the living room without a glance at her mother. Jean rose and held out her hand to Stella-Jean for the bag.

'I'll talk to her,' she said firmly. 'You stay here please, Stella-Jean.'

Jean hurried toward the car. 'Angie!' she called, and Angie, who was sitting with her hands on the steering wheel and the engine running, waited for her mother to give the bag to Finn, in the back seat. She could have driven away then, but she didn't.

'Come back inside,' said Jean, bending to the open driver's window. 'At least have the courtesy to come back and apologise to your sister.'

'Oh, this is *my* fault, is it?' Angie cried. 'What about *him*?'

'Gerry didn't start that, miss.'

Angie gave a screech of frustration. 'You've never taken my side, have you? Not once. You never cared about me, you never listened to me. *You never loved me.*'

Sternly, her mother told her, 'Angie, that's just not true.'

'Say it then. Say it! Say you love me.'

Jean closed her eyes momentarily. 'Don't be ridiculous. Of course I love you.'

'Say it like you mean it,' Angie cried with passionate heat. 'You don't *mean* it. You don't!'

Jean stepped back a pace from the car window, face set. 'Grow up, Angela, for heaven's sake.'

Angie glared furiously at her, rammed the car into gear, and drove off.

FIFTEEN

Finn wasn't exactly hiding, but no one knew he was there, crouched on the floor with big puffy curtains around him, squeezed into the space between the wall and the end of the couch. Lots of rooms in Pastor Tim's house, lots of couches, and today being Christmas Day, lots of people too, visiting in between services at Faith Rise. No one was going to notice him, curled up out of sight. Mum thought he was upstairs with all the other kids but Finn felt safer here. Upstairs was Lily and Grace: dangerous.

He had his new puzzle for company. As he moved the bits of plastic around, trying to figure out how many ways he could make it work, Finn half-listened to his mum, still talking about what had happened at Stella-Jean's house. She'd told everybody but she was still upset, he could hear it in her trembly voice. She didn't want to stop talking about how awful it was, having a family who weren't Christians, how Uncle Gerry never liked her and Jeejee never loved her, how they both said bad things about God. Now Pastor Tim and Gabriel were sitting there on the couch with her. Finn stayed very still.

Pastor Tim's voice was all round and fuzzy, just like in church. Sticky, like those fuzzy seeds that stick to your socks. 'You know, Angie, many dear members of our Faith Rise community have families who have caused them, too, great suffering. And this is the message I share with them, from the twenty-seventh psalm: "When my father and my mother forsake me, then the Lord will take me up." The Lord feels your pain, dear girl, and he can heal every wound your family has inflicted on you.' There was a rustle of movement; Finn twisted carefully around, and could see Pastor Tim's hands extended across the low coffee table, holding his mum's hands. 'Let the love of God, like healing balm, pour into your heart.'

His mum said thank you, thank you, in a warm, wet voice, and Pastor Tim's hands patted hers. After a while he got up and went somewhere else. Mum was having a little soft cry.

Then Gabriel started speaking, and his voice wasn't smooth and slidy like it was when other people were around. There was that other edge to it that Finn knew, that angry edge that made him shiver.

'I know what it's like to have a family who wants to drag you under,' he said, snaky and hard. 'Destroy you, bury you. There's something else our Lord Jesus Christ said that you should know, Angie. You should learn this by heart. Luke, chapter fourteen verse twenty-six: "If any man come to me, and hate not his father, and mother, and wife, and children, and brothers, and sisters, and even his own life also, then he cannot be my disciple." Know *that* truth, Angie. It set me free, and it can free you, too.'

Angie was silent for a few moments. Finn hardly breathed as he waited, wanting so hard to hear Mum say that it wasn't right, you mustn't hate your children, you mustn't hate your mother. But instead he heard his mother take a big deep trembly breath, and let it out, *ohhh*, as though she'd finished doing something really hard. 'I wasn't ready to hear that before,' she said, 'but – oh, Gabriel, it's true. It's so *true*.'

'Yes, hate,' said Gabriel, sounding satisfied, like she'd just given him a present he wanted. 'We have to hate everything and everyone who keeps us from God's love.'

'I never understood before that God *wants* me to hate my mother,' his mum said. 'All this time I've been fighting it – I didn't know that it was *right*.'

Hate your mother. Hate your children. Behind the curtain, Finn hugged his knees very tight and closed his eyes. *No, don't. Don't.*

'Mothers!' said Gabriel, almost spitting the word out. 'Mothers should know how to protect their children, but they don't. They let the enemy in, and bow down before him thinking that he's God.'

Finn thought, *That is true. That is the only true thing I have ever heard him say*. His whole body twitched, like he was trying to shake off something crawling and horrible – and suddenly the curtains were thrown back, rings rattling, and Finn was exposed.

'You little sneak!' hissed Gabriel, looming above him.

'Finnie!' said his mother, leaning over the edge of the couch, her face full of surprise.

'What sort of child are you, hiding so that you can eavesdrop on your elders?'

Finn quailed.

'Finnie, why don't you go upstairs?' said his mother quickly. 'Go and play with Grace and Lily and the other kids, honey. It'll be much more fun than sitting around down here with all the boring grown-ups!'

Finn went slowly up the carpeted stairs and sidled into the room where the kids were watching a movie on the enormous TV. Something with princesses, and Grace was sitting up in a chair that had all gold on it, like a throne, with her yellow party dress spread out around her. Lily was sitting in the middle of a big couch, in a dress just the same but blue, with other girls crammed in by her, trying to be the ones who sat closest. There were a few boys there too, not on the couch. Finn sat on a chair a little bit away from everyone.

Some private signal went between Grace and Lily, and pretty soon no one was watching the movie any more. They were circling Finn, too close, and firing questions at him, first Grace, then Lily, and Lily again, then Grace.

'Where does he stay at your house? What room is he in? Are you allowed in when he's playing guitar? What about when the band is practising? Does he practise just with your mum? Does he close the door? Does he go into her room and close the door?'

Grace reached out her shoe, a pretty shoe, and tapped Finn's sneaker with it. 'What does he look like when he's not wearing his special cripple shoe?' she asked.

They were all standing too close to him, Grace and Lily and the other kids, all of them in the room at the top of the stairs. Finn hated being crowded in like this.

'Does his cripple leg look horrible? Is it all twisted up and *deformed*?'

'I don't know,' Finn muttered. Why did they care about Gabriel and his stupid leg? He tried to move away but the others wouldn't let him, they all crowded close.

'We can't hear you, Finn!' Lily jabbed him suddenly with her elbow. 'Tell us!'

'*I don't know*,' he yelled, raising his head. The encircling faces were alight, hungry. 'I never *see* him!'

Grace gave a high-pitched laugh. 'You never see him! What, is he invisible? Do you think Gabriel's *invisible*?' The other children joined in, laughing at him.

'He always has the special shoes on, all the time,' said Finn desperately.

'He has to take them off *some*times,' said Grace knowingly. 'He has to take them off to have a shower, doesn't he? He has to take them off to go to *bed*.'

Lily put her face right up to his. She had slightly popping-out eyes, just like Pastor Tim. 'Does your mum take his special shoes off for him? Does she? When they go to *bed*?'

'*Oo-ooh!*' chorused the other kids, thrilled to bits.

'Hey, Finn? Tell us! Does your mum —'

He had to get *away*. Finn shoved Lily aside, then another kid; he made a dash for the door and was almost to the stairs when Grace, in her yellow dress, caught up with him, slipped in front and wouldn't let him past. He tried to dodge around her; she was faster. To the other side, but she was there first. He could hear the others behind them, laughing. She had him trapped. *Get away, get past.* Finn raised both arms and shoved Grace, hard, out of the way.

Grace seemed to take off, flying, arms windmilling as she landed on a step halfway down, and then to the bottom, where she stumbled a few paces before folding gracefully to the floor like an origami bird. Lily began screaming and the other children joined in. They were clustered now in a shrieking crowd at the top of the stairs, clutching at each other, while slowly, stiff-legged, step by step, Finn went down. His eyes were fixed on Grace lying there, still. Still − except for one hand, which reached down and smoothed the hem of her yellow dress so that it sat nicely just above her knees, then rested again like a delicate seashell at her side.

A thunder of feet as the grown-ups came running. They were all calling out, all yelling at once, and the kids were still shrieking from above. The racket pinned Finn back against the wall. As Helen threw herself to the floor, snatching her fallen daughter into her arms, Grace's eyes fluttered open, and she shot a quick triumphant look at Finn before allowing her lids to half-close again. 'Mummy,' she whimpered piteously.

'What happened?' cried half-a-dozen adult voices.

Lily's voice rang like a bell. 'Finn pushed Gracie down the stairs!'

'No!' It was Angie. His mum was coming toward him, her face bunched up with fright. 'It must have been an accident! You didn't mean to push her, did you, Finnie?'

An awful, avid moment of silence. Finn nodded, slowly, up and down. He had to. *Yes.* Up and down. *Yes, I did.* Angie made a sound that was like something being torn, and her legs went sideways, as though she was going to fall over, but instead she stumbled backwards and knocked into another person, who propped her up.

'He was talking about Gabriel,' said Lily in the ringing tones of someone who'd heard preaching all her life. 'He kept telling all these horrible stories about Gabriel's poor leg. He was calling him a *cripple*. Gracie didn't want to listen so he pushed her down the stairs.'

Gasps, murmurs. And then Gabriel's arm whipped out, a striking snake; he grabbed Finn by the shoulder and spun him around, bending him face forward, folded in the middle, in that grip Finn knew to be inescapable. He struggled anyway, twisting around to try to get free.

Gabriel gestured Angie to come forward. As she did, Finn caught a glimpse of her anguished face before Gabriel swung him around again and then tapped, twice, on the backs of his legs, bare below his shorts.

'Punish him.'

His mother started crying. 'He didn't — No, it wasn't —' Their voices sounded somehow as though they were talking only to each other, yet Finn could *feel* all the others, every single person in that crowd: their hot eyes, their eagerness to see him hurt.

'"Withhold not correction from the child",' said Gabriel. His voice didn't even sound angry now, just cool and hard. 'He could have killed her. You must punish him, Angie. You.'

'But he's just a little boy,' she pleaded.

'It's the *enemy* inside him, and you know it!' Gabriel said more loudly. 'Proverbs nineteen: "Chasten your child while there is still hope, and let not your soul spare for his crying." *While there is still hope*, Angie! Will you not save your own child?'

Angie was still crying. Finn, twisting his head, could see her stepping closer, jerkily, as though forces were struggling inside her. Her face was screwed up tight, she raised her arm, and turned her face away as, with a tortured exhalation, she brought her hand down on to his bare legs. Not very hard; it didn't have to be hard to hurt him, shame him. Finn cried out wildly with the shock of her betrayal.

Four times, she did it, while Grace and Lily and all the other children watched. While Pastor Tim and Helen and all the other adults watched. With the second smack her crying seemed to grow less, and her resolve greater. After the third, she looked at Gabriel and he told her with his face, *one more*, and she raised her hand and smacked Finn one more time.

Then she stepped back, and Gabriel let him go, and Finn rolled himself into the smallest ball he could form, arms curled around his head, trying to hold himself together.

SIXTEEN

Susanna groaned.'Oh, can't you just stay there at the sewing machine for a few minutes longer, sweetie? I just need to get the arms right.'

'No, Mum,' said Stella-Jean severely. 'I can't *pretend* I'm doing something just so you can take four hours to draw it. Take photographs, why don't you? Don't most artists do their drawings from photos?'

'Working from photographs isn't the *same*,' Susanna moaned. She knew she was sounding petulant but it was so frustrating. Here she was nearly at the end of the summer holidays and her 'Women and Work' idea was still nothing more than a collection of sketches, most of them incomplete. *And all of them second-rate, if that.* 'I took a whole lot of photos of my friend Andrea from book group, working at her potting wheel, but they just don't have the — I don't know. The *vitality.*' A life drawing class, that's what she needed, like Jean had suggested months ago. *I could've enrolled in a summer school, and had weeks with a life model. Why didn't I do that?*

'If we'd gone to *Bali* for the summer, you could have had all the women you needed, working away right in front of you,' said Stella-Jean snarkily. 'Women in Bali are working all the time. And for a few bucks you could have paid someone to pose for you all day, if you wanted.'

Susanna refused to rise to the bait, even though she was sick of hearing about how they should have gone to Bali. Stella-Jean had been crabby and argumentative for weeks. Bored, that was Gerry's theory, without her brother to scrap with, Seb being away at a tennis camp his coach was running down at Portsea. And no Finn to look after, Angie having rung a few days after the Christmas Day fiasco to announce they were going to Tasmania for the holidays; Gabriel, she told her sister rather frostily, had been invited to be the musical director of a month-long Christian youth symposium. Or something like that. Susanna had mostly felt thankful to have a break, and concentrate on her art.

'Just one more sketch?' she wheedled. 'Half an hour?'

'Sorry, Mum, but I've got to get over to Tessa's. We're trying to build up stock for the market next Sunday, it's the first one since Christmas. You're taking us, yeah? And picking us up?'

'I suppose so, if it's my turn.' Susanna and Tessa's father Leo alternated the chauffeuring duties.

'I could ask *Dad* to do it, for once,' said Stella-Jean. There was a testing pause. 'He never does any of the driving-us-around stuff.'

'Your father's very busy, you know that,' Susanna said. 'He's got this New York trip in a couple of weeks, he's trying to get ahead of things before he goes. *And* he's working on plans for here, too.'

Stella-Jean snorted eloquently. 'That'll be the day!' she muttered.

'No, I think this time he really is going to make it happen.' The ironic thing was, Susanna privately wished Gerry *wasn't* so determined that this was the year for their big home renovation. A whole second storey, and the entire ground floor completely revamped. A showpiece! He'd declared he'd take out a mortgage to pay for it, if he had to, at the same time assuring her that Visser Kanaley was doing fine and a mortgage wouldn't be necessary. All Susanna could think was, *more disruption*.

Stella-Jean lifted a corner of the blind and cast a look at the searing day outside. 'First day back at school on Tuesday,' she griped. 'Why do they always start school again in the middle of a heatwave? Like,

145

every year. And Dad reckons this is the worst heatwave *ever*, like, on record. Did you know that?'

'Yes, I know.' said Susanna. It was so hot she'd even relaxed her principles on running the air conditioner, even at night, although she continued to feel guilty about it. 'It's tinder-dry all over the state, it's very worrying.'

'Yeah, so – can you give me a lift over to Tessa's now?' asked her daughter hopefully. 'So I don't, like, melt into a puddle?'

Susanna agreed; what was a little more procrastinating, when her alleged work was already so far behind?

When she'd returned to the quiet and cool of the house, Susanna looked at her drawings. *Maybe I should give up on figures? Maybe I should concentrate on still lifes?* She wandered disconsolately from room to room, looking for subjects. Those ripe red tomatoes in their deep blue bowl? The pale yellow soap sitting slimily on its metal dish? Gouaches, perhaps, would suit those colours . . . But it all seemed so banal; nothing raised even a flicker of excitement. She turned on the computer and spent an hour flicking through the websites her students had introduced her to, checking out the latest work and admiring the insouciant disregard for boundaries of form and media. *I wish I was an art student now, it would be so much fun.* But here she was, bound by her own tedious limitations, without even a model to draw.

Tired of berating herself, she went into her bedroom to lie down. She decided she'd be cooler naked, and as she pulled the cotton dress off over her head and dropped it to the floor, her eye fell on the reflection in the long mirror on the far side of the room. She kept watching the woman she saw there as she unhooked her bra and stepped out of her underpants. *I could draw her. Look at all that flesh!*

Observing her own familiar body so objectively, drawing it, she no longer felt disheartened by the rolls of flesh around her middle, the dimpled thighs, the sagging of breast and jawline. Rather, she felt grateful that this generously built, accommodating model was prepared to move in any way the artist wanted, assume a pose for as long as required, wait patiently while she shaded or erased or simply gazed consideringly. *As long as I'm prepared to be here and work, she will be too. And this is work. My work, at last.*

Several hours went quickly by, and at the end of that time Susanna had almost a dozen sketches, a few of which, she thought, had real potential. She smiled to herself. *Portrait of the artist as a middle-aged frump.* Not cutting edge, or even fashionable, but something.

A few days later Seb returned from the tennis camp, and he and Rory became engrossed in planning their study regime – at least, that's what they claimed to be doing. Gerry showed off his raft of plans for the house. All their lives began to pick up pace after the somnolent summer break, though summer's parching breath was unabating. On the last Friday of January, a slight cool change came through; Gerry and Seb, about to attend their much-anticipated weekend of the world's best tennis at the Australian Open, were volubly relieved.

Susanna kept waiting for Gerry to make some comment on her frank self-portraits, which she left clipped to her easel on the far side of the room, where his clothes were kept. But despite the fact that he'd begun his usual meticulous packing, and his suitcase was on the floor right next to the easel with all his warmest winter clothes spread about, he'd said not a word. She felt pretty sure, though, that he'd flipped through them, at least once.

His silence made her yearn all the more – childishly, perhaps – for feedback. *Just another adult's comments. They don't have to be an expert, just interested.* That made her think of her mother. So, within minutes of Gerry and Seb heading off for the Rod Laver Arena on Saturday, she dialled Jean's number, but was disappointed to only get the answering machine.

Just ten minutes later, while she was bucketing grey water in the back garden, Stella-Jean came out, holding out the phone. *Mum,* Susanna thought as she took it, but Stella-Jean said, 'It's Auntie Ange, they're back,' and she was mouthing Finn's name and making gestures that said, *Tell her to come over.* Susanna asked her sister to come by, adding quickly but casually, 'Gerry's out for the day.'

'Okay,' said Angie happily.

Ten minutes after *that* call came another, and when Susanna heard her mother's voice she felt slightly panicked. This was not the moment for Jean, who had not mentioned the Christmas fiasco since it happened, to meet Ange again. Even as she was trying to think of a reason why, having just left a message inviting her mother to visit, she must now put her off, Jean said apologetically that she couldn't come over, as she and Leonard were just about to leave for a few days out of town. 'We're going to stay in a guesthouse up at Marysville. It'll be so much cooler up there. I'm sorry darling, we only just decided.'

Susanna felt relieved, and then immediately ashamed of her cowardice, and wished things weren't so darn complicated. Yet when Angie arrived, full of good spirits, her holiday tan set off by a lacy white shirt, Susanna felt only pleasure to see her again. As they sat talking at the kitchen table, it dawned on Susanna that her sister was inserting Gabriel's name into almost every sentence. *She's in love,* she realised, and her heart gave a little skip of gladness. *Angie with Gabriel, Mum with Leonard, Seb with Aurora . . .* The notion that every person she loved should themselves be loved was like a vision of heaven to her.

Finn, so tanned he appeared to have been rolling in dirt, had scampered off the moment he arrived to join Stella-Jean in the games room, and soon they both came barrelling back out to the kitchen. 'Can I take Finn in to the city with me on the train? Just for, like, an hour,' said Stella-Jean breathlessly. 'I just got a call from the place that's making my labels, they're ready to be picked up!'

'What labels?' asked Susanna and Angie together.

'Clothing labels. For my range. *Stella-Jean,*' she said, tracing a short line with thumb and forefinger in the air. 'I'm going to sew them into every single garment I make. Can Finn come?' she asked, directly of Angie this time. 'Two hours, max.'

Angie agreed and minutes later, the cousins were yelling 'Bye!' from the front door, and clattering off.

'I think we've just witnessed the birth of an empire,' Susanna said.

Angie agreed. 'A Coco Chanel moment.'

Now. Susanna stood up. 'Come with me,' she said, beckoning her sister down the hall. 'There's something I want to show you.'

Angie went through all the self-portraits, twice. Looking at the drawings with her, Susanna could see them afresh: their weaknesses, but also their strengths. *Not bad. Not bad at all.* But Angie's praise seemed hesitant, uncertain.

'What is it?' Susanna asked. 'There's something you don't like about them, isn't there? It's okay to tell me.'

'It's just that . . .' Angie's teeth caught at her bottom lip as she looked again at the topmost drawing: an unsmiling Susanna standing with one hand fisted on a hip, tummy pouching, cellulite dimpling her upper thighs. 'Susu, you've made yourself look . . .' But she couldn't bring herself to say it.

'Fat,' Susanna said for her, and then went the step further. 'Ugly?'

'But you're *not*!' Angie cried. 'I *love* the way you look, I think you're beautiful!'

Susanna chuckled. 'That's so sweet of you,' she said. 'Bless your little cotton socks, Ange. But this *is* the way I look. I want to draw what I see. No: I want to see who I am.'

SEVENTEEN

Stella-Jean and Tessa were as noisy and gleeful as a pair of rainbow lorikeets when Susanna picked them up from the Sunday market. The owner of a boutique in Degraves Street had approached them, wanting to stock Tessa's felt cuffs and Stella-Jean's elaborate floral brooches. 'We're *made*,' they crowed. 'It's the hippest location in the city!' Susanna glanced in the rear-view mirror at the two jubilant girls, enjoying the endearing contrast between tall Tessa with her heavy-lidded goth elegance, and Stella-Jean like a little tan terrier, all yap and energy.

But once they'd dropped Tessa off at her place, she noticed that Stella-Jean, now in the front seat beside her, went quiet. 'Is there something about the offer from this boutique you're not happy with?' Susanna asked tentatively.

Stella-Jean kept tapping her fingertips together. 'It's just that . . . Tess's cuffs are brilliant: really clever, really simple. We can make ten of them in, like, a couple of hours. But my brooches take *days*. They stop the traffic all right, but my return on them is just . . .' She blew out noisily through her lips, like a pony.

'But won't you be able to sell them for more, in a boutique like that?'

'I *wish*! No offence, Mum, but you really haven't got a clue about retail, have you?' She shook her head at her mother's naivete. 'They'll *sell* for twice as much, but we won't *make* any more. The shop's gotta put on their mark-up.'

'I see.' Pausing at an intersection, Susanna cast a glance at her daughter, who sat now flicking her thumbnail back and forth against her front teeth, narrow-eyed, cooking up some scheme. There was a contradiction, Susanna mused, between how her daughter looked, rounded and soft-haired as a kewpie doll, and her personality: direct as an arrow from the bow. *Stella-Jean*: she'd stayed up last night till who knows how late, sewing those new labels into all her garments. They would be in the outfit she was wearing now: one of the 'headlights' singlets that had been her best seller of the summer – this one's panel splashed with ric-rac braid and a scattering of cute buttons – and an elastic-waisted flippy rayon skirt.

'What are you thinking about?' Susanna asked.

Hitching one leg up onto the seat, Stella-Jean shifted around to face her. 'I'm thinking, if I got a half-a-dozen Knitting Nancys and maybe twenty of the *big* spools of ribbon in different colours, and took them over to Bali with a couple of samples, the girls who work for Putu could be whipping up those brooches in no time.'

Susanna looked at her, mouth agape, then back toward the road. 'You have got to be kidding me,' she managed.

'No,' said Stella-Jean. 'Why would I be? I'm not asking you and Dad to pay, I've got the money. I can go by myself, it's not like I'm going somewhere *foreign*.'

'Okay, that's it,' said Susanna grimly, and pulled over. They faced each other. 'Stella-Jean, you are *not* going to Bali on your own. It *is* a foreign country, no matter how familiar you feel you are with it, and you are fifteen years old.'

'Nearly sixteen,' her daughter muttered.

Susanna held up one hand. 'Enough. Apart from the . . . *absurdity* of the idea, has it slipped your mind that you started back at school a few days ago? *I* may have a couple of weeks more holiday before college resumes, but you, my girl, are now in Year Ten and you are going to focus on your schoolwork.'

'Oh, Mum, we're not doing any *serious* classes yet. I'd just be gone, like, a few days! And I'd take some other samples too, like this skirt for instance.' She plucked at her bright rayon hem. 'The whole trip would pay for itself in no time.'

'Stella-Jean, are you *deaf*? I am saying *no*. En–oh. No!'

Her daughter harrumphed, slumping into her seat and folding her arms crossly. Susanna put on her blinker and rejoined the stream of traffic.

'Well anyway, there's something else I wanted to talk to you about,' said Stella-Jean after a couple of minutes. 'A family thing. And it's really important.'

Susanna slid her a sideways look. 'Go on.'

'Yesterday with Finn . . . Mum, I know you and Dad think his manners have improved and Gabriel's been a good influence and everything, but I'm *really* worried.'

'Why?' asked Susanna, deciding to give her the benefit of the doubt. 'What is it, exactly, that's making you feel worried?'

'Haven't you noticed how Finn's got this kind of . . . *hunted* look?'

Susanna hadn't. 'Honey, they've been away for a month. He's probably just unsettled.'

'But this was before they went away, too. And it's worse now. And also, it's the way he's clammed up. With *me*! It's like he's scared to talk.'

'He's always been a bit like that. He's just not the world's most communicative child.'

Stella-Jean made an impatient noise, but pressed on. 'And, Mum, when we were on the train, I was mucking round with him and I went like this —' she demonstrated an arm raised as though to deliver a smack '— just kidding, you know, and he ducked. Not just ducked, he went all white around his mouth. He was really *scared*.'

Susanna frowned. That didn't sound right. Finn had never, as far as she knew, suffered any kind of physical punishment. Sometimes, in private, Gerry had expressed to her the view that a smack on the behind might do the kid good, but neither they nor Angie would ever do such a thing.

'Angie doesn't believe in smacking children,' she reminded Stella-Jean.

'I know. But what about Gabriel? I'll bet *he* does! Mum, I want you to talk to Auntie Ange. Please. Just ask her to — I dunno, to keep an eye on how Gabriel is with Finn. She really respects you; no one else could say it to her, but you could.'

Susanna thought about it. 'Okay,' she agreed. 'I'll catch up with her later in the week.'

'And you'll talk to her about Finn?'

'I will.'

'Promise?' Stella-Jean persisted.

'I promise.' Her daughter's face cleared, and Susanna cast about in her mind for some way to maintain this amity. 'Sweetie, my bag's somewhere down by your feet,' she said. 'I think there's an invitation that one of my students sent me. A show at some new arts studio. Could you check the date for me?'

Stella-Jean hauled the bag onto her lap and fossicked. 'Is this it?' She was holding up a card, a jewel-bright painting of a jowly white boxer dog dressed in a sparkly tutu and sitting on a flying trapeze. A pink banner above the dog's head read *Come fly with us at Studio Lulu's Annual Summer Show.* 'That's pretty cute,' she said.

'When's the opening? Today?'

'Yep. All day, ten a.m. to ten p.m.' Stella-Jean flipped the card over. '"Studio Lulu, where artists fly",' she read aloud. '"Star-spangled group show, studios for rent, new class schedule". What sort of artists?'

'All sorts, I gather.'

'Are you going?'

'I was thinking I might, yeah,' Susanna said casually. 'It's quite close to here, up near the bridge. I think a few of my students will be there.'

'Yeah? Can I come with you?'

It was exactly what Susanna had hoped she'd say. 'If you like,' she shrugged, cool as any teenager, as she turned smoothly into their driveway. 'Sure.'

Stella-Jean nodded. 'Mum?' she said.

'Yes?'

'Can we go to Bali at Easter, then? Just for a week?'

Susanna turned off the engine and dropped her forehead to the steering wheel with a soft thud. 'You don't let up, do you?'

'Pretty please?'

Susanna sighed. 'Maybe.'

'Is that like a sixty-per-cent-yes maybe, or eighty per cent, or . . . ?'

'It's a be-incredibly-nice-to-your-mother-and-we-might-discuss-it maybe.'

'Cool,' said Stella-Jean. 'I'll find out about sending Putu some samples ahead of time.' She started hauling the market gear out of the back of the car. 'Maybe I can even bring some new stock back with me!'

Could I have just a quarter of your confidence? That'd be all I need.

Within minutes of arriving at Studio Lulu, Stella-Jean, freshly outfitted, was mingling seamlessly with a gaggle of young people, a couple of Susanna's students among them, all talking and laughing animatedly as they admired the eclectic range of art on show. From the other side of the crowded gallery, Susanna caught her daughter's eye and signalled that she was going to explore upstairs.

The large building was a former factory, close to the river in a part of town that had left its industrial past well behind. The gallery area shared the ground floor with a printmaking workshop and a picture framer's; a floor plan showed the artists' studios and classrooms on the two floors above. Susanna made her way up the broad wooden staircase, ducking round knots of people who'd stopped to have conversations halfway up or down. She overheard several references to a person called

Vinnie who was, she gathered, the owner or the manager – or both, perhaps – of the complex. She pictured a guy rather like Gerry: smart and charming, with all the vision and drive you'd need to put together a place like this. When she asked about the classes that had been mentioned on the invite, she was directed to the far end of the top floor.

STUDIO LULU 2009 CLASSES – STARTING FEBRUARY was emblazoned along the top of a noticeboard, with a big arrow pointing to classroom B, adjacent, where one could sign up. A cluster of people studied the board's notices. 'Rita Olsen – I've heard she's a really good teacher,' said one, pointing, and when they'd moved away Susanna stepped forward to look at the notice they'd been reading, with that shivery sense that she knew what it was going to say. Yes! *Life drawing*. A fetching graphic of the white boxer, dressed this time in an artists' smock and standing at an easel drawing another dog, unclothed and with one paw behind its head in a classic life model's pose – plus the more practical information, like dates, times, cost.

In classroom B, a woman of about forty with shaggy, dark, shoulder-length hair was showing the group who'd been at the noticeboard around. Susanna tagged along unobtrusively, and when they'd written down their names and contact details and left, she stepped forward. The woman gave her a broad, welcoming smile and Susanna noticed a flash of gold and a big gap between her two upper front teeth. *Germaine Greer, that's who she looks like. If Germaine Greer had decided to become a pirate.*

'Are you interested in one of the classes? Ask away!' the woman said.

'Oh, I — yes, actually. The life drawing class.'

'Excellent!' A clipboard full of enrolment forms was right beside the woman, on a tall table, but instead of asking Susanna to fill one in, she hoisted herself lithely to the table and sat there, swinging her legs in their faded blue jeans. 'So, tell us about yourself. Done any life drawing before?'

To her own surprise, Susanna found herself explaining not only about teaching at the college, but about the exhibition she was

155

committed to having, and even about the difficulties she'd been having in getting going with it.

'You don't have a studio of your own to work in, then?' the woman asked.

'Not really,' said Susanna, leaning her hip against the table. 'At work I'm – well, I'm at work. I used to have a studio at home. Once upon a time.'

'Don't tell me: and then you had kids. Right?'

'Yeah. And what with one thing and another . . . And then, once I didn't have my own space, I seemed to slowly just . . . stop painting,' Susananna confessed. The woman was nodding knowingly. 'Familiar story, huh?'

'My, my, it sure is. Half the artists renting studios here are women desperate for a bit of space that's not the kids'. Or the partner's.'

'Is that so? I didn't realise I'd become part of a . . . I don't know, a *syndrome.*'

'It kind of sneaks up on you,' the woman said, and was about to say something further when a young man interrupted, waving at them from the door in apparent relief before turning to call to someone behind him, '*Here* she is, Lulu!'

A white dog, a boxer, raced up, wagging her stumpy tail so hard her whole back end sashayed from side to side. 'Lulu! Couldn't you find me, baby?' the woman cried, jumping down from the table to greet the dog, who rested its front paws on her thighs, jowly face wreathed in a toothy canine grin.

'There's a photographer from the local paper downstairs, Vinnie,' the young man said. 'Shall I send her up?'

'Nah, I'll come down,' the woman said. 'Just give me a few minutes to get my make-up on.' They both laughed at her joke, and the guy disappeared.

'*Vinnie*?' Susanna said. 'You're Vinnie? Are you the —' She made a big circular motion to indicate the whole building.

Vinnie grinned, showing that gap in her teeth and the bold

buccaneering flash of gold. 'Yup, that's me. Vinnie Loggia; I run this three-ring circus.' She stuck out her right hand; Susanna shook it and introduced herself, admitting too her assumption that Vinnie would be a guy. The woman waved her chagrin aside.

'And now,' Susanna said, 'I must go and find my daughter. She's downstairs somewhere, soaking up the ambiance.'

'Oh, no, you don't!' said Vinnie. 'You're not getting out of here without signing up for the life drawing class. I reckon you should do Rita's, she's an outstanding teacher. So outstanding, I'm doing the class myself. Again!'

Susanna began filling out the form, pleased to think she'd be seeing this vivid, welcoming woman again.

'Rita's class starts next Thursday evening, seven till nine. No time for second thoughts or cold tootsies, Susanna Greenfield, mother of two, teacher. *Artist.*'

Susanna handed her the completed form, grinning with oddly embarrassed delight.

'And on our way downstairs,' Vinnie went on, 'I'll show you a couple of studios. There's none spare at the moment, I'm afraid, someone just signed up for the last vacant space, but your name'll be at the top of the waiting list.'

'Oh, I don't need – a . . . studio . . .' Susanna's voice trailed away.

'The very top of the list,' Vinnie repeated, giving Susanna's shoulder a little shake and grinning her gap-toothed grin.

Throughout the Nadal–Federer final that evening, both Gerry and Seb had texted Susanna nail-biting bulletins from courtside. By the time they got home at two a.m. they were still wild with excitement and woke Susanna, who'd fallen asleep watching it on the TV. She listened, blinking, to their blow-by-blow description, until eventually she felt compelled to remind Gerry that he was flying to New York in the morning.

'S'right, Dad,' said Seb. 'And it's the middle of winter there, right? You're gonna get off that plane and be freezing your arse off.'

'Ah, I'm looking forward to it,' said Gerry breezily. 'Refreshing, after roasting here all summer. You've never seen snow falling, have you, Sebbie? It's amazing. Beautiful.'

'Right, sure, I believe you,' said Seb, and after reminding Gerry again of the brand of T-shirt he wanted him to bring back, he hugged him, and Susanna too for good measure, and went off, yawning hugely, to his room.

'Seb's a good kid,' Gerry said with satisfaction as they were getting ready for bed. 'They both are.'

'They've got a good dad,' said Susanna fondly.

'Their mum's not half bad either,' he said, winking at her. 'What'd you get up to today, Suze? Anything exciting?'

She told him briefly about Stella-Jean's coup with the Degraves Street boutique. 'And then we went to an art show together, at a local gallery. Quite interesting.'

'Sounds good,' he said, pulling her close for a cuddle. He would be away for two weeks; they made comfortable love.

Afterward, when he was spooned around her and she couldn't see his face, she screwed up her courage to say, 'Gerry, can I ask you . . . what did you think of my drawings?' The easel with her self-portraits clipped to it was still standing in a corner of their bedroom, unremarked on.

'These new ones? Of yourself?' He was hedging. *He doesn't think they're any good.* 'Well, pidge . . . I think you look better than that. I *like* your curvy bits, you know,' he said, and she smiled to herself, thinking how much he would hate knowing that he and Angie had said almost the same thing. 'But they're honest, I guess, and that's you, eh? Honest.' He dropped a couple of kisses on her shoulder. 'An open book, that's my Suze.'

'Yes,' she said slowly. She would've liked more, but – what had she expected? *They're not art critics.* She decided to be pleased. Both Gerry and Angie had confused their feelings for her with their opinion of the work, but that was all right. *And it's true: I am an honest person.* She liked that her husband had said that. The fact that she had neglected to tell him about the visit from Angie, or the talk with Stella-Jean about Finn, or that she'd put her name down for a studio, did not occur to her. Nor did it strike her as an instance of possible dishonesty that she had just, for the umpteenth time, faked an orgasm.

Contented in their embrace, they fell asleep.

EIGHTEEN

One of the perks of being in Year Ten, Stella-Jean had realised, was that you started to get more choice about subjects, and thus, if you were smart, more opportunities for what she liked to call 'creative time-tabling'. Thursday afternoons, for example, she'd managed to wangle not only a double free period but a (theoretically) foolproof method for skiving off, with Tessa primed as backup should her absence be noticed. This was her first chance to try it out, and so far, so good.

She pedalled her bike through the blazing afternoon, relishing the quiet roads and her illicit freedom, heading for the suburban shopping strip where her favourite opportunity shop, supporting the Cat Protection Society, was located. They were only open on weekdays and closed at three, but today she'd have plenty of time to scope the bargains, drop them home, and still be on time to pick up Finn from school. Afterward, she might take him into the city again; she needed to stock up on various supplies, and maybe drop into the Degraves Street boutique to check it out.

The Cat Protection Society op shop was true to form; she bought four old straw hats (tarted up with a length of ribbon and a felt flower, they'd sell in minutes at the market this Sunday, which was forecast to be even hotter than today), plus a gorgeous beaded cardigan, a set of embroidered serviettes that she could already see as cute pockets on skirts, and a pair of brand-new red silk curtains, still in their packet, which she would make into . . . skirts? Tops? Something fabulous, anyway. And the whole lot cost less than twenty measly dollars! She thanked the old ladies profusely, stroked the ancient chewed-up puss who ruled the place (with due care, mindful of his unpredictable claws), and pedalled off again. The sun was burning her to a crisp; she wished someone would design a bike helmet that gave you some shade. *Maybe I should?*

Stella-Jean coasted into the driveway and along the side path to the back of the house. She propped her bike against the door of the shed, hooking her helmet by its strap over the handlebars, and had just paused as she went by the straggling veggie garden to pop a few hot juicy cherry tomatoes into her mouth when she noticed the back door was standing open.

She stopped dead in her tracks, seeds and juice dripping down her chin. *Uh-oh.* Had it been left open this morning? Or had someone broken in? If so – a prickling started in her scalp, right above her ears – might they still be in there?

Careful not to make a sound, Stella-Jean crept back along the side path to peep in through the living room window. Well, the fancy flat-screen TV was still there. And she could see her mother's camera sitting on the coffee table, in the cool blue Crumpler case Seb had given her for Christmas. So, no burglar. *Maybe Mum's home from work early?* Oops. Having this Thursday break-out sprung on its first day would be tragic. She cast an eye back toward the bike, wondering if she could still sneak off unseen, if necessary. But – phew – there was no sign of the car out the front. The back door must've been left open by accident. Unless — Seb had nicked off from school too. She clicked her tongue. So obvious!

She put her bags down in the kitchen and went down the hallway. *Shh*, she told herself. *Quiet, like a little brown mouse.* The house definitely had that indefinable occupied feeling. *Is that a noise?* Yes. *From Seb's room?* Yes.

Tippy-toeing to his open door, Stella-Jean was ready to back off in an instant if it turned out he was in there with Rory, getting hot 'n' heavy – but the only occupant of the rumpled bed was Tigger, curled up sound asleep. There was Seb, the big dork, sitting at his desk, just the top of his head visible above the high back of his chair. Playing one of his dumb computer games, most likely. She sneaked closer . . . closer: this was childish, but she was going to enjoy going *Boo!* and scaring the crap out of him.

Seb remained oblivious. Three metres, two, one: she peeked a look at the computer screen. Not a game after all: he was watching a video clip, or maybe a movie; it was —

'*Ow!*' As though she'd grasped hold of something burning hot, Stella-Jean let out a shriek of raw surprise.

Seb jumped like his chair was electrified. '*Fuck!*' he yelled as he spun around, his face fractured with alarm and shock. 'Jesus, Stella! What the fuck are *you* doing here?'

Pointing at the screen, she yelped, 'What is *that*?'

'What's it look like?' he snarled. '*Sesame Street*?' He swung around again and with a click of the mouse the images disappeared from the screen.

'Seb!' Stella-Jean's eyes were popping. 'That was – *porn*.'

'Really? I hadn't noticed.'

She registered that he was busy zipping up his jeans and yowled again.

'Fuck *off*, Stella, you little sneak!' he yelled in a frenzy of embarrassment. 'So it's porn, so fucking what? What the fuck are you doing here, anyway?'

'But Seb, that was *guys*.'

He roared out of his chair and Stella-Jean leapt in the air like a cartoon character and started running. Ooh, he was mad enough to *really* clobber her! She slammed the door of his room behind her so hard the wall shook and took off down the hall and through the kitchen, feet skittering on the cork-tiled floor, and didn't stop till she was at the far end of the backyard. With her hands on the wooden fence, ready to swarm up and over, she dared a glance back.

He wasn't chasing her. She sagged, panting, and skulked around out there for a while, until, driven indoors by the heat, she stole back in to her bedroom. With hands that hadn't stopped jittering, she laid her op shop haul out on the bed, but she couldn't get the images she'd seen on Seb's computer screen, briefly but all too clearly, out of her mind. Quite apart from the fact that there had been *three* guys, all into it together, she was flabbergasted by the size of their — *sheesh!* Did ordinary guys' dicks really get that big? It wasn't just gross, it was kind of . . . scary. Hopefully they were, you know, exceptional, and that was why they were in porn films.

Guys looked at porn, well, *duh*, she knew that! Girls looked at porn too, some of them. Stella-Jean hadn't, and she hadn't had a boyfriend yet either, let alone sex – unlike at least half the girls in her year, or so they claimed. She was too *busy* to waste time getting involved with guys. Well, okay . . . she had a secret crush on Dylan Sweeney, who was in Seb's year, but only Tessa knew about that – and not even Tess knew that she liked to imagine Dylan kissing her and . . . and doing other things when she touched herself.

But what about Seb? He was on with Rory, she knew that for a fact, which meant he was — well, *did* it mean that he was straight? If a guy looked at *gay* porn, did that mean the guy was gay? Maybe straight guys watched gay porn too; guys could be pretty weird when it came to sex. Maybe he was bi? She felt completely out of her depth just thinking about this stuff. Maybe he —

A thump on her door. Seb shoved it open and stood there with his arms crossed. 'Let's be abso-fucking-lutely clear on this, dumb-arse,' he said grimly. 'You say a *word*, to *any*body, and you are dead. I will kill you outright and bury you in a shallow grave.'

'Are you are out of your *mind*? Like I would *want* to tell anybody! I don't even want to be having this conversation, I've got —' Stella-Jean looked at the clock beside her bed – 'Oh, shit!' – and jumped up. 'I'm outta here! I've gotta pick up Finn.'

She ran, even though it was stinking hot. 'Sorry, Finn, sorry!' she called, spotting him sitting in a corner of the almost deserted school-yard, just staring at the ground. *He looks so sad, like all the fun's leaked out of him. But nobody cares about that, as long as he stays quiet and behaves himself.* Poor kid. When was Mum gonna have that talk with Auntie Ange? She'd *promised*!

'No dusty old playground for us today, Finnsterino,' she told him as they walked along. 'We're going on an adventure. Into the city, on the train.'

Finn stopped short. 'No, Stella, no!' he said, pulling his neck down into his shoulders like a turtle. 'I can't go without per-*mission*.'

'But hey, we did it last Saturday, remember?' Stella-Jean nudged at him to keep moving, out of the sun. 'You're with *me*, you've got *my* permission.'

Finn looked desperately twitchy. 'But if *he* finds out, I'll be in trouble. He'll get *angry* with me.'

'What happens when he gets angry?' Stella-Jean stopped in a patch of shade and crouched down in front of him. 'When you're in trouble, what does Gabriel do?'

Finn's face twisted up as though he was in agony. 'I can't say anything. I can't talk about *anything* about him.'

'All right.' Stella-Jean pushed out her bottom lip and blew a big breath up over her face, trying to get her hair to lift off her sweaty forehead. 'Here's what we'll do. I'm going to text your mum and ask *her* permission for you to go on the train with me, okay?' She'd already pulled out her mobile phone and her thumb was clicking like a hyperactive cricket. 'And if she says yes, then we'll go.' She clicked send. 'Done! And meantime, we're gonna go in to that milk bar over there and get a couple of ice-cold chocolate Billabongs. One for you, and one for me. Okay?'

Finn had been listening to her very seriously. ''Kay,' he said, nodding. They walked toward the milk bar. 'Stella? Don't tell Mum I told you I can't tell you.'

'But . . . you *can* tell me stuff, Finnster,' she said. 'It doesn't matter whether Gabriel says you can or not. He can't *make* you keep things secret, you know.' But looking at her cousin's small, scared face, she understood that she was wrong: secrets were exactly what Gabriel was making Finn keep. *If Mum can't get through to Ange, I'm going to have to do something about Gabriel myself.* Stella-Jean didn't know what, exactly, but she'd figure it out. She'd have to.

By the time they reached Stella-Jean's place, Angie had texted back saying *Yes fine xx*, their ice-creams were dripping down their hands faster than they could lick, and Finn was looking a lot chirpier. Just as they turned in at the front gate, Seb was heading out with his sports bag slung over his shoulder.

'Where you going?' Stella-Jean asked.

'Coaching,' Seb said, not looking at her. He wouldn't even have stopped if he hadn't had to readjust the stuff in his bag. 'Not that it's any of your business.'

'At the tennis centre? Till when? Is Mum picking you up?'

'Who wants to know?'

'Don't be a pain, Seb.' Fat drops of melting ice-cream were splotting on to the footpath; she slurped what was left into her mouth and let it slide in a cool sugary lump down her throat. The tennis centre where Seb had his coaching sessions was right on the edge of the city. 'I'm going into the city too. Me and Finn can meet up with you, and then Mum'll get us pizza on the way home. You know, from the place that does that excellent garlic bread.'

'Whatever,' Seb shrugged, but she saw she'd fed the spark of his robust appetite. He knew the pizza place she was talking about, and would be slavering at the thought. 'I finish at seven-thirty.'

'Cool,' said Stella-Jean. 'We'll meet you outside that side gate. Okay?'

He gave her the briefest of glances and a short nod, picked up his sports bag again and swung off. Turned his back again, just like that. *Don't be mad at* me*!* she felt like yelling after him. *I didn't do anything!*

'See ya!' she called, and he raised his left arm without turning around. For a moment she felt better, and then she saw the single raised middle finger. *Yeah, well, screw you too.* She turned to Finn, who was giving his ice-cream stick a final comprehensive lick. He had chocolate from nose-tip to chin, and all the way down his arm to his elbow.

'Come on, buddy,' she said. 'Let's hose you down and then we'll go have our own adventure.'

NINETEEN

The network of little laneways and arcades lacing the heart of Melbourne had always been one of Susanna's favourite features of the city, but she had forgotten how crowded it would be at peak hour. Hard to enjoy window-shopping while being jostled by the throng of commuters heading home, as well as meandering shoppers and knots of students chatting to each other in Chinese, Hindi, Indonesian, and other languages. How the city had changed since she was a child, making the rare trip in with her parents for special occasions: viewing the Christmas windows at Myer, for instance. Nobody actually lived here in those days; you seldom saw a non-European face, and there was hardly a restaurant in existence, let alone an outdoor cafe.

Susanna walked down a short flight of stairs, into narrow, European-looking Degraves Street, and edged around a knot of tourists taking photos of a wall of street art – she knew better than to call it graffiti, these days. She cast an admiring eye over it herself, rather proud of her recently acquired appreciation of the quality of Melbourne's stencils. Amidst the other tiny shops, she spotted the boutique which was going to stock Stella-Jean's brooches, and dawdled at the window, looking at their display of bags and clothes and jewellery. She would go in there, later, with Angie, after their coffee and their talk. That was part of her plan.

There it was, the cafe where they'd arranged to meet. It was more crowded than she'd expected; she had to wait for a table, and as she waited her anxiety grew. *Is this really the right thing to do?* The very care with which she'd planned this meeting now gave her a sense of guilty unease. The innocent-sounding proposal for a coffee during the hour Angie had off from work at the department store before Thursday's late-night trading, at this cafe in Degraves Street (a safely public place) with the convenient pretext of showing her sister the boutique. And if things got uncomfortable when she had raised the difficult subject of Gabriel and Finn, Susanna could divert the conversation, tell Angie about Studio Lulu and the life drawing class she was about to begin that very evening. Innocuous; easy . . .

Seated now, she sipped a glass of water and scanned the stream of people flowing and eddying in the narrow lane. When Angie was late, Susanna found herself hoping she wouldn't come. *Wuss!* she told herself. *You just hate confrontation, that's what this is.* Poor Ange, she'd been so delighted when Susanna called her. She had no idea her sister was about to suggest that her . . . her what? It had never been made clear what Gabriel was to Angie. Nevertheless, Susanna was certain that her sister loved this man. And here she was, about to suggest – on no evidence, only (as Susanna had no intention of revealing) Stella-Jean's intuition – that he was being abusive to Angie's own son.

What if she gets angry with me, and makes a big scene – here, in public? Now Susanna wished she'd thought to broach this subject at home. *I could just go, while there's still time.* Eyeing her bag on the table beside her, she pictured herself grabbing it, dashing out and —

'Hi, hi, here I am!' Angie flung herself into the chair opposite. 'Sorry I'm late! Oh, I'm glad you got a table inside, it's *stinking* hot out there.'

They air-kissed into the space between them. Angie was flushed and breathless; looking at her, Susanna was filled with the old protective feelings for her erratic and flighty but good-hearted sister. *Yes, she is good-hearted.* Ange would never allow anyone to harm Finn. *I can't say this to her. It's like accusing her of harming Finn herself.*

They chatted, then, of this and that: inconsequential small talk, while they drank their lattes. 'Shall we have a look at this boutique, then?' Angie said. 'I've still got twenty minutes before I have to be back at work.' She ducked down, reaching for the bag which she'd put on the floor at her feet. At that moment, through the window, Susanna thought she saw Stella-Jean and Finn going past. She gasped, and Angie's head bobbed up again, blocking the view.

'What?' said Angie. Seeing her sister's startled expression, she quickly turned to look out into the narrow street herself. Nothing untoward. 'What, Susu?' she asked again, puzzled.

'Oh – nothing. I just thought I saw someone I know,' Susanna said. She felt shaken; it was as though she'd been sent a reminder that she must keep her word to her daughter, and say what she had come here to say. 'Angie: there's something I have to talk to you about.'

Speaking as though they were her own concerns, she raised Stella-Jean's observations about Finn: that he seemed nervy, on edge. Angie brushed them off. '*Frightened*,' Susanna insisted then, and, pretending she had witnessed it herself, she described Finn flinching in fear when a hand had been raised to him in a mock blow.

As though a cloth had been wiped over her face, Angie's smile disappeared. 'What are you saying? That I've been hitting Finn?'

'Not *you*, Angie! Not you! But, possibly . . . Gabriel? You know, it's not uncommon, sadly, that a mother's new partner —'

Angie's cheeks flamed. She drew a quivering breath in through her nostrils and drew herself up. Susanna quailed, recognising the telltale signs of Angie's temper, and knowing too late that she had said completely, utterly, the wrong thing. 'What do you mean, "new partner"?' Angie snapped, her empty coffee cup rattling on its saucer as she pushed it away. 'You have no idea what you're talking about. You don't know a *thing*!'

'Angie, I'm sorry, I didn't mean —'

'Gabriel has done nothing but good, for Finn and for me and for *every*body. He cares about me and Finn more than anyone in my own family does. Including *you*, apparently!' Angie was trembling, literally, with emotion.

'No one cares about you more than I do, Angie,' said Susanna in a low, heartfelt voice. 'You know I've always —'

'You've always been Mum's favourite, that's what you always!' Angie flung at her, and Susanna, stung, drew back. 'Always the *good* one! How dare you accuse Gabriel of doing anything bad? Or wrong? The discipline he's given Finn is in the *Bible*. It says in the Bible that smacking a child when he misbehaves is the *right thing to do*.'

'Well, I'm sorry,' said Susanna, unaccustomed anger rising in her own voice, 'but if that's true then the Bible is a very sick book. Let me ask you, have you ever *really* looked at all those images of Christ on the cross? Really thought about what they're depicting?'

Angie stared at her, confused. 'They're — He — *You* don't care, that Christ suffered and died for *us*. Our sins. God gave his only begotten son for our salvation.'

'It's child sacrifice, Angie; has that ever occurred to you?' asked Susanna hotly. 'It's sick! A father having his own son tortured and killed? *That's* sin!'

Angie looked at her, her face working with disbelief, rage, disgust. 'So that's what you really think. Now I know.' She brushed her hair back fiercely from her flushed face. 'You and that disgusting husband of yours. You want to see sin, Susanna? Take a look at what your precious Gerry's up to!'

'I didn't —' Susanna stopped, beginning already to regret that she had spoken her mind so harshly. 'Look, I know Gerry behaved badly on Christmas Day, and I'm sorry about it. But that doesn't —'

Angie swatted that aside. 'This isn't about Christmas Day. It's about the girl I saw him with in Sydney. A week *before* Christmas.'

'What . . . girl?'

'I don't know who she was,' said Angie with a tight relish, 'but I can tell you that he couldn't keep his hands off her in the hotel lobby. I can tell you how he was fondling her backside. How he was taking her up to his room – I saw him get the key, Susanna, I watched them get in the lift – at midnight.'

Susanna started shaking her head, and kept shaking it. How had she and Angie got to this awful place? 'No. No,' she said decisively. 'You've made a mistake.'

'Oh, I wish I *had* made a mistake, but I haven't. Gerry and that woman – she was tall, she had long, red hair – were hell-bent on *sin*.' Angie spoke fiercely, pronouncing the phrase with a preacher's precision.

Susanna recoiled. 'This is ridiculous! Gerry wanted me to come up to Sydney with him that weekend. He was *disappointed* when I couldn't. Now, why would he have wanted me to come with him if he was meeting some – some floozy?'

'I don't know. I don't know whether this was arranged beforehand or if she was somebody he'd just picked up. But I know what I —'

Picked up! Susanna's hand flew up, palm out: *Stop!* 'You don't —' she began, but she was so upset she had to stop, swallow hard, and try again. 'You don't know what you saw! Or *claim* you saw. My husband put his hand on some woman's back – maybe – and now you sit here and —' She could hardly go on. *Why is she saying this stuff? Why?* 'What are you trying to do, Angie? Do you want to destroy my marriage, is that it? Do you hate Gerry that much?'

'I don't hate anyone!' Angie cried. 'I just want you to know the *truth*!'

Susanna leaned toward her. 'Bull – fucking – shit,' she said, each word as precise and conclusive as a card slapped down on the table. *I have to get away, before I —* She stood up, fumbling in her bag, pulling out her purse, tossing down a five-dollar note. Angie reached out her hand, urgently wanting her to stay, to sit down again, but Susanna jerked her arm away. '*Don't*,' she said, and knocked into another table, and a chair, in her hurry to get out.

Oblivious to the crowds, to everything but her own shock and anger, Susanna walked through a city that might as well have been a ghost town, for all she noticed. She had no idea how she found her way back to her car, and when she got there she had to sit for some time before she trusted herself to drive. *I am not going to let her upset me. I am going to Studio Lulu, and I am going to draw, and I am going to behave as though this meeting never happened.*

Carefully, Susanna put the car in reverse, backed up, joined the stream of traffic. She saw her hands, trembling like leaves on the steering wheel, but they looked distant, as though they were someone else's. *We have a good marriage. We have good sex. My husband loves me.* A traffic light turned red, and as she waited in the column of cars she made herself take deep, calming breaths. *I would know if there was any problem.*

TWENTY

Jean lay her pencil down beside the notebook. An ordinary, lined, spiral-bound notebook, no different to the thousands she had filled with shorthand in her forty-five years as a secretary. But this one was not filled with sentences dictated to her by men: these words were her own.

She had finished a letter which was, quite probably, the most important thing she'd ever written in her life. A letter which just six months ago, she'd simply not had the words for. *Oh, I had the vocabulary, all right,* Jean reflected. *It was the heart's capacity I lacked.* Flipping back through the notebook's early pages, reading the loops and dashes of her neat, confident shorthand as fluently as ordinary written English, she could see with humbling clarity just how far she'd come. Such changes, both in tone and content, since she'd started taking Leonard's measured thoughts about forgiveness and reconciliation seriously. What she'd first written, she saw now, was little more than self-justification of her stance toward Angie. Not forgiveness: blame. Just another chorus of that tired old song: *You did this, and you did that,* banging the drum of accusation, even though she'd thought she was exploring a new way forward.

There it was, the very moment: *When you came back from overseas that first time, it was your father who welcomed you home, not me.* Below those words, a blank. Jean remembered clearly the shock of seeing the implications of what she'd just written, how she'd almost stopped there, not gone on. But then: *I never once went to the airport to see you off or welcome you home, did I?* Another blank, longer, and then, all by itself, the sentence: *I never welcomed you.*

Jean sat in her peaceful living room, late on this hot summer afternoon, recalling that revelatory moment and allowing herself a quiet sense of . . . achievement. *That was where I began to make progress*, she thought. In the months since writing those words – and especially since the row on Christmas Day – she'd gone from accusation and justification, to admission, and from there to honest confession. Finally, to apology. *I'm sorry.* Writing those two little words, the hardest thing she'd ever done.

Oddly, a matter of national importance had stiffened her personal resolve. For years the country had been wrangling internally on whether an apology should be made to the generations of indigenous Australians whose lives had been harmed, even destroyed, by government policies. One prime minister had begun the process of atonement, the next had steadfastly, scornfully, refused to carry it on. How Jean had despised that small-spirited, self-righteous man – and how chastened she had been when she recognised that her own uncompromising attitude toward Angie was not very different. Now, a new prime minister had made the apology, and brought some measure of healing with the gesture. *Perhaps that will happen for us too, in our own family*, she thought. She hoped.

A separate letter, to Susanna, would follow, but nothing would be as difficult again as writing this first one. Now, Jean knew, she must steel herself for the next challenge: overcoming her habits of privacy, of discretion, and, yes, of pride, and giving this letter to — oh, that was a daunting picture: giving it to Angie. Mightn't her daughter's first response be unwelcoming, angry, rejecting? *Yes*, Jean told herself, *and Angie is entitled to be all that.*

She would show it to Leonard first. Or read it aloud to him, more precisely, since he couldn't read shorthand. Dear Leonard, so considered and wise; he would offer her support and wise advice. *If not for Leonard, I would never have been able to come this far.* He was curious, she knew, about what she had been working on, especially these past few days they'd spent together in the guesthouse at Marysville, in the cool of the hills. Jean hadn't told him though; just smiled enigmatically. *Wait.*

Jean lifted her gaze, looking around uneasily. While she'd been preoccupied with her notebook, dimness had crept in to the room. She blinked several times, and rose, walking a little stiffly (she'd been sitting down for too long) to the back door. The long summer day was drawing to a close. Magpies and ravens were calling to each other from the tall trees around the village. Stepping into her courtyard, Jean raised her face toward the sky, where a pearly sheen was beginning to soften the uncompromising blue. Lately, she'd found evening's approach unsettling. *These darn cataracts;* in diminishing light, they affected not only her vision, but her sense of wellbeing. Perhaps she should have that operation sooner, rather than later? Susanna would be upset that she hadn't been told. But Susie was so busy; Jean didn't want to worry her. *Or perhaps that's pride, too. I just don't want to be seen as old and vulnerable.*

She wished for Leonard's rational, comforting presence. *I'd like to read him the letter tonight.* Peering at her large-faced wristwatch, she saw that it was now a little after seven. Leonard was at his chess club meeting this evening, till eight. *I'll go over to his unit and leave a note; ask him if he'd like to come and have a little supper with me.* He would like that, she knew he would. *Perhaps he'll stay the night.* How nice it was to have a man with whom to share her life again. An intimate companion. Indeed, even in her marriage, much as she and Neville loved each other, his illness had meant she'd not felt able to . . . *lean* on him, the way she could with Leonard. Neville's illness – and their cold war over Angie. *I punished him, too, poor Neville. Why am I only seeing these things now?*

Jean went inside again and wrote the note she would leave for Leonard. In the bathroom, she quickly brushed her hair and put on a little lipstick, barely glancing in the mirror as she did so. She knew perfectly well what she looked like, which was no better or worse than might be expected. Jean felt sorry for those of her female contemporaries who grieved for their lost good looks – or, sadly, tried to pretend they still had them. Such a treacherous gift, beauty. Angie, she suspected, would find it hard, when her looks finally went. Catching herself mid-thought, she did raise her eyes to the mirror. *Stop!* she told the old woman there. *Stop judging her!*

Standing on her porch, just about to close the front door behind her, Jean heard the phone ring. She hesitated, tempted to let it go – the answering machine was on – but then stepped inside again.

'Hello?'

'Oh, Mum! Thank heavens you're there!'

'Hello, Susie. Is everything all right?'

'I'm in a bit of a pickle actually, Mum. I've just realised I'm supposed to be picking up Seb at the tennis centre in fifteen minutes and – I – I'm on the other side of town, in a drawing class. I don't know how this happened, I just completely forgot.' Susanna sounded ragged and upset; quite unlike her. 'Even if I left this instant, I wouldn't —'

'Now, now, no need to panic,' Jean said lightly, reassuringly. 'I'm very pleased you've found a drawing class. And you mustn't leave; your work's important.'

'But you see, I've just realised there's a text message from Stella-Jean, she's there too. With Finn! I tried to call them but I can't seem to get *through.*'

Jean was taken aback. Her capable daughter, on the edge of tears? 'It's perfectly all right, Susie,' she said. 'I can go.' Yes, she could visit Leonard later. He could read her letter to Angie tomorrow; there was plenty of time. 'You pick him up by the gate just after the Queens Avenue corner, don't you?'

'Yes, exactly. Oh, Mum, *could* you go? That would be fantastic. I'd ask Gerry but he's away at that conference, and Angie's – um – she's at work.'

Jean suddenly remembered her eye doctor's instructions. *No driving except in full daylight.* She looked out through the open front door at the sky and the light, and pressed her lips together nervously. *But I've said yes now.* And really, it was still daylight, more or less; it wouldn't be properly dark for a good hour.

'I'll just get my car keys and be on my way,' she said.

'Oh, thank you, Mum, so much! What would I do without you? I can't —' Susanna's voice seemed to hit a snag.

'It's fine, Susie, really. Everything's fine,' Jean said, each phrase smooth and calming as the stroke of a loving hand. 'But I'll want a thank-you present. Would you give me your first drawing from this class? I'd love that.'

Susanna drew a long shaky breath. 'Of course I will, Mum,' she said, sounding more like herself. 'I hope I can do one that's good enough.'

'It will be. Off you go then. Bye-bye.'

'Bye, Mum. Don't let them give you any cheek if you're a bit late. Thanks again. I love you.'

With all three of her grandchildren in the car, Jean concentrated hard on driving, doing her best to ignore the tense atmosphere caused by Seb's foul mood. Surely it wasn't just because he'd been kept waiting for a few minutes? More likely, judging by the way he'd been snapping at Stella-Jean, he was resentful of his sister being there. Jean had always found her grandchildren more enjoyable one by one than together – except for Finn, of course, who was impossible on his own, and needed Stella-Jean to keep him in line. *But I've been prejudiced toward him because of his mother,* she admonished herself. *I haven't been fair to him, poor little boy.*

Seb, in the front passenger seat, turned around abruptly. 'Finn! Stop kicking my seat!'

'Don't yell at him,' snapped Stella-Jean.

In a tired whine, Finn said, 'Sorry, Seb.'

'Be nice, everybody,' said Jean. Which exit did she take at this roundabout? She would prefer to take them straight home, but they would all be in a better mood with food in their stomachs.

A few moments later, she heard Stella-Jean say, 'Don't scratch it, Finnster. You'll just make it worse.'

'Itchy,' he groaned.

'It's just a titchy itchy.'

'No! Not titchy. It's *not* a titchy itchy.'

'Shut *up*!' roared Seb.

'Please don't shout in my ear, dear,' said Jean firmly. 'And you'll have to tell me where this pizza shop is. I'm afraid I'm a bit lost around here.' In the deepening twilight she blinked hard, trying to clear her vision.

'You go straight on here, Jeejee,' Stella-Jean said. Her voice was close behind Jean's head; she must be leaning a long way forward.

'You do all have your seatbelts on, don't you?' Jean asked. No one responded. 'Don't you?' she repeated anxiously.

''*Course* we do,' Stella-Jean answered. 'We always do.'

'Through these lights,' said Seb, 'and then you take the next left.'

The traffic light was green. Jean had just entered the intersection when a truck, coming toward her, popped its headlights on. It was like a phosphorus bomb going off in her eyes: the light exploded and spread instantly, a blinding halo surrounding that dazzling centre. *Stop, stop! I have to pull over!* But in her panic Jean slammed her foot down not on the brake but on the accelerator and her old car leapt forward —

'*Stop*, Jeejee!' Seb cried. 'What the —'

The brake! The *brake!* She jammed it down and the car went into a skid across the intersection. Shouts, screaming, surrounded her. They were headed straight toward the truck's dazzling headlights and Jean jerked the steering wheel hard around and the car spun, screeching hideously. In slow motion, it seemed, the truck went sailing by them and their car slid onward before slamming into the pole on the far side of the intersection, metal crashing on metal with an explosive roar.

A man was calling out. 'Hello? Hello?' He was asking something. Asking if someone could hear him.

Who is he calling to? Why don't they answer? Jean tried to answer, but the man probably couldn't hear her because of this other noise, a sound that was all around her, so loud it seemed to be right inside her. Frighteningly loud, and fast; it was making the ground shake, and she was shaking with it. *Ba-boomp, ba-boomp, ba-boomp, ba-boomp.* Slow down, slow down! It was so close, and getting closer. Horses' hooves! That's what it was: the thunder of horses' hooves. Many, many horses; it must be an enormous herd. Look out, look out! Which way were they coming? Wild horses, they could drag you away —

'What is your name?' the man was asking, but he was fainter now, further away, while the thunder of the approaching herd was louder, louder — *oh!* She could see the faces of the riders now. There was her father, right in front! Look at his smile, he was so happy to see her again. She hadn't seen her father for so long. Or was it Neville? *Neville!* She tried to call out to him.

In a wild burst of scarlet light she heard her husband calling, 'Forgive her, Jeannie. Won't you forgive our little girl?'

I have, she cried, but she knew there was something more. The burst of red light had knocked her off her feet and she was falling, a long, long way. *Now, do it now!* With a mighty effort Jean held herself from falling long enough to cry, 'Forgive me! Angie, forgive me!'

There. She had said it, she had said it in time, and now she was falling again and then she understood, for just one perfect gleaming instant, that words didn't matter. *It's love that matters. Only love.*

And then every word, and love itself, was gone.

AFTER

TWENTY-ONE

He'd heard the dragon's hunting cry, howling and screaming as it bore down; he'd tried to hurl himself from its path – but it got him. Its savage burning teeth ripped at his shoulder, its talons tore at his back.

'*Get away!*' Seb screamed, but with his face pressed into the dragon's spongy hide, his voice was a muffled blur. He couldn't see. He struggled to jerk free, to turn his head, but with one arm wrenched behind his back and the other pinned in front of his chest, he was trapped, helpless. The monster bit hard and deep, trying to rip him apart.

He fought against the searing pain to move something, anything. A crack appeared, and through it he could see his sister, wedged into the back seat of a car. Whose car? *Jeejee's*. No, the back seat was too small. But Stella looked smaller too, tucked in on herself like she was trying to make room for the ridged metal pole which had somehow forced its way *inside* the car, shoving her aside. She was still, completely still.

We've had a crash. Jeejee crashed the car.

'Stella!' he yelled, but she didn't move, maybe because his voice was still muffled. She was so close: if he could just get his arm free he could touch her, shake her knee, wake her up. Then, through the gap between the car seats, he saw his sister's hand being lifted and held tight by two smaller ones, a kid's hands. *Finn; that'll be Finn.*

How come I'm corkscrewed around like this? Seb was trapped. Through the rear window he saw shapes, movement: people. He tried to call for help. Heard urgent voices at a distance, drowned out by sirens. Then the strobing of lights, blue and red.

'Hello? Madam, can you hear me?' a man's voice shouted. He was very close: over on the driver's side. Jeejee's side. Seb tried to twist back around, reversing the corkscrew, but the pain was too hideous. He decided to hold still, but from the corner of one straining eye he could see part of the driver's seat, and his grandmother's shoulder. She seemed to be leaning toward the door.

'What is your name, madam?' the man said, very loud and very clear. Seb, his own face still jammed against the seat, could just manage to see the outline of the speaker's head and shoulders leaning in through the open driver's window. He thought he heard his grandmother reply; just a murmur, perhaps not even that. It could have been anything. Red light flashed on the man's glasses as he leaned in further through the window, his head right up against Jean's face. He thought he heard, briefly, something else: a high whimpering, like a puppy, or a bird fallen from the nest.

The overlapping urgent voices outside the car were clearer now.

'Any response, Andy?'

'Jo, go round the other side!'

'How many are there?'

'Joanne? Over *that* side! There's a kid there, conscious.'

The guy had disappeared from Jeejee's window. Seb managed to lift his mouth just clear of the seat, enough to shout as loud as he could, 'Somebody help my sister!' Couldn't *somebody* hear him? 'She's not moving!' he yelled desperately. '*Stella!*'

Nothing. All he could do was let his head drop forward again, peering with one eye between the seats. Stella-Jean was in shadow now – he hoped it was shadow, not blood, darkening the side of her face, her neck.

Finn started yelling, 'No! No!' Then screaming, '*No, no, no, no!*' Seb could see him trying to scoot closer to Stella-Jean, away from whoever must have opened the door.

'It's all right, it's okay,' said a woman's voice, trying to calm him. 'What's your name? We'll just get your seatbelt – it's *okay*.'

'No! *No!* Stella!' Finn was clutching convulsively at her arm.

'Finn,' called Seb, trying to get his attention through the gap between the seats. 'Finn, let them help her. *Finn!* You've got to get out of the car, so they can help her.' He was in an agony of fear and impatience. '*Ste-lla!*'

The door on his side opened; he couldn't see it but he could feel the change in air, in pressure.

'Hello there, mate. I'm right behind you, right here,' said the same guy who'd been talking to Jeejee. He had a British accent. 'You can hear me, can you? What's your name?'

Seb lifted his mouth clear again. 'Sebastian Greenfield Visser.' It seemed important to say his full name.

'Sebastian. Right-oh. Is that your little brother? Flynn, is that his name?'

'My cousin. Finn.'

'Jo, the lad's called *Finn*,' he heard the guy call. 'Okay, Sebastian, I'm Andrew.' He must've put his mouth right up to Seb's ear; he could feel the warm breath, hear every syllable. 'I need you to do something. Can you move your feet a bit for me? A little soft shoe shuffle?'

'My sister's not *moving*,' Seb said, incredulous. *What kind of idiot is this guy?*

'Don't worry, we're getting to her,' Andrew said, infuriatingly calm. 'How're those feet?'

Seb moved his feet to and fro just to shut him up.

'Oh that's beautiful,' said Andrew. 'Champion.'

Seb could hear other voices now, outside the car, calling orders, advice, instructions, only some of which he could understand.

'And this hand – can you wriggle these fingers for me?' Seb felt a touch on his right hand, the one twisted behind his back, its shoulder still gripped tight by the dragon's teeth. 'Twinkle, twinkle, little star?'

Twinkle, twinkle? Jesus! But Seb moved his fingers around.

In his narrow slice of vision he saw Finn's hands being prised from Stella-Jean's arm and, still protesting wildly, the kid was lifted away from her and out of Seb's sight. Immediately, a woman in a white uniform climbed into the back seat with Stella-Jean, close, putting one hand up to her mouth. Seb understood that she was feeling for his sister's breath, and held his own as he waited for what seemed an age.

'Respiration's good,' the woman called, and Seb let out a sob of air. Now the woman had two fingers on Stella-Jean's throat. 'Pulse is strong, steady.'

'Her name's Stella,' the guy behind Seb called.

'Stella-Jean,' Seb amended, even though he used his sister's full name less than anyone else in the family. Andrew repeated it in his British voice. *Scottish, that's what he is.*

'*Stella-Jean!*' the woman yelled, very close to her ear. 'Stella-Jean, can you hear me?'

Open your eyes, Stell, Seb willed her. *Please, open your fucking eyes!*

Did her eyes flick open? Yes? No? Seb thought they had, but now they were closed again.

The woman picked up Stella-Jean's hand and pushed the edge of what looked like a pen hard against the bed of her fingernail. Seb saw his sister's arm jerk up and try to pull away.

'Hey, you're hurting her!' he yelled. 'What the fuck are you doing?'

The woman glanced toward him briefly, and lowered the hand. 'Stretcher,' she said, backing swiftly out of the back seat, and out of his sight. Seb heard her yell, outside the car: 'Stretchers, spine boards!'

'Right-oh then, Sebastian,' said Andrew, behind him. 'Time to get you out of here. This seatbelt is well and truly fooked, so I'm cutting it. Hold still, okay?'

Seb grunted assent, and a moment later he was, not free exactly, but no longer trapped in that corkscrew twist. Andrew's hands were guiding him, his arm bracing and supporting, and he was being moved out of the car. He could see Jeejee now, just sitting there in the front seat, head back and turned aside, none of the ambulance people doing anything with or to or for her – and then, as his right shoulder and arm swung back, Seb screamed. The pain, *holy shit*! The pain!

And now he was almost out of the car but he couldn't see Stella-Jean. For the first time, Seb panicked. This Andrew dude was trying to move him, trying to take him away from Stella, and they were doing stuff to her, hurting her —

'Fuck off!' he yelled as Andrew tried to ease him around. He managed to raise the arm that had been squashed between his body and the seat, and swung it across like a club, trying to punch the guy away. Only his forearm connected; Andrew's head, already moving back, caught the edge of the clumsy blow.

'Whoa! Go easy, tiger,' he said, nudging his dislodged glasses back into place with his upper arm. 'We're here to help, Sebastian. Trust me.'

Another person was there, and then a third, easing him from the car and onto some kind of trolley, fiddling and fussing and strapping him in and then he was being wheeled away. There were cops and ambos and onlookers. He was wheeled past the open back of one ambulance where Finn sat with a uniformed woman beside him with her arm around his shoulders. He looked like a little kid in a war film. *This is freaking surreal. It's like I'm in a TAC ad on TV.* Only the pain made him know he was really there, actually *in* it, not just watching. He was holding his breath against the pain and Andrew leaned close.

'Keep breathing, Sebastian,' he said, and did a few big breaths – in-and-out, in-and-out – to demonstrate. Seb fixed his eyes on his face, the coloured light glinting on his glasses, and copied him. He had to. Andrew nodded. 'That's it, stay with it. We need your help. The coppers'll need to call your family.'

'My mobile . . .' said Seb. Where was it? 'It's in my bag. The big sports bag. It's in —'

He tried to turn his head, to look back toward the car, but couldn't. His head seemed to have been braced or something.

'We'll get it. You're a champ. You just keep steady with those slow, deep, breaths.' Andrew touched his chest, very lightly. 'Grrreat!'

They were wheeling him away from the car. Away from Jeejee, away from Stella-Jean. Seb took another breath, a slow deep breath that turned into a ragged tearing sob.

TWENTY-TWO

In Vinnie's kitchen, behind the framing workshop on the ground floor of Studio Lulu, half-a-dozen of people were getting in each other's way as they prepared an impromptu dinner after the life drawing class. 'Two minutes, everybody!' yelled the woman who'd just tested the penne, while another stirred the sauce and someone else tossed a big bowl of salad at the table. Vinnie was chopping parsley with an enormous knife while Susanna, standing next to her, grated a big chunk of parmesan. Everyone was talking, all at once.

'So, you liked the class?' Vinnie asked her over, or rather under, the hubbub. 'What did you think of Rita?'

'She's terrific,' Susanna assured her. 'Though . . . it was a bit confronting, the way she told me so severely, "You heff not turnt off your teacher brain!"'

'Ah.' Vinnie's mass of dark hair swung with her as she flashed a grin at Susanna. 'And that was her solution? Getting you to lie on the floor and draw?'

'Yep.' Again Susanna imitated Rita's European accent. '"Moofe *in*. Moofe in ker-loh-ser!" Gawd! How much closer could I get? The poor model, she was starting to look quite nervous.'

'Nah, don't worry, Lisa's an old hand,' Vinnie said as she scooped up the finely chopped parsley with the flat of her knife and dumped

189

it in a bowl. 'I saw the drawing you did: *so* Venus of Willendorf, all those rising mounds of flesh.'

Susanna nodded agreement. 'Actually, I've been doing a few self-portraits lately. Maybe that's where the —'

'Coming through!' one of the others called, lugging the enormous pasta pot from the stove to the sink. 'Hot hot!' Steam billowed as she poured the pasta into the waiting colander.

'Somebody's phone's ringing,' a voice sang out. 'He-llo – somebody's phone!'

Susanna glanced across at the bag dangling from the woman's hand. 'Oh, that's mine. Ta!' She darted over. This would be her mother, or one of the kids, or Gerry wondering where she was. *No, not Gerry: he's in New York.* And it would certainly not be Angie, not after — no. As she flipped her phone open, Susanna tightened against the memory of that awful meeting with her sister. She would *not* go there.

But the voice, a man's, was unfamiliar, and she couldn't make out what he was saying. 'What?' she said, walking away from the racket around the table, over to a quieter corner. 'I'm sorry, I didn't catch that.'

From the far side of the kitchen, Vinnie saw Susanna stop dead, heard the terror in her voice as she cried, '*An accident?*' All the women froze. 'What do you mean?' In the sudden silence, her voice was shrill and penetrating. 'What sort of accident?'

Someone murmured, 'Oh, no,' and a moment later they all flinched as Susanna screamed, '*Oh no!*'

Vinnie had her bag over her shoulder in an instant. 'Carol, will you make sure the place is locked up when you go?' The woman she'd asked nodded quickly. 'Please, all of you: stay and eat. I'm going with Susanna.'

Susanna insisted on driving, but after only a few hundred metres she pulled over. 'Would you?' she asked Vinnie in a shaky voice. 'I need to make phone calls.'

They changed places. 'Which one first, Northern General or St Vincent's?' Vinnie asked.

Susanna said tensely, 'Northern General.' Then, anguished, '*Why* would they take them to two different hospitals?'

'Facilities? Specialists?' Vinnie hazarded. She could hear Susanna sucking air in strongly through her nose, sensed her struggle for control. 'Hang in there,' she said, taking one hand from the steering wheel to give her arm a squeeze.

'I know,' Susanna said. 'I know. I'll keep it together. It's right to go to Northern General first. Isn't it? If Seb's conscious, I can at least talk to him.' She stared at the mobile phone she was holding in her hand. 'What —Vinnie, what time is it in New York?'

'Um – mid afternoon? I'm not sure.'

'We don't usually call each other when he's away.' Susanna made no move to key a number. 'International . . .' she said uncertainly. 'My brain's not functioning.'

I'm not surprised, thought Vinnie. 'If he's set for international roaming, you shouldn't need to dial the code. Just his usual number.'

'Oh.' Susanna pressed a couple of keys, put the phone to her ear, waited, took a big breath. 'Gerry, it's me,' she said. 'Could you give me a call, as soon as you get this message?' She paused. 'Urgently. I'm – ah – there's been an accident.' She took the phone away from her ear, eyeing it doubtfully, then added, 'Um – bye. Bye, darling,' and closed it. 'Should I have said that?' she asked Vinnie. 'That there's been an accident?'

'Yes. He needs to know it's urgent.'

'He's at a conference. He has to give a talk. I don't want to worry him.'

She doesn't want to worry him. Vinnie was incredulous. 'Susanna, that was a good message,' she said firmly. 'He needs to know.'

'Okay. All right.' Susanna was staring at the phone again. 'Now I've got to call my sister.' She pressed a couple of keys and held it to her ear, waiting. 'Voicemail,' she muttered, then, rapidly, 'Angie, it's me.

I'm on my way to Northern General. The police called me, they said they've already spoken to you: I guess you're probably at St V's now. I hope Finn really is okay; the guy I spoke to said they were keeping him in for observation. I don't know . . .' She started crying. 'Angie, I'm sorry about this afternoon, I really am. We were both upset.' For a moment she couldn't go on, and then she managed, 'I'll be there as soon as I can. See you.'

She held the phone down in her lap, arms stiff and back rigid, and let out a howl of anguish. 'Why wouldn't he tell me about my *mother*? What's *happened* to her?'

'Hang in there, Susanna,' Vinnie said again. 'We'll be there soon.'

'I want to talk to my *mother*!' Susanna cried. 'I want *her* to tell me what's happened. What to *do*!' She clutched her arms around herself, making wordless sounds of distress. '*Why* did I call her earlier? Why did I ask her to go and get the kids? They could've got the *train* home, they're not *babies*!' She was rocking back and forth.

'Susanna . . .' Vinnie didn't know whether to tell her to let it all out, or pull herself together. 'Susanna, if you *could* talk to your mother, right now, what would she say? What would she tell you to do?'

Susanna made a whickering sound of protesting helplessness, but she'd heard. She stilled herself, and on her next breath raised her head as though listening for something, then exhaled slowly. 'You're right,' she said. 'She'd say, "Don't panic, Susie, stay calm." She'd tell me to be strong.' It was remarkable, how her voice had steadied. 'I have to be strong.'

'You can do it,' Vinnie said.

Afterward, Susanna could remember very little of that night. At the time, it felt like she was deaf, or else the police and the hospital people – and it was hard to be clear who was who: doctors, nurses, surgeons, admissions staff – were talking in a language other than English, one she didn't understand. She watched their mouths moving but could make no sense of what was coming out of them. Time and again she had to turn, literally, to Vinnie, for interpretation.

What she did remember most vividly later was her first sight of her kids: Seb's face when she arrived, his relief so naked, so child-like, despite his pain. They were going to operate on his shoulder the next morning. 'It'll be okay, Mum,' he said, but he was crying. And the moment – was it hours later? – that she saw Stella-Jean, the small part of her face one could see instantly recognisable – *my little girl, my baby* – despite the swelling, the bandages, the tubes. They had already operated to relieve the pressure in her brain; Susanna thought they told her that a piece of skull had been removed and was now refrigerated (though this turned out, later, to be an option that had been considered only) and Susanna felt a wild desire to go to that fridge and hold that piece of bone, cradle it as she couldn't cradle her daughter.

Coma: an incredibly easy word to lip-read. Someone said "induced", but what did that actually mean? She couldn't understand: was Stella-Jean unconscious because of the accident, or the anaesthetic from the operation?

She had no memory of any forms, yet in the days and weeks that followed she saw her signature on so many. The amount of infor-mation she'd apparently been able to impart was astonishing. She'd even thought to enlist Marcus to make contact with Gerry in New York; poor Marcus, he was distraught, and wanted to come to the hospital, but she told him that since she had to switch her mobile off inside, he was more useful on his phone at home. All this, she was reminded of later.

She could remember being told that her mother was dead, but not who told her, or the words they used. Vinnie and Angie were able to fill in those missing words for her later, but she had a persistent sense of shame at not being able to remember them herself. Nor what she had said when she was told. Had she said anything? Had she wailed? She did remember hearing herself protesting, '*I can't! I can't!*', like a piteous child when they told her that it was necessary to officially identify her mother's body. And Angie taking a step forward and saying, with calm assurance, 'It's all right. I'll do that.'

Angie embracing her, taking charge; their roles reversed. For Susanna, crawling across a trackless and terrifying desert, it was like her sister holding a glass of cool water to her lips, saying *Here. Drink.*

But the desert still stretched on.

TWENTY-THREE

'Who are you?'

The guy sitting in the chair beside Seb's bed looked up from the magazine he'd been reading. 'Hello there, Sebastian,' he said, closing the magazine and placing it on the floor beside him. 'Awake, are we?'

'Se-*bus*-tyun,' mimicked Seb. The way the guy said his name was kind of familiar, and so was the guy himself. Tall, red buzz-cut hair, wire-rimmed glasses. 'Where do I know you from?' he asked, and the words seemed to float out of his mouth, soft, like bubbles.

'I scraped you up off the road last night. No, I exaggerate,' the guy said, leaning forward. 'No scraping required. You just needed a bit of assistance releasing your seatbelt.'

Seatbelt . . . A sudden jumble of images spilled through Seb's mind, like floodwater swirling with debris. Seatbelt; truck lights; howling dragon; shoulder; pain. *Whoa.* Too much! He closed his eyes for a moment, gasping like a fish. *Car crash.* Coloured lights, flashing off those glasses. 'You were there. You're like, an ambo or something. Yeah?'

'That's right,' the guy confirmed, nodding. 'Well done, Sebastian.'

'What's your name again?'

'Andrew.'

'Unn-drrrew,' said Seb. It wasn't the way an Aussie would say it. 'Scottish.'

'More just a mongrel Brit, unfortunately.'

A power pole in the back seat; Stella, not moving. Was it fact, or nightmare? Trapped, he'd been trapped, and now, as he tried to heave himself upright so he could meet whatever was coming, he was *still* trapped: his whole right side — arm, shoulder, neck — was wrapped up tight, like a rolled roast at the butcher. 'Why can't I *move*?' he cried.

'Take it easy, tiger. You've just had a shoulder op a few hours ago.'

'Shoulder op.' Seb saw a chain of little bubbles floating in front of him, popping open to release strange images and words. 'Anterior dislocation.'

'Correct.'

Pop, pop. 'From when that fucking dragon tried to rip my arm off.'

Andrew nodded agreeably. The lad's eyes were almost all pupil; no doubt post-operative pain relief was being generously administered.

'They couldn't get it back in. What do they call it, when they can't get a dislocated shoulder back in?' Seb asked.

'Irreducible.'

'Irreducible, yeah. So they had to operate. Doesn't even hurt, not now, anyway. Did before. But I saw my mum after that, after the op, I mean. Was I awake before? Was my mum here?'

'Aye, she was just leaving when I arrived. She had to go back to the other hospital, where your sister is.'

Stella, not moving. 'Is she okay? My sister?'

'She's in the ICU at St V's. They're looking after her, Sebastian.'

Seb kept looking at the guy's eyes: nice eyes, steady; they'd kept him afloat in the flood. *Keep breathing*, he'd said. Seb took a deep breath in. 'But Jeejee's dead. My grandma. Isn't she?'

Andrew made no reply, but his gaze didn't waver.

For Seb, the silence confirmed it. 'No one was helping her,' he said flatly. 'That's how I know. 'Cause that was you at the window, right? And you were trying to talk to her. And after that . . .' Seb's face buckled and a kind of lost crooning sound came wandering from the back of his throat. Andrew sat there like a rock, like a lighthouse, like there was nowhere else he needed to be. 'My mum's gonna be messed up,' Seb whispered eventually, and then for a while he seemed to float away.

A nurse entered, wheeling a trolley stacked with bed linen and cleaning gear. She proceeded to raise the bed next to Seb's by stepping repeatedly on a foot pedal; with each step it protested loudly, *scree-ah, scree-ah*. They watched as she wiped down the rubber covering of the mattress and every inch of steel rail with disinfectant wipes. She didn't once look at them.

'Friendly, some folk,' said Andrew when she'd left the room. Seb's gaze flicked back to him.

'Your accent's Scottish,' Seb said. 'I went to school with a kid from Scotland.'

'North of England, actually.'

'Did you already tell me that? Yeah, you did. Hey, I just remembered: I had this dream. You know what I was dreaming?'

Andrew shook his head.

Seb licked his dry lips. 'Can I have some water?' When Andrew held the tumbler to Seb's mouth, some spilled, but it didn't matter. He felt like all he had to do was open his mouth and streams of words would just spill out, and he could watch them.

'A volcano . . . I was dreaming this volcano had erupted, and all this lava was flowing down the street and I was trying to get my stupid sister out of the way. She was standing there with her hands on her hips just refusing to move. I was screaming at her, "Run, run! Get out of the fucking way!" But she wouldn't. You wanna know *why*? Just because I wanted her to. That's the only freaking reason. I just . . .'

The stream of words dried up; his eyes wandered the room, as far as that was possible given that he could barely turn his head. Of the four beds in the room, only one other was occupied. A middle-aged man lay watching the TV suspended from an angled steel stalactite above his bed. The man looked very tired.

'She is the stubbornest little . . . face-ache,' said Seb softly.

'When I was trying to get you out of the car last night, you didn't want to leave her. D'ye remember trying to punch me out, Sebastian?'

'No! Fuck! Did I?' Seb looked at Andrew, asking if this had really happened. Andrew nodded. 'Sorry! Must be hard enough being an ambo without some idiot trying to punch you out.'

'I thought it was very touching, actually. *Ste-lla*, you were yelling. Just like Marlon Brando. *A Streetcar Named Desire.*'

'I saw that movie,' Seb said. He felt like he could just float off now, into the cosmic river. 'He was a knockout, that guy. So fucking hot. Not as hot as Clarence, though.'

'Is that so?' said Andrew, leaning back in the chair, resting his jaw in a propped hand. 'Who's Clarence, then?'

'He was my doubles partner. We won everything. We were *more than the sum of our parts*. You know what that means?'

'Tell me. What's it mean, Sebastian?'

'It means we were amazing. Fucking amazing.' Seb's sigh was as long and heavy as a steel cable being lowered to the seabed. 'And now he's gone.'

'And where has Clarence gone?' asked Andrew gently.

'Hong Kong. His uncle had a massive stroke and now his dad's gotta . . . Anyway. He's not coming back.'

'You miss him,' said Andrew. Not a question.

'Yeah.' Seb lay his head back, looking up at the bright ceiling lights for a few moments before closing his eyes. 'He's beautiful,' he said simply, and tears leaked out from below his lids. Andrew sat, silently watching.

For a few moments, Seb seemed about to say something more, and then he squinched his eyes hard several times to push the teardrops on their way. 'This is pretty fucked up, isn't it?' He laughed, a short harsh bark.

'No,' said Andrew. That was it, just no.

They held each other's eyes, briefly. Seb gave a big snorting sort of sniff. 'Anyway, Stella could wake up any minute. Couldn't she? Maybe she has already. They're gonna call me . . .'

He looked toward the door, and, at that moment, as though summoned, a nurse entered the room. But she went straight past Seb and Andrew to the empty bed next to his that had been cleaned and prepped. Behind her came other nurses wheeling a trolley; the young man lying on it gave Seb and Andrew a wave and a woozy smile as he was trundled past. One leg, bruised and stitched and swollen, was enclosed in what looked like a hideous medieval torture device. Seb had a glimpse of flesh pierced by metal rods before a nurse, giving them a brief and businesslike smile, flicked the curtains across. 'What the fuck?' he said softly, shocked.

'Iliazarov apparatus,' said Andrew in his matter-of-fact drawl. 'I'd put money on a motorbike somewhere in that picture.'

'Axillary nerve damage,' said Seb. The words had just floated into his brain, each one in its bubble, and gone *pop, pop, pop*. 'That's what they said about my shoulder. Hey, Andrew, what d'you know about axillary nerve damage?'

'Not a great deal,' Andrew replied evenly. 'Except there's a lot can be done to repair it, these days.'

'Yeah?' said Seb. 'That's good.' Every time Andrew said something, he felt like someone had reached out into the river's current and steadied him. 'But my dad's gonna freak out,' he said suddenly. 'Oh, boy. He's gonna really freak out. My tennis career's prob'ly over before it's really gotten started.'

'I see,' said Andrew. 'And what about you, Sebastian? Are you freaked out about your tennis career?'

'My tennis career.' Seb stared at him, trying to concentrate. Weird; a big *whoosh* had come out of nowhere, almost swamping him; he was feeling too tired, all of a sudden, to keep swimming. 'I have no idea,' he said slowly. 'I have no idea who I fucking am.' His eyelids drifted down, fluttered up, drifted down again.

'Sebastian.'

With a mighty effort, he cranked his eyes half open.

'I've got a shift starting soon,' Andrew said. 'So I have to get going now.'

'That's a shame,' Seb murmured.

'Is it?'

'Yeah. It's really good, knowing you're sitting there.'

Andrew reached out and curled his fingers round Seb's hand, and held it. Just held it. 'It's really good,' murmured Seb again.

'I'll come back, then, if you like. But I don't know when that — Sebastian, listen: there's going to be some extreme weather tomorrow. Highest fire danger Victoria's ever had, they're saying.'

'Yeah? But I thought the heatwave was over . . .' Seb's eyes were closed now, his voice drifting.

'It's building up again. If it's bad as they predict, I might not be able to come in for a few days. Till after you've gone home.'

'No. I want to see you again . . .'

'Do you? Really?'

'Yeah . . . I do . . .'

'Right you are then.' Carefully, Andrew released Seb's hand, stroking the back of it with the tips of his fingers, twice. 'You will. Don't you worry, Marlon. You will.'

TWENTY-FOUR

The instant he pushed clear of the revolving doors Gerry was rocked back on his heels by a wolfish blast that had arrived in New York direct from the Arctic. His face felt like it was being pistol-whipped with icicles, but despite the shock he forged ahead. Anything rather than go back inside that damn conference centre.

Gerry had just delivered his paper, *Mind the Gap! Reconfiguring Interstitial Space in the Public Domain*. His audience, sprinkled across a two hundred and sixty-seat auditorium, had consisted of less than twenty people. Seventeen, to be precise: he'd counted them as he waited to be introduced by a young conference lackey who read stumblingly from a publicity handout and mispronounced his surname – Gerry *Vise*r – twice. 'Hey, no one walked out,' said this genius afterward, and Gerry had smiled tightly, preferring to conceal his furious humiliation.

On his way out he passed the crowded bar where one of the giants of architecture was throwing a cocktail party. *That's* what his session had clashed with. He had an invitation – every single person at the conference had an invitation, to judge by the whooping and holler-ing crowd – but even though he was in great need of a consoling Scotch, Gerry stalked regally out into the sub-zero blast. In less than a minute his face was aching, right down inside the cheekbones, as he tried unsuccessfully to hail a cab. In imminent danger of being frozen solid if he stood still, he started walking back to the hotel, his unsuitable shoes slipping sickeningly on the ice. *That'd be all I need, to go arse over tit and end up with a fractured skull.*

He'd imagined that winter in Manhattan would be glamorous. He'd indulged, god help him, in fantasies of a scintillating reunion with the lovely Marianne Zavos from the Prague conference of a few years before. Walking arm in arm into the Palm Court at the Plaza, laughing, brushing snowflakes from each other's hair; holding her hips as he fucked her while looking out at the spire of the Chrysler Building glowing against a steel-grey sky; rocketing her to another yowling climax via the combined pleasures of his cock and a few selected toys from the little bag he always packed for conferences. *Ha!* He might as well have left the toy bag locked up in the filing cabinet back in his office in Melbourne, because Marianne Zavos had said no. *No!* Flashing her wedding ring at him like a crucifix at a vampire, shocked, as though that hot little wanton of Prague had been someone else entirely; as though she hadn't responded warmly to the friendly email he'd sent her a few months ago. 'Deceitful bitch,' he snarled into the unpleasant, humid woolliness of the scarf wrapped across his mouth.

Just like Justine. Gorgeous, smart, ambitious Justine, whom he had loved to distraction. Yet when he proposed to her – held a bloody diamond ring out to her, sitting in a tiny black box on the palm of his stupid hand – she said she needed to think about it. *Think about it!* Even walking down this freezing Manhattan street, dark already at five o'clock in the afternoon, Gerry grew hot with rage and shame.

Shit, what street's this? He blinked hard, slitted eyes watering from the cold, at the sign. Fifth Avenue. *Damn.* He turned around and a guy immediately behind nearly collided with him; they had to grab each other's arms to prevent a fall. 'Sorry, sorry,' Gerry said, feeling like a hick. Without a word, the guy manoeuvered away and walked on. *Where's the bloody hotel?* He spotted it, half a block away, and felt a disproportionate surge of relief. A hot shower before frostbite set in, and a change of clothes. And then that drink.

Half an hour later he was in the bar, warmer, calmer, and halfway through his first Scotch, when a woman walked up and put her glass down on the granite counter beside his.

'Your paper,' she said without preamble, 'was excellent.'

Gerry's head jerked up. 'Why, thank you. You – ah, you heard it?'

'I did, Mr Visser.' She was about his own age, and as well-maintained: black and silver hair cropped elegantly short, a gym-toned, full-breasted figure. Her black pants and jacket, her sleek silver jewellery, all were understated and expensive.

'Gerry,' he told her, half-rising from his bar stool, extending his right hand. 'I'm sorry, I don't —'

'Susanna Delgado,' she said. It was on the tip of his tongue to tell her that his wife's name was Susanna, but — no.

'That auditorium should have been full,' she said, sliding her trim backside onto the stool beside his. 'Their loss.'

'I didn't expect much of an audience,' Gerry shrugged, doing offhand self-deprecation. 'Who's heard of some Aussie with a thing for using what's already there, eh?'

'*Yet*,' she appended, and he inclined his head, acknowledging her compliment. She took a sip from her glass, and he noticed that she too was a Scotch drinker, and that she wore no wedding ring. 'One must make allowances for Americans,' she said. 'Despite being so thrilled with themselves for electing Obama, they're desperately parochial. And New Yorkers, of course, don't really want to listen to anyone else but themselves. I —' she tapped her sternum, just below the silver necklace, '— am Canadian. And *I* find your ideas extremely interesting.'

They had their second drinks sitting in comfortable leather armchairs in a quieter corner of the bar. Susanna Delgado, he soon learned, was a senior policymaker in the Canadian government's civic planning authority, whose current brief was to explore means of extending the useful life of aging public buildings – hospitals, prisons, museums and galleries, colleges – thus, the government hoped, saving billions. 'Your concepts – utilising the interstices, revitalising infrastructure, creating new forms of connection – appear to be a *very* good fit with our project priorities.'

Sleek, alert and intelligent, she put Gerry in mind of a raven. She was clearly a woman of considerable energy and, he suspected, considerable influence. The humiliation of his poorly attended session was already being reconfigured into a very different story. Could that be a bunch of Canadian government commissions for Visser Kanaley he saw on the far horizon?

'How very fortuitous,' he said, with his easy charming smile, 'that you decided to forgo the pleasures of the Bauer cocktail party and come to my little talk instead.'

'Cocktails I can have any time,' she said, swirling the ice cubes in her glass. 'Your talk I'd diarised the moment I read the abstract. And then . . .' She looked straight at him with keen dark eyes. 'I noticed you at the reception on the first evening. And I thought, that's the most . . . *interesting* man at this conference. Without a doubt.'

A pause, of several beats, as Gerry joined the dots. Susanna Delgado could have approached him at the end of his talk, but instead she must have followed him from the conference centre. When he came into the bar, she'd been waiting. He allowed his smile to deepen, become more sensual, letting her know by the subtlest movements that, although his eyes were still on her face, his awareness had expanded – at her invitation – to her body.

She would be wearing, assuredly, the classiest of lingerie. Her skin would be soft, lacking youthful resilience but expensively maintained; there would be a luxuriant heaviness to her breasts. Gerry despised those puerile men who slavered over girls young enough to be their daughters, even their granddaughters. A woman like Susanna Delgado, in middle-age, offered a depth of sexual savvy no high-tittied lass of twenty could possibly emulate. A woman of this age appreciated *him*, too: his good looks, hard cock, full head of hair. Gerry liked being appreciated.

From the bar to the hotel restaurant, and dinner. One minute they were quoting Joni Mitchell lyrics to each other, and the next discussing retro-fitting the heating systems of massive buildings. *We're compadres*, he thought. *Her intellect is as big and bold as mine.*

'You're a rare woman, Susanna Delgado,' he told her. Their plates had been cleared away but they had been enjoying their conversation too much to make a move. Till now.

'I am,' she said, smiling, slyly confident.

The next sentence, he thought, *will be —*

'Would you care to have a nightcap, Gerry Visser, in this rare woman's room?'

He went back to his own room just long enough to brush his teeth and collect the emerald-green toy bag. On the coffee table sat his laptop, and the mobile phone still plugged in to the charger beside the bed; he made the decision, thrilling in itself, not to even glance at them. Tonight there were no emails, no phone calls, no messages, that couldn't wait. Right now, he was on his way to a rare and different place.

About three in the morning they agreed that the final sessions of the conference could manage perfectly well without them. At last they slept, and when they awoke were in no hurry to do anything but talk more, have more terrific sex (enjoying Susanna's toy collection, as well as his) and demolish an eclectic meal ordered from room service: coffee and mimosas, oysters and danishes.

It was past noon when Gerry finally left Susanna's room, each wanting to get some work done. They would meet again toward evening – an evening, they both understood, which would again be enjoyed together.

When Gerry got out of the lift on his floor, he felt like he really had been off on a different world: his head seemed to be not quite attached to his body, while his body felt like it had experienced some other atmosphere than Earth's. But he felt good; oh yes, he felt very, very good – right up until the moment he opened the door of his room and saw the dozen notes left there. He snatched a couple up: *Mr Visser to ring Mark S. Karnaley immediately*, and *Urgent!! Mr Visser to call this number . . .*

He dived for his mobile phone – *37 missed calls* – flipped it open, swearing furiously, and jabbed in Marcus's number.

Less than two hours later he was at JFK, in the first of many queues. As Gerry shuffled toward the security check, he thought of something else. He hadn't yet spoken to his wife: no phones on in ICU, for which, under the circumstances, he was grateful. He called Marcus again.

'This is what happened, why no one could reach me: I changed rooms, but the desk clerk forgot to enter it into the computer.' From the other end of the line, silence. 'Got that, Marco? I changed rooms, but the —'

'I heard you,' answered Marcus, not sounding pleased.

'Just tell Susanna that, okay?' said Gerry testily, and snapped the phone shut. His panic and guilt were only bearable if he could transmogrify them into bad temper. 'Don't give me a hard time,' he muttered under his breath.

He'd been following this bloke in the blue uniform down vinyl-floored corridors for what seemed like hours, scurrying after him like a rat new to the maze, angry and anxious and exhausted and with his goddamn suitcase screeching like a hungry seagull as he towed it along behind him. A moment was all it had taken to catapult him into craziness, then twenty-four hours to go from one side of the world to the other, from below freezing to what felt, when he'd stepped out of the airport in Melbourne, like an oven in hell.

Eventually, the nurse keyed the two of them past some sort of security lock and was ushering Gerry swiftly through a room that looked like a cross between NASA's control centre and a dormitory. *Rark, rark*, went his case, embarrassingly loud. He'd paid a fortune for the damn thing, what the hell was wrong with it? The nurse halted at one set of curtains and flicked them back abruptly.

Susanna gasped and lurched up from a chair beside the bed. 'Gerry!' Tottering toward him with her arms outstretched, she pressed her face to his chest and started crying, a thin drizzle that sounded as though she'd been holding it in so long it had lost all substance.

Looking over the top of her head to the figure in the bed, Gerry felt his blood go icy. If he hadn't known it was his daughter he would never have recognised her. *She looks like she's been bashed*. He wished there was someone he could hit, punish, *kill*, for doing this to his daughter. He let go of Susanna and hunkered down beside his little girl. Poor swollen face; tubes everywhere, stuck on her hands and chest, snaking into her mouth and nose. With the tenderest of touches, he traced the line of close-shaved scalp visible below the helmet of bandages.

'You're going to be all right,' he whispered. 'I swear, Stellabell, you are going to be all right.' His face worked as he struggled not to cry.

'Gerry? I didn't know where you were,' said Susanna in a broken mew. 'I had no idea.'

Oh god, don't say that! 'It was just a stupid stuff-up,' he said, keeping his eyes on Stella-Jean. 'I turned my phone off for the lecture and forgot to turn it on again.' That was true, more or less.

'But we got them to look in your room,' Susanna said with a pleading insistence, 'and you weren't there!'

'Didn't Marcus tell you about the room change?' Gerry straightened, turning to look his wife squarely in the face, and got a shock almost as great as when he'd seen his daughter. *What's happened to her?* Susanna looked sixty, not forty-five. Her face had gone all ... baggy. Her whole body seemed to be drooping. And the way she was staring at him, with those desperate drowning eyes – it was awful.

'About the — what?' she faltered.

'I changed rooms, but the desk clerk forgot to enter it into the computer.' *Why hasn't Marcus passed that on?* 'I'm so sorry, Suze.' He took her in his arms again, hugged her properly this time, stroking her hair. 'It's all right, I'm here now,' he murmured. 'The kids are going to be all right.'

'All right?' said Susanna, her voice muffled, confused. Not just confused: she sounded stupefied. 'But what's "all right"?'

'They're *alive!*' he said, hearing his own voice full of strength and reassurance. 'And I'm telling you, sweetheart, they are going to be all right.'

A wrenching sob tore from her. *But her mother's dead.* Jesus, how could he have forgotten that? And he loved Jean! But the ferocity of his fears for his children had kept this other terrible news, somehow, from registering fully in his mind.

'Oh, honey,' he whispered. 'I'm sorry.'

She felt like dough in his arms, heavy and spongy: he had a sudden ominous sense that her exhaustion was a black hole which would suck up all his energy and determination. *She can't deal with this*, Gerry realised. *I've got to talk to the doctors.* He had to find out what was happening, here and at Seb's hospital. He had to ask questions, demand answers, decide on courses of treatment. *Now!* It was time for him to take over.

'How long since you had a sleep, a proper sleep?' he asked. 'How long since you've been home?'

'Home?' Susanna shook her head. 'Not since it happened. I've been here the whole time, here or with Seb.' She looked around vaguely. 'Angie was here . . .'

'Suze, *I'm* here now,' said Gerry firmly. 'You need to go home and get some sleep.'

She started crying again. 'I haven't . . . I haven't seen Mum yet. They needed someone to identify her —' Susanna's lips made movements but she couldn't say the word *body* '— and I just *couldn't.*'

'Don't worry. I can do that.'

'No, Angie did; Angie did that. But I need to *see* her.'

Well, well; he wouldn't have thought Angie had the backbone for something like that. 'If you want, I'll go with you, tomorrow,' he said gently. 'But right now, you need sleep.'

Slowly, she nodded. 'Yes,' she whispered.

He saw, with relief, that she was giving way. 'You need a cab, babe? I think there're cabs outside. Or they can call one.'

'No.' She lifted her head, looking around as though reassessing her location. Her gaze lingered on Stella-Jean's face and then she forced her eyes back to him. 'My car's here,' she said. 'I can drive.'

He kissed her doughy cheek, her lined grey forehead. 'Drive carefully,' he said, and with this innocent, well-meant phrase the reality of the crash was horribly present again. They came together in a fumbled hug, parted clumsily.

Pausing by the gap in the curtains Susanna said, 'I'll take your suitcase with me, shall I?'

'Sure,' said Gerry. He'd already plucked the clipboard from its hook at the foot of the bed and was scanning it, trying to make some preliminary sense of the charts and notations. 'Thanks.'

She gave a tiny wave, shy and mechanical in her exhaustion, and walked away, trundling the suitcase – *rark, rark, rark* – behind her through the strange and focused hush of Intensive Care.

TWENTY-FIVE

A parching wind buffeted the car as Susanna drove home. Each time she had to stop at a traffic light she listened to more messages on her mobile phone. So many voices full of concern and sympathy, so many helpless offers to help. How had all these people learned of the crash in the — how long since it happened? *Thursday night, to . . . is it Saturday morning?* Her slow brain took ages to figure it out. *Thirty-six hours.* The messages made her want to cry again. She stopped listening to them.

So tired. Her body was almost not under her control, as though she was drunk, and when she parked safely in the driveway of her home it was with a drunk's sense of undeserved good luck at having made it. The day was already so hot; the air seemed to crackle, as though all the oxygen had been sucked out, leaving it starving and savage.

She heaved Gerry's suitcase out of the car and dragged it up the three broad stairs to the front porch, just as Tigger leapt in front of her, miaowing frantically, pushing himself hard against Susanna's legs. 'Oh, Tigger, I'm sorry. Were you scared you'd been abandoned, poor thing?' The ginger cat charged through the front door as soon as she got it open, than ran back out and looked searchingly toward the car. Tears filled her burning eyes. 'He'll be home soon, Tigger. He will, I promise.'

Trust

The house was cool; the kids, she realised, must've left the air conditioner on, and the knowledge that she would've yelled at them for that almost crushed her. After shaking out some dry food for the hungry cat, she trundled the suitcase through to the bedroom. *Shower.* Suddenly she was desperate to be clean. *I never want to wear these clothes again*, Susanna thought as she stripped off and scuffed them aside with her foot. She slumped against the wall of the shower, tempted to sit and let the water just pour down on her – but if she did that, she might not be able to get up again.

The bed, not neatly made, looked so horribly normal. *Can I sleep there again? Ever?* Putting on her old cotton nightie, she spotted the easel standing modestly in a corner, and paused, regarding the top-most self-portrait with hollow eyes. *That's me; I drew that, only a few days ago.* It seemed impossible. Ludicrous.

She couldn't lie down, not yet. Susanna wandered the house. Along the hall, she noticed for the first time in years the remnants of drawings the kids had done when they were naughty toddlers. *We can't repaint*, she realised. If they repainted, these drawings would be covered over, and her heart would turn to dust.

In the games room, Stella-Jean's garment rack was filled with clothes she'd made. Susanna ran her fingers softly along them, and stroked the dress tossed half-finished on top of her new sewing machine. In Seb's room, she collected a crumbed plate and a couple of glasses from beside his computer, as she'd done so many times before. She swore to herself that she'd never growl at him about that again.

The kitchen was so quiet that the crackling of the electric jug when she put it on sounded like a roaring fire. She held the white teapot in both hands and gazed at the blue phoenix on its side. *Mum gave me this teapot.*

Now, with a cup of tea, she would be able to climb into bed and go to sleep. But first, she'd just unpack Gerry's suitcase, standing in the middle of the bedroom. Susanna eased it onto its back, knelt down and unzipped it. His black wool and cashmere coat was on top, then jumpers, shirts, trousers, barely folded. She imagined him hurling things in there in a panic once Marcus had reached him with the news. How dreadful to have been so far away; she wished she hadn't complained about not knowing where he was.

Susanna picked up one item after another and put it in its pile, taking a weary solace in the familiar motions of sorting and folding. Beneath the clothes, a few books, a folder of notes, a bottle of duty-free Scotch, hardly touched. Shoes. A soft, green, drawstring bag that Susanna recognised as one of the half-dozen she and Stella-Jean had bought in Bali last time: jewellery bags, silk-lined, with little pockets round the inside for rings and brooches. *But what use does Gerry have for it?* She picked the bag up, sat it on her lap and drew the silk-tagged strings apart. It opened smoothly, like the mouth of a large obliging frog.

The first object she withdrew was as long as her index finger, pink and bafflingly feminine, shaped to resemble a daffodil, with petals around the base and a softly knobbled head. Made of – latex? Puzzled, she dropped it back in the bag and felt around. Was this jewellery? She drew out a string of metal beads, which had no clasp and were only moderately flexible. How odd. Then a pair of clips joined by a cord, presumably a spectacles tether, but she'd never seen Gerry use anything so naff. A stretchy blue band – yes, latex, surely – with a smaller band holding a silver cylinder. It looked rather playful; could these be children's toys? She fiddled with the tiny black base of the silver cylinder and it started buzzing in her hand. She gasped, tossing the thing away from her in fright.

Not children's toys. *Adult* toys.

'Oh my god!' she cried aloud, the bag falling from her lap to the floor, the toys scattering. With shaking hands she picked up the stretchy blue band and twisted the base again to turn the buzzing off. *A cock ring.* She'd heard of them – was this one? Could it stretch that much? Little square packets of condoms lay scattered on the floor.

She picked them up: *For her greater pleasure*, it said on one. Another: *Super sensitive. Rough rider.*

And the daffodil, the sweet little daffodil? Gingerly, Susanna picked it up again and peered at the underside of its stalk. Yes, small round batteries were stacked inside. *A vibrator.* A blush worked its swift way up from the base of her throat, racing over her jaw and up toward her hairline. Was she the last woman in the western world to actually see a vibrator? It was small; smaller than she would've imagined. This would never fill a vagina; where, then, did it go? And then: *Where has it been?*

And now, Susanna got it. *Angie was telling me the truth.* The story Susanna had rejected so furiously was not malicious fiction. Angie really had seen Gerry in Sydney with another woman.

He's having an affair. The woman – a redhead? *Didn't Angie say she was a redhead?* – she too must be an architect, and she too had been at this conference in New York. *That's* why his phone had been turned off for so long, why he hadn't been in his room at the hotel. *He was with his lover.*

Susanna sat there on her heels, blank, gutted, gripped by a nauseating sense of shame and humiliation. *I've been such a fool. Mum will be so disappointed.*

No. No, no. An awful noise tore from her mouth. Her mother would never know. Her mother was dead. *Dead.* Susanna toppled to her side on the carpet, wrapping her arms around herself. 'Mummy!' Tears gushed from her eyes; she groaned, rolling to and fro. 'Mummy, Mummy!'

But within just a few minutes, real though her agony was, another part of her, the onlooker, became aware of what she was doing. *Carrying on*, her mother would have said, disapprovingly. How many times had she heard Mum snap at Angie, *Don't be such a drama queen*. Pressing her hands to her eyes, Susanna made herself literally swallow her tears; she could actually hear them sloshing and gurgling in her stomach.

When she opened her eyes, there right in front of her was the emerald-green bag. 'I cannot deal with this,' she said aloud. 'Not right now.' And a voice said, *You don't have to.* She levered herself up to sitting. If she told no one, then it would be as though it hadn't happened. She could shut it down. Shut herself down.

Quickly, she replaced the horrible little things in the bag, the bag in the case, and then the books, the Scotch, the stacks of clothes both clean and worn: shaking them out, refolding them roughly, just as they had been. The cashmere overcoat was the last thing to go back in. Everything restored and concealed. She jostled the zipped suitcase to the far side of Gerry's wardrobe, where she would not see it from the bed.

Her own unsmiling face was watching from the easel. *Honest*, he had said. *That's you.* She couldn't bear to look at it, her honest, stupid face. Unclipping the thick sheaf of drawings, she mashed each one into a ball, tossing them one after another into the wicker laundry basket which she carried down the hallway to the rubbish bin in the kitchen.

The bin? No. They must be burnt.

She stepped out into the backyard and cried out at the shock of the terrible heat. It was insane, as well as illegal, to even think of lighting a match on a day like this. *Maybe I am insane.* She went back in to the kitchen and collected the gigantic pasta pot and a box of matches. Down at the far end of the backyard, in the negligible shade of the lemon tree, she squatted down and dropped the first scrunched drawing into the pot. The flame of the lit match flared terrifyingly high in the ravenous air, and in a flash the drawing was devoured. One after another, Susanna burnt them all to ashes, glimpsing now and again the shape of her arm, or her mouth, just for a moment before it blackened and disappeared.

Then it was done. She left the pot there, sitting charred and smoky under the tree, stumbled inside, fell into her bed, and slept.

Trust

The room was blissfully cool after the scorcher outside. Even with the curtains drawn, more than enough afternoon light filtered in for Gerry to see his wife's huddled form. *Sleeping.* He looked around for his suitcase, shoulders sagging with relief when he located it, unopened, on the far side of the room. *Thank fuck for that!* It had given him a nasty jolt when, hours after Susanna left the hospital, he'd remembered what was in it.

He noticed an untouched cup of tea on her bedside table. Showed how exhausted she'd been, poor girl. He left the room quietly, and made a fresh cup with a teabag. 'Suze,' he said, sitting on the edge of the bed beside her. Lightly, he touched her hunched shoulder. 'Suze, cuppa tea here.'

She burst from sleep in a panic, jolting upright. '*Whaa?*'

'It's all right,' he soothed. She was staring at him as though she didn't recognise him. 'It's all right, honey, it's me.'

In Susanna's dream, or nightmare, she had been in a helicopter that was racketing out of control toward power lines. She was terrified. If it hit those lines, they would all be killed: her children, her parents, everyone she loved. Gerry was in the pilot's seat. She'd been trying to scream, *Gerry, you don't know how to fly,* but no sound would come out of her mouth.

No, Gerry was here, sitting looking at her, holding out a mug. She took it, stunned, lifting it automatically to her mouth to sip. Too hot. She put the mug down and rubbed her eyes, then peered at her husband, at his moving mouth, trying to make her ears and brain connect.

'. . . Glasgow Coma Scale . . . eighty-seven per cent . . . only a few days . . .' she heard. None of it was making sense. Gerry smiled at her encouragingly. 'Two to four weeks, max!'

'What?' she asked him. 'Two to four weeks what?'

'Till Stella-Jean wakes up! That's the statistical likelihood. And Seb's going to be home in a few days. He's comfortable, they're keeping the painkillers up to him. They'll know soon whether the axillary —'

'What are you doing here?' Susanna said, and started getting out of bed.

'Whoa, whoa, stay there,' he said, motioning her back, but she ignored him. 'You don't have to get up. Let's get some —'

'You left Stella-Jean on her *own*?'

'She's not on her own! She's in the ICU, she's *surrounded* by people. Not just people, specialists! Highly trained —'

'I'm going in there.' Susanna was pulling clothes from her cupboard, fumbling and stumbling but getting dressed. 'I've got to be with her.'

'Susanna, don't be ridiculous! Were you listening to —'

His wife left the room.

'She's *unconscious*!' Gerry shouted after her from the doorway. 'Susanna!'

No reply.

Susanna sat hunched in the vinyl chair by her daughter's bed, elbows held in tightly to her sides, rocking minutely to and fro in distress. She wasn't thinking of her husband, her mother, even her own children, but of another family. In a newspaper, years ago, she had read about a family of four – mother and father, daughter and son, just like her own – on holiday in the Blue Mountains, who had visited a lookout. The mother, taking photographs, had turned to see one of the children perilously close to the edge. She had rushed, grabbed, intending to rescue, but her momentum had carried both herself and her daughter over the cliff. The father and the other child had seen them plummet to their deaths.

Susanna could remember the awful hollow feeling she'd had reading the brief article. How quickly she had turned the page. But the story she'd pushed out of her consciousness now wouldn't stop replaying in her mind. She could see them, the family on their holiday, picnicking, making jokes; pausing along a bush track to admire some bird or flower, then the scene at the lookout unfolding in all its horror: the mother's dash, the tipping point, the two screaming, clutching at each other as they fell. The father rushing forward, helplessly watching his wife and child in freefall. Had he seen them hit the ground, far below?

Susanna saw it from every angle, from every viewpoint. She couldn't look away. *That woman was just like me*, she thought. *I was trying to be a good mother, and instead I destroyed them.*

Her own tragedy melded with all the tragedies that befall families everywhere, every day. Guilt, pity, and the dreadful awareness that people's lives, their sufferings, their deaths – all are soon, or finally, forgotten. *Mum will be forgotten. Me, too.* Her solitary horror so overwhelmed her that she couldn't even cry.

The nurses, who had been quietly coming and going all the while in their regular monitoring of Stella-Jean, now gently asked Susanna to go to the nearby visitors' room while – and they gestured to Stella-Jean's tubes, her catheters, the various bags that nourished and drained her. Silently, Susanna went. Other patients' families, sitting in clusters in the visitors' room, nodded a welcome, but resumed their own sombre conversations when they saw that Susanna wasn't up to talking. She heard someone say *the hills*, and *bushfires*, and realised that she had no idea what had been going on in the outside world for the past few days. *I have to get a grip, somehow; I have to take hold of something.*

Allowed back into the ICU, she went first to the nurses' station. One of the small clutch of staff huddled by a computer screen gave her an inquiring smile. 'I was wondering if you might have some spare sheets of paper?' Susanna asked. 'Blank paper?'

Sitting beside the bed where her daughter lay, Susanna took a black pen from her bag and began to draw the story that had unfolded in the Blue Mountains years before. *I don't know your name*, she told that mother, *but I remember what happened to you*, and one image followed another, from happy innocence to grim death, exactly as they played out before her inner eye.

She drew and drew, and when she had drawn it all Susanna put the sheets in her bag, stretched, rolled her tight shoulders, flexed her fingers. She felt sad, and calm, and resolved, as though something she'd been putting off for a long time had finally been done.

In that strangely peaceful state, she rested; perhaps she fell asleep. Something roused her: a touch? A voice? She sat up, looking around. No one else was there except Stella-Jean. Her darling face: was it a little less swollen? Susanna bent over and gave her daughter's cheek a feather-soft kiss. She looked at her watch and saw to her surprise that it was after nine o'clock at night.

The sounds on the other side of the curtain, she became aware, had shifted, become more urgent. Looking into the ward, she saw that some change had occurred in the focused calm of the intensive care unit. Additional nurses and other staff had appeared and were busy moving equipment and beds purposefully around, making room for more. She beckoned to a passing nurse and asked her what was happening.

'We've got word that the bushfires are even worse than anyone expected,' the young woman told her in a low voice. 'All the major hospitals are preparing. We're expecting a large number of casualties.'

TWENTY-SIX

Finn's mum said, 'Be careful not to mess anything up, honey,' in a low voice. She'd just finished tidying up the living room after the Faith Rise Band rehearsal, but Gabriel was back in his room with the door closed, so it was okay for Finn to linger in the living room with her. His mum had been home with him all week, since the accident, and he hadn't had to go to school. He wouldn't be going till after tomorrow, after Jeejee's funeral; that was when everyone would say goodbye to Jeejee, and her body was going in the ground.

They could hear Gabriel playing his guitar, trying to get this new song right. Little changes each time to the music, or to the words he was singing.

'Calling them home
Calling them ho-oh-ome
He sent the angels, through the fire,
He's calling them home.'

'You know what that means?' Angie asked. 'The angels calling them home?'

Finn was pretty sure, but he shook his head anyway, because he wanted his mum to go on talking to him. It was better, having her near, and talking.

'It means that all those people who died in the fires have been

219

taken up to heaven. God sent the angels to bring them to live with him, in *his* home. So they're all safe and happy now, with Jesus.'

Finn frowned, his fingers plucking uneasily at a frayed spot on the arm of the couch. 'But – what if you didn't die in the fires?'

'Oh, the angels still come, baby,' she assured him, smiling sadly. 'You still go to heaven and live with Jesus, no matter how you die.'

'So . . . Jeejee's gone up to heaven, too?'

He was watching his mum's face, and saw her smile go tight. 'You have to believe in God before you can go to heaven. And Jeejee didn't believe in God, I'm afraid.'

'So she's not in heaven?' Angie shook her head *no*, in big slow side-to-sides. 'But what about the people in the fires? How does *he* know —' Finn's finger jabbed briefly in the direction of Gabriel's voice '— if all *those* people believed in God?'

Angie started to say something, then seemed to change her mind. She started again. 'The important thing is that *you* believe in God, Finnie, and you know he's watching over you, all the time.' She sat down on the edge of the couch, right by him, putting her face very close to his, and her hands draped softly on his shoulders. 'It was *God* that spared you. He let you – just you! – walk away from the car crash without a scratch, didn't he? You see? There's a reason for every single thing that happens.'

'What's the reason?'

'The reason? That you were spared?'

Finn nodded.

'Because when you're a good boy and love the Lord Jesus, then he loves you and takes care of you. You see?'

'Why didn't God spare Stella? Stella is good.'

'Well . . . maybe because he wants her to be *truly* saved.' His mum was looking right into his eyes, very seriously. 'Maybe when Stella wakes up, she'll take God into her heart too. Like you.'

'But she should have been spared!' Finn's voice had risen, and Angie raised a warning forefinger to her lips. He whispered fiercely,

'I really *want* her to wake up.'

'I know, honey,' she whispered back. 'And I know this is hard for us to understand, but sometimes God has to teach people a very big lesson, so they learn they mustn't waste a single day longer not believing in him. He might even have to *punish* them sometimes, before they learn.'

Suddenly Gabriel's voice, clear and commanding, came from his little music room down the hall. 'Angie! Come in here please!' Mother and son jumped apart from each other.

'You just keep praying for our Stella, Finnie,' she said. 'My special little guy,' and hugged him quickly and hurried from the room.

Finn waited till Gabriel's door had closed again and then slipped quietly to his bedroom. He looked at his books on his shelf, and his toys, but he didn't feel like reading or playing. He lay down on his bed and pulled the cover over him and tried to figure it out. Why did God care if people believed in him or not, as long as they were good? Wasn't being good the most important thing? Why would he want to punish someone like Stella? That was just mean. That was *bad*.

He could hear his mum singing with Gabriel, and then just Gabriel's voice again, a new bit of the song:

'He said, *Suffer the little children,*
And bring them unto me . . .'

Finn held very still. *Suffer the little children.* God said that, Jesus Christ our Lord. Why did God want little children to suffer?

Maybe he knows what I really think of him. Maybe he's spared me just so he can punish me for thinking he's mean. The more Finn thought about this, the more likely it seemed. *That's why he sent Gabriel here. Gabriel is God's big lesson, come to punish me.*

Susanna invited Leonard Styles to do two things: deliver the eulogy at Jean's funeral, and have dinner with her the evening before, in Jean's unit. He replied, in his courtly fashion, that each would be an honour.

The car seemed almost to drive itself to the retirement village and, stepping inside her mother's front door, it would have felt so natural to call out, *Mum? It's me!* Susanna didn't: she just stood there, looking, taking in the orderliness, the care, and the quietness. She put down the shopping she'd brought and silently counted the nights since her mother had stood up from that chair, picked up that phone, and then closed this door behind herself for the last time. *Five.* Five nights, since the world spun off its axis.

A cup and saucer, a bread and butter plate, a knife, rinsed and sitting in the dish rack. Susanna replaced them in the cupboard. On the coffee table the TV guide was folded to last Wednesday's program. A spiral-bound notebook was on the table, a pencil lying at a neat diagonal across its cover. Susanna picked it up, flipping through the pages, but it was all in shorthand, of which she didn't understand a single squiggle.

In the bathroom, she picked up her mother's hairbrush, put it down again, unscrewed the top from the bottle of Oil of Olay, the only moisturiser Jean had ever used. It smelt familiar, but it wasn't quite the smell of Mum. *Because it's not on Mum.* What would become of this bottle, of the hairbrush, and of the silver hairs caught in its bristles? Throwing any of it away seemed unendurable.

She went into the bedroom, stood looking at the aqua slubbed silk bedspread, drawn up precisely over the pillows. It had graced her parents' bed in the old house as well, before Dad died and Jean moved here. There were neatly folded clothes in a laundry basket sitting on a chair. Susanna opened the wardrobe door: she was familiar with every single garment. Inhaling, she caught her mother's smell. This cardigan, this dress: she gathered them to her face, one by one, and then, impulsively, stepped inside the wardrobe, and pulled the door to behind her. There was no one to see her, no one to call her crazy. With the soft swish of Jean's clothes touching her face, her body, she drank in that sweet, clean, adored perfume. *Oh Mum, stay close to me.*

When she emerged from the cupboard, feeling like one of the

children who went to Narnia, she felt a little better, a little strength-ened. She could just about hear Jean's voice: *Leonard will be arriving soon, dear. Time to get dinner ready, there's a good girl.*

Leonard's face, when he knocked at the door promptly at six-thirty, looked thinner, older. As she welcomed him in, both understand-ing, with an exchange of sad smiles, that this would probably be the last time Leonard visited Jean's pretty, tidy home, Susanna knew this had been the right thing to do. She could feel the warmth of her mother's approval.

Over a glass of wine, they discussed the funeral arrangements. Susanna had told everyone it would be simple, as her mother would have wanted, and Leonard agreed that Jean would, indeed. 'However,' Susanna said, 'my sister wants her pastor to speak.' There was a note of apology in her voice; she knew that Leonard too was an atheist. 'It's very important to her. I felt — I didn't feel I had the right to say no.'

'Quite so,' he said.

'Mum told you Angie's a Christian?'

'She did. I used to joke that it was her cross to bear,' said Leonard, and they smiled.

Susanna served grilled lamb chops, boiled potatoes, a lettuce and tomato salad. It was, Leonard commented, the sort of plain-cooked meal Jean would have enjoyed. Their conversation over dinner sur-prised her with its effortlessness.

'Do you know, I think I'm going to stay here for the night,' she said impulsively. Leonard nodded solemnly, chewing. 'I feel . . . peace-ful, here. I . . . I've found it hard to sleep in my bed at home since it happened.' She didn't know why she was telling him this. 'Mostly I sleep in a chair by —'

Abruptly, she stopped.

'I imagine you and your husband are at the hospital a great deal,' said Leonard gently.

'Yes. This is actually the first night I haven't been with my daughter. And my husband . . .' But Susanna couldn't go there, couldn't go near the reason she hadn't slept with — *no*. 'My husband's coping by being busy, twenty-four hours a day. He's everywhere at once; he knows every nurse and every doctor, in both the hospitals. Every acronym. What all the machines do.' She sighed softly. 'And then there's his work. His company. He can't just go on leave.' As he'd snapped at her, earlier today.

Leonard gave her a judicious look. 'Yes, I see. That certainly sounds like the way many men cope with what might otherwise overwhelm them.'

'I'm overwhelmed,' said Susanna simply. It was a huge relief just to say it.

He reached out his thin, veined hand and touched hers. 'This has been a terrible week, and not only for us. I think the whole state feels overwhelmed. The country.'

'Yes. Leonard, this might sound . . . I don't know, discourteous, or masochistic, or even ghoulish, but I have to watch the seven o'clock news. I have to know what's happened with the fires.'

'Of course,' he said.

They sat side by side on Jean's floral couch, looking at the catastrophe that had befallen the hill towns – outer suburbs, almost, they were so close to Melbourne – the Saturday before. *Black Saturday.* Fires were still burning. Thousands of homes had been destroyed and more bodies were being discovered each day. The death toll was nearing two hundred, with fears it could climb much higher. Footage of Marysville appeared. The pretty little resort town had been wiped out as if by a massive bomb blast.

'You and Mum were there,' said Susanna softly, turning to him. 'Just last —' Silent tears, she saw, were coursing down Leonard's face. They held each other's hands and cried, watching the images of the firestorms, listening to the stories of families incinerated in their homes, or in their cars as they tried to escape, and the terrifying tales of those who'd managed to survive.

When the news ended and the television was turned off, Leonard said, 'I'm sorry, my dear. In the face of this vast tragedy, my own grief over your mother's passing seems almost selfish.'

Susanna shook her head. 'Not at all. Please. Not at all.'

'I had come to feel so close to Jean. I'd hoped to become . . . more.'

'I know.' Susanna felt a new kind of pain, for the relationship that had ended so prematurely.

'May I . . . may I make you some tea?' he asked, and she had to smile. It was precisely the thing her mother would have asked, at such a moment. *They were so well matched.*

'Only if you let me tidy up the kitchen while you do,' she told him.

As Susanna was putting things away, her eye fell on her mother's notebook. *I wonder what Mum was writing?* On an impulse she asked, 'Leonard, do you know anyone who can transcribe shorthand?'

'I do,' he said promptly. 'My former secretary, Mrs Henderson. Why, if I may ask?'

Susanna showed him the very ordinary lined notebook, explaining where she'd found it. 'Did Mum say anything to you about what she was writing?'

'Nothing specific,' said Leonard. But Susanna saw in his face that some thought had occurred to him.

'What is it?' she asked.

'Some . . . musings, perhaps. Things she was considering.'

'Would you ask Mrs Henderson? If that's no trouble? I'd be more than happy to pay her, of course.'

'It will be no trouble, Susanna. None at all.'

After Leonard had gone home, she called Gerry and told him she was staying the night at her mother's. He seemed barely to be listening. 'I'm still at the office, I haven't been off the phone all day. The Kansas City people want to pull the pin.' He sounded like he was at the end of his tether. 'The fires: we've got four or five clients who've lost houses, plus that beautiful winery we did a couple of years ago in the Yarra Valley. And Marcus has bloody gone AWOL; some crisis with John.' He paused, but Susanna could think of nothing to say.

'Just make sure you're at Northern General in the morning to pick up Seb,' Gerry went on. 'I've done all the paperwork.' And he hung up, even before she had a chance to ask if they would be going to the funeral home together.

Susanna stood outside in the little courtyard, thinking about the people Gerry knew who'd lost their homes; homes he'd designed, and they'd loved, and everything in them. *Loss, loss; so many things to lose.*

The gardenias she was staring at, she realised, and all the other plants, were gasping for water. Quickly, hoping they'd not been left too long, she filled the watering can again and again. *Mum will be so upset if her garden —* She caught herself. All the plants could die, every one of them, and Jean would never be upset, or plant more, or do anything, ever again.

It's not fair, it's not fair! And then recalled what Leonard had said. 'My own grief seems almost selfish.' *None of it's fair. Fairness has nothing to do with it.* She thought of all those families, reading the Saturday papers, cleaning up after children's birthday parties, enjoying a weekend in the cool of the hills . . .

Susanna knew where her mother kept blank typing paper, pencils, pens. She fetched some, sat at the table, just where her mother had sat writing in that notebook, and began to draw.

The drawings were not only of the horror, but of what the horror had roared in upon. Small things at the heart of it, like the crockery found piled on the passenger seat of a woman's car overtaken by the fire. Susanna imagined that scene unfolding and showed it, covering sheet after sheet as rapidly as her pencil could draw: the woman watching from her verandah as the inferno approached, sheltering in her house, frightened, brave. The flames taking hold. The frantic dash to the car clutching the box of her mother's crockery (Susanna assumed it was her mother's crockery), the desperate drive, her little dog in her lap with its paws on the steering wheel. The road blocked by the fallen tree, the ravenous flames —

Every part of the story was important: the life, as well as the death.

How could she show it all, in one drawing? *Not one drawing*, she realised. *Many drawings, on one page, that's how.*

Scissors. She cut her drawings into various shapes – hacking, almost, she was so eager to see how it might work. Using the back of an old poster laid face down on the table, she moved the pieces around. Not a collage, more like — a comic. *I'm making a comic.* At the thought, she gave a little snort of laughter: brief, faint, but still an actual laugh. Her students popped into her mind: she pictured Bianca giving a cool nod of approval, Angelo crowing, 'Totally sick, miss!'

Susanna had no idea how long she worked. *Captions, I can have captions, too.* Hours went by. Yet when she stopped, she felt that same restfulness, a sense of something resolved, that she'd felt after making those other drawings of the family in the Blue Mountains, as though an overdue task had been completed, or perhaps a promise kept. She yawned, an immense stretched-out yawn. *And now, I could sleep.* She brushed her teeth with Jean's toothbrush, put on one of Jean's nightgowns, lay herself down in Jean's bed.

She'd almost managed to forget that when she woke up, she would be burying her mother. But just before dawn, Susanna was woken by the sound of desolate sobbing: her own.

TWENTY-SEVEN

Tessa rubbed the fabric of Stella-Jean's hospital gown between her thumb and forefinger, shaking her head sorrowfully. 'Sorry about this, Stellarina,' she said. 'I have told them and *told* them.'

'Told who what?' asked Seb.

'Hi, Tessa,' said Rory.

'Hey there.' Tess gave them a little wave. 'I've told the nurses that she is *not* happy about wearing this! I mean, *synthetic*? And what is this colour? Beige? Not something Stella would ever wear!'

'Tess, come on.' Okay, the girls had their big fashion thing, but this, Seb thought, was just plain ridiculous. 'Right now, I don't reckon she gives a rat's arse what colour it is.'

Tessa rolled her eyes as if *he'd* said something ridiculous. 'Guys!' she said in a scornful aside to Rory, who nodded regretful agreement. But Seb instantly forgave her this small disloyalty: Rory had actually asked to come with him to visit Stella-Jean, for which he was more grateful than he felt able to say. Seb found standing around his unconscious sister's bedside horribly depressing, even though the doctors kept saying 'no longer critical' and 'positive indicators' and crap like that. *Hello, people? She can't wake up!* Two weeks since the crash and he'd only visited her . . . twice. Not what you could call a lot, really.

Now Rory was checking out all the stuff crammed on to the shelf and the top of the steel locker. This place was almost as craft-crazy as Stella's real bedroom. 'Well, at least there's all these really pretty things here for her,' she said to Tessa. 'Oh, wow, look at these gorgeous little dolls.'

'One of Susanna's students did those. Aren't they divine? Hey, Seb, I've been talking to your mum about doing fine art at her college in a couple of years, that would be *way* cool.'

'Sure sure. Where is my mum, anyway? I thought she was gonna be here.'

'She's just gone downstairs to phone in today's update,' said Tessa. 'You know, for the Google group.'

'Oh, she could've used my iPhone,' Rory said.

'Only if you pressed every key for her,' said Seb. 'My mum's a tech-free zone. Her students set up the Google group because she was going nuts trying to keep up with everyone who wanted to know what's happening. Otherwise she'd still be sending out . . . I dunno, handwritten letters or something.'

'Those updates are really good,' Rory said. 'All the medical info is so *precise*.'

Seb nodded. 'My dad puts all that in. Mum just phones in the touchy-feely stuff to . . . someone.'

'But that's beautiful,' said Tessa. 'Touchy-feely is what mums are for!' The wide sleeves of her top floated out as she wafted her long arms around in a touchy-feely way. There were shiny things in her hair: crystals, or beads, or something, and about a kilo of eyeliner on her eyelids; Seb wondered how she kept them open. He remembered one time hearing Tess describe her style to Stella as 'fairy goth', and he'd said, *Better than mangy parrot, like Stinker-Bean*. That had earned him a whack in the arm. 'Your mum's *lovely*,' Tess insisted. 'Look how she's brought in all Stella's talking books, and her fave CDs, and —'

'I know,' said Seb, holding up both hands. 'I know.'

'Plus the way she always goes off and does something else while I give Stella the goss. So I don't have to, you know, censor.'

Rory carried a plastic bucket chair over to the head of the bed and folded herself gracefully into it. *Every movement she makes is graceful,* Seb thought. 'It's Rory here, doll, in case you hadn't picked that up,' she told Stella-Jean conversationally. 'I wanted to tell you, I was thinking the other day about that Mother's Day stall you and Tessa had, the first year you were at high school.' Tess, leaning on the other side of the bed, chortled. 'Remember? You guys got this spare table out of a storeroom and hauled it into the corridor at lunchtime, and started selling stuff. Little bags, and earrings and . . .'

'Ooh, the velvet eye-masks – they went like hot cakes,' said Tess.

'Oh yes! Then one of the senior-school teachers came up and told you you had to stop because you didn't have permission. And I'll never forget, you just looked him straight in the eye and said, "No, we're not going to, sir. Because as you can see, we're *showing initiative.*"'

All three of them burst out laughing. '*And,*' added Tessa, 'providing a service!'

'He didn't know what to say!'

'Kids kept coming up to me all week going, "Did you hear what your sister did?"' said Seb. 'This shrimp in Year Seven. God, what an embarrassment – I wanted to wring her neck.' *But at the same time I felt incredibly proud of her. I kept thinking, she's got more guts than anyone else I know.*

'Ooh, ooh!' squealed Tessa. 'She smiled! Did you see that? She *definitely* smiled.'

The girls leaned over so their faces were right up by Stella-Jean's. Seb couldn't tell if there was something like a smile or not. 'Well, I think she did,' said Tessa uncertainly. Gradually they drew apart; Rory floated her bottom back into the chair.

'Let's tell you some other news, then,' she said. Throwing Seb an inquiring glance, she asked, 'Have you told her about your grandma's funeral?'

'*No*,' said Seb, with a very creeped-out expression. 'Why would I do *that*?'

'Because it's important!' Rory and Tessa had both attended Jean's funeral with their parents. 'I mean, I know it was a really really sad day, but it's also really sad that Stella-Jean couldn't be there, exactly *because* it's her grandma!'

'I think Mum read her the thing Mr Styles wrote,' Seb conceded after a few moments. 'You know, the eulogy.'

'Which was really beautiful, but she needs to know what it was *like*.' Rory looked across to Tessa for confirmation.

Tess nodded. 'Rory's right, Seb. Don't be such an Anglo.' Tess's parents were Italian. 'Okay, I'll start. So, Stella: your Jeejee's funeral. It was awesome!' She and Rory went on to describe everyone who'd been there, the flowers, the music, what was said, what had made people cry (and how much), and any other details that occurred to them.

Seb added the occasional item, like Auntie Ange's *friend* (said meaningfully, with air quotes) singing 'Amazing Grace'. 'He wasn't bad, either. Not a dry eye in the place – except Dad's, of course. He was spewing.'

'And after the service,' said Rory, 'we went back to the retirement village. They had a fabulous afternoon tea thing – is that a wake? – in this hall they've got there.'

'The Lodge,' Seb put in.

'Yeah, the Lodge. There were lots more old people who hadn't been able to come to the funeral. They were really sweet.'

'And they were all wearing name tags. Gladdie, and Verna, and Betty.'

'The food! Oh my god, I ate like a pig.'

'Fantastic sausage rolls,' said Seb.

'Tell her about that nice ambulance guy who came,' said Tessa. 'I thought that was so sweet of him. What was his name, Seb?'

'Andrew,' said Seb shortly.

'Yeah, Andrew. And he's *cute*, too.'

'He is *not*! Don't be so —' Seb stopped short, suddenly aware of how angry he sounded. 'He's – um, he's like, twenty-four. Way too old for Stella.'

'Gee, Seb,' said Tess, making a face at him. 'Johnny Depp is like, fifty, and Stella thinks *he's* cute. It's not like this Andrew guy's gonna front up here and ask her out on a date or anything!'

'Course not,' muttered Seb. *No, it's me Andrew's asked out.* 'Forget about it.'

Rory rose from the chair at the head of the bed. 'Tell her *your* news,' she urged Seb. 'Go on. Sit down here and just crap on to her.'

Seb twisted his good shoulder in refusal. 'I feel like an idiot.'

'That's not the point, Visser.' She rattled the back of the chair. 'Go on!'

Reluctantly, Seb sat down. 'Um . . . well . . .' He looked down at his sister's face. It was much less swollen than it had been a week ago, less bruised. 'I'm going to see this physio. He wasn't taking new patients but Dad crowbarred me in. I don't actually like him that much but Dad reckons he's the best in the state . . .' He snuck a look over his shoulder at Rory, who was standing with her arms folded. She was trying to look encouraging. 'Anyway . . .'

'You know, Seb,' Rory said, 'maybe Tess and I might go and get a coffee. I feel like we're kinda cramping your style here.'

'No! You don't have to go.'

But the girls already had their bags slung over their shoulders and were heading out the door. 'Back in ten,' Rory called.

'We'll bring you a coffee,' said Tessa.

Seb hunched his shoulders and shifted about in the plastic chair. 'Right. Okay. So: me and Mum were talking about you the other day. That world music show was on the radio, that one you really like with the dorky presenter. Remember how you used to go *off* when I'd do imitations of him?' He chuckled, waiting for a response from Stella-Jean. When none came, he went on at a gallop. 'And Mum said that next time she was in here at the right time, she must remember to turn it on for you, and I said, it's downloadable, Mum, you could play it to her any time. She looked completely bahzoolied. I reckon she still thinks podcasting is something you do with peas.'

No response. He knew there wasn't going to be any, and it made him feel stupid, and hopelessly inadequate. *I've only ever been mean to her, no matter what I really feel.* He jockeyed the chair closer. 'That afternoon, before the accident, when you and me had that big fight . . . okay, I know we've had plenty of big fights, but that time . . .' He stopped and shook his head. 'But the thing is, afterwards, when we were waiting outside the tennis centre, you were trying to be friends again, and I wouldn't. I just gave you the big freeze.' He rubbed the hand not pinioned in its sling roughly over his face. 'Why did I have to be such an arsehole?' He hunched down, low and miserable, his voice sinking to a whisper. 'Nobody knows about it. Not about that fight, or why we had it; not about anything. I just wish there was *somebody* I could talk to.'

If he wasn't so scared, he could talk to Andrew. Andrew had texted him after the funeral to say that anytime Seb wanted to talk, or get together, just let him know. *I'm here,* that's what he'd said. Seb closed his eyes. *I want to, but I'm too scared.*

He opened his eyes and gazed at his sister's unchanging face. *Can she hear me?* he wondered. *Will she remember anything that happened?* Seb leaned all the way forward and rested his forehead on the bed beside her shoulder. 'I'm sorry, Stell. That's all I can say, I guess. I'm really sorry.' Raising his head, he looked at her face. Her eyelids were quivering, but that was all. 'After you wake up, I'll never call you Stinker-Bean again. Face-ache, maybe, yeah. Not Stinker-Bean. Promise.'

What an incredible relief to hear the music of the gamelan, tinkling and donging into the darkness. *I'm in Bali, at last!* As soon as she heard the music, Stella-Jean knew she was safe. She felt like she'd been travelling for weeks. Something had gone wrong at the start, on the way to the airport. The taxi? Did the taxi have an accident? And all those days in the transit lounge, unable to move or go anywhere: waiting, waiting. The flight itself had gone on and on, so long she'd almost forgotten where she was going.

Let the gamelan music guide her: she would find the members of the orchestra – rice farmers and shopkeepers by day – rehearsing, sitting cross-legged at their instruments in the open-sided village hall. Even though it was completely dark, she had no fear. Some people, when they heard the name *Bali*, immediately thought of the terrorist bombings, but Stella-Jean knew the Balinese were the kindest people in the world. The Balinese always watched out for you, made sure you were safe. Even walking down a pitch-black road, like this one, they would be watching out for her.

Finn would be really happy to be back here, too. 'Finn!' She groped for his hand in the darkness, and then heard a voice, calling her. Not his. A hand took her own, but it was an adult's hand, not Finn's hard little paw.

'Stella-Jean? Stella-Jean, look at me. Open your eyes.'

She opened her eyes. The light was ferocious: a spotlight, shining straight at her. Protesting, she closed them tight, and then her mother's voice was calling her. She sounded upset, and Stella-Jean opened her eyes again. *Is that Mum?* It was hard to tell, there was just an outline against the glare. She should be happy to be here in Bali too. 'Where are we staying, Mum?' she asked.

'What, darling? What did you say?' Urgently, 'What did she *say*?'

But Stella-Jean was back walking along the velvet dark road in Bali, toward the sound of the gamelan. *Tomorrow I'll find Putu. I'm supposed to be meeting Putu. She won't mind that I'm late.*

'*We be of one blood, thou and I.*'

She was kind of surprised, at first, to be listening to *The Jungle Book* here, but then on second thoughts it made sense. The stories were set in India, and Bali had so many ties with India: all that Ramayana stuff, and Hanuman the Monkey King rescuing Sita. They loved stories with animals and adventures, and they loved kids, of course, so naturally they'd like the stories of Mowgli and his wolf brothers, Baloo the bear, and the elephants. Someone was reading from it now, aloud, here in Putu's workshop, to entertain all the girls who were busy sewing.

The storyteller's voice stopped. 'No, keep going,' Stella-Jean said, but someone else had come into the shop. They wanted her to do something – couldn't they see she was busy?

Numbers . . . This pushy person was asking her to count. A stock-take? Obligingly, Stella-Jean started counting, standing by the racks and flicking through. Nyoman, Putu's sister, had looped the hangers together in groups of ten. Wow, look how many garments have been completed! Thirty, forty, fifty . . . Oh, she was very happy with these designs . . .

'Keep trying, Stella-Jean,' the voice said. 'One, two: what comes after three?'

Three? What an idiot! Surely they could see that the rack was full? Three . . . three . . . Well, if they wanted her to count to three. 'Satu, dua, tiga,' she told them.

'What did you say, sweetheart?' Mum's voice? Hooray, Mum had made it here too! Stella-Jean opened her eyes, smiled a welcome at her.

'Look! Look!' Mum cried. Look at what? Stella-Jean tried to turn her head but it seemed stuck, somehow, or too heavy, or . . . She looked around as much as she could without moving her head. She could see Mum, and other people too. How come she wasn't in Putu's workshop? Maybe she was in the house they rented, in the village. Where was Finn?

'Where's Finn?' she asked, and her mother's face loomed large. Too large to take in; Stella-Jean closed her eyes again. Finn would be safe here, he would be happy. No one would give Finn a hard time in Bali.

Ow, ow, ow! The Balinese were expert at giving massages, but gee, sometimes they were too hard. Usually they asked you if it was okay, but sometimes you had to say.

'Too hard,' Stella-Jean told the person who was lifting her leg, rubbing, hurting. 'Too hard!'

Why on earth was she even having a massage right now, when she'd been — what had she been doing? She'd been meeting with the girls who were making the new flower brooches, that was it.

'Larissa! Can you come here? I think I got a little response from our girl.'

The Balinese liked *Winnie the Pooh*, too, apparently, and *The Hobbit*. Oh! Maybe Mum had brought them with her, all the old talking books Stella-Jean had listened to since she was a kid. That would explain it. Stella-Jean looked at her mother, sitting there beside the bed, drawing, wiping away a tear now and again. Why was Mum crying?

'Mum? Why are you sad?'

Susanna's face kind of leapt open and she jerked closer.

'Stella-Jean, do you see me? You do, don't you!'

She was calling for a nurse, saying, 'She was looking at me, really looking at me. She tried to say something, I'm sure she did!'

Tried to say something? What, had Mum gone deaf? *Maybe I was talking in Indonesian, I've been speaking that so much lately.* Stella-Jean tried to reassure her mother in English that everything was okay and there was no need to be sad, just because she was busy . . . But her eyes got too heavy, and she had to close them again.

TWENTY-EIGHT

Susanna slumped listlessly in the chair. 'I've got the flu,' she told her GP, known to the whole family as Doctor Gillian. 'I've had it for weeks, and it's just getting worse.'

Doctor Gillian listened patiently as Susanna described her symptoms: aches, lethargy, sore eyes, no appetite. 'How are you sleeping now?' she asked.

'Okay, if I take one of those tablets. But I don't like to do that too often.'

Doctor Gillian nodded. 'Susanna,' she said, 'you've been feeling like this for . . . some weeks now?' Susanna nodded agreement. 'Since the accident?'

'I suppose so,' she agreed reluctantly.

'I don't think you have the flu, Susanna.'

Don't talk about the 'grief process'. Please don't.

'We'll examine you, do some blood tests if you like, but I think the symptoms you're experiencing are probably all part of your grief process.' Doctor Gillian's smile was full of sympathy, and Susanna was shocked at how irritated she felt by it. By all the sympathy, all the kindness. Yesterday when she got home from the hospital, there'd been yet another white box on the verandah, another splendid cake left by Jo from the book group, and Susanna had felt the urge to kick it to bits.

'People have been so kind,' she said carefully. 'Incredibly kind. Over these past few weeks I've had cards and flowers and offers of help from people I hardly know.' She was looking at her hands, holding each other in her lap. 'This woman I used to play tennis with, Wendy, I always thought she was quite a hard nut, but she called me and she said, "You'll find people want to help. My advice is, say yes to everything, it's so much easier." So my freezer's full of casseroles and my garden got weeded and Seb has people driving him to physio, and I've got a pile of books this high —' she lifted one hand almost to chin height '— on bereavement and spirituality and bad things happening to good people. And sometimes – I'm sorry, Gillian, but sometimes I feel like if I hear or read the words "grief process" one more time, I'm going to scream.'

'I understand,' said Doctor Gillian, and her smile became even kinder and more sympathetic.

No, you don't. 'I just don't feel like my grief is a process,' Susanna said. 'It's part of my *life*. I don't want to get over it! My son *is* injured, my daughter *is* in a coma, my mother *is* dead. I feel like saying, "Leave me alone, let me wallow in it." If I get over it, do you know what that means? It means my mother will be *gone*.' She touched her hand to her chest as she said this, over her heart, and kept it there for some seconds. *Is there anything left in there?* she wondered.

Gillian wasn't smiling any more. She listened, and thought, and tapped a pencil. Then she asked Susanna whether she had discussed these feelings with Gerry.

'No,' said Susanna flatly. 'I have not. Gerry is very busy. I try to stay out of his way. Mostly, I succeed.'

'I see,' said Doctor Gillian. 'So, ah – how are you two getting on?'

Susanna hesitated. 'Not great.'

'I see,' said Gillian again. 'That's . . . I'm sure you know that's not surprising, under the circumstances. The terrible loss you've experienced, the ongoing stress – it's tough. It's tough on even the best marriages.'

Susanna nodded. She was beginning to wish she hadn't come.

'Susanna, I'm concerned that you're not seeing a therapist. You should be seeing someone.'

'I already saw somebody at the hospital. And when the accident first happened we all had this — what did they call it? Mental intervention? Mental first aid? Something.'

'You didn't find it helpful?'

Susanna shrugged. The hospital therapist had a bushy beard and red wet-looking lips that she'd found repulsive. She'd also felt no rapport with him whatsoever, but she didn't care. 'Besides,' she said, 'there are so many people who've gone through much worse than me.'

'Comparisons are odious,' said Doctor Gillian firmly as she wrote on a pad. 'Your whole family should go, preferably. Oh, and I believe the Traffic Accident Commission will cover costs. Talk to Leigh about it.'

She tore the little sheet off and handed it to Susanna. 'This is his number: Leigh Fermor. I've recommended many patients to him and he's a *really* good counsellor. Family therapy, couples, grief counselling, individual issues . . .'

'Issues,' said Susanna softly, looking at the number.

Doctor Gillian heard the hint of derision in her voice, and suppressed a sigh. 'Why don't you just give him a call, Susanna? You really need to see a counsellor at a time like this.'

No, I don't. What I need is my old life back, and that's completely, totally, utterly impossible.

'Hello there, lovely girl!' said Angie as she approached the bed. 'Oh, that is a *pretty* haircut!' She kissed Stella-Jean's cheek, stroking her fuzz of hair. Finn was wriggling in beside her and she moved back to sit in the chair Susanna had pulled up beside her own.

'She looks *so* much better without those horrible tubes sticking up her nose,' Angie whispered.

Susanna nodded. 'She's getting better nutrition now too, direct to the stomach.'

'And much nicer being here in her own room, too,' Angie said. She leaned in close to her sister and lowered her voice. 'That intensive care ward was scary. I didn't like to bring Finn there.'

'I know. But you came, Ange.'

'And you're here with her, Susu, every time I've come,' said Angie. 'Do you ever take a break?' This was not said critically, Susanna understood, but with love and genuine concern. The sisters had never spoken of their awful argument in that cafe in Degraves Street, nor of any of the matters that had been raised so painfully. All had been swept aside by the crash, and their amity restored.

Nevertheless, Susanna thought wryly, *Take a break: just what Gerry's always suggesting.* Though of course she wouldn't say that now: in fact, Susanna did her best not to even mention Gerry's name to Angie, and it seemed that Angie, similarly, took care to speak of Gabriel as little as possible too. 'I do take breaks,' she said somewhat defensively. 'And it's only been three weeks. The statistics say she's extremely likely to wake up within four weeks.'

'And she will,' Angie hastened to assure her. 'Of course she will.' They both looked over to where Stella-Jean lay, as still as ever. Finn had wriggled in so close to her side, he was almost *on* the bed, and was whispering in her ear. Susanna felt ashamed that she had never made more effort to understand this unusual little boy. *My only nephew. Stella-Jean's only cousin.* 'He must miss her so much,' she said softly.

'It's a special thing they have together,' Angie said. 'Like we did.' She touched Susanna's hand. 'Like we *do*.'

Just then, *The Jungle Book* CD, one of Stella-Jean's favourites since childhood, finished playing. Intending to change it, Susanna made to rise, but Finn bounced up saying, 'Let me choose!' and began sorting through the pile. A minute later, the atonal chiming and tinking of a gamelan orchestra filled the room. With a note of something like defiance, Finn said, 'Stella likes *this* one best of all.'

'She does,' Susanna said. 'You're right, Finn.'

They were quiet for a while, listening to the gamelan. 'I've been trying to figure out why she's always had this thing about Bali,' Susanna said to her sister. 'You know, I don't think we would've kept going back there all these years if she hadn't formed such a strong attachment to the place.'

'I think it just suits her personality. She's always loved being busy making things and the Balinese are like that too. That's what I thought, the couple of times I've come with you. And that lovely girl who looked after them, I always thought she was like Stella-Jean's big sister.' Angie gave Susanna a wistful smile.

Susanna recognised Angie's observations as accurate, and perceptive, which took her aback. She did not expect perceptiveness in her sister. *You've underestimated her*, she told herself. *She sees things, better than you do sometimes.* 'Angie,' she said suddenly, 'I've got something to tell you.'

'You do?' Angie leaned in eagerly toward her.

The urge to confide bubbled up in Susanna like a spring. 'I've been offered a little studio to paint in, at a kind of arts centre quite close to my place. I think I'm going to take it.'

'That's wonderful! You *must!*' said Angie. 'It's exactly what —'

Finn gave a piercing squawk. 'She's woked up!' he cried as they jerked around, startled. And yes, Stella-Jean's eyes were open, and seemed to be focused – but not on any of them. Gently, Susanna explained that her eyes opened sometimes, but it didn't mean she was awake, or could even see them. Sure enough, after staring into a high corner of the room for a while, Stella-Jean's lids drifted down. Finn, who had been holding her hand the whole time, now turned his face right away from them, and Susanna was pretty sure he was crying.

'Oh dear,' she said very quietly. 'This can't be — oh, Angie, I want him to visit, of course, but this can't be good for him. Has he had any – any counselling?' *Counselling! You hypocrite!* 'At the school, perhaps?'

'They suggested it,' Angie replied in an equally low voice, 'but Finn said he doesn't want to talk to anyone. And we . . . I . . . well, we believe that faith and prayer are the greatest healers. We're all praying for Stella-Jean, you know, Susu.'

She means well, Susanna told herself firmly, *she means well*. 'Thank you, Ange,' she said. 'I know you love her, too.' She touched her sister's hand. 'We all just want the best for our children, don't we?'

Vinnie was in her framing shop on the ground floor of Studio Lulu, measuring tape in hand, marking off lengths of bevelled-edge timber with a slash of her pencil.

'Hi there, gorgeous,' she called when she saw Susanna hesitating in the doorway. 'Come in. I've just got a couple more things to finish off here.'

Susanna drifted round, checking out frames, wondering about prices. The biggest expense in putting together an exhibition is the framing, that's what she'd always heard. Brochures and price lists lay scattered on Vinnie's messy counter. Susanna started sifting through them, getting distracted by the many invitations and catalogues for shows at other galleries. *So much art*. The pictures on the cover of a small square catalogue peeking out near the bottom of the pile caught her eye. She tweaked it out and had started flipping through the pages before she realised what was familiar about it. The little sculptures, the jewellery, were no such thing: these were the same sex toys that had been in the emerald-green bag, hidden in Gerry's suitcase!

'What's up?' asked Vinnie. Susanna must have gasped, or made some noise. Vinnie was coming over, and Susanna first made to stash the catalogue again under the pile, but that was too . . . childish. Instead, she held it up bravely.

'What's this?' she asked, and was embarrassed to hear the squeak in her voice.

Vinnie peered at it, and grinned. 'Catalogue from Toys in Babeland,' she said. 'Best products, best range, and thank the goddess for mail order. You want to borrow it?'

'No!' said Susanna with a level of vehemence that made her blush. 'I didn't — I've never —'

'You've *never*? Not ever?' Vinnie teased, the tilt of her head seeming to complement the rakish gap between her teeth. 'Well, do yourself a favour, girl!' She reached over, plucked the catalogue from between Susanna's fingers and dropped it into the open top of the bag hanging from her shoulder. 'Satisfaction guaranteed. That husband of yours'll love you for it, too. Trust me.'

My husband's already well acquainted with these products, Susanna thought. Suddenly she wanted to tell Vinnie about what she'd found, how devastated she'd been, how she'd suppressed all the — but Vinnie, after giving her a big wink, had already moved on, and was beckoning Susanna to follow her up the wide wooden stairs.

'Let's go and inspect your new studio then, eh? You want a space to yourself, right, not shared? Right.' Vinnie led the way through the warren of partitions on the second floor. Some studio doors were open, a few people calling out greetings as they went past. 'Here you are.' She opened a door and stood back, allowing Susanna to enter first. 'If I may say, I do believe it will suit madam nicely. You don't have to keep that ancient table if you don't want it, obviously.'

Susanna put down the large black folio she'd been carrying. Except for the scarred and paint-spattered wooden table pushed up against one off-white wall, the space was bare bones. A single window faced south. 'It's perfect.'

'Knew you'd say that,' said Vinnie, leaning against the wall with a proprietorial smirk. 'And now that we've lured you into a studio, I want you to come back to the life drawing classes too.'

'I don't know if I can manage both. This studio and classes.'

'Susanna. I know this is a – a very weird, difficult time for you, but think about it. The classes are good; you like Rita. You *need* to draw. And you need to prepare work for that exhibition, yes?'

'Yes.' Susanna pressed her lips together. *Come on, you have to start somewhere. Vinnie's the perfect* — She opened her mouth and the words seemed to jump out, eagerly. 'Vinnie, I *have* been drawing. New stuff, completely new.'

'You have?' Vinnie straightened, alert as a gun dog at point. Her eyes lit on the black folio. 'Show me.'

'But they're not life drawings,' said Susanna. 'I guess they're —' She was having trouble with the word 'comics', it seemed so undignified. 'They're more like — well, not graphic novels, more like graphic short stories. And they're really rough, just cut and paste at this stage. What I plan on doing —'

Vinnie snapped her fingers impatiently, twice. 'Okay, so they're rough. Let's see 'em.'

Susanna was still standing in front of the folio as though guarding it. 'And I need to warn you: they're awful. I mean, they're of awful things. I don't know —'

'*Show* me!'

'Here, then.' She hoisted the folio on to the table.

Vinnie drew out the topmost sheet. Blinking, she dipped her head to peer at it more closely. 'This is in . . . Bali?'

'Yeah. Part of the dark side of Bali's history,' Susanna said. 'Up until about a hundred years ago, when a prince or sultan died, the widows and concubines were expected to throw themselves onto the funeral pyre and be burnt to death.'

'I had no idea.' Vinnie, aghast, but riveted, hunched over the rows of black-and-white images, all of varying sizes, some captioned. A drawing in a circular frame was in the centre. She was looking, reading, for several minutes, shaking her head occasionally. 'This is so – god, it's like being an eyewitness. Were there photos?'

'No. I read a description years ago, by a Dutch observer; he described these five young women walking one by one out along a kind of bridge above the funeral pyre and jumping in to the flames. He said they seemed to be in a kind of trance. I'd forgotten about it, but then just a couple of weeks ago I was thinking – I don't know, about how Stella-Jean was nagging me to go back to Bali, and the bushfires, and how there's ... how there's a dark side to everything.'

'Boy oh boy. All the preparation: the dances, the girls making offerings. It's ... you know, it's fascinating, but then you see what it's all been leading up to and that's *so* horrible.'

'I know. I warned you.'

Vinnie took the next sheet out of the folio. 'In a village in Guatemala ...' she read aloud, and then after a little while she gasped. 'Oh! *God*.'

'Again, something I read about years ago,' Susanna said, amazed that she could talk about these things at last, and in such a matter-of-fact voice. 'Just an ordinary Guatemalan peasant woman whose village was suspected of being used by guerillas. A gang of para-militaries raped her two teenage daughters and then flayed them alive, in front of her.'

'Oh *no*. How could anyone ...' Horrifed, Vinnie still examined the whole drawing, every frame. 'Oh, and their lives were so ... well, we can see what they were: hard, but beautiful, too. You show us that, as well as the – ugh. What those men did.'

'I've never been able to get that story out of my mind. Well, that's not really true: I put it *right* out of my mind, or at least I thought I had. For ages.'

Vinnie looked up from the drawing, directly into Susanna's eyes. 'How *is* it that human beings are capable of such cruelty?' she asked.

'I don't know. I think I understand some of the whys, but *how* – no. I can't figure that out, at all.'

'It's so awful.'

'You don't have to look at any more of them,' Susanna said, moving toward the folio as though to remove it, but Vinnie fended her off.

'No, I didn't mean the drawings,' she said, and took out another.

Susanna leaned across to see what it was. 'Well, this is a different sort of awful. This happened right here, in Melbourne. A Japanese woman who'd been living here with her husband got in the car with her young son one morning and drove flat strap all the way along Station Pier and straight off the end. The people who saw her said she was screaming the whole way. And here, the car's going down: you know how murky the bay is. They both drowned.'

'Look at her, poor thing,' Vinnie sighed, taking in the woman's memories of childhood, then her foreign isolation, her husband's long hours and coldness. 'So *lonely*.'

'And so ashamed. That's what I figure: she was ashamed of having failed,' Susanna said. 'I know what that's like. I've been feeling so ashamed myself, Vinnie.'

'Ashamed? You? What on earth would *you* feel ashamed about?'

'Lots of things,' said Susanna heavily. 'That I called my mother that night, that I didn't know about her eye problems. That I —' *That I was such a fool about my marriage. That I'm too gutless to face my husband with the truth*. Susanna gestured at the densely covered sheets of paper. 'I feel like the only thing I really know about is this. The way people's lives can be destroyed in just a single, terrible instant. And then they're gone.'

'But *look*, Susanna,' said Vinnie, who had been frowning intently as she listened. 'Look at what you've been able to do. All these people may be gone, but at least they're not forgotten. Because you've remembered them.'

Susanna went quite still. 'How strange you should say that. That's exactly what's been going through my head every time I do these drawings. Like there's a thousand little voices and they're all saying, I was here, this is what happened. *Remember me*.'

'Bearing witness,' Vinnie said. 'That's what you're doing. Bearing witness to other people's suffering.'

She gets it, Susanna realised, and a tremor of excitement rippled invisibly through her. She went over to the window and looked out; there was building work going on next door, men in hard hats, trucks, activity, but she wasn't seeing any of that. *And if Vinnie gets it, maybe other people will too.* 'Bearing witness ...' She turned around. 'Yes, that's exactly what it feels like.'

'So,' said Vinnie, nodding. 'This is your exhibition.'

'You really think it could be?' Susanna asked, facing her. 'I've wondered if it isn't just some ghastly form of – you know,' she made air quotes, '*letting go of my pain.* Art as therapy. The bloody grief process everyone goes on about. Sorry. I don't mean to sound bitter.'

'You can sound bitter. Why the hell not? And so what if it *is* partly letting go, getting it out, self-therapy – so what? What do you think it should be, Susanna: pure art?' Vinnie tossed her head impatiently, flipping her shaggy hair back from her face. 'Pure art doesn't exist.'

'But Vinnie ...' Barbs of doubt pricked at Susanna again. 'Can I really show this? I don't know. It's such awful stuff. No one needs to see this.'

Fiercely, Vinnie said, 'I think *every*one needs to see this.'

TWENTY-NINE

'Well, I want to see you doing some serious work on that arm over the weekend. I mean it, Seb!' Still barking into the phone, Gerry motioned Marcus in to his office with an impatient wave. 'Playing video games isn't going to get you back into championship tennis.' Pause. 'All right then, I'll see you tomorrow. And you better not have a bloody hangover!'

He slammed the phone down, hissing exasperatedly through his teeth.

'Don't tell me Seb's finally turned into a normal teenager?' said Marcus.

'Get this. I ring him to find out why he hasn't told me anything about this new doubles partner his coach has lined up, and you know what he says? "What's the point?" What's the fucking *point*?' Gerry plucked a yellow highlighter from his desktop and arrowed it across the room. 'And *then* he tells me he doesn't want to keep going to this physio I busted my arse to get him to, the best in Victoria. Too rough! I told him, listen, son, no pain, no gain. And now he's heading over to his girlfriend's place with a bunch of mates to eat pizza and no doubt get shit-faced.' A blue highlighter followed the yellow one.

'Cut the kid some slack, Gez. The past month can't have been a lot of fun for him.'

248

Gerry muttered to himself and looked out through the glass wall to the main part of the office. 'Everyone's cleared off, I see.'

'What do you expect? It's gone six o'clock on the Friday of a long weekend. Most places, the staff would've rostered off by midday. Or taken a sickie.'

'Not these days. Not if they want to keep their jobs.'

Marcus widened his eyes at him, and hoisted a sixpack of Coopers Pale Ale in the air. 'Come and have a beer out the back, Mr Cranky, it might improve your mood.'

Grumbling, Gerry followed his partner out to the small courtyard, where a tall lemon-scented gum planted in the centre made the inner-city air smell tangy and fresh. Marcus settled on the wide jarrah step. 'So, fill me in,' he said, handing a stubbie to Gerry, who'd sprawled on the wooden folding chair. 'Better you get it off your chest now than take it home to Susanna.'

'If Susanna *is* at home. And if she hears a word I say in any case, which is unlikely. I probably shouldn't say this, but Susanna's next best to a zombie these days.'

'Zombie!' Marcus clapped one hand to his forehead. 'I hope you don't say that to *her*.'

'Course I don't. But honestly, Marco, she spends all her time just sitting in Stella-Jean's room wringing her hands, yet she knows no more about the kids' medical issues – TBI, for instance, or brachial plexus injury – than she does about nuclear physics. I try and talk to her about test results or treatment options, and she just looks at me blankly.'

'Maybe she's depressed,' suggested Marcus. He poked at a broken half-brick lying next to the step with the toe of his shoe. 'Remember in *Six Feet Under*, the little Latino guy, what was his name? Rico, that's right. Remember when Rico's wife's mother died, she went into this total depression? Just wanted to sit by her mum's grave? And then she started self-medicating, because she was a nurse, and totally lost it, and they split up and —'

'Whoa!' Gerry held up his hand. 'I get the picture. But *I* haven't switched myself off, have I? She's on leave from teaching, you know, but *I* haven't stopped working.'

'Yeah, I know. But it's not your mother who got killed, is it?'

Gerry's mouth was open, about to say something, then he closed it and stared off into the shaded corners of the courtyard. 'You're right,' he said. 'Jean was a terrific woman. Somehow I keep forgetting how close Suze was to her.'

'Yeah. Must be hard.' The two of them drained their beers in thoughtful silence. 'I don't want to sound like a marriage counsellor, Gez, but what with everything else – have you been paying much attention to *her*?' Marcus asked, handing him a fresh stubbie. 'You know, one on one?'

Gerry took a big gulp. 'One on one? Not what she's interested in, mate. We haven't had a shag since this happened. It's been weeks.'

Marcus looked appalled. 'There are *other* reasons to spend time alone together, you know. How old are you again? Nineteen?'

'Oh, shut up,' Gerry growled, embarrassed.

'Suggestion: why don't you do something just with Susanna this long weekend? Get her away somewhere; drive down the Great Ocean Road, for instance. Romantic. You could stay at Lorne, or Apollo Bay.'

'This weekend? I was going to come in here and get some work done. No phones ringing, no interruptions. Get a push on the Sydney stuff.'

'This is the *Labour Day* long weekend, Gerald, commemorating the eight-hour day and fair conditions for the working man – if you can remember such an archaic notion. *I'm* not coming in, I can tell you right now. John and I are going up to the Trickey's vineyard, there's a big working bee on. Place looked like a write-off straight after the fires but they're soldiering on.'

'And John's wife's really ended it? For good?'

'Yep. Moved the boyfriend in and all,' said Marcus cheerfully.

'All this time, she had somebody else on the side too.' Gerry slowly shook his head. 'Fucking amazing.'

'Isn't it? I always thought it was pretty suss, the way she was so slow on the uptake. Turns out it was *his* wife she was waiting to see off!'

'So how's John taking it?'

'Rather well, actually,' said Marcus smugly. 'Settled right in, already plaguing me with his *hideous* notions of redecorating.' He didn't sound unhappy about this.

'Queer eye for the bi guy, huh? Good for you, buddy. Bottoms up,' said Gerry, raising his beer in congratulation.

'So to speak,' Marcus leered.

Gerry rolled his eyes. 'No, seriously. You must feel great. God knows it's been a long time coming.'

'Oh, *stop!*' said Marcus with a queeny flap of his hand, and they both laughed helplessly.

'But enough about me,' said Marcus eventually. 'What are you going to do about *your* marriage?'

Gerry's face sagged. 'It's not just my marriage, mate, it's my kids too. My *family*. Stella-Jean should've woken up by now!' Anger had crept into his voice; Marcus grunted sympathetically, knowing it was there to mask the fear.

'Look, you're doing all you can for Stella-Jean, and so are the doctors and what have you. And Seb: same there. It's Susanna you've got to concentrate on now.'

'You know what she said to me the other day?' said Gerry, moodily rolling a bottle cap round and round between his fingertips. 'I asked her when she was going back to work, and she said, "All I want is my old life back. Can you give me that, Gerry?"' He flicked the bottle cap away; it pinged against the wall and bounced back into the courtyard. They both watched it roll along the uneven brick paving and come to a stop. 'How can I give her her old life back, Marco?'

'I don't know, Gez,' said Marcus softly.

'I *can't*. It makes me feel completely fucking . . . *useless* when she says that.'

'Yeah, I can imagine it does.'

They were silent together for a while, drinking their beers, all the companionable ghosts of their decades of friendship sitting quietly there with them.

'Just give her time. You two've been married for twenty years.'

'Yeah. I know.'

'Tell her you love her. That can't hurt.'

'I guess not.'

Everything should have been going swimmingly. Gerry had phoned Susanna's mobile, told her he'd pick up some Thai food (her favourite), even bought a bottle of the grassy sauvignon blanc she liked. But halfway through dinner, he made a regretful discovery. *It's not possible to flirt with your wife: she knows you too well.* Uncomfortably, he realised he'd assumed Susanna would *always* look at him the way she used to: that eager-to-please, adoring expression. *Devoted, like a dog.* Except that now she seemed more like a cat, aloof and unamused.

Give her time, Marcus had said. All right, he would. He even went to the cupboard and got out a second bottle of wine. Finally, she started talking. Nothing world-shattering, just about a letter she'd got from the management at the retirement village, saying they had a waiting list of retirees wanting to move into the village, and asking her to make her mother's unit available for sale as soon as possible. 'It was in Mum's contract, apparently. Three months,' Susanna said. Her words had the fuzzy edge of too much drink.

Gerry nodded encouragingly. 'Well, that's good news, Suze. That means we can get stuck into the renovations without having to borrow money.'

'The renovations?' Susanna said. There was a long pause. 'I thought — weren't you going to fund that?'

Gerry smiled. 'It's *our* house, babe. Why should I be the one to pay for it all?' Abruptly, her expression closed down. 'Jean would've been more than happy,' he added, feeling a flicker of impatience. *Don't clam up again, damn it.*

Susanna reached for the bottle of wine. 'That's empty, Suze,' he told her, but she upended it over her glass anyway and was cartoonishly amazed by the three feeble drops that trickled out.

'Shit,' she said, holding the bottle up to the light to peer at its patent emptiness. 'How did that happen?' She looked at the clock on the wall. 'Shit,' she said again, 'is that the time?' As she stood up, she pushed the table away from her a bit too hard. Their empty glasses wobbled.

Yep, she's pissed, thought Gerry. *I am too, a bit.*

'I've got to get to bed.'

'I'll join you,' Gerry said, wondering if a boozy screw might still not be out of the question. Worth a try. He came up behind her as she stood at the sink filling a tall Duralex glass – the one she liked to have on her bedside table – with water, and put his arms around her, curving his frame around hers, snuggling his crotch against her bottom. 'Mmm, you feel good,' he murmured into her hair. 'Check this neat little waist. You're getting your girlish figure back, baby.'

Susanna snorted as she turned the tap off so hard the plumbing gave a small shudder. 'Yeah. Fabulous what tragedy can do. I should recommend it to Weight Watchers, eh?'

He chuckled – humour, always a good sign – and crossed his forearms across her torso, holding one of her breasts with each hand. 'I think a closer inspection is highly recommended,' he purred.

Brusquely, she knocked his hands away. 'I'm exhausted,' she said flatly. 'I'm going to bed. To sleep.'

A flush of anger prickled Gerry's skin. 'Exhausted? How can you be? All you've done is sit in a chair all day.'

'Is that so?' Susanna said. 'Actually, that's *not* all I've been doing.'

The way she was slurring her words was almost comical, but Gerry wasn't about to laugh, no way. Laughing at her would totally cruel his chances. *Give her time*, he remembered, and leaned against the counter, inclining his head at a disarming angle. 'Well . . . so, tell me, Suze, what else have you been up to?'

'Drawing,' she said. She was gripping the benchtop so hard her knuckles gleamed whitely.

'Oh? What have you been drawing?' *Relax*, he urged her silently, and reached across to stroke the back of her hand.

She gave him a guarded look. 'Work for the exhibition I'm supposed to be having. Remember?'

'Exhibition? Hasn't that been cancelled?' He saw immediately that he'd made a tactical blunder. 'No. Right. The – ah, the exhibition, at the . . . council gallery. Great! So, show me what you've been drawing.'

'You want to see?' It sounded like a challenge rather than an invitation. 'Really?'

'Sure. Of course.'

Susanna bumped against the couch as she walked a little unsteadily through the living room. Gerry leaned against the kitchen bench, waiting. She went outside. He heard the car door slam, then she was back, carrying a large black folder, which she thumped down on the kitchen table.

'Here!' she said. 'You might as well have a look.'

As Gerry approached, he had a presentiment of what he would find in there: portraits of their daughter in her coma. He paused. Her stillness, so terribly like death. *Am I okay with this?* He squared his shoulders and used both hands to withdraw the contents of the folder, all the sheets of paper, all at once.

The drawings that confronted him, a mix of pencil and pen and ink, were not what he'd expected. Not at all. He lifted one after another, each sheet stiff with other bits of paper that had been glued on, dense with detail, hand-lettered text here and there. 'What the hell is this?' he asked, baffled. He looked up at Susanna, who was watching him with a defiant expression. 'These are like comics!' He looked at another sheet. 'War comics . . .'

'You could call them comics,' said Susanna stiffly. 'Or chapters in a graphic novel, maybe?'

'Bloody hell,' said Gerry wonderingly. 'These are horrible.' He didn't see her face, her whole body, tighten. He pulled one sheet to the top of the pile. 'The SIEV X,' he said, pointing to a line of large text. 'I remember that.'

The central panel showed the heart of the tragedy: the stormy sea, at night, and a small ship, foundering. Amid the waves a mass of women and children struggling to stay afloat, clinging to each other, to anything floating, including the bodies of those already drowned. Gerry winced and turned his face aside from the heart-stopping terror on their faces, then looked back at the drawings through unwilling, narrowed eyes. Before the storm, there had been the perilous journey out of war and hardship; before that, the lives, the marriages, the births.

'Yes,' said Susanna. 'Suspected Illegal Entry Vessel X, as our wonderful government of the day called it. They knew about it, they knew it was leaving Indonesia. Three hundred and fifty three people we allowed to drown that night. Mostly women and children.'

'*We?* Don't ever say that,' said Gerry angrily. 'I didn't vote for that little prick Howard, and nor did you.'

'No, but did we do *anything*?' asked Susanna, standing back from the table, her arms crossed high over her chest. 'To protest? Some people did, but not me, or you. The government of this country – *our* country – treated refugees worse than criminals, for *years*, and you and I were too busy with our comfy little lives to even write a letter saying, "Excuse me, that's not nice. Please don't do that."'

Usually when Susanna had too much to drink she either got maudlin or turned into a giggler. Never this sort of challenging aggro. Gerry did not appreciate her attitude one little bit.

'What exactly is your point here, Susanna? Going for middle-class guilt trip of the year award, are you?'

She gave an insolent shrug. 'Maybe. Maybe I am.'

Gerry shook his head. 'Well, isn't that marvellous.' He pulled out another sheet at random. 'What is *that*?' he cried, rearing back.

Susanna peered at the drawing. 'In Rwanda. Tutsi women and girls were gang raped and then sliced to ribbons with machetes and broken bottles. From the inside, as you see.'

'That is *disgusting*, Susanna,' he cried, truly appalled. 'That is worse than the worst pornography.'

'Yes, I agree,' she said. 'It is disgusting. What people do to each other is often disgusting. Well, what *men* do, for the most part. No getting away from it, Gerry. It's mostly men who do this disgusting stuff.'

Gerry slapped the offensive drawing face down on top of the others. He turned his back on them to confront her. 'Tell me you are not thinking of exhibiting these.' His voice was loud, and getting louder. 'Tell me you're not even remotely considering putting this horrific *shit* on the walls of the council bloody gallery, and inviting people to come and look at it.'

'Yes. I am.'

Gerry ran his hands tensely through his hair, then held his palms to his temples for a moment, seeing how disastrously the evening had gone off the rails, realising that he needed to calm things down. *Reason with her*, he told himself.

'Susanna, I know you've been through a lot. We both have. But it's *your* mother who died, I understand that, on top of what's happened to the kids. You're traumatised. Depressed.' She was staring at the floor. *Does she get it?* 'You just can't show this stuff, Suze,' he said persuasively. 'Comics, about war and torture and genocide? It's sick! You'd be . . . you'd just be making a fool of yourself.'

'They're not finished,' she said calmly. 'These are just rough drafts. The final versions will look . . . quite different. Sharp. I'm going to work on them in my studio.'

'What – studio?'

'The space I've just rented at the art centre near here. Studio Lulu.' For a few moments, Gerry couldn't actually say anything. 'And when,' he managed finally, '*when* were you planning to tell me about this studio? Let alone show me these hideous drawings you've been doing, while sitting, let me just add, at our poor daughter's bedside.'

Susanna seemed to be considering this. 'I don't know, Gerry. When were you planning to tell me who you were with on the night our poor daughter, and our poor son, and my poor mother, were in a car crash?'

'What on earth are you talking about?'

'I'm talking —' and suddenly her deadly calm was gone. 'I'm talking,' she yelled, 'about your fucking *girlfriend*.'

'Girlfriend?' Gerry repeated, genuinely mystified. 'What the hell? I don't have a girlfriend!'

She rushed at him, fury making her face ugly, hardly recognisable. For a moment Gerry thought she was going to take a swing at him, and he was ready to grab her arm if she did.

'Someone saw you, Gerry,' she hissed. 'Someone saw you with her at the hotel in Sydney.'

There was a momentary blank, and then he had a lightning-quick image of Monica, the redhead with the luscious arse. 'Sydney?' he said. 'Right. The developer's PR person interviewed me at the hotel. I can show you the story she wrote for their corporate newsletter. Nothing happened. I've never laid eyes on her again. Susanna, I do not have a girlfriend.'

His wife's face suddenly crumpled. Gerry saw that he was off the hook and the adrenalin flooding through him kicked into triumph. *I've won!* Watching her struggling for control, Gerry prepared himself to accept her tearful apology, and rested a solicitous hand on her bowed shoulder.

She wrenched herself away. 'Don't lie to me,' she snarled. 'She was with you in New York. I found your cute little bag of toys.'

Gerry's skin, all over his body, tightened, but he was a good liar. His face never gave him away. 'Toys? Susanna, I don't know what's going on here. This is getting very weird.'

She glared, and he looked back at her with concerned innocence, while assessing his options as fast as the shock, and the alcohol in his system, would allow. The game was suddenly knife-edge – but he could bluff this out. He knew the toy bag was safely locked in his filing cabinet under the desk in his office. 'I have no idea what you're talking about.'

'A green silk bag? From Bali?' Susanna sounded dangerously calm again. 'Full of – sex toys.' The way she said it sounded prissy, a bit lame, and she pressed her mouth down hard in dissatisfaction.

Okay, fuck. So, she'd found the toy bag. *Fuck.* Could she have unpacked the suitcase that day, after all? Adrenalin pumped faster through his system. *But she doesn't have it now.* Therefore, no evidence, and if she'd only seen it that once, in the traumatised condition she'd have been in —

'Honey, I don't know what you thought you saw,' he said, shaking his head, puzzled, worried. 'I'm no more familiar with sex toys than you are. Yes, I do have a green bag. You mean the one with a bunch of little pockets round the inside?' he asked. She nodded. 'Yeah. I use it to keep my tech gadgets in – USB hub, connection cables. Stuff like that.'

Susanna made a rolling motion with her hand, for more information. *What else? What could feasibly be mistaken for a sex toy?* 'iPod extras . . .' he offered. He could feel his mind running out of track. 'I dunno. Spare batteries . . . I'll bring it home from the office and show you, if you like.'

'That's all?' She sounded disappointed. She walked back over to the kitchen bench, looked at the glass she'd filled earlier, picked it up, glugged down the water, wiped her mouth with the back of her hand. 'That's the best you can do? You really do think I'm a moron, don't you?'

She raised the arm holding the now empty Duralex glass behind her head, like a softball pitcher. Instinctively, Gerry ducked, but she wasn't aiming for him. The heavy glass hurtled through the air and struck the big window at the far end of the kitchen, the one that looked out onto the backyard. The window shattered with a sound like a rifle shot.

'*Holy shit!*' yelled Gerry, spinning around to see. Another huge jolt of adrenalin made his heart feel like it had suddenly doubled in size. Cool night air rushed into the room. 'Jesus fucking Christ! Susanna, have you gone *mad*?'

'That's how fragile our marriage is,' she said. She was holding her own forearms in a kind of monkey grip; she was shaking.

'You're *nuts*,' he said loudly, going over to the window. Though very little glass had come into the room, the brick paving outside was covered in shards. 'You have lost your mind!'

'Why would your iPod need condoms, Gerry?'

No evidence, she has no evidence. 'I am not going to indulge this madness. You need help, Susanna.'

'No, *we* need help, Gerry. If this marriage isn't already shattered into a million fucking pieces, that is. We need to see a counsellor, and you need to start telling the truth.'

'I can *show* you that bag,' he shouted in a fury, convinced now by his own righteous shock. 'And I'm telling you, there are *no* condoms and no sex toys in it. You are *sick*, blaming men for every bad thing that's ever happened in the world. Blaming *me*.'

She looked at him in a way he'd never seen her look before. With disgust. 'I'm sleeping in Stella-Jean's room,' she said, and left the room.

THIRTY

'It could be post-traumatic stress,' Rory suggested. 'Don't you think? From the car crash?'

I wish, thought Seb. He rolled his head from side to side, *no,* on the pillow. 'That was a month ago.'

'So what? Seb, a month is nothing, to get over something like that. And it's *ongoing*: your shoulder, your tennis, your sis—'

'*I know,*' he interrupted loudly, and then repeated in a much quieter voice, 'I know.'

'Oh, mate, I'm sorry,' she said.

'No, *I'm* sorry, Rors. I didn't mean to yell at you.'

She moved closer and manoeuvered one arm under his neck, pulling his head across to rest on her shoulder. The way she offered *him* comfort; he didn't deserve such a sweet girlfriend. 'Sorry,' he murmured again, turning his face to touch his lips to her inner shoulder, and she stroked his hair.

'Anyway,' she continued after a while, 'I *do* think it's got something to do with stress. The nerve damage, too, that's got to be affecting you.'

'The nerve damage affects my ability to get my arm up, Rors, not my dick. Don't laugh!' he said, when Rory sniggered. 'Anyway, they can fix the nerve damage, if I have another operation. Or it might improve on its own.'

'Another operation, that's another stress factor,' she pointed out.

He moved his sore shoulder restlessly, and sat up, looking around at the stuff in her older brother Tony's bedroom. It was the first time he'd stayed the night at Rory's house since they were little kids; her parents were in Townsville for the weekend, settling Tony into university there. Seb and Rory and their friends had spent the evening watching TV, eating pizzas, playing video games, arguing about bands – and it was all cool, till the others left. Then Seb got nervous, anticipating what would happen in her brother Tony's queen-size bed, where she'd suggested they could spend the night. Rory would lead, and he would follow – but only to that certain point, and then his dick would go no further. He wished he hadn't been right.

'I feel like some ice-cream,' he said. 'You got any ice-cream?'

'Yeah, sure.'

There's something wrong with me, Seb thought as they sat at the Fengs' kitchen table digging into huge bowls of ice-cream. *I'm not really traumatised by the car crash, the way I should be.* He'd hardly even cried. And there was another reason he knew it wasn't post-traumatic stress that was stopping him getting it on with Rory.

A week ago, he'd watched his own fingers texting Andrew, like they had a mind of their own. *Wanna catch up?* They'd gone out, they'd had a great time with other friends of Andrew's at a club in the city with a fantastic DJ. Sitting in Andrew's car at the end of the night, the two of them, just talking – and Seb had leaned across and kissed him. He'd been wanting to do it all night; he'd even got Andrew to park right up the other end of the street from home. *That kiss*, like no other kiss he'd ever had or imagined. And then he freaked and said, 'I have to go!', and jumped out of the car and ran off. But he couldn't stop thinking about it. And every time he did, he got hard in a nanosecond. And if he was by himself when he imagined what might've —

'Seb?'

What? he asked Rory with his eyebrows, since his mouth was full of ice-cream.

'Have you ever, um, considered your sexuality?'

His guts flopped over like a fish. He took his sweet time softening and swallowing that ice-cream. 'How do you mean, "considered my sexuality"?' he asked finally, trying to make it sound like it was something that had never even remotely occurred to him.

'Just that,' she said. 'No biggie.' But he knew her just as well as she knew him, and both of them knew it *was* a biggie.

'I've considered *sex*,' he said. 'Is that the same thing?' It was just something to say; he hoped she wouldn't ask what it meant, because he didn't even know.

'I don't think so.' Rory shook her head. She wasn't accusing him of anything, she was *worried* about him, he could see it in her face, hear it in her voice.

He chased the last bits of runny ice-cream round the bowl, and put his spoon down. 'I don't want to consider my sexuality, Rors. I just wanna be able to have a good time. With you.' And suddenly, horribly, he felt like he might be about to start crying. 'You're a really great person, Aurora Feng, you know that?' And then, bloody hell, he *did* start crying.

She jumped up and came around to hug him. *Stop crying*, Seb ordered himself, screwing his face up hard. *Stop.* He picked up a paper serviette and blew his nose on it. 'Sorry,' he muttered.

'You wanna talk about it?' Rory asked tenderly.

Seb gave a shuddering exhalation. How he wished he could say *yes*.

'Nah,' he said. 'I just want to go to sleep now. I feel buggered.'

They did sleep, for a while, but after a few hours Seb was awake again. He lay there in the darkness of the unfamiliar room beside Rory, his good and lovely friend, thinking his unhappy thoughts. Ben Folds Five's *Brick*, the saddest song in the world, was on a loop in his brain, repeating and repeating the lines about finding someone and feeling more alone than ever before.

When he was a kid it had all been so simple: hit the ball, have a laugh with your mates, do okay in school, give your sister a biff when Mum wasn't looking, watch sport on TV with Dad. And then all those fantasies of being a famous doubles star, with Clarence. Now he could see real life, adult life, stretching out before him, and it was a freaking maze of traps and danger. Lying to everyone, terrified of the truth, tortured by the constant risk of being found out. And he *would* be found out, and then he'd be an outcast. Alone, for the rest of his life.

Did he doze? Maybe. When he opened his eyes again the quality of light there in Tony Feng's bedroom had changed, and he could hear the first notes of birdsong outside. He looked at Rory: still sleeping, curled up around a pillow. Just watching her, Seb felt guilty. He couldn't keep lying there. Stealthy as a thief, he slid out of bed and gathered up his clothes. He dressed in the living room, wrote Rory a note saying he'd remembered he had an early morning training session *(liar)* and quietly left the house.

It was six or seven kilometres to his place. At the end of the Fengs' block, Seb did a few stretches and then began to run, a steady jog, then a short sprint, and back to jogging. His bad arm lagged and tried to droop, and he tried not to let it. There was a cool tang in the air, and some of the trees he passed were starting to change colour. Magpies warbled. Everything was so beautiful and so familiar, and yet everything had changed so much and it would never be the same again. He didn't think he could bear it.

Gerry, having slept badly alone, heard Susanna get up at dawn. He listened to the muted, familiar sounds of her making tea in the kitchen; she would bring a cup in to him soon, as she always did, whether he drank it or not. No doubt she'd clean up all that broken glass first, though; she wouldn't want the evidence of her craziness staring her in the face.

He was still lying in bed, anticipating her entry, her ashen apology, when he heard the front door close, and then the sound of her car backing down the drive. *What?* He jumped up, and reached the window just in time to see her driving away down the street.

What the hell? Maybe there was no milk in the fridge for the tea, and she'd gone to get some? He went swiftly to the kitchen, which felt and sounded weirdly different with the smashed window letting in the air. Nothing from the night before, including the broken glass, had been touched, and there was plenty of milk in the fridge.

Gerry showered, dressed, made his very much-needed cup of espresso. Drank it, glaring at the space where the window used to be, thinking about how hard it would be to get a glazier to come on a long weekend. Still Susanna wasn't back. Was it possible she was already sitting at Stella-Jean's bedside, drawing more of those hideous scenes? She had her mobile on most of the time in there these days – it wasn't like the ICU, where the no-mobiles rule had been strictly enforced – but he was buggered if he was going to call her.

By the time he'd finished his coffee, he couldn't stand it any longer, and quickly swept up what little glass there was inside before going outside to deal with the worst of it. *Bloody hell, how can there be this much glass from that one window?* He set to work, furious at being landed with this mess. Not like it was of *his* making.

'What happened?' said Seb's amazed voice, behind him. Gerry was so startled he almost dropped the jagged shard he'd just picked up.

'What does it look like?' he growled, not turning round.

'Broken window. But how'd it get broken?'

'How?' Gerry dropped the shard into the cardboard box beside him and stood up. For a moment he was disoriented: Seb's T-shirt was dark with patches of sweat and he was breathing pretty hard; how come he'd been out running already? No, that's right, he'd been staying at his girlfriend's last night. *Well, welcome home, son!* With a certain satisfaction Gerry said sternly, 'Your mother threw a glass through it. One of those Duralex ones.' He pointed at the evidence: the heavy tumbler still lying, unbroken, in the parched herb garden.

'*Mum?*' Incredulity creased Seb's forehead. 'Threw a *glass*?'

'Correct.'

Seb shook his head. 'Mum wouldn't have *thrown* it. It must've been an accident.'

'It was no accident, Sebastian. She was throwing it all right, at *me*. Your mother's having some sort of breakdown, I'm afraid.' Gerry felt wonderfully righteous, saying these words, but the look of utter devastation that swept over Seb's face shook him. 'Don't worry, mate,' he added quickly. 'It's just, you know, a reaction to everything that's happened. I should've seen it coming, really. She's been trying to soldier on but . . . We'll get her to Doctor Gillian, get her on some medication.'

'Where's Mum now?' Seb asked anxiously. 'The car's not in the drive.'

'I, uh —' Gerry hesitated. Would it sound uncaring to say he didn't know? Yes, it probably would. 'She's gone in to the hospital.'

Seb looked around him as though at some completely unfamiliar place and then walked quickly inside. *You could offer to give me a hand*, Gerry thought, but let him go and continued clearing up the glass. A few minutes later, Seb was back.

'Where's Tigger?'

'I don't know where Tigger is,' Gerry said, trying not to sound impatient.

'Was he here last night?'

Gerry had no idea whether the cat had been around the night before, and said so. Seb went into the house and his father could hear him calling, 'Tigs! Tiggsy! Come on, Tigs!'

'I can't find him,' Seb said, standing at the back door again.

'I'm sure the cat's fine, Seb. He's just —'

'Maybe he got locked in the shed.' Seb was off to the back shed, creaking the door open, and again the insistent calling. Then back again, like a yo-yo. 'I can't find him,' he said again, querulously.

'Don't worry about the bloody cat, Seb. Did you run home from what's-her-name's?'

'Rory's.'

'How did the arm take it?'

'It's okay,' Seb said, raising and lowering his right elbow to the side like a bird trying out an injured wing.

'Lift it straight out, in front. Now straight up.' Gerry watched his son. 'Huh. Have you been doing those exercises the physio gave you?'

Seb looked away. 'No.'

'Why the hell not? Why wouldn't you be doing everything you can to improve that arm? You've got to *work* on it to fix this nerve problem.'

Seb had his bottom lip stuck out. He looked like a sulky toddler. 'Dad, I really don't wanna go to that physio any more. It hurts.'

'Of course it bloody hurts!' Gerry snapped. 'Don't be such a sissy!'

Seb's head jerked back as though he'd been hit. 'Shut up! It's not *your* arm!'

'Don't tell me to shut up!' Gerry yelled. 'Who do you think you are?'

'*You* weren't in a car crash! You don't know what it's *like*!' Seb's voice cracked, as it hadn't done in a year or more. He looked like he was about to burst into tears.

Christ almighty, thought Gerry, *they're all going off the deep end, the whole bloody lot of them*, and all the fury and frustration he'd been feeling for weeks boiled over.

'You're eighteen now, you're a man, for god's sake,' he snapped at Seb, his upper lip lifted scornfully. 'What if you were in the army, would you be having hysterics like this over a dislocated shoulder? Or a bloody missing *pet*? "Oh, where's my pussy cat?"' he mocked in a high mincing tone. 'What are you? Some kind of *poofter*?'

Seb's face just collapsed, and with a whimpering cry of outraged despair he turned away and stumbled into the house.

'Oh, *fuck*,' muttered Gerry in disgust, and finished clearing up the broken glass, seething. A run, that was the only way to settle himself down. He changed into his running gear, peeling and chomping down a large banana as he did so, and set off. Crossing the road, who should he see sauntering along the fence between Mrs Parthanopoulos' and the new people's place but Tigger, the errant ginger cat.

'You!' he called crossly, jogging on the spot. 'Get home!'

Tigger stopped and looked at him with narrowed, impertinent eyes. Gerry muttered an exasperated inaudibility, and crossed the footpath to the side fence. 'Tiggsy, Tiggsy!' he wheedled. 'Come on, you little bugger, you're wanted.' The cat looked off into the distance, considering, and then, with the haughty insouciance of a runway model, stepped the remaining few metres along the fence rail. '*Per-rrow?*'

'Yeah, yeah, miaow yourself.' Gerry plucked him from the fence and tucked him firmly against his chest. 'Come on, pest.'

Seb's door was closed. 'Someone to see you, Sebastiano,' Gerry called, opening it with one hand. He scooted Tigger in there and was about to close the door again, but on an impulse so rare he hardly knew what it was – the impulse to make amends – he went in instead.

'Seb, I just wanted to say —'

His son, sitting hunched on the bed, faced the door for just an instant, and the look of hunted anguish Gerry saw there shocked him to the core. Seb's face, wet with tears and glazed with snot, was that of someone on the edge of the pit. Gerry had seen this look, just last night, in Susanna's drawings. The faces of those people, staring at death, were at the same pitch of despair as his son's.

'Seb!'

Seb held up his arms, sobbing like a child, and Gerry saw the pill bottle he was holding. Aghast, he forged across the room as though to pull him from a raging torrent and wrapped his arms around the boy, holding him tight. There was another bottle of pills lying on the bed: he recognised Seb's own powerful analgesics, and a foil of Susanna's sleeping tablets. But the tops were still on the bottles, Gerry saw with a gut-loosening sensation of relief, and only a couple of tablets had been popped from the foil.

'Dad,' Seb wailed. He sounded like something inside him had broken. 'Dad . . . Dad.'

'Oh, Sebbie.' Gerry rocked him in his arms. 'I'm sorry, mate, I'm sorry,' he crooned, and for once in his life he meant it, with all his heart. 'You're right, you're right: I wasn't in the crash, it's not my arm. I *don't* know what it's like.'

'No, *you're* right,' Seb sobbed. 'I *am* a poofter. I'm gay, Dad, you know I am. You hate me!'

'No, no, I could never hate you. Never. Don't ever think that. You're my son, you're my life.' Gerry held his boy away from him so that he had to look at him. 'Do you get that? You're my bit of the future. I *love you.*'

Seb started crying again but in a different way, in release, acknowledging his father's words, and Gerry pulled him to his chest.

'Sebbie, you have to tell me: did you take any pills? Any at all?'

Seb shook his head against his chest; the storm of weeping abating a little. 'I was just going to. I thought you'd gone out.'

Thank you, Tigger, thank you, thought Gerry fervently. His big handsome son, his baby. He'd been trying to do his best for Seb, for all of them, but it had gone wrong. He'd missed something terribly important. Maybe lots of things. 'Is this about the girlfriend?' he asked tenderly. 'Rory?'

'No! No, it's not about her. It's about *me*.' Seb sat up a little straighter, chest and shoulders heaving. 'I really like her but I don't wanna . . . I can't *do* it, it's just — I *can't.* And I know why: I'm gay. I can't lie any more, it's true, I am.'

Gay? Only now did Gerry register what Seb had already said. *How do I handle this?* The immediate crisis: that, he saw in a flash, was what he needed to get Seb through. 'Every teenager goes through a stage of thinking they're gay,' he said with absolute conviction, even though he had no idea if this was true or not. Seb was leaning against him now, and Gerry had his arm around him. 'It's perfectly normal.'

Seb pulled away slightly and looked at him, not sure whether to believe his father or not. '*You* didn't, did you?' he said, then grabbed a handful of tissues and wiped his glazed face and blew his nose, hard, several times.

Gerry frowned. 'No,' he admitted. 'But . . . most teenagers do. It's just . . . a stage.'

'Dad, it's not a stage,' Seb said. 'Not for me.'

Teenage hyperbole. Gerry didn't see how Seb could possibly be gay; he was his *son*, for god's sake! But this was not, tactically, the way to go, not right now. 'And what if you *are* gay?' he said. 'So what? Big deal!'

'Big deal?' said Seb. He sounded outraged. 'It *is* a big deal! You said it yourself, you called me a poofter!'

'I'm sorry, mate. I did say that, and I'm sorry. But listen: have you forgotten who my best friend is? Best friend and business partner?' Gerry could see that, oddly, this had not occurred to Seb. 'Do I have a problem with Marcus being gay? Does anybody?'

'I guess . . .' Seb murmured. He shook his head slowly.

'You want me to call Marco?' Gerry offered. 'Maybe that'd be good, maybe you could talk to him . . .'

'Maybe.' Seb tried to think about it. 'Not right now.' He yawned, hugely. The luxuriant, irresistible tiredness that follows an emotional cyclone was seeping in. 'Dad, I think right now I just want to sleep.' Hadn't he said this to Rory a few hours ago? But this time it was true. 'I hardly slept at all last night.'

Gerry looked at him closely. The boy was indeed clearly exhausted; sleep would be the best thing for him. 'Fair enough. But I'm putting these pills under lock and key, okay? And I'm going to be sticking my head in here and checking on you, just to make sure you're okay.'

'You don't have to do that. I won't . . .'

'Good. But I'm going to, anyway,' Gerry said, picking up the bottles and the foil of tablets in one hand. 'Promise me you're not going to try – anything like that, again.'

'Promise,' said Seb, yawning mightily again. He lay down on his side, head on pillow, and Tigger, who seemed to have been waiting for this signal, sprang from the desk to the bed. 'Tiggsy,' Seb said, and pulled the cat to nestle in against him.

Gerry leaned over, hugged his son, kissed his cheek. 'I'm not going for a run, or anywhere else,' he told him. 'I'll be right here. If you want anything, or if you start to get the heebie-jeebies, just sing out.'

'Okay. Dad? Thanks.'

'I love you, Sebbie.'

'Love you too, Dad.'

The boy let go, Gerry could see it. Probably asleep before he even got to the door. He left it open a crack, went straight to the bedroom where he'd slept alone the night before, and was astonished to see from the clock beside the bed that not even two hours had passed since he'd woken up. He picked up the phone from its base and popped the number for Susanna's mobile.

She didn't answer; he hadn't expected that she would. After her recorded voice invited the caller to leave a message, he spoke in a rush, before he could reconsider. 'Susanna, what I said last night about not having a girlfriend is true, but a lot of the other stuff isn't. You were right. Those *were* sex toys in that bag you found. I have been having – adventures, with other women. Nothing that threatens *us*, believe me. But – yeah. We do need to see a counsellor.'

He paused. What else should he say? 'I love you.'

THIRTY-ONE

Angie stood stock-still in the kitchen, make-up on, all ready to go to work in her saleswoman's demure black dress, staring glassy-eyed at the phone sitting on the bench near the window. Willing it to ring. For years she had daydreamed about how one day the phone would ring, and she would pick it up:

Hello?

Angie? her mother's voice would say. *Oh Angie, I've been such a fool. You're a wonderful girl, and I love you so much.*

Now her mother was gone, and that call would never happen.

Strange, the great surge of relief she'd felt at first. Soaring, like she'd lifted off at last: that's how she'd felt at the funeral. When Gabriel sang 'Amazing Grace', those were tears of joyful release Angie had been weeping. Once lost, but now found. Once bound, but now free – for the first time in her life, *free* from that wretched sense of her mother's eye upon her, watching, judging, criticising. *You're not good enough.* For forty years that had weighed her down, but she was free now.

So why, why do I still feel so empty?

Surely the Lord saw that she was worthy of love? Of Gabriel's love? Wasn't Gabriel God's angel, sent to deliver the message of his love? That's what he did for Christ's mother Mary.

That fluttering that she felt, somewhere deep inside her, a fluttering

271

in the emptiness – Angie placed a hand on her stomach, just below the waist, gazing down at her own palely freckled hand on the black fabric – maybe *that* was the angel? Or a baby? God had sent Gabriel to give her a new baby, and that baby would be the messenger. *Not just for me, for the whole world.*

But the angel spoke to Mary. *Why doesn't Gabriel speak to me?* Why did he come to her at night, join their bodies together, but never say any of those words she longed to hear? So much so that she whispered them to herself sometimes: *I love you, Angie.* In the dark, alone, whispering: *Angie, will you be my wife?*

Or that fluttering in the emptiness could be the enemy. A tumour growing inside her, come to kill her and rid the world of her deepdown wickedness. *That's what Mum wanted.*

No. No, Susu would tell her that was crazy. Maybe she was going crazy, and that was how God was testing her?

'Mum. Mum.' Someone – Finn was shaking her arm.

Find that bright smiling face, Angie. Put it on. 'Finnie! I've — you're all set up, aren't you, honey? For the day? All your – your drawing things?'

'Mum, take me to school, *please*,' said Finn urgently.

'But school's closed today,' she said, bending down to him and taking both his hands. 'It's a pupil-free day, remember? No kids.'

'But there'll be *teachers* there,' Finn said. 'And I'll be good, I will.'

'Honey, you just have to stay home today and be good here.' Angie gave him a kiss on his cheek. 'Gabriel's going to look after you.' She dropped her voice. 'But you know to be mousey-quiet, don't you? Sweetheart? 'Cause Gabriel has to work on his music. And I have to go off to work now too, I really do.'

Finn drooped.

She'd have to hurry now to catch the train. At the door of the small room in which Gabriel worked on his music, Angie paused, fingers picking anxiously at the zip fastener on her bag. 'Finn's in his room, he won't be any trouble, Gabriel,' she said. 'I'm so grateful to you for looking after him like this.'

'Who else will have him, Angie?' said Gabriel coolly. He leaned forward to the music stand, turned a sheet, and then fixed his green gaze upon her. 'Can he go to Tim and Helen's house? No, not after he tried to kill their daughter. Does he have any friends from school? No, not one. Can he go to your sister? No.'

'I'm sorry,' Angie murmured.

'The question is, will he interfere with my work? Will he interrupt me, or has he learned how to behave?'

'He *has*, Gabriel; he won't be *any* trouble. Thank you!'

Finn had played with his toys, done some drawing, and sneaked out of his room just once, to go to the toilet. Now he lay on his bed, watching all the teeny bits of dust floating in a beam of sunlight coming through his window, thinking about how it was lunchtime. He was hungry. He'd been hungry for a while. He went to his door and opened it a crack, listening to the sound of Gabriel's guitar, and his voice. The same song he'd been singing all morning, again and again.

'Take what is ti-ny, take what is ten-der,
Take what can ne-ver, be taken away . . .'

Yes, it was safe. Finn stole silently down the hall to the kitchen and got out the bread, the butter, the honey, carefully so as not to make a noise. But when he was easing the cutlery drawer open to get a knife, somehow he pulled it too far and the whole thing fell to the floor. Ker-*rash*! Finn nearly jumped out of his skin; he cast a frightened look over his shoulder and was desperately trying to fit the drawer back onto its runners, when he sensed the man's approach.

'Your mother said you wouldn't be any trouble.'

Finn got the drawer in, keeping his back turned. It was like having a monster under his bed: *don't look, don't look.*

'But you're always trouble, aren't you?'

Finn's shoulders hunched defensively.

'I *said*, you're always trouble, aren't you?' Gabriel shouted right in his ear.

Finn was drawing his breath in little gasps, and trying to keep the gasps quiet, staring at the benchtop. *Capilano Honey*, said the label on the jar: red and yellow, and a stripey black bee. Gabriel gripped his shoulder and forced him to turn, then thrust his hand in front of Finn's eyes, pointer finger curled up tight behind the thumb tip. 'You,' Gabriel said, and then he flicked his finger, hard, against the end of Finn's nose. Face screwed up in pain, Finn jerked his head back but he was trapped, his back hard up against the bench. 'Are,' said Gabriel, and flicked him hard again, on the cheek this time. 'Always,' on the other cheek. 'Trouble,' on the tip of his nose again. 'Aren't you?' he shouted.

'I *hate* you!' Finn screamed. 'I *hate* you, you're *evil*!' He ducked under Gabriel's arm and streaked away, heading for the backyard. He'd made it to the back door and was dragging it open when Gabriel caught up with him.

'*Mum!*' Finn shrieked as he was lifted clear off his feet. Angie had left some clothes soaking in the laundry trough. Face down into the water Gabriel thrust him, holding him there with one hand on the back of his head and one pressing down between his shoulderblades.

Finn was still screaming when his face hit the water and it rushed into his throat, his chest, his lungs, choking and burning. Wet cloth pressed horribly against his face. He kicked and squirmed, arms flailing, his chest pressing against the rounded metal edge of the trough. He could feel the hatred, a living murderous thing, coming through Gabriel's hands as they held him down. *Kill him*, those hands were saying.

And then, just as suddenly, Finn was hauled free of the sucking water. The hands released him and he fell to the floor, fighting for air, water pouring off him and out of him, gushing from his mouth and nose.

The man stood motionless in front of him: his legs in their jeans, and his plain black shoes: one ordinary, one built up high. 'Say you're sorry,' came his voice, from what seemed a great distance, but Finn, gasping and choking, couldn't manage a word. The built-up shoe nudged him. 'Say. You're. *Sorry.*'

'I'm – sorry –' Finn gasped. A pause, and then a towel was dropped, half on top of him and half on the floor.

'Get to your room. Be quiet. Don't make me tell your mother what you did.'

'It may be a small seed, it may be a great need . . .'

Finn had to push with all his might to get the window in his bedroom up, and as it lifted it made a thin screeching sound. He froze, terrified, listening not just with his ears but with his whole body.

But Gabriel continued to sing in his room down the hall.

'It may be the one last hope that you hold . . .'

Without waiting another second, Finn pushed his backpack through the window and slid out after it, heart thumping, then ran as fast as he could go, all the way to the train station. There he waited, huddled in a corner, hidden by a machine that you could buy drinks and chips from, if you had the money. Finn had some money, but not enough for stuff from a machine.

When the train came he did just like Stella-Jean had shown him: he stood well back until it stopped and the doors opened, then he took a giant step inside. Safe inside. A few last drops of water trickled warmly from his ear. Gradually, his trembling stopped. Tucked up small on a seat in the almost deserted carriage, he looked out the window at backyards of houses whizzing by, and cars lined up behind white boom gates waiting for the train to go past, and thought about that last time he'd been on a train, when Stella had taken him into the city after school. They'd had a good time, just like she'd said they would, just like they always did. Then they met up with Seb, and they all waited for Jeejee. They were going to get pizza but they never did, because the car crashed.

Finn knew now why Stella-Jean didn't get spared: God didn't like her because she didn't suck up to him. It was just like with Lucas Beal, or Grace and Lily: people said nice things about God because they were scared that otherwise he'd get them. All the things Gabriel said in his songs – he didn't mean any of them, he just sang them to suck up to God. But if God was really so good, and so powerful, he wouldn't care what people said about him; he wouldn't care about Gabriel's songs. *If God believes that stuff Gabriel says, he's just stupid.* Stella had never believed Gabriel. And Stella never, ever, said anything she didn't mean.

The train stopped at the big station in the city, and Finn climbed the stairs amid a whole crowd of people, feeling scared again, and small. At the gate he remembered you were supposed to put your ticket in to make it slide back and let you through. But he didn't have a ticket, and the man in a uniform, standing to one side, was looking right at him. *I'm going to get caught.* Then the man reached down and pressed a button and the gate slid back, letting Finn go through even without a ticket.

A lady told him which tram to catch to the hospital; he watched carefully and got off at the right stop. Walking up to it from the road, the building loomed, much bigger than the times he'd come there with his mum to visit Stella. Then, they drove in to the car park and walked across on the bridge thing. *This is supposed to be the same hospital they brought me to that night in the ambulance,* but Finn couldn't quite believe that. This was Stella-Jean's hospital.

He walked in the big front doors, past all the people and the desks and the wheelchairs wheeling in and out, and straight over to the lifts. He knew the way up to her room; people always said he didn't pay attention to things, but he did. In the lifts Finn suddenly thought, *What am I going to say if Stella's mum is there?* She'd been there every time they'd visited. But when he sneaked a look around the door there was only Stella-Jean.

He stepped inside and closed the door softly behind him. He said,

'Hello, Stella,' and picked up one of her hands and gave it a squeeze; her eyes kind of flickered but that was all. 'I got here all by myself,' he whispered. 'I came on the train all by myself. I climbed out my window and I ran away.' Leaning on the bed, propped on his elbows, Finn told her what had happened, every single thing, even the name on the honey jar. The way the water had seemed to *burn* inside him. 'Then he made me say *sorry*,' he told her, and hot tears plopped from his eyes. He lay his head down next to hers. 'I only said it because I was scared. But you know what, Stella? It was a lie!'

She was listening to everything. He could *feel* her listening.

'You believe me, don't you?' Finn said.

Stella-Jean said, 'Mmm, mmm.'

Finn gasped and jerked up. 'You said *yes*, didn't you, Stella?' he said. 'You said, yes I believe you!' His mouth was wobbly from trying not to cry. 'Thank you, Stella,' he said in a little squeaky voice.

'Mmm, mmm,' she said again.

A nurse came in, stopped, frowned.

'Hello,' she said in a loud voice. 'Who are you, dear?'

Finn said nothing, just stared at her, holding Stella-Jean's hand. And then it was like Stella poked him, not really with her finger, but – inside his head, somehow. *Tell her you're my cousin*, he heard her say, except he didn't actually hear her.

'I'm her cousin.'

'Oh, her cousin. I see,' the nurse said. She was looking around the room. 'You're here on your own?'

'No, my mum's here,' said Finn. 'She just went down to the cafeteria.'

'I see,' the nurse said again. 'Well, it might be a good idea for you to go down to the cafeteria too. Tell your mum it's Stella-Jean's bath-time, and there are other things we have to do too. No point coming back for a good hour. Okay?'

'Okay,' said Finn, and skedaddled.

As soon as he got near the cafeteria and smelt the food he realised how hungry he was. He'd been here with his mum and auntie, he knew what to do. You took a tray and joined the line, and then put the things you wanted to eat on the tray, but before you could go to a table and eat it, you had to pay. But what if he didn't have enough money for the food he picked? Then he would get in trouble and they'd find out he wasn't meant to be there. Finn hesitated, rubbing the sore part of his chest where the laundry trough had bruised him, as he wondered what to do. Just then, a man sitting at a table just in front of him got up and left, having barely touched any of the fried chicken and chips on his plate. When he was sure the man wasn't coming back, Finn sat down and ate everything he'd left, even the mushy peas and carrots.

As he waited in the cafeteria till he could go back to Stella-Jean, he got out his drawing of Robo-Boy and together they played out what *should* have happened in the laundry. This time, when Gabriel tried to catch Finn and hold his head under the water, Robo-Boy grabbed hold of Gabriel and held *his* head under the water instead. Robo-Boy held Gabriel down till he was finished. Dead. *You're dead now, Gabriel*, he said in his big strong robot voice, and then he threw him away, dropped him in the wheelie bin and said, *Good riddance to bad rubbish!* That was something Jeejee used to say. And then Finn's mum came home and thanked Robo-Boy for putting Gabriel in the rubbish and saving her son. 'He's my special little guy,' she said, and Robo-Boy said, *I know*.

'That's right, Robo-Boy,' said Finn softly. 'Good riddance to bad rubbish. The End.' He put the drawing of his one-armed protector away again, safe till next time.

The cafeteria didn't have any windows, but on the way back to Stella-Jean's room he passed some and saw that the day was almost over. He wondered if Stella slept with the light on – but she was asleep all the time, no matter whether it was daytime or night-time, so she probably didn't care. Finn was nervous. It seemed like there were more people around, nurses and visitors, but there was still no one else in Stella-Jean's room. He closed the door behind him. 'I've gotta stay with you, Stella, so Gabriel can't get me.' There was a cushion on the chair that his auntie usually sat in, and a knitted rug: he took them and his backpack and quickly, before anybody came in, he slipped under Stella-Jean's bed and curled up as small as he could, right up against the wall, with his thumb in his mouth and Robo-Boy standing guard beside him.

He slept, he didn't know for how long, and was woken by the door being pushed open in a rushing sort of way, and a loud voice saying, 'I'll check her room, just in case.' Bright lights were snapped on: he could see shoes and legs and the bottom part of a nurse's uniform come in, stop, and turn around in a circle. The nurse was looking, carefully. For him.

Stella-Jean's hand suddenly appeared, hanging over the side of the bed. *Hold my hand, Finn.* He scooted silently toward it on the cool vinyl floor, and slid his small hand into hers.

The shoes, the legs, walked over to the bed. A sideways face appeared, looking straight at him. The woman's eyes and mouth went very round with surprise and she said, '*Oh!*' Then the face disappeared, the legs ran to the door and the voice called out, 'He's here! That kid they rang about, he's *here.*'

More legs ran in, more faces appeared. They were calling to him, and yelling, all of them at once.

'Come out from under there!'

'Finn? Are you Finn?'

'What on earth are you doing there?'

'Let go of her hand! Come out! *Now!*'

Finn shrank away from them, hard up against the wall, clinging to Stella-Jean's hand. The room seemed to be full of people now, poking and pulling, trying to get him out from under the bed.

And then a strange creaky voice said, 'Lea' him alone.'

All those people poking at him went very, very still. Their eyes stopped looking sharp and hard at him; instead they looked at each other and one of them said very quickly, 'What was — ?', and another, 'Did you — ?'

Again came the voice, more definite this time. 'Lea' him *alone*.'

As they stood up Finn heard those nurses call out, all at the same time: 'Oh!' and, 'Oh my god!'

'Le' him stay,' said Stella-Jean. She was holding his hand, and she was not letting go.

THIRTY-TWO

'I feel *angry*,' said Susanna, and the harsh word seemed to leave her mouth and launch itself into the therapist's pleasant room like a ... a weapon, a blunt object. Her eyes widened. *But it's true*, she thought. *And he did ask, how do you feel?* She hoped very much that the therapist, Leigh Fermor, would not say something about anger being a normal part of the grief process, now that she and Gerry had gone through the litany of awful events which had brought them there. 'And,' she added, 'I feel scared.'

'You feel scared, as well as angry,' said Leigh, and Susanna relaxed a little. She liked his even voice, and his way of repeating things so temperately. She'd been impressed, too, that he'd responded so quickly to the phone message she'd left on the weekend, once she found his number on Doctor Gillian's note, and by the way he'd offered calmly to see her and Gerry as soon as possible, even after-hours. So here they were, just a few evenings after the hideous row, telling their worst secrets to a stranger. Yet there was something about this stranger – a man around her own age, with a squarish face and large wide-open hazel eyes – that seemed familiar. *It's the way he looks at us*, she realised. The same way an artist looks at someone, or something, they were drawing: observant, but neutral. A kind of measuring curiousity.

'Yes,' she said. 'I'm angry at all I've lost, and scared I'm going to lose more. If I lose my marriage too, I'm scared I – I'll be —'

'You're *not* going to lose your marriage,' said Gerry forcefully. 'I don't know why you'd even think that. I have never once considered ending our marriage.'

Leigh's calm observant eyes turned to him. 'Gerry, you don't feel that your relationship with Susanna is threatened by your affairs.'

'Not *affairs*,' said Gerry, waving the word away. 'That makes 'em sound more important than they were. Just little adventures.' He was sitting at one end of the dark-brown leather couch, she at the other, while the therapist was on the other side of a low table, in an armchair. 'No, they're not a threat. They weren't before Susanna knew about them, and they're not now.'

'But you've *lied* to me,' Susanna said, swinging around to accuse him. 'As *well* as screwing all these other women, you've been lying to me, for years. I still don't know how many years. Don't you see what that means?'

Gerry looked away from her, around the room.

Leigh wrote a few words on his notepad. 'Gerry, can I ask you about when you first met Susanna,' he said in his mild way. 'What was important and unique to you about her? What were your expectations of the relationship?'

'Well, I knew she'd be a lot different to the woman I was with before, that's for sure! Justine.' Gerry gave a small scornful grunt. 'Justine was gorgeous, but completely unreliable. After the bust-up with her, I realised I didn't need to marry somebody who was brilliant, or ambitious, or glamorous. I realised what I really wanted was a *family*. You need to understand,' he said, leaning forward to emphasise the seriousness of his point, 'I was really keen to have kids. People never think about a bloke wanting to have kids, but I did. That was me.'

'You were ready to marry and start a family,' said Leigh, 'with the right partner.'

'Absolutely.' Gerry nodded emphatic confirmation. 'After the fiasco with Justine, I decided to look for someone who wasn't so, you know, so full of themselves. Someone who, ah . . . I probably shouldn't say this, but someone who didn't have as many options.'

There was a small silence.

'Someone who'd be eternally grateful for your approval,' said Susanna, with acid in her voice.

'Don't take this the wrong way, Susanna, *please.*'

'I kept asking myself back then, why is this incredible guy interested in *me*? Now I get it.'

'You're deliberately misunderstanding me. I chose you because of who *you* are, specifically.'

'Safe. Plain.'

'Why do you always put yourself down like that, Suze? You're better looking than you think. It's part of her family's mythology,' he told Leigh. 'Her younger sister's the pretty one, so Susanna's always seen herself as the plain one – which is bullshit. The important thing is, we *both* made the right choice. Careers, good marriage, two great kids. Up until the accident, everything was fine.'

'Everything was fine,' repeated Susanna. There was something about Leigh Fermor's presence, she realised, that allowed her to question Gerry's assertions in a way she hadn't done in years. Perhaps ever. 'Wait a second. Our son was in despair over his sexuality, which we had no idea about, and you had a whole secret sex life going on, which *I* certainly had no idea about.'

'Well, you only have to look at who Seb chose to come out to, don't you, to see who *he* thought had some understanding of him.'

Susanna stared at him, suddenly confused. 'What?'

'You're saying that . . . there's a particular reason your son Seb first came out to you, Gerry, rather than to Susanna?' the therapist asked.

'Pretty obvious, isn't it? I mean, coming out's a big deal, and Seb did it with the parent he feels closer to. I've always gone that extra mile with the kids, right from the time they were born, no matter how busy I was.'

'And you're saying I *didn't*?' Susanna was shocked. 'Wait a second. First you say everything was fine and you approved of me, now —'

'I'm just saying that on a personal level, I was more engaged. As a parent.'

'You've been a wonderful father, Gerry, no one would ever deny that. But you know, sometimes I used to listen to you laughing and playing with the kids while I was busy cooking and cleaning and getting things ready for the next day, and I used to envy you. I remember thinking, he does what he *wants* to do, and I do what *has* to be done.'

'Oh,' said Gerry, raising his eyebrows coolly. 'Envy me, huh? Now the truth's coming out. Maybe this *is* all about resentment of males. Because let's face it, Suze, since the accident you've hardly been there for Seb at all.'

'That's not true!' she cried. 'Are you trying to say that because I've been going to see Stella-Jean every day, I haven't —'

'But you don't go in there just to be with Stella, do you? What about those ghastly drawings you've been doing?' Gerry turned to the therapist with a troubled expression. 'The fact is, Leigh, that Susanna's had a breakdown,' he said in a sad but authoritative tone. 'It's totally understandable, of course. But that's why we're here.'

Susanna felt like she'd been slapped. What had happened to the admission her husband had made just a few days before? What had happened to *I love you, Suze*?

But Leigh Fermor looked as calm, as unfazed as ever. 'Gerry, you feel that the traumatic events your family has undergone have resulted in a breakdown of some kind for Susanna. That's what you're saying? And, Susanna, can I ask you now: what do *you* feel are the issues that have brought us here?'

He actually wants to know, Susanna realised, looking into Leigh's impartial, interested face. *And he hasn't talked about the grief process once.* She drew a deep breath. 'I want to know what's been going on. My husband has been lying to me about his sex life for years, maybe for as long as we've been married. When I first found out, it was just a day or two after the crash. My mother had just been killed; my kids were —' She stopped. *Don't cry*, she told herself. *Don't stop: go on.* 'And I tried to pretend that I could put it aside and just try and deal with – with everything else. But I can't. I need to *know*. I need to know what he's really been doing, and with whom, and *why*.'

She and the therapist had been holding each other's gaze while she spoke. Now, both turned to Gerry. His face was turned away, twisting his lower lip between thumb and forefinger as he stared out of the window.

'Gerry?' said Leigh mildly.

He moved restlessly in his seat, crossed his right ankle over his left knee, put the leg down again. 'Yes, I've had occasional adventures,' he said to Susanna. 'But I keep telling you, *they're not important*. What's important is our family. Can't you see that we have to stick together, at a time like this? Help each other, not tear each other down. How on earth do you think that sneaking off to this hidey-hole you've set up —' He broke off and turned to Leigh. 'She's gone and rented a studio, for god's sake. At a time like this, she's drawing these *comics*, full of gruesome, violent, man-hating images . . .' Gerry paused just long enough to draw a deep accusatory breath. 'And *then*, after she'd finally shown me these things the other night, she turned on me! Attacked me, physically!' He subsided, slowly shaking his head. 'I probably shouldn't say this but – Susanna's sick. I'm frightened for her, I really am.'

Leigh wrote in his notes for a minute or two. It struck Susanna as distantly amusing that, despite all their animosity, pain and protest she and Gerry both waited dutifully for the therapist's attention before continuing. Finally he rested his pen. 'Gerry, I'd like to talk about secrets, and privacy,' he said. 'Do you feel, for example, that your having sex with other women equates to Susanna not showing you her drawings?'

Gerry's expression said *yes*, but then he reconsidered. 'Well,' he said cautiously, 'not precisely, maybe. But the point is: yes, she keeps secrets too.'

'I know you don't approve of my drawings,' Susanna said, 'but, Gerry, they aren't an attack on you. They're . . . they're something I *have* to do.' She heard the note of pleading in her voice, and suddenly recognised how much she needed him to accept them, accept her creating them. *They come from my deepest, darkest place*, she cried out to him in her heart. *If you could hold my hand while I go there, while I come back, we could be all right.*

'Oh, and if you *have* to do something, then it's okay?' said Gerry with a corner of his upper lip curled. 'What if I *have* to screw someone, is that okay too?'

She slumped back in her chair, wounded. 'How can you be so crass?'

'Susanna; Gerry,' said Leigh, summoning their attention. Obediently, the two of them sat up straight on the couch. 'There's a couple of phrases I've heard each of you use, which I think it would be worth examining. I'd like to spend the time we have remaining in this session unpacking them.'

With lifted eyebrows, he asked for their agreement, and they gave it, nodding and settling. 'Susanna, you've talked about approval several times, or being approved of.' Leigh paused; she nodded again. 'It seems to be important. Can we talk about approval, and what it means to you?'

Gerry crossed his arms and leaned back, watching his wife closely.

'Approval . . .' she said hesitantly. 'Well, it – it underpins everything, doesn't it? How people get along . . . their values . . .'

'Approval is the underpinning, the foundation perhaps, of personal relationships,' said Leigh. 'That's how you see it, Susanna?'

'Well, yes,' she said. *Isn't it obvious?* She tilted her head as she asked the therapist silently for confirmation. 'It's one of the first things you learn, as a child. My mother approved of what I did when I was good, and that's how I learned to be good.'

'So being good, and therefore approved of, is very important?'

'Of course! And I *have* – I've been a good wife, a good mother, good daughter, good sister. And a good teacher. Or at least, I've tried to be.'

With gentle gravity, Leigh asked, 'Can you tell me what a relationship would be like, in which approval didn't matter?'

Susanna looked taken aback. 'Well, it wouldn't be much of a relationship, would it? If you don't care whether someone approves of you, then it means you don't care much about *them*.' This seemed so self-evident, she wondered if perhaps it was a trick question. 'How else would people show their . . . love?'

A little silence stood in the room, waiting, and Susanna saw that Leigh was about to suggest another possibility.

'Can you imagine a loving relationship in which approval was not a prerequisite?' he asked.

She wanted to say yes, because she had the sense that was the better answer. *The answer he would approve of*, she realised. Slowly, she shook her head. 'No,' she said. 'Not for me. I – need it . . . too much.'

Leigh smiled, without judgement or demand. Susanna glanced quickly at Gerry, and was surprised to see the interest and – was it concern? – in his face, his eyes. Softly, into the fecund silence, she said, 'I needed Mum's approval like I needed air, or food. I've grown up assuming it was as necessary as . . . love. Or that it *is* love.'

Gerry gave a murmur of satisfaction. 'That's right,' he said. 'You know, Suze, I probably shouldn't say this but —'

'Stop!' Leigh exclaimed, holding up one hand. Gerry stopped. 'Susanna, thank you. I know you'll think about this, and we'll come back to it in our next session. And Gerry, thank you, too, because you've just presented us with the phrase of yours which I felt it would be worthwhile to examine.'

Gerry looked at him questioningly.

'"I probably shouldn't say this, but",' quoted Leigh. 'What's the significance of that phrase, to you? What are you thinking about when you say it?'

'Well, uh . . .' Gerry thought about it now. 'I guess it signifies that I'm about to say something particularly truthful, and honest.'

'And why do you preface it by saying that you probably shouldn't say it?'

'Because people don't like to hear the truth, do they? For the most part, they don't like honesty.'

'Why do you think people might not like to hear the honest thing you're about to say?'

Gerry chuckled. 'Because they don't like to get their precious feelings hurt.'

With a kind of forensic delicacy, Leigh asked, 'Are people's feelings really precious, Gerry?'

'They are if they're mine,' he shot back, adding a short hearty laugh. 'Joke!' He sat back again, knees confidently apart, arms relaxed. 'Look, everybody's feelings get hurt sometimes. It's all just part of the cut and thrust of life.'

'So when you say something you know may hurt the other person's feelings, you see that as being just an everyday comment?'

'Sure. Everybody does it.'

'Do you think Susanna says things, knowing they may hurt another's feelings?'

Husband and wife looked assessingly at each other, and then Gerry gave a dismissive shrug. 'No. Susanna's too concerned with being *good*,' he said, giving the word a derisive emphasis.

'And you're not?'

'Look, I'm a bloke, and a competitive sort of bloke. I play to win. Susanna doesn't.'

Leigh rested his forehead on his steepled fingers for a few moments, then took his hands away. 'And what if she did? What if there was, say, one issue, that Susanna played to win? That she was *determined* to win?'

Susanna watched as the skin around the corners of Gerry's mouth tightened. 'Then she wouldn't be the Susanna I married. She wouldn't be the Susanna I know.'

But if you don't know me, then who does? She felt a lurch of fear, as though an unimaginably deep and wide chasm had suddenly opened up in the earth before her, and she was looking across it. *If I'm not the person you married, who have I become? If I am not your wife, who am I?*

'Well, that was really interesting,' Gerry was saying with enthusiasm as they walked back toward the car. 'I reckon he —'

'*Sh, sh!*' said Susanna fiercely.

Gerry hated being shushed. Scowling, he swung his head toward his wife and saw that she'd stopped in her tracks, her mobile phone to her ear. Gerry halted abruptly too, reaching for his own phone which, like hers, had been turned off, at Leigh's request, during the session. Then Susanna jerked as though a bolt of electricity had shot through her.

'She's woken up!' she yelled, and started running for the car. '*She's woken up.*'

THIRTY-THREE

Susanna watched her sister standing, absorbed, before each of the three watercolours hanging in a neat row on their mother's living room wall, and felt ashamed that for years she'd barely glanced at their father's landscapes. At heart, indeed, she'd been dismissive of them because they weren't . . . very good. *As if that matters*, she thought now.

'It'll be ten years, this November,' Angie said, touching her fingertips softly to the spidery signature: *Neville Greenfield*. 'The sixteenth.'

'Yes.'

'Mum always blamed me for Dad's death. Even though he'd had that heart condition since he was a kid, she still blamed me.'

'I know,' Susanna said quietly, instead of denying, or defending, or changing the subject, and her sister shot a surprised glance over her shoulder. 'It wasn't fair.'

'You didn't, though. I knew you didn't,' Angie said, her face softer.

Susanna gestured at the row of paintings. 'You must have them,' she said.

'Not all of them,' protested Angie. 'You take one, at least.'

'No, keep them together. It's right.'

'Well, you have the portrait,' Angie said, going over to the painting of the two of them. 'It's so special.'

'How about we share: I'll have it for a year, then you?'

Angie agreed, and they moved over to the pile of flattened cardboard boxes. 'And keep an eye out for anything else you'd like as we pack,' Susanna added. 'I really appreciate you helping me do this, Ange. I just couldn't face . . .'

'Packing all this up on your own? No, of course not.' Angie began assembling boxes, one after another. 'You just tell me where to start, 'cause I don't know. I've only been here a couple of times.'

'Start with the books, maybe?' Susanna suggested, as she taped one end of each box. *She's only been here a couple of times*, she thought wonderingly. Jean's unit had been like Susanna's second home, and she was struggling to come to terms with the fact that soon it would be sold, and she would never be able to come here again.

Angie, kneeling by the bookcase, asked, 'How are you feeling about selling this place?' and Susanna started. It was as though her sister had read her mind.

'Oh . . . not great, to tell the truth. But we have to.'

Angie settled a batch of books into the box and paused, her forearms resting on its edge. 'I hope this doesn't sound mercenary, Susu, but – I am *so* looking forward to paying off my mortgage. That is going to be such a huge weight off my back.'

'That's what you're going to do with your share? That's *great*, Ange.'

Angie gave a brief laugh. 'Look at you, so relieved. You thought I was going to give it all to Faith Rise, didn't you?'

'I — oh, not really, I hadn't . . .'

'Well, I am going to make a donation, but not a big one. The mortage is where most of it's going.' Angie smiled ruefully. 'It's what Mum would've wanted, isn't it? Finally, I'm doing *something* that Mum would have approved of.'

Approved, Susanna thought. 'Do it for yourself, Ange. Because it's what *you* want.'

'I am. What about you, what are you going to do with your half?'

'Maybe renovate our place,' Susanna said, keeping her eyes on the cups she was wrapping. 'Put on a second storey. That's, um . . . that's what Gerry wants to do.'

Angie, watching her, asked, 'You don't?'

Susanna shrugged. 'I'm, ah – I'm not sure. I don't know that it's a great idea to put in stairs, you know, with Stella-Jean. How is she going to handle them? But she *is* progressing amazingly, so maybe it won't be an issue . . .'

Angie was nodding. 'Finn's so happy she's coming home. He doesn't say much, but he's missed her terribly.'

'She's missed him, too.' Susanna kept packing the contents of Jean's china cabinet, uncomfortably aware that she was being evasive. She had never told her sister that it was Stella-Jean who had raised concerns about Gabriel and Finn. *All the things I don't talk about*, Susanna thought. *Even now.*

The sisters worked steadily for a couple of hours, making good progress. Everything was so orderly; Jean had left no messy drawers, no broken items tucked away in cupboards. Susanna tried to be tough with herself and keep only the minimum: the photograph albums, of course, a few boxes of books and treasured knick-knacks like the old tea caddy with the paintings of camellia blossoms painted on the sides. A few items of furniture were going to her house: Stella-Jean had asked for the floral couch, Gerry the pair of wooden bookcases, and he'd also suggested the walnut cabinet for Seb's trophies. Everything else, including kitchenware and clothing, right down to the pegs in the peg-basket, would be collected by a charity Leonard Styles was involved with, helping to resettle refugees who had arrived with nothing. *Mum would have approved*, Susanna thought, and smiled wryly. What significance that word possessed for her now, ever since that first session with Leigh Fermor —

And still Gerry won't tell me when he started fucking around. The thought crashed into her mind like a rock – or a duralex glass – through a window. *Right from the beginning? I still don't know.* She stood, frozen, in her mother's bedroom, a pair of Jean's slacks half-folded in her hands, possessed again by the shock and anger of those unfolding revelations of Gerry's betrayal. She saw herself spitting denial at Angie in the cafe in Degraves Street, just hours before the crash; the fear and confusion when no one had been able to reach him in New York; saw herself opening that green bag, jumping back in fright from the buzzing cock ring. *Naïve fool!* Hurling that glass through the window in a blind rage at Gerry's stupid, stupid lies; the harsh rasp of her voice when she said 'I'm angry' to Leigh Fermor. *Angie doesn't know about any of this. Nothing. I'm still pretending I've got the perfect marriage.*

It hit her that if she wanted to hear the truth – from Gerry, Angie, her kids, anyone – then she'd have to get a lot better at telling it. She'd been trying to, but . . . Susanna dropped the clothes she'd been folding and walked quickly toward the kitchen, where Angie was working. But Angie had stood up from the box she was filling and was already walking toward her.

'Angie —' she said, just as her sister was saying 'Suse —', with equal urgency, then they both smiled and Angie said, 'You go first.'

Not letting herself pause, Susanna said, 'Ange, you were right. About seeing Gerry in that hotel in Sydney, with another woman – you were right.'

'I knew it,' Angie gasped. 'Oh, Susanna. Who is she?'

'He says she's not anyone special. That's the thing. He's been playing around for years, he still won't say how long. Maybe the whole time we've been married.'

Angie clapped a hand to her mouth. Her eyes above it were very round. Then she stepped forward and put her arms around Susanna. 'I'm so sorry, Susu. I'm so sorry.'

With the hug, Susanna very nearly lost it. A noise, something between a moan and a whimper, sounded in her throat, but she kept her lips clamped tight, fighting for control. 'So,' she said at last. 'There it is.'

'What's going to happen?' Angie asked, without a trace of righteous triumph.

'I don't know.' Susanna shook her head. 'We're seeing a counsellor. I've only told one other person, the woman who runs the art studio, and now you know too. I suddenly felt like I was being such a hypocrite, not telling you. Anyway. What were you just about to tell me?'

Angie closed her eyes for a moment, gathering herself. 'I was about to tell you that *you* were right, too.'

'What do you mean?'

'There's something not right about how Gabriel treats Finn. The discipline is – oh, I *know* Finn's behaviour is so much better, everyone can see that, but . . . I keep wondering, why *did* he run away that day? Was it really just that he was missing Stella? It's true: he's scared. And he won't tell me why.'

That's exactly what Stella-Jean said, Susanna thought.

Angie pressed her lips together tightly, and sighed. 'I don't — I haven't said anything, but I don't leave him alone with Gabriel any more.'

Susanna nodded, several times. 'I think that's wise,' she said.

Angie caught her hand. 'Have I – Susu, have I been a bad mother?' she pleaded.

'No! Angie, sweetheart, you've been a wonderful mother.' It was Susanna now who hugged her sister. 'You've done the best you could, always. We can't ask more of ourselves than that, can we?'

'Mum thought I was a bad mother,' said Angie, starting to sob.

Tears came into Susanna's eyes as well. 'Never mind,' she murmured, rocking Angie gently. 'I know how much you love him, Ange.' She wished she could say that their mother's approval didn't matter, but in truth, she knew all too well how much it did.

Leonard Styles had invited them to lunch, and as they walked through the quiet retirement village, Susanna described him to her sister, who couldn't remember meeting him at Jean's funeral. He had been, she said, their mother's . . . she hesitated over the appropriate word. *Beau*, she chose in the end, and Angie repeated it, with a tiny chuckle. He welcomed them warmly into his unit, which was just as Susanna had expected: lots of books, a functional masculine simplicity.

After they had eaten and the table was cleared, Leonard produced a manila folder and sat leaning forward a little with his hands clasped on top of it, looking very much the former magistrate. Susanna, sitting beside her sister on the opposite side of the table, had a sudden image of movie scenes in which a will is read. *Was there a second will? Did Mum change her mind and not leave half her estate to Angie?* Instantly, she knew that if that was the case, she would defy her mother's wishes and split the proceeds of the sale with her sister. *And I don't care if Mum would've approved or not!*

'Susanna,' said Leonard solemnly, and she braced herself, 'do you recall showing me, not long after your mother's death, a notebook in which she had been writing?'

'Yes, I do,' Susanna said. 'All in shorthand.'

'I offered to get it transcribed. I do apologise that it's taken rather longer than I'd anticipated.'

Susanna made a gesture to say it didn't matter. 'I'd completely forgotten about it,' she said quickly, which was true.

'My former secretary, Mrs Henderson, has kindly transcribed the entire notebook. I have it all here.' He tapped the folder, then opened it and drew out several pages. 'This, however, appears to be the final draft of what Jean was writing. It's a letter. Even though the letter addresses itself to one of you, you will see that it concerns you both. Such was my certainty that you would want to read it together, I have taken the liberty of making two copies.'

He separated the sheets he was holding and, with a tiny bow, handed two pages to each of them simultaneously. 'I'll just be in my garden,' he murmured, rising, and left them.

The sisters looked at each other wonderingly, and Susanna lifted open palms: *I've no idea.* They both began to read. At one point Angie exclaimed, 'Oh!' and her hand flew to her mouth; Susanna reached for her sister's other hand and clasped it momentarily. Then they read on together, silently.

Dear Angie —

I am writing this letter with all the humility that I, a woman not practiced in humility, can muster. I only hope that whatever you make of it, you will read it through to the end.

I have been thinking a great deal about what has happened in our family over the years. I have found much to examine. It has not been easy. I always thought I'd wanted my daughters to be good, and thus to have a good life – good, that is, according to my terms. I suspect now that what I really wanted was for my daughters to be like me.

What a simple and terrible demand that is: 'Be like me!' Foolishly, fearfully, we demand it of our children in the vain hope that if they are sufficiently like us, then we will somehow cheat death.

I lacked the wisdom to see that being not-like-me did not mean being bad. Your father tried to make me understand this but I refused to see it. You insisted on being yourself, Angie, and I punished you for it. In the name of responsibility and duty, I punished you by withholding my affection, my approval, my love. Susanna I rewarded with all those things, but I see that this was a false reward. I never asked myself, "Who is Susie, really? What does she need?" And when she stubbornly continued to love you, never once colluding in my campaign against you, I resented that. How I wish now that I'd had the grace to learn from her, then.

All I can do now, Angie, is to say I am sorry. I have been a selfish, self-righteous woman, too proud to see my faults. I've been an inadequate mother, and now I am fearful that you will reject my apology, and me, as you would indeed be justified in doing. You are angry with me, rightly. Nevertheless, I do apologise, and ask for your forgiveness.

I will ask your sister's forgiveness too. You were right; I pushed her toward becoming a teacher, wanting her to choose those things I prize so highly: respectability and security, not the riskier path of creativity. And in my treatment of you, I also threatened her with what could happen if she chose to tread a different path. I threatened, implicitly, that I would withdraw my love. Is there a worse threat any parent can make?

I take solace in one thing: that you and Susanna have each other. The love you share — and I can take no credit for it — is a gift that will sustain you all your lives.

Gandhi said that forgiveness is choosing to live. Angie, please, when you are ready: can you forgive me?

With love, finally,
your mother

THIRTY-FOUR

Rory was engrossed in the window display of the shop they'd stopped in front of, but Seb was more interested in what he saw reflected in the glass itself. 'Look at those two,' he said, nudging her in the side without letting go of her hand. 'Pretty convincing, huh?'

She shifted focus to their reflection. 'Absolutely,' she agreed. Watching the happy teenage sweethearts from the corner of her eye, Aurora Feng rose on to the balls of her long ballet dancer's feet to plant a kiss on the side of Sebastian Visser's open, tanned face. 'Young love.'

They regarded themselves for a few seconds more, then Year Twelve's most devoted item strolled on through the busy shopping mall. 'You sure you want to keep this ball in play, Rors?' asked Seb. 'You could have a real . . . you know, something real happening. You could have anyone you want!'

'Will you cut it out, Visser? I've told you, I'm not looking. This is the Plan, and as far as I'm concerned, it's working perfectly. Anything changes, I'll let you know.'

'Okay.' They stopped to look in another window. 'Um, you know . . . Andrew reckons it's the smart thing to do too,' Seb said. 'He totally agrees, it'll be much, much easier for me to come out once I'm at uni, or at least once I'm not at school.'

'See? Mr Andrew's got his brain in gear, too. You have good taste.

And, Seb, seriously: those mid-semester results *prove* it's working, yeah? Study-wise, we da bomb!'

'Rors. If I hadn't been working with you I would've failed everything.'

'That's just crazy talk,' she said briskly. 'Besides, Visser, I like hanging out with you. Especially now we're being straight with each other.'

'I don't know that "being *straight* with each other" is exactly . . .'

'Oh, that is *so* lame,' she said, giving his shoulder – his good shoulder – a biff. 'So tell me, what's happening with Mr Andrew?' she asked with a suggestive gleam. 'We getting any of that hot ambo action yet, huh?'

'I *wish*!' Seb showed gritted teeth, exaggerating – or perhaps not – his frustration. 'I should never have told him about the thing with the pills, it totally freaked him out. He's been like, whoa! we're not rushing anything; you have to be totally a zillion per cent together. Nearly four weeks of just *talking*, not even a —' He made a kissy mouth.

'Well, what do you expect? The thing with the pills totally freaked *me* out, too. I know, I know,' Rory held one hand up as he started to protest. 'You didn't actually take any. But you were *there*, right on the freaking edge and you hadn't told *any*body. You reckon Andrew wants to jump in at the deep end with some, like, suicidal teenager? I don't think so.'

'Gee, Rors, that's a bit rough,' said Seb, pretending to be offended. 'Actually, I think I've got him convinced I'm not a nut case. He's got next weekend off and he's kind of asked me down to Venus Bay with him.'

'To, like, stay?' Rory was alight with curiosity. 'Overnight?'

'Yup, I gather that's the plan. Some friends of his live down there.'

'Ooh-ah!' she leered, and then pulled up, frowning. 'Wait up – isn't your sister coming home from hospital next weekend?'

'Nuh-uh. Week after. They're keeping her in for a few more tests or something. Or else she's just piking.'

'Your sister is *so* not a piker. So, your folks cool with you going to Venus Bay?'

'My folks?' Seb looked puzzled. 'Why would they have a problem with it? I haven't even told them yet; it's just a weekend.'

'He-llo? This is with *Andrew*. Your brand-new potentially first *boy*friend. You can't not tell 'em, not after what they've been through. Specially your mum.'

'I dunno . . .' said Seb, looking uncomfortable. 'Um, look, there's something else: they're not having such a great time right now. They're seeing a, like, a marriage counsellor guy. I mean, it's all super-nice and civilised and stuff, at least when I'm around, but . . . you know. I don't wanna . . .'

Rory shook her head. 'All the more reason your mum needs to know, and *not* two minutes before you head off. Trust me here.' When Seb continued to look doubtful she asked, arching her eyebrows, 'Have I been wrong before?'

'No,' said Seb, with an only slightly reluctant smile. 'Feng the Infallible. Okay – I'll tell 'em.'

His mother was standing down by the lemon tree in the backyard, staring off into the distance. Seb walked right up to her and she still hadn't noticed him. 'Hey, Ma,' he said and she jumped like he'd yelled *Boo!*

'Oh! Seb!'

'Yep, that's me. Your son.'

She gave him a kiss on the cheek. 'Sorry, darling, I was miles away. What are you up to?'

'Talking to you, right now.'

'I got *that*, smarty. You know what I mean.'

'Actually, I just wanted to let you know I'm going away for the weekend, with Andrew.'

To his surprise, her face changed completely, swept by a sudden fright that made her look weirdly like someone you saw on the TV news, or maybe a movie: someone who'd been ambushed. 'With Andrew? What – where to?'

'Ah, Venus Bay? Some friends of his have got a place down there.'

'No – no. Seb, really, I don't think you should,' she said in a panicky voice.

'Don't worry, Ma, it's just a weekend. We'll be back Sunday. It's not far.'

'That's not the *point*. What about —' she looked around wildly, as though enemies might be coming over the back fence, '— and anyway, you hardly *know* Andrew.'

'I've known him for a couple of months now. And this is how I get to know him better,' Seb said, not unreasonably. Thinking she must be freaked out about the car thing, he added, 'He's got a really safe car, he's a really good driver. He's an *ambo*!'

Susanna shook this assurance off, and started pulling lemons off the tree like she was angry with them. Suddenly she swung around to him. 'What about Aurora? You go off with someone else and you just *dump* her? I thought you —' She looked like she was going to cry. Seb was stunned. 'What has *she* ever done, might I ask, to deserve being treated like this?'

'Whoa, Mum. Whoa,' he said. There was no point trying to figure out what was going on; instead, Seb took a large, swift step forward and wrapped his arms round his mother, rocking her a little as he hugged. At first she held her arms stiffly to her sides, with a couple of lemons clenched in each hand, and then she started to relax. 'Rory's my best friend,' he said to the top of her head. 'Seriously. She knows about me, she knows about Andrew, she knows about us going away for the weekend. She was the one who told me I should tell *you*.'

'Oh,' Susanna said. Seb could tell she'd changed gears, but he kept hugging her. 'It's just — I'm okay,' she said, and he carefully released her. 'It's just that . . . Seb, you have to be careful of people's feelings. Sometimes men aren't.'

Seb had a pretty strong suspicion this wasn't about him, but he had zero desire to find out any more. 'I am, Mum. Careful. I try to be.'

She handed him the lemons and they began walking up the path toward the house together. 'And besides,' she said suddenly, 'Andrew's a *lot* older than you. What, seven years? I think that's too big an age difference, when you've only just turned eighteen. Oh, wait a minute, I want to get some rosemary,' she added distractedly, detouring to the herb bed where she plucked a few pungent sprigs, then some thyme, and mint, while Seb stood patiently by.

'Dad's *eight* years older than you,' he pointed out.

'But I wasn't eighteen when I met him, I was twenty-three. There's a very big difference, darling. And there's something else: the fact that Andrew is the paramedic who got you out of the car that night – I think that makes you . . . vulnerable.' Her forehead was crinkled with concern. 'I really don't think you should be going away for the weekend with him. I am not happy about this.'

'Is it because he's a guy? Is it because – I'm gay?' Seb didn't much like the way that sounded: defiant, a bit childish. But how else could he say it?

'No, it is *not!*' his mother shot back. And then her face clouded. 'I worry for you. I just want you to be happy, and I worry that it'll be harder for you to be happy if you're . . . gay.'

'Ma,' he said gently. 'It was gonna be *impossible* for me to be happy otherwise.'

'Yes,' Susanna said slowly. 'Yes, we both understand that, your dad and I. As long as you're happy,' she repeated, and Seb had a little memory flash of Clarence commenting that Australian parents said that all the time, and Chinese parents never did. Clarence: he'd hardly thought about him in weeks. 'Has anyone said anything at school?' his mum asked, and he explained Rory's strategy of continuing to hang out, supporting each other socially and deflecting complications. Susanna asked more questions; she was looking a lot less worried. *Infallible Feng strikes again*, thought Seb, impressed.

In the kitchen, he dropped the lemons into the blue ceramic fruit bowl on the table. Susanna put the herbs on the wooden chopping board and got a leg of lamb out of the fridge. 'And about the age thing,' he went on, 'it's not like Andrew's *forty* or something. He's not, you know, trying to pull some kind of power trip on me. Andrew's totally not that kind of person.' And then, again verging on defiance, 'And I *am* going away with him for the weekend!'

'Okay, I think I get that,' Susanna said, rubbing the lamb with olive oil and rosemary and a few pinches of salt. 'So – what would be the chances of having Andrew over here, say, for dinner? *Before* you go away with him?'

'Like tonight?' said Seb, eyeing the leg of lamb. 'He's not rostered on till later.'

'I think tonight would be perfect. Your dad's going to be home soon, he's just in at the hospital going over Stella-Jean's home program with the team.'

'Oh, wow,' Seb said. 'I can't wait to have my adorable little sister back home.'

Susanna frowned. 'Are you being sarcastic? I can't tell.'

'You know what? Neither can I.'

'It'll be a while till she's giving *you* what for again, anyway.' She hefted the leg of lamb into a baking dish. 'Now, why don't you go and give Andrew a ring? Ask him if he's any good at making gravy.'

'Thanks, Ma.' He'd come to stand very close to her, and she glanced up inquiringly, sensing he wanted to say something more. 'He's a really, really nice guy; he's really *sane*. You don't have to worry, Mum.'

They gazed at each other, a long and fond moment of exchange. 'Mothers always worry, darling,' she told him. 'It's part of the job description.'

Gerry was enormously pleased to have someone, outside the hospital, whose eyes didn't glaze over the moment he mentioned Functional

Independence Measures and Clinical Outcomes Variable Scales, even by their acronyms. He and Andrew discussed these and other methods of assessing the extent of TBI (Traumatic Brain Injury) in depth throughout the meal. Gerry was also pleased to discover that Andrew knew exactly what Seb's latest scores were on the SPDI (Shoulder Pain and Disability Index), and that he was clearly knowledgeable about the most effective rehabilitation practices.

'Very impressive, Andrew,' he said, sitting back, finally sated with information. 'I had no idea that a paramedic's training involved all this.'

'It doesn't, really,' said Andrew in his easy, unfussed way. 'More that a cycling mate of mine got hit by a car a couple of years ago, and we've formed a rehab team, working with him. You get pretty involved. I have, anyhow.'

Gerry nodded several times, looking at Andrew thoughtfully. 'Good for you,' he said. 'That's great to hear.'

When Andrew was out of the room, Seb said, 'You like him. Don't you?'

'I do, I do. He's smart, he's focused, he's knowledgeable. I reckon he's just the bloke to get you motivated again, young Sebbie.' Gerry grinned. 'I'll put money on him having you back on the courts inside a month.'

Wordlessly, Seb asked his mother's opinion. She'd been listening to Gerry; now she gave a little half-smiling shrug, nodding several times, and then Andrew re-entered the room. 'Apricot tart?' she asked, rising.

When they were all eating dessert, she asked politely, 'So, Andrew: what made you decide to become an ambulance driver?'

'Well,' said Andrew, leaning forward, and Seb saw the wicked glimmer in his eye, behind the sober metal-framed glasses. 'I always wanted a job where I get to turn on a big loud siren and drive really fast through red lights. I thought about becoming a copper, but I didn't want to go through life with everybody hating me.'

For a moment Gerry and Susanna both stared at him, mouths-open, spoons half-raised – then Gerry gave a short shout of laughter, and they all cracked up.

'Sorry,' Andrew said, still completely straight-faced. 'That was my evil twin speaking.'

Susanna giggled. 'Could the non-evil twin tell us, then?' she said. 'Seriously.'

He nodded. 'Seriously, then: it was because of me brother. He has severe epileptic seizures, our Craig. They'd happen anywhere: school, shops, on the bus. They were pretty full-on; bit frightening for most folk, but when I was still a little feller I realised I had no problem dealing with 'em, whatsoever. One time we were on holidays in Majorca and Craig had a seizure while we were in the swimming pool. It was really early in the morning, just him and me, no one else around, and I was able to hold him up and get him to the side. I saved his life; I knew I had. Mum and Dad were that proud of me – I liked that.'

'Wow!' said Seb. 'How old were you?'

'Eight or nine.'

'I'd have been proud of you too,' said Susanna. 'So you decided saving people's lives was your . . . vocation, when you were only eight or nine?'

'Aye. Joined the St John's Ambulance Brigade: cute little junior cadet, I was. Long way from that to being a qualified ambulance paramedic, though.'

'And when *did* you qualify?'

'A year and a half ago. Still the cute little junior on our team,' Andrew said, with a big cheesy grin.

By the end of the meal, Seb had the distinct impression they would *all* like to go away for the weekend with Andrew.

They drove down the highway with the Cat Empire's first CD blasting out of the sound system, singing their heads off to 'How to Explain?'. When they got to the bit about having all the pairs – of hands for

climbing, knees to spring, balls for strength and lungs to sing – Seb
stretched out in the passenger seat giving double air-punches to the
sky, and as they rounded the corner of the South Gippsland Highway
at Kilcunda and got that first stunning view of the mighty ocean,
they were bellowing, *'Music is the language of us all!'* into the wind.

'You know what I was just thinking?' Seb said after they'd stopped
in Korumburra for a couple of pies and a milkshake, and were back
on the road, burping. 'I was thinking how weird it is that if it hadn't
been for the car crash I never would have met you. And that means
somehow that the accident wasn't a totally terrible thing. I mean it
was, obviously it was. My grandma got killed and my sister nearly
did too. But here I am, on the way to Venus Bay on a sunny day, and
I'm with you and I am so fucking *happy!*'

'That's good,' said Andrew in his might-be-ironic way.

'*Rah!*' yelled Seb, a roar of joy. '*Raaaah!*' Suddenly he stopped. 'Is
it good? Or do you think it's weird?'

'It's good, and it's weird, and it's also true, but most of all it's bloody
fantastic.'

'Yeah! My auntie would probably say it was all part of god's plan
or something. I don't believe that stuff, or that things are "meant to
be", even, like some people say. But it's just —' Seb narrowed his eyes,
trying to sort it out '— it's just *amazing* how you can feel all these
radically different ways about one single thing that's happened. Or
one single person.'

'Ah, yes. Ordinary life, Marlon, in all its quivering complexity,'
said Andrew, and Seb turned the sound system back on. They let the
music fill the last part of their journey.

When they arrived at the Venus Bay house, a plain weekender
elevated among the ti-tree and banksia on a sandy, sloping block,
the half-dozen people on the deck of the house all turned to look,
then waved and yelled greetings. Seb felt a moment of awful shy-
ness. 'Oh, shit,' he muttered, but Andrew gave him an encouraging
wink and then they were walking up the steps and he was being

introduced. There was Johnny, the mate of Andrew's who'd had the cycling accident (Seb noticed the two crutch-like sticks he used for walking) and his boyfriend, plus his sister and her husband, who were the owners of the house, and another gay couple, and two German girls who'd been hitchhiking and been invited to join the party. It became apparent that Andrew had told his friends about Seb; they'd been looking forward to meeting him, and were curious, in a friendly way, to see what he was like, which he found simultaneously flattering and nerve-racking.

They drank a few beers, they talked; a few of them went for a walk on the beach with a black dog that barked madly at wheeling seagulls. Back at the house, a barbecue had been set up; they ate, drank a few more beers. Dusk fell, and an impromptu joke-telling competition sprang up, of which the German girls, unexpectedly, were the outright winners. A couple of joints went round. Johnny's sister played the ukelele and sang 'If You Like a Ukelele Lady' with a red hibiscus tucked behind one ear and a winsome smile, and then accompanied her brother who sang 'Dream a Little Dream of Me' with cheesy vocal flourishes. Then Andrew turned off all the lights but one, so that he was spotlit on the verandah, and produced a set of soft colourful juggling balls, adding to them one at a time till he was juggling six at once and everyone was cheering wildly.

Seb lay on his back on the grass and saw two shooting stars and thought he had never been happier in his life, until Andrew came over and hunkered down beside him and said, 'How are you doing there, Marlon?', and Seb grabbed him by the front of his shirt and pulled him down and they kissed and they kissed, and Seb knew that he was happier still than he had been just minutes before.

There was a small bungalow out the back of the house; that's where they were sleeping. 'Look at this,' said Andrew as he lit candles. 'The great romantic, me.'

Seb was lying back in jeans and a T-shirt, a little bit zonked but not too much, just gazing at the sculpted lines of Andrew's tall, lean body. 'Romantic's good,' he said dreamily. 'It's all good. Better than good.'

'Sebastian.' Andrew sat down on the edge of the bed, solemn-faced, the candlelight reflecting in the lenses of his glasses.

'Can you see me if you take them off?' Seb asked, lifting a hand toward the glasses.

'Sebastian,' said Andrew again, seriously, moving his head back out of range. 'Listen. I want you to understand: we don't have to do anything. We can just sleep. We don't have to —'

'Shut up,' Seb said. He pulled his T-shirt off, then leaned forward and tugged at Andrew's. Andrew drew in a quivering breath and took his shirt off. Seb lay his left hand flat, palm down, over the ridge of Andrew's collarbone and drew it down over his chest, evenly, over his nipples and ribs and stomach. 'Oh,' he murmured, 'fuck.' He did it again, this time twinning the long, slow touch with his right hand on his own chest. The sensation was dizzying, overwhelming; he had to close his eyes. It was like coming to a place he'd never been before and finding it utterly and beautifully familiar; like coming home. He took Andrew's hand and laid it over his own crotch, pressed it down.

The sound of music came from the house. Were they singing, in there? It sounded fresh, and wonderful, like people who didn't have a care in the world.

'Do you hear that?' he asked Andrew.

'The music? I do.' Andrew took off his glasses.

'You see me?' Seb breathed.

'I see you.'

THIRTY-FIVE

Crazy shit, thought Stella-Jean as she lay in bed, waiting for the next lot of therapy – occupational, physical, speech, recreational, whatever was up next. How could she believe stuff had happened when she had absolutely no memory of it? How was she supposed to get her head around all the impossible things people had told her? *It's like being in one of those dodgem cars, trying to zoom around really fast while other cars keep crashing into you.* You were in a real car crash – *bang!* – and Jeejee got killed – *bang!* You weren't in Bali at all, you were in a coma for a month – *bang!* – and now you can't walk or talk properly – *bang! bang!* Oh, and by the way, while you were out to it, almost two hundred people got burnt to death, just outside of good old safe Melbourne, the city you've lived in all your life. *What?*

And the one thing she could remember apparently hadn't happened. Someone tried to drown Finn. *No they didn't, Finn's fine.* But he told me. *You told me, didn't you Finnster?* Finn shaking his head, *no, I never said anything.* Very, very weird. She was going to have to sort it out. Get up, get walking, get talking, and get to the bottom of what was going on. *And don't tell me it's just confusion because of the TBI,* Stella-Jean felt like yelling. Yes, her memory had holes in it and yes, bright light gave her a shocking headache and yes, when she tried to talk it was like there was a wet sock in her mouth, but Finn was lying and she *knew* something was badly wrong.

Seb was visiting. He watched her transfer herself laboriously into the wheelchair, then he walked slowly alongside her down the corridor, with his friend Andrew. Andrew the Ambo. They had a thing going on, she knew they did. Andrew was cute; she liked him.

The therapist had to help her get up out of the wheelchair and on to the walking machine. 'Come on, Stell,' Seb called from where he was leaning against the wall. 'You're supposed to be coming home this week. What, you expect us to carry you over the threshhold or something?'

'Shu' up,' Stella-Jean grunted. No *way* was she going to get carried in!

'You're doing really well, Stella-Jean, you're doing fantastic,' the physical therapist crooned. This was the nice therapist, who always said sweet, encouraging things. Bit drippy, actually. 'You're our brightest little star, you really are.'

'You'll never motivate her that way,' said Seb. 'Tell her she's pathetic, that'll get her going.'

I'm going to get off this thing and punch you in the nose, said Stella-Jean's look, and he beamed at her, delighted. She picked her feet up, working her kitten-weak leg muscles for all they were worth. *Just you wait.*

Cute Andrew just shook his head and smiled quietly to himself.

She swung her legs out of the car, gripped the handles of the walking frame and hauled herself up. Along, just a couple of metres: that seemed to take about five minutes. And now those three steps, up to the front porch. Mum was standing at the top, wanting so badly to help her up those stairs; Stella-Jean could feel the power of Susanna's want coming at her. She shot her mother a warning look, *Don't*, and saw her dad put his arm firmly around Mum's shoulders. Dad understood; good. In between each step, Stella-Jean leaned her weight onto the frame, breathing hard. *Three crappy little steps*, she thought. *You're not going to beat me.*

'Nice work, Stell,' her dad said casually when Stella-Jean made it to the front door, and she lifted her head and flashed her parents a grin of pure, naked triumph.

A few nights later, Susanna lay in bed picturing that grin. It was so like Gerry's own, and recognising how much of Gerry was in their daughter gave her heart. Having his driving will, his sense of purpose, would help Stella-Jean deal with all that lay ahead of her.

She was lying with her husband's sleeping arms close around her. It was becoming uncomfortable, but she was not yet ready to move from his embrace; she felt polite with him, and a little nervous, as though he were a stranger. *Making love to strangers* – she could hear that line, sung in a wistful male voice, but couldn't place the song. Except that she and Gerry weren't strangers; coming together again had been more like a meeting between old schoolfriends, someone you'd once been close to and weren't sure if you could be again. But they – their bodies – were becoming more familiar to each other each time.

It had been reading Jean's letter of forgiveness – a week ago? No, longer: almost two – that had made her see she must stop turning away from Gerry. What good would staying closed and angry do? Better, surely, to embark on that journey of forgiveness, as her mother had. She remembered Jean at the book group meeting saying, 'I don't know anything about forgiveness,' but she'd found a way. Susanna resolved to do the same, to find her way to forgiving Gerry and putting his betrayals behind them, but it wasn't easy. Even while they were in the midst of sex, even while, having put in maximum effort, she was coming, she felt self-conscious. Even though he called her his sweet little pigeon and said nice things about her body, part of her wanted to demand, *How do I compare to all those other women? Are they better in bed than me? What did you do with them, that we don't?*

And something else. *What are those toys like?* That little square catalogue Vinnie had dropped into her bag: Susanna had studied it, furtive and embarrassed, but increasingly curious. Do yourself a favour, Vinnie had said. *What if I were to order some of those things, myself?* She imagined Gerry's face if she were to reach under the pillow and produce her own buzzing vibrator one night. Wow! Or she could just put the catalogue on his pillow, that would open up the subject – but she felt too shy. *Good girls don't play with toys like that, is that it?* she asked herself.

Responsible, respectable. Yes, she'd earned her mother's approval. *I wanted it too*, Susanna thought. *I chose security.* And now more than ever, her family needed it. Anger and bitterness would tear her and Gerry apart, leave her – and her children – exposed and unprotected. Susanna had glimpsed the terrible chasm that lay down that road, and she was afraid. Crossing to the other side? Impossible! And even if, by some means, she managed the feat, who would she be then? Another dumpy middle-aged single woman with a precarious job, going out sometimes to concerts or galleries with other women like herself. Getting old alone, longing for her children's occasional duty calls.

She lay there listening to her husband's breathing, the regular, faint *pfh . . . pfh . . . pfh* of exhaled air pushing out his top lip. Susanna had always loved listening to that sound; she still did. In spite of everything. Needing, finally, to change position, she eased carefully out of Gerry's embrace. He muttered something in his sleep and rolled on to his other side, and, suppressing a sigh of relief, she flopped onto her back and crossed her arms loosely on the pillow above her head.

And what will happen when he goes to his next conference? Part of her wanted to assume that Gerry wouldn't do it again — 'do it' meaning, fuck other women. But she'd made too many assumptions in the past. Gerry had to say it, swear to it, himself. Why was it still so difficult to raise these subjects with him, except, to some extent, in the safe haven of Leigh's room? Very well then, she decided: that's where she would raise the question: at Leigh's, the next time they went for a counselling session. And she would demand an answer.

Sleep now, she told herself, *sleep*. Consciously relaxing all her muscles, from the toes all the way up her body, and trying to concentrate on just her breathing, Susanna invited sleep to come. But instead new images kept appearing in her brain: small things, apparently random. A branch of pink peach blossom, hanging broken from the tree; the bright beads of a necklace scattered on the ground; a child's blue sandal lying on its side by deep tyre tracks. A hand, curled in restfulness or death; another hand, reaching out to touch. *What is less or more than a touch?*

What a lovely phrase: where was that from? It seemed familiar. So did the images. Then she recognised them; she'd seen every one of them before, not in colour but in black and white. They were in her drawings; each one was a tiny detail from the graphic stories, the comics (she still didn't know what to call them). *Remember me*.

Paintings, Susanna realised. *I have to paint these, too.* It wasn't just an idea, more like an order, though where it came from – inside her brain, or outside – she couldn't tell.

Any notion of sleep had evaporated. She had to get this down, and now.

She slid from between the sheets without disturbing Gerry and padded down the hallway toward the kitchen. Her hand was on the light switch, about to flip it on, when she heard a noise, a tinking sound rather like a little bell, of something being moved. She stared, heart thumping, into the dark room, and gradually made out the shape of a person sitting at the kitchen table, faintly silhouetted against the big window. Susanna blinked.

'Stella-Jean?'

The person turned slightly toward her. 'Hi Mum. Don't turn it on.'

'Sweetheart, why are you sitting here in the dark?' Then Susanna remembered her daughter's sensitivity to light, one of the odd symptoms of the brain injury. She made her way across the kitchen, hands outstretched for the guiding touch of wall and bench, to sit at the table beside her daughter.

'It's not that dark,' Stella-Jean said.

It'th noh that dah. Her speech, though still thick and woolly, seemed much better already, her mother thought. Or was that just wishful thinking? As Susanna's eyes adjusted, she realised with surprise that it was not, indeed, that dark: the light coming in through the window enabled her to see fairly clearly. Stella-Jean's eyes might be light-sensitive, but perhaps everyone else's had been made lazy by electricity.

She looked around for Stella-Jean's walking aid, but couldn't see it. The *tink* sound came again: the clink of spoon against bowl. Had she got all the way here from her bedroom, made herself something to eat and brought it to the table, without help of any kind? So it seemed.

'What's that you're eating?' she asked.

Stella-Jean looked down into the bowl. 'Cornflakes,' she said, scooping a brimming spoonful into her mouth.

'Why are you eating breakfast at one o'clock in the morning?'

'I just felt like 'em. Mum, can I ask you something?'

'Yes, sweetheart, of course.'

'Weren't you going to talk to Auntie Ange about Finn? Ages ago, I mean, before the accident?'

'You remember that,' said Susanna, greatly excited. 'You see? That means you're recovering memories. That's a *very* positive sign.'

'Sure sure,' said Stella-Jean impatiently. 'But *did* you talk to her?'

'Yes, I did,' Susanna said, composing herself. This was the first time she had mentioned that conversation to anyone. 'It was just before the accident, actually. I, um – oh, I made out they were *my* observations, by the way, I didn't want her to be cross with you – I expressed my concerns to her about the things you'd told me, that Finn seemed scared of Gabriel, and so on.'

'And?'

'She didn't, ah, she didn't take it all that well. Which was to be expected, really, Stella-Jean.'

Reluctantly, Stella-Jean seemed to concede that.

'*But*,' Susanna went on. 'Angie and I had another conversation, just the other day, and she said she's come to some . . . Well, she told me she's been rethinking the situation re Finn and Gabriel.'

'Rethinking how?'

'Well, she's keeping a close eye on it. And, she doesn't leave Gabriel in charge of Finn any more.'

Stella-Jean nodded. 'Good. Now. Can Finn come here soon? Maybe stay over?'

Susanna decided to ignore all the uncertainties, responsibilities and complexities already pressing upon her. *Stella-Jean needs this.* 'Yes,' she said. 'Yes, he can stay over, next time Angie asks.'

'Or *I* could ask *her!*' said Stella-Jean eagerly. *Ah cou' arth her!*

'Could we just get you a little bit settled first, darling?' asked Susanna faintly. 'See how your rehab program's going, how tired you get?'

'Okay,' said Stella-Jean. Acquiescence! Amazing. Susanna leaned over and gave her a grateful kiss on the cheek, and then, to her mother's even greater surprise, Stella-Jean put her arms around her, hugging her tight.

'Thank you,' said Stella-Jean's muffled voice. 'You're a great mum.'

'Am I?' Susanna asked softly, her eyes prickling.

'You bet. The best.' They cuddled for a while, the longest time Susanna could remember since her daughter was a much, much littler girl. Then Stella-Jean wriggled a bit and they released each other. 'What did you come out here for anyway, Mumsie?' she asked.

'What did I come out here for?' wondered Susanna. 'Oh, I know! I had an idea. Gosh. Thanks for reminding me.' She got up and started fossicking in the drawer where paper and pens might be found. 'Do you mind if I turn the lamp on? Not the overhead light, just the side lamp.'

'I'll do it,' said Stella-Jean, levering herself from the chair and lurching the couple of steps to the side table and the lamp, which she flicked on. 'There!' she said with satisfaction. They sat together at the table again. 'So, what's this?' she asked.

'Just a tick, sweetie . . .' Susanna didn't look up for several minutes, hurriedly covering pages with sketches and scrawled words. *What is less or more than a touch?* she wrote along the top of one page, and drew a kind of banner around it. 'There!' she said, unconsciously echoing Stella-Jean. 'I think these are going to form part of my exhibition, along with — hmm. I haven't told you about the drawings I've been doing, have I?'

'I don't think so,' said Stella-Jean. 'Not that I remember, anyway.'

'Well . . . I wonder if it's time I did?' mused Susanna, looking at her daughter consideringly. 'Um – where did you get that gorgeous nightie, by the way?'

'It's not actually a nightie, it's the lining out of an old evening dress. Fab, huh? *So* good not to have to wear that crappy hospital stuff any more.'

'Beautiful,' said her mother. 'Well, these drawings. They're very, um – confronting, Stella-Jean; some people don't like them at all. I don't know that your – ah, that some adults would think you should even see them.'

'*Really?* Oh, cool!' Stella-Jean looked thrilled. Susanna told her something of how the drawings had come about, and what they contained, and described the unusual format she had chosen – or rather, as she felt it, that the stories themselves had demanded.

'But I still don't know what to call them,' she said. 'Comics sound too lightweight, somehow, and they're not actually a graphic novel. I thought of graphic short stories, but that's too cumbersome . . .' Suddenly her face lit up. 'Graphic narratives! That's what they are! Oh – is that a term already in use?'

'Doesn't matter. Graphic narratives sounds great,' said Stella-Jean. She pointed at the new drawings, lifting her eyebrows in inquiry. 'And these are . . . ?'

'These are selected details, from within the, um, narratives. I see these as small paintings' – Susanna held up her hands and shaped the size – 'acrylic on canvas, a textural contrast or counterpoint to the density of the black and white drawings. Like pools of colour or beacons of light. One small bright painting for each dark story.'

'This is pretty cool, Mum,' said Stella-Jean. 'Wow! You're an *artist*!'

Susanna's sudden delighted cackle surprised them both, and she covered her mouth for a moment, still smiling. 'Maybe,' she said.

'So, this is what you've been doing in this . . . studio?' asked Stella-Jean. 'Tell me about that.'

Susanna told her about Studio Lulu, reminding Stella-Jean of the opening party there, and described the little room she'd rented. 'But I've been thinking, perhaps I should let it go and work on these new paintings here at home. Because I won't have that much time, once I start teaching again, even if it's just part-time, and you're out of hospital now, and there are . . .' Susanna trailed off.

'No, 'cause I wanna get back to school, and you *need* that studio,' said Stella-Jean. It was remarkable how decisive she was able to sound, despite her woolly speech. 'If you're here, you'd be thinking all the time about me, and Seb and Dad, and the house, and dinner. You just *would*!'

'Mmm . . .' Susanna leaned on her crossed forearms and thought about it. 'You know me pretty darn well, don't you, sweetie?'

'Well, I know what it's like trying to make things,' said Stella-Jean. 'I know you need a proper space.'

Susanna sat back in her chair. 'The kitchen table will do.'

'It will *not*,' said Stella-Jean with considerable heat. 'Mu-um!'

'Oh, that was a quote. Years ago, when you were just a baby, I did a study of a Melbourne painter called Clarice Beckett. She died in 1935; I think she was in her thirties. She lived with her parents all her life, but even though they were well off – her father was a bank manager – and there was always at least one room in the house virtually unused, she never had her own studio. "The kitchen table will do", that's what her father used to say.'

'Huh. Well, not for *my* mum,' Stella-Jean declared. 'I wanna come and see you in your own proper studio. I wanna see these weird drawings! I wanna come to your *show*!'

'That's very sweet of you,' Susanna said, giving her another quick hug, and wondering what Stella-Jean would think of the 'weird drawings' once she'd actually seen them. 'And now, bedtime, my lovely girl. Do you need a hand getting back to your room?'

Stella-Jean began her preparations to stand. 'No,' she said. 'I can do it.'

THIRTY-SIX

Angie was standing in front of her mirror, holding a dress on its hanger in each hand. She held one up against herself, and then the other. 'I just can't decide,' she murmured, then spun around. 'Which dress should I wear for the big concert, Finnie? This one – or this one?'

Finn was sitting on Angie's bed with a long loop of red wool stretched over his fingers, playing a complicated string game Stella had taught him. He looked solemnly at his mother and at each dress, then shook his head. 'Stella will know. You should ask her when you take me to her place.'

'There won't be time, honey, we'll just be dropping you off and going straight to the airport,' Angie said. 'The minute Gabriel gets back from Pastor Tim's, we'll have to —' and just then they heard the sound of his car pulling up. Their eyes met; Finn was about to scramble down from his mum's bed and back to his own room, but Angie said, 'You can stay here, Finnie, this is my room.' Hastily, she folded both dresses into her suitcase.

They listened to the slightly uneven sound of Gabriel's footsteps coming down the hallway, then he was in the doorway of Angie's room. Just standing there.

'I'm packed, Gabriel,' she said brightly. 'Just need to put my bathroom bag in and we're all set to —'

Gabriel looked at Finn. 'Out,' he said, with a single jerk of his head. Finn slid quickly off the bed, and sidled past Gabriel without touching him. He went into his own bedroom and closed the door but then let it come open again, just a crack, and stood there listening, the red wool drooping from his fingers.

'Is everything all right?' he heard his mother ask nervously.

Silence. Then that cool slithering voice. 'Should you be coming to Brisbane, Angie? Should I allow you to appear on stage with me?'

'Gabriel!' she cried. 'Why *not*? I've been . . . Why would . . .' She was so shocked, she was stammering.

'What have you been saying to Helen?' he asked.

'Helen? I haven't been saying *anything*, Gabriel, I swear I haven't.'

'Lies, that's what you tell. Lies, Angie. Should I allow a liar to sing with the Faith Rise Band, in front of thousands of good Christians?'

Finn could hear that his mum had started crying. 'I didn't, I swear. I don't know what Helen said but . . .' There was a sound of rushing footsteps and then Angie's voice sounded much closer; she must be right there, in her doorway, with Gabriel, up close. 'Please,' she said, 'please believe me. Please let me come with you.'

'Why would you want to give Helen the impression that you're a slut, I wonder? A dirty, sinful, slut? And worse: that I am a filthy sinner too?'

'But I didn't *say* anything!' Angie cried, and then, 'Ow,' like she'd been hurt. Like he'd pulled her hair or something.

Go in there, Finn told himself. *Go in there and stop him, don't let him hurt Mum.* But he couldn't move, he was too scared.

'I've never. Touched. You,' Gabriel said, and his voice was so clear and cold it made Finn cringe to hear it. His mum's bed made a loud squeak, as though she'd sat down heavily on it, or been pushed.

'I'm sorry,' she sobbed. 'Oh Gabriel, please, I'm sorry.'

'Very well, Angie. One chance. I'll let you come to Brisbane; I'll let you sing with us. But let me never hear disgusting rumours like this again. *Whores* are liars!'

Finn closed his door with the quick stealth of fear. He knew his drawing of Robo-Boy was already safely in his backpack, along with his clothes and stuff for the weekend at Stella-Jean's, but he checked anyway. Then he put his backpack on and stood there in the middle of his room, twitching involuntarily as he listened to the sound of his mother crying really hard on the other side of the wall.

Her parents had gone off to a party at Marcus's place, a kind of housewarming because it had been totally redecorated. 'I suppose we'd better get used to calling it Marcus *and John's* place,' Stella-Jean heard her mum say as they were leaving, and her dad said something about lashings of leopardskin, and they both laughed. Then Seb and Rory, who'd been studying together, went off with a bunch of their friends to a movie. As Finn was going through all the old DVDs piled up in a cupboard, Stella-Jean talked on the phone to Tessa about plans for their new improved market stall, and also how they could start selling stuff on etsy.com and reduce their overheads.

Now, Stella-Jean was curled up on the couch with Finn, watching *Who Framed Roger Rabbit?* which she hadn't seen for a million years. Finn, who'd been quiet as a little mouse all evening, even laughed a few times. Other than that, he only took his thumb out of his mouth to eat some of the popcorn from the huge bowlful they'd made. Stella-Jean dozed off, till Finn shook her awake for *Roger Rabbit's* final scene of dreadful danger and wild revenge. And then they went to bed, with him on the fold-up bed that took up what little space there was in her room. But that's where he'd asked to sleep, and he seemed to conk out the moment his head hit the pillow.

Stella-Jean sat up in bed and drew some new ideas for bags – small-ish, with a long strap that would go across the body so you didn't need to hold them. *Not bad,* she thought, assessing the sketches; her fine motor skills were improving heaps, every day. She turned out her light, punched her pillow into the shape she liked, and settled down to sleep.

'Stella?' It was Finn's small scratchy voice that had woken her. 'Stella?'

'What's up?'

'Can I hold your hand?'

'Here.' She put her hand out from the covers, felt around, found his. 'So what's up, huh?' she asked softly.

A little silence. 'He's just like Judge Doom,' Finn whispered.

Stella-Jean didn't need to ask who he was talking about. Gabriel might not look like the extremely tall, bald and scary bad guy in *Roger Rabbit* – in fact, maybe the scariest thing about Gabriel was that he actually *looked* like a nice guy – but yeah, he was Doom-like, definitely. 'I know what you mean, Finnster.'

'He put me in the Dip, just like Judge Doom.'

'The Dip? You mean, like the time he tried to drown you?' Stella-Jean held her breath. Finn had denied telling her that, ever since. She felt the two very definite nods of his head all the way down his arm.

'He wants to disappear me,' he said in the smallest, scaredest voice she'd ever heard.

Stella-Jean's heart clenched. 'Hey Finnster. Wanna climb in here with me?' As he clambered out of the folding bed, she scooted herself closer to the wall, and he settled his skinny self into the warm place she'd made for him. Finn lay with his pyjama-clad back to her and she put an arm around him.

After a minute or two he said, twisting his head toward her over his shoulder, 'And Stella, you can't tell anybody, 'cause then he'll put me in the jail for bad kids, and they'll never let me out. I'll *die* there.'

That'd be right. The bastard. 'That's not gonna happen, Finnster,' she told him. 'Relax now, you've got the whole weekend here with me. We'll figure something out.'

'I had to tell you,' he murmured. Pretty soon he was asleep again, and Stella-Jean lay there trying to figure out what to do. She could try talking to her mum again, but maybe she should talk to her dad. Dad couldn't stand all those churchie people, so he might be better.

But he still thought Gabriel had done wonders improving Finn's behaviour. What about Andrew? He was such a cool guy, and he must've seen a lot of bad stuff, being an ambo; he knew how horrible life and people could be. But Andrew wasn't, like, family. And besides, no matter who she told, Gabriel had Finn too terrified to talk. *That's how child abusers get away with it.*

Even if she *could* persuade Finn to talk, there wasn't a shred of evidence, not even a mark. Just the word of one notoriously difficult child, and her, a teenager with brain damage. Oh, it was *so* frustrating! *But we've got all weekend*, she reminded herself, just as she had Finn. *Sleep on it.*

She slept, and she dreamed. She dreamed she was in Bali again, walking down the village street. An old guy carving on his verandah waved to her; his little grandson was beside him learning how to carve, chubby hands holding some insanely sharp tool, but he was all right, nothing bad would happen. In her dream, Stella-Jean called out '*selamat pagi,*' good morning, and walked on. A girl about her own age in sarong and sash was making offerings outside her house, freshly bathed with her lustrous black hair combed and looped up, her lovely face fixed on the thread of smoke rising from the incense, her graceful fingers wafting it on its way to gain the attention of the gods, making everything safe for her home and the people within it.

And there was Putu, beautiful, broad-shouldered Putu, who Stella-Jean couldn't ever remember not knowing. She was standing in the open doorway of the sewing room, from which came the sound of the half-dozen machines and the chat and laughter of the girls who worked there. '*Selamat pagi*, Putu,' called Stella-Jean, and the young woman's face lit up. *Come, come*: she was beckoning Stella-Jean in, and Finn who, she now realised, had been walking beside her the whole way. *Come in; you'll be safe here.*

Stella-Jean woke up. She lay there, Finn deeply asleep beside her, figuring something out.

Everything depended on them all going out: Mum, Dad and Seb, and all at the same time, on Saturday afternoon. Well, it didn't just depend on that: it depended on a lot of things. The more unlikely it seemed that everything would fall into place, the more determined she became that it would. It *must*.

Seb went to a training session and then to catch up with Andrew. Susanna, somewhat reluctantly – 'Are you sure you and Finn are okay, sweetie?' – went to her studio. Dad was off to meet a client and then put in a few hours at the office. *Yes!* Three hours, at least, more like four. Stella-Jean printed out the bookings she'd made online in the middle of the night, got the bag she'd packed out of the cupboard – it was a backpack, just a small one; she could buy everything she needed once they got there – and Finn put his on, and she called a taxi.

First, to his house. Now everything depended on whether Auntie Ange still kept important things in the same place. Straight into her bedroom, to the built-in wardrobe that went all the way to the ceiling. 'There,' she pointed. 'On the very top shelf. We might need a ladder to —' but Finn was already scaling it like a monkey, from a wooden chair and up, a toehold on a shelf here, another, then clinging as though magnetised to the top one while with one skinny arm he felt around for the fabric-covered box she'd described.

'I've got it!' he squawked, winkling the box forward. He was down on the floor again in a flash. Stella-Jean took the lid off, flipping through the contents with bumbling, hurried fingers. *Passport, please let his passport be* . . . Yes, here was Angie's – and this was Finn's, and it was – she held her breath as she opened it – current for another eighteen months.

'Ah, *sweet*,' she said. 'Finnbar Greenfield O'Reilly, see? That's you, buddy. Let's go!'

When they got out of the taxi at the airport, she reminded Finn that he shouldn't have to say anything. 'But if they ask you,' she said as they went inside the big busy glass building, 'remember, I'm your cousin. Our mothers are sisters, they're already there on holiday, they're going to meet us. We've been there before. Everything's fine. Okay?'

They joined the check-in line. Finn was breathing through his nose in a puffing, determined sort of way. She tried to lean on the walking stick as casually as possible, like it was just some cool accessory. No problem with check-in or seat allocation. The line for security wasn't too long, and soon they were through that too. They didn't hang around the duty-free shops; Stella-Jean could feel herself getting tired, lurching a little more, and she didn't want to attract attention.

Tessa was always saying how you should visualise the outcome you desired, so Stella-Jean pictured herself and Finn in their seats on the plane, buckling their seatbelts around them. Finn would listen really carefully to the safety precautions, and study the laminated cards for ages. There would be the whoosh and roar of the plane taking off. She pictured all that so clearly: no way could it not happen.

With plenty of time before boarding, they went through the big doors and into the immigration section with its maze of roped-off queues. Stella-Jean filled out the forms for both of them, very carefully. As they stood in line she whispered to Finn to stay close and let her lean on his shoulder a bit, so she didn't look wobbly. The queue snaked slowly forward until finally they were at the front and then were called up to one of the little booths. The man in uniform looked at their passports, looked at herself and Finn, looked at the passports again.

Say, go through, Stella-Jean willed him. *Say, go through*.

'Just a moment,' the man said, and called over another person in uniform, a woman. Together they did all the things the man had just done, looking at the passports, at Stella-Jean and Finn, and back at the passports. Then they both stared at the computer screen, murmuring to each other.

The woman beckoned Stella-Jean closer. 'You're unaccompanied minors,' she said. 'Where are your parents?'

'I'm not a minor, not for travel,' Stella-Jean said, trying with all her might to make her speech sound uncluttered, clear and confident, hoping her wobbly brain wouldn't forget some simple word and make her look like an idiot who couldn't be trusted to get herself and an eight-year-old on and off a plane. 'Mum checked. I'm sixteen, so I can legally accompany a child.' The woman nodded reluctantly, but she still didn't tell them to go through. Discreetly, Stella-Jean crossed her fingers for good luck and gave the woman the line about her and Finn being cousins, about how their mothers were awaiting their arrival. 'They're meeting us at the airport,' she said.

The woman pressed her lips tight as she considered. 'I think I need to confirm this with a parent or guardian,' she said.

'Mum's mobile doesn't work there,' said Stella-Jean, quickly. *That is brilliant!*

'I see. What about your father? Where's he?'

'He's, um, he's in . . . New York. At a —' *What's the word? What's the word?* 'He's on business.' Finn was pressing close to her side. *Go through*, she willed the woman to say, *Go through*.

'I see,' the woman said again. She cocked her head at Stella-Jean's bag, sitting on the high narrow counter between then. 'Do you have a mobile phone with you —' she glanced down at the passport she was holding in her hand, '— Stella-Jean?'

She could check the numbers in memory. She'll call Mum, or Dad. 'No,' she said, shaking her head.

The woman tapped the end of a pen against the passports, *tok tok, tok tok.* 'Well,' she said eventually, 'I suppose —'

And at that moment, the mobile in Stella-Jean's bag started ringing. Loud: incredibly, hideously, deliberately loud. They both jumped and stared at the small bag, going off like a fire alarm right there on the counter between them, then Stella-Jean snatched it away out of sight. Finding the phone by touch, she switched it off, even though the knowledge that it was too late was sitting in her stomach like a great big lump of cold porridge.

'We're going to —' the woman started.

'You *have* to let us go to Bali,' Stella-Jean interrupted. 'Please! We've got our passports, I've paid for our tickets, it's all legal.'

Finn, who had been standing there the whole time vibrating with nerves, like a piece of twanged elastic, now grabbed her arm. Standing on tiptoe he whispered, 'He's gonna *get* me,' in her ear, in a voice very close to tears.

'I *have* to get my cousin away,' Stella-Jean told the woman urgently. 'It's the man who's living with his mum, he's really horrible. He's been abusing him.'

The woman exchanged an alarmed glance with the guy who had first looked at their passports. 'I see. Right. Okay,' she said in a rush. 'We need to call in some assistance here,' and she picked up a phone that Stella-Jean hadn't noticed before, tucked under the counter ledge. Finn started crying, and Stella-Jean was very close to it herself.

Finn talked. Once he'd been assured by the officials that no one could send him to a prison for bad boys, and that in fact there was no such prison, he talked. He told them everything Gabriel had done, the yelling, the ways of hurting that hardly left a mark or bruise, the hours he'd made him kneel and pray, the day he'd nearly drowned him. He told them how he'd heard his mum crying, before they went to Brisbane. Stella-Jean told the police and the social worker what she knew too, with Susanna and Gerry listening to everything.

By the time Angie was located at the big evangelical festival in Brisbane, it was too late for her to catch a plane back to Melbourne. But she got the first plane the next morning, and then, when she was with them in the living room, he told her, too. Everything, right down to what had really happened with Grace and Lily, upstairs at Pastor Tim's house last Christmas Day.

As he talked, Finn stayed right next to Stella-Jean, sitting together in the middle of the couch. Angie, who looked like she'd been crying all night, like she was nearly all cried out, was facing him, sitting way forward on the very edge of the armchair she'd pulled close. She listened, and her mouth trembled, and she sniffed and made little noises and kept wiping her eyes. Then, when Finn had told her everything, she slid forward off the chair and kneeled down in front of him. Her fingers touched his knee lightly.

'I am so sorry, Finnie. All the way through, every bit of me, right down to the bottom of my heart, I'm sorry. I should have seen what was happening, I should have — oh. So much.' Angie covered her face with her hands for a few moments, shaking her head, but then took her hands away and said, 'He's never coming back. Not even for a single moment.'

'What are you going to do?' asked Finn, his voice thin but suddenly hopeful. 'Are you gonna throw him away? Like rubbish?'

Angie nodded, making a quick gesture of hurling something aside. 'Yes, exactly. Good riddance to bad rubbish!'

A smile suddenly lit Finn's face. 'Good riddance to bad rubbish!' he repeated loudly, and threw himself forward into his mother's arms.

'My special little guy,' Angie said through different tears, 'I love you so much.'

'I do too, I love you, too. It's okay, Mum. It's okay now.'

When Angie lifted her head at last, she turned to the person in the room everyone would've least expected.

'Gerry,' Angie said. 'Can you help me do something?' Gerry raised his eyebrows in surprised inquiry. 'Would you come to my house and throw every single thing that belongs to that man – every bit of musical equipment, every book, every scrap of clothing, his *toothbrush* – into his car, and drive it away?'

'With pleasure,' said Gerry. 'I'll drive it off a bloody cliff, if you like.'

'No, just to Faith Rise. Leave it outside the church. Those people stood and watched me hit my own child, and I am never, ever going back there again.'

THIRTY-SEVEN

'I really don't see the *point*,' said Gerry. He was looking at the window in the far wall of Leigh Fermor's room, the place where he often fixed his eyes, Susanna had come to realise, when something came up that he didn't want to – well, *to look at*, she supposed. 'Just when things are getting back to normal for us, what's the point of raking over stuff that's only going to upset you?' He swung his head around to give her a challenging stare. 'What's the point, Suze? It's stupid.'

'Susanna?' Leigh asked after a little pause.

'Maybe it will upset me,' she said. 'That may very well be so. But let's face it, I already am upset. I don't think it's stupid; I think knowing more will help. I *need* to know.'

Gerry's gaze went to that window again, his mouth pouchy and sullen.

'Why won't you tell me?' she persisted. 'Just the facts: when these affairs started, how often, who with.'

'Why do you have to hound me about it? Why can't you just let it go?' he snapped.

'In my experience,' said Leigh, who was sitting in his usual chair, making occasional notes, watching them, unflappable, 'it's very often the case that someone whose partner has had sexual encounters with others wants to know more than, simply, it happened. They often want not only the facts of who, when, and where, they also want to know exactly *what* took place, as well.'

'I don't know why you want to know *any* of it,' muttered Gerry. Pause.

'You're reluctant to give Susanna information about your liaisons with other women,' said Leigh.

'Yes, I am!' said Gerry. 'Because it won't help anything. And it's – my business.'

'Your business?' said Susanna. She felt the anger again, a physical thing. 'Gerry, you can't be serious. This is our marriage: twenty years of what *I* understood to be a monogamous relationship, but it turns out – you were lying to me the whole time. How can that not be *my* business, too?'

'You insist on thinking I did this stuff because of something to do with you, don't you? You just can't accept that it's got nothing to do with you,' said Gerry, matching her hostility and raising it some. 'These adventures were *my* thing: not yours, not ours, not the family's. Just one thing that was *mine!* Why is that so bloody hard to understand?' He wasn't looking out the window any more: their eyes were locked together in heated contest. 'The minute I roll over and tell you who or when or where, I've lost that. I've *lost.*'

'Lost?' Susanna snapped back. Oh, the courage, or at least bravado, that came to her in this room! 'You better think very carefully about what you could lose, Gerry. Because if you won't tell me, you could lose a hell of a lot more than your secrets.'

Gerry glared at her. 'What's that supposed to mean?'

'Me. Our marriage.'

'Is that so? You're saying you'd throw our marriage away for – what? For insufficient information?'

'It's about respect, or lack of it. About not respecting me enough to tell me your secrets, and not acknowledging that it *does* affect me. That's what could destroy our marriage.'

'Don't make idle threats, Susanna,' Gerry said, his face hard with scorn. 'They could backfire on you.'

'Gerry,' said Leigh. They'd almost forgotten he was there. 'Have you ever known Susanna to make idle threats?'

Gerry was forced to consider this. Susanna knew that in any other context, he would have left the room, or intimidated her; blustered his way out of it somehow. Now, she watched him realise that he had no choice but to give his secrets up. Rapid-fire, then, uncrossing his arms from time to time in order to tick things off on his fingers, he told her when the affairs had started – around the time she started teaching at the college, he said, when the kids were little and she was exhausted all the time – and where – never in Melbourne, always when he was interstate or overseas – and something about who with: mostly women he met at conferences, where everyone had an eye out for a bit of action. He gave her the names he could remember, though these, he claimed, were few.

'What about the woman you were with that night, the night of the accident?' Susanna asked. 'Who was she?'

'Just someone from the conference.'

'Yes, but *who*?'

'Some architect.' Gerry gave an impatient shrug. 'Susan something. She was from Chicago, I think. Like I've told you before, a thousand times, these are just . . . flings. Not one of them has been ongoing, or important.'

Susanna had been expecting worse. At four a.m., lying in bed beside her husband, unable to sleep, her imagination had spared her nothing. She took a deep breath. 'And now?' she asked. 'What happens after this?'

'Now, I sincerely hope we can put this behind us and get our lives back. What else would you want?'

'I want to know what happens next time you go to a conference.'

Gerry sighed heavily. 'Well, I've been sprung now, haven't I?' he muttered.

'What does that mean, that you've been sprung?' she asked. 'To me, that implies you see the problem as being that you got found out, not that you were having affairs in the first place. Do you plan to just cover your tracks better next time?' She had never challenged him like this before.

'No, I get it: I have to give up my little adventures. So,' he said, sitting up straighter as he challenged her right back, 'what do *you* give up?'

That, Susanna wasn't expecting. 'What do *I* give up?' He nodded. She had no idea how to respond.

'Gerry,' said Leigh. 'You feel that if you are being asked to give up having sex with other women, Susanna should give up something as well?'

'Yes. Fair's fair, after all,' he said. 'And it should be something that *matters* to her, too. Something that's just hers. Like, her art.'

'My *art*?' Susanna gasped.

'Yes. Why should I be the one who loses out while you get to do whatever you want?'

'Because you, Gerry,' Leigh cut in, and his voice had an edge to it Susanna had not heard before, 'are the one who lied to and betrayed your partner.'

Susanna could hardly believe her ears. To have it *said*, just like that, and that her husband had to hear it! She felt as though the room had suddenly got much bigger, as though she might be able to lift off and fly around in it, like a bird. *Now we can go on.*

Gerry, however, had withdrawn into himself; he was looking down at the carpet between his feet, tapping his fingertips on his thighs, silent for what seemed like a long time. 'Okay,' he said finally. 'You win.'

'But it's not a matter of winning!' Susanna was appalled. 'Gerry, we're — I'm your *wife*. I don't want to *win*. I want us to have a good marriage, that's all. For both of us.'

'I know,' he said heavily. He sounded deflated, defeated. 'I know.'

Leigh was saying something, but for once Susanna wasn't listening: she was staring at her husband, asking him silently, *Isn't that what you want too? A good marriage?* Willing him to look at her, to smile. *I love you,* she told him silently. From beneath the lids of his downcast eyes she saw a slow tear trickle, and then another.

'Gerry?' she whispered. 'What is it?'

Now he looked at her, but his face was full of sadness and loss. 'I'm not supposed to say it.'

'What? Say it anyway.'

'I'll never have that kind of sex again. The adventure's over.' There was no bluff, no brashness in him; he had given up.

'What sort of sex *will* you have, Gerry?' asked Leigh quietly.

A few more tears spilled down his face, to be wiped away. 'Married sex,' he said, his voice tender but terribly sad.

She could have protested, but Susanna realised that she had never seen her husband like this. This wasn't the brutal 'honesty' of 'I probably shouldn't say this but'. He was revealing something about *himself*, something she'd had no idea about. She sat as still as a birdwatcher, hardly breathing.

'You don't think that married sex can be an adventure too?' Leigh asked him.

Gerry shook his head. 'I've tried,' he said. 'Susanna's not interested. She's a wife, not a —' he stopped.

What was he about to say? A wife, not a lover? 'When did you try?' she asked. 'When did I say I wasn't interested?'

'A few years ago. I asked you to . . .' He turned his head away, discomfitted. 'To . . . give me a blowjob. You see?' he cried. 'I can hardly even say it in front of you!'

Susanna was trying to recall such an incident. She couldn't, but that didn't mean it hadn't happened. She'd hardly ever – *done that*, in her life. In fact, she felt self-conscious just saying the word *cock*, let alone sucking one. Maybe in the early days, when they were courting and she was trying to impress . . . But wasn't their relationship proof you could have good sex without – that? *Your relationship isn't proof of any such thing. And stop assuming you know what's good.* 'What did I say?' she asked, humble and curious.

'You looked at me like I'd just proposed something completely . . . ridiculous. You said, "Why would I do that?"'

333

He wasn't mocking her, yet Gerry's imitation of her tone of voice was so precise that Susanna not only recognised the words as hers but suddenly remembered the distant, fleeting incident itself, and could even see the look on his face immediately she'd spoken: the bruised sadness as he relinquished something. A hope, perhaps. 'Oh,' she said softly. It had been a lot longer than a few years ago – ten, perhaps, maybe more – but it was true. 'Gerry. I'm sorry.'

'A blowjob,' he said to her, with a small and rather sweet smile. 'It's not really that out there, you know, Suze.'

'I guess not,' she said. They were both quiet for a while. 'All these years I've been so proud of our sex life,' she went on. 'I've been kidding myself. I had no idea how much I was saying no to. I wasn't even aware I was saying no.'

Gerry moved closer to her on the couch, touched her hand, stroked it sadly. 'Don't get me wrong, Suze. I like what we do, I like it a lot. But it's always . . . vanilla.'

'Vanilla,' she admitted. 'Bland.'

'That's what I mean: married sex.'

'Susanna,' said Leigh. They turned to him, both their faces open, hiding nothing. 'What might happen if, one night when you're in bed together, or in the mood for bed, Gerry was to invite you to go on an adventure with him?'

'*Me?*' she said, and blushed to hear her tone.

'Yes,' Leigh smiled. 'Why not you?'

Is this what had been missing in their relationship: sexual adventure? *What would he want me to do?* she asked herself nervously. And then: *what am I so afraid of doing? Stepping outside of my narrow vanilla good?* She took a breath, high into her chest, and looked boldly into Gerry's eyes. 'Only if we can go to the toyshop first.'

How long since she'd heard Gerry laugh like that? Really laugh! It seemed a very long time.

It was like having a handsome suitor, going all-out to win her. *No, not 'like' that: Gerry* is *my handsome suitor.* He'd secretly packed her bag, with her favourite going-out dress and her only pair of high heels, and a taxi delivered them to the door of a boutique hotel in the heart of the city. What awaited, in their suite? A bottle of excellent champagne, of course. On the bed lay a flat pink box, extravagantly ribboned, with the name of a legendary lingerie shop written in a flourish of gilt across the lid. Within the box, and the layers of tissue, a luscious Italian bra and matching silk knickers that were sensuousness itself. And when she emerged from the bathroom wearing them and – *oh, why not!* – the high heels, Gerry's response, very visible through his own new designer underwear, made her giggle like a teenager. 'And now,' he said a couple of minutes later, in a growly murmur, 'I get to take them off you.' Which he did, slowly, with nuzzling digressions.

The toys they had chosen together, but Gerry had sneaked in a few extras to surprise her. Somewhere amid the delicious delirium Susanna recalled Vinnie's voice saying, as she'd dropped the catalogue into her bag, 'your husband will love you for it'. *My husband?* she thought. *I love myself for it!*

She waved goodbye to some inner censor she'd never even been aware of, and let herself be noisy: gasped and moaned and, at one point, even screamed – a small shriek, really, of surprise rather than pain. There had been nothing, Susanna realised, to be afraid of. *Not in this adventure. Not with him.*

Afterward, both fell briefly into a post-orgasmic sleep, deep as though they'd been dropped down a well. When they awoke, the evening was still young. Susanna exchanged languor for glamour, enjoying the rare thrill of dressing in her finest clothes and carefully putting on mascara as well as lipstick, to dine in a many-starred restaurant with this beautiful man. *Her* man.

Over dinner, as Gerry regaled her with one story after another illustrating his wit, his talent, the esteem in which he was held by people whose opinion counted, Susanna suddenly put her finger on it. *You're flirting with me. Showing off.* Why did this feel like a revelation? *You don't have to impress me,* she felt like saying, but instead she smiled and made appropriate noises of admiration. Susanna knew perfectly well how the game was played, but was surprised that instead of truly finding it enjoyable, she felt an inner niggle of resentment. *Is this what he always does when he's flirting? With a new woman?*

When Gerry had finally finished describing the rapturous response to some designs he'd done for a project in Canada ('setting the standard for retro-fitting large-scale buildings throughout North America', apparently), she tried to introduce some topics of more mutual interest – the kids, and their progress at school, for instance; some gossip about Angie's new-found interest in Buddhism – but he brushed these aside with a charming, careless smile. 'We can talk about the family any time, Suze,' he said. 'Tonight's for us!'

Is it? she began to wonder. *Or is it for you?* Throughout the meal she waited in vain for Gerry to ask *her* questions, to show any curiosity about her work at the college, or what she was doing in her studio. None. But he *did* ask when the purchasers of Jean's unit were likely to settle, which led directly to what they would spend the money on: the house renovations. *I don't want to talk about this, again.* Susanna decided to make a bold move to change the subject.

'Gerry, could I ask your advice, about a professional problem?' she said, while they waited for the arrival of the dessert they'd decided to share.

'Absolutely,' said Gerry, always pleased to give advice. 'Go ahead.'

'Lucy Simonic, the curator of Booradalla Art Gallery, is getting some serious opposition to mounting my show there.'

I told you so, said his look. 'Too bleak for them, right? They want family viewing, not torture and pornography.'

Steady, she told herself. 'Booradalla *is* a conservative gallery, as Lucy has reminded me. Being funded and administered by the council, and with councillors always mindful of the next election – yes, they're not exactly at the cutting edge of contemporary art. Lucy's already been called in to a meeting about my work, and she's shown me the follow-up letter. It's, ah . . . they're pretty serious.'

'So, what's she reckon? Pull the whole show, or just the most offensive bits?'

Wow, you really don't like my work, do you? It took Susanna a few moments to compose a cool response. 'Pulling the whole show isn't what we want to do, though a couple of the most conservative councillors would like that. Lucy suggests withdrawing some of the more . . . confronting works.'

'Sounds reasonable,' said Gerry, nodding his agreement. 'What's your problem?'

'Well . . . that feels like a cop-out to me.'

'People are going to *hate* that stuff, Suze,' said Gerry. 'This gal Lucy's right: you've got to take out pieces like that Rwanda rape thing. At least rework it so it's not so hideous, or put a great big sticker saying *CENSORED* over the top of that – ugh! Do *something*!'

'Right,' said Susanna thoughtfully. 'Thanks.'

'Though I reckon you'd be better off cancelling the whole thing, myself.'

'I think I kind of get that idea,' said Susanna, resting her chin on one hand as she gazed at him. *Why don't you want me to have this exhibition?* She hadn't been able to come up with a convincing answer to that question, no matter how she puzzled at it. Then a dry voice inside her head said, *There's only room for one creative genius in this marriage, and that's Gerry Visser.*

She sat up straight. 'Oh!' she said.

'What?' he asked.

'Nothing, nothing. Look, here's our dessert.'

'Fabulous!' said Gerry, lifting his spoon. 'I'll have an espresso, too,' he told the waiter, who looked questioningly at Susanna. She asked for peppermint tea.

Back in the hotel room, Gerry said he'd stay up for a while and catch some of the play at Wimbledon. Susanna went to bed. She took off her lovely dress, her stunning new lingerie, and lay propped up on the abundant snowy pillows, staring at the small hillock of her bent knees. That dry, unsentimental voice that had spoken inside her head at the end of the dinner was intent on conversation.

So, it asked her, *you really think adventurous sex is what's been missing from your marriage? Everything'll be hunky-dory now?*

Reluctantly, Susanna found herself admitting to the likelihood that, for her at least, it probably wouldn't. *Not that sex like that isn't fantastic*, she assured the interrogating voice, *and wonderful.*

What is it you're really missing, then?

I think it's . . . something else entirely.

What?

Oh – it sounds so pretentious.

What? What do you really need, Susanna?

Acknowledgement of my creative side, and support for my own work.

With this admission, a still space opened up inside her, and Susanna looked into it for a long time, trying to find some sense of optimism that Gerry would be able to give her this acknowledgement, this support. But there was none.

Gerry sat on the other side of the wall, on the natty leather couch, staring at the TV, wondering whether hot sex with Susanna was really going to satisfy his need for sexual adventure. Reluctantly, a part of him was coming to the conclusion that the frisson of triumph he felt at what he'd done with her this evening wasn't going to last. *Not that it wasn't fantastic. It was.* But the thrill of the chase – that's what was missing. The heady moment when he knew he'd won a new woman's consent, the exploration of unfamiliar flesh, the raw animal rush of getting his hard cock into a body he'd never fucked before.

He sat there, hands propped on his knees, looking down the barrel of a future without any secrets, any adventures, any such triumphs. It seemed a desolating prospect.

THIRTY-EIGHT

'Susanna, Susanna!' Vinnie's voice was almost yelping with excitement. 'Where are you? Can you get yourself in to Studio Lulu inside half an hour?'

'Inside half a minute, if you like,' Susanna said. 'I'm just out here in the car park, running over one of the drawings.'

'Running it *over*?' Vinnie shrieked. Susanna held the mobile away from her ear. 'What are you *doing*?'

'Relax, Vin, everything's okay. There's method in my madness. So, what's up?'

'Just come — oh, I'll meet you! I'm walking out to the car park now.'

Excited though she was, Vinnie insisted on first inspecting the drawing Susanna had run over. 'Oh, thank god, it's not wrecked.'

'Of course it's not wrecked, it just had to have tyre marks on it. Come on, what's the big news?'

'First, you have to tell me this,' said Vinnie, taking hold of Susanna's elbow, her dark eyes glittering. 'Do you want to be on national television?' Susanna goggled at her. 'Because in half an hour – less, twenty minutes – a producer and a reporter from *Arts Week* are going to be here —' at this point Vinnie started literally jumping up and down, '— to look at *your work!*'

'Huh?' This didn't make any kind of sense. Susanna shook her head as though trying to clear it. 'No.'

'Yes!' Vinnie was striding along, propelling Susanna toward the framing shop. 'Come on, I want to get all the pieces I've already framed out for them. Then we'll get the others down from your studio.'

'Vinnie, please, explain to me what's happening. How does *Arts Week* even have a clue about me? Or my work?'

As they hurried to assemble Susanna's graphic narratives, and the small paintings that complemented each one – almost thirty pairs now, in total – Vinnie breathlessly explained that Anna, whose studio was two along from Susanna's, had got a phone call from the *Arts Week* reporter (who happened to be her sister) as she and her producer were driving back to Melbourne after a segment they'd been planning to film in Ballarat had suddenly gone pear-shaped. She'd told Anna they were going to drop in on their way through and asked if, by any miracle, she knew of an artist whose work would fit with — and here Vinnie was a little unclear. 'But whatever they need it to fit with, and whatever Anna told them about your stuff, they seem to be interested. *Very*, Anna says. And they're on their way here *now*.'

Susanna didn't even have time to get nervous before the door buzzer sounded and they were there, Melita the reporter and Megan the producer, both in their thirties, with smooth asymmetric haircuts, stylish clothes in shades of grey and black, and friendly but analytical eyes. Suddenly Susanna felt very conscious that she was wearing an old blouse of Jean's, pale blue with a neat little round collar, which made her look like a Sunday school teacher, tucked into jeans with a desperately old-fashioned high waist. As the pair looked at her work, Susanna, as casually as possible, untucked her blouse.

Melita beckoned her over. 'Susanna, can you tell us about this one? Why these tyre tracks?' she said with an interviewer's smile, indicating the piece Susanna had just run over in the car park.

'Right.' Susanna took a deep breath. 'I added them because it was a truck that took the bodies away,' she began. 'Some years ago,

I read a Bosnian woman's description of the massacre of about fifty women and children in her village. She described how her youngest child had run to her when the soldiers came into the hall and started firing, how he had been hit just as he reached her. She described the noise of his breath leaving his body: *Oof.*' As she talked, Melita and the producer were glancing back and forth between the drawing itself and Susanna's face. 'This woman was shot too, and thrown onto the back of a truck – she found herself lying on top of her own mother's body – but she wasn't dead. She jumped off the truck before it got to the place where they dumped all the bodies. So I — I felt it needed tyre tracks. Brutally, running over it. This,' she added, picking up the small painting of a child's blue sandal lying on its side on a muddy road, 'is the detail painting that accompanies it.'

'And there's one painting for each of the graphic narratives?'

'Yes, they're paired,' Susanna said. 'A tiny bright spark, to light each dark story on its way.'

'Mmm,' murmured Melita. 'Like that phrase. And the idea to present your work as – I keep thinking of Alison Bechdel's subtitle of her graphic memoir, "a tragicomic" – where did that come from?'

'Probably my students.' Susanna briefly described her epiphany about their online work, and the essay she had written about it – just published, in fact. 'There's a link to it on my website,' she said, 'which, I have to admit, is completely my students' doing: the whole website. They said they'd be too embarrassed for me not to have one. "If you're not online, miss, you're nowhere," quote unquote.'

Melita flashed a look at her producer, who pursed her lips and gave several confirming nods. 'Great story, Susanna,' Megan said. 'And I hope this doesn't sound – er ... but, well, visually, the contrast between the way you look and the work you're showing is ... striking.' She grinned.

'The students influencing the teacher thing is such a neat little twist – plus having a council gallery like Booradalla showing work like this,' said Melita.

'Oh yeah.' Megan was now texting furiously on her BlackBerry. 'Good. Topical. We could certainly give Booradalla a plug.'

From the other side of the framing shop, Vinnie gave Susanna a double thumbs up. As the *Arts Week* pair went from drawing to drawing, painting to painting, Vinnie sidled up to her. 'A plug like this?' she hissed in her ear. 'The councillors will love you. We won't hear another peep out of them.'

'And this one,' Melita said. 'Tell us about these stamps, *REFUSE* and *DENY*, across the — oh, I get it. This is the story of the people on the SIEV X. Wow.'

'You'll see words stamped on several of the narratives,' Susanna pointed out. '*CENSORED. UNKNOWN.* Well, they're not actual stamps, of course, I've painted them on.'

'Nice layer,' said Megan briskly. 'Effective.' She was checking her messages. 'Mm. I'm sorry to rush you, Susanna, but for various boring but unavoidable reasons, we're in urgent mode here. We'd like to shoot an interview with you; it won't go to air for several weeks, but because of our production schedule we need to shoot it – tomorrow. Here at Studio Lulu. Around ten. Can you do that?'

'*Yes!*' said Vinnie, and Susanna nodded.

'Yes,' she said.

In a way, Susanna felt that her exhibition opened the Sunday afternoon before the official one, when she was sitting in Leonard Styles' living room, crowded on to his couch with Stella-Jean and Finn and Angie, with Seb and Rory sharing one armchair and Leonard in the other, watching *Arts Week*. After the program's debonair presenter introduced the story, the screen suddenly filled with Susanna's face and Stella-Jean let out an ear-piercing squeal. 'That's *you*!'

'I know, darling,' Susanna said calmly, even though part of her was asking, *Is that me?* and she felt queasy with nerves. One of her graphic narratives flashed up: a Black Saturday bushfire one, the story of a well-known journalist and his wife fighting, unsuccessfully, to save their home. Susanna's voiceover, explaining something, and then the painting: a hand, that of the journalist's daughter, reaching out to touch the charred black body of her beloved dog, found curled beneath the remains of a favourite chair. Rory murmured, 'That's so *sad*.' Then Melita's face with its intelligent smile, interviewing her: just a few sentences, it seemed, which Susanna couldn't quite take in. Another drawing, the camera moving around it to show the panels, the captions. Lucy Simonic, curator of Booradalla Gallery, talking artspeak; segue to a montage of the paintings. Susanna felt quite startled: the work looked strangely familiar, but not like her own. And then the segment was over and the debonair presenter was back, saying, 'And you can see Susanna Greenfield's remarkable graphic narratives in her debut exhibition, *Remember Me*, at Booradalla Gallery in Melbourne, opening on . . .' He gave the date, paused, and moved on to the next item.

Everyone had been sitting forward tensely in their seats, and now, like marionettes released, they all flopped back. Then Angie turned to her sister and flung her arms around her. 'That was *beautiful!*' she said. She was crying, Susanna realised, which made her feel like she might start crying too.

'Hooray!' yelled Stella-Jean, and Finn yelled hooray too, and then again, for good measure.

Seb said, 'You were fantastic, Ma.'

'I couldn't be prouder of you if you were my own daughter,' said Leonard, and Susanna, who had met his daughter, an eye doctor working in Africa, thanked him sincerely. 'I've taped it,' Leonard added, 'so your husband can watch it later.'

'Wow, you've still got a video machine?' said Seb.

Susanna said, 'That's so thoughtful of you, Leonard.' The program would be repeated in a couple of days, but Gerry might be busy again then, too.

'Ga-*zillions* of people are going to come to your opening now,' said Stella-Jean with relish. 'I hope the council's organised heaps of catering.'

The following Thursday at five o'clock, as the caterers were bringing in what certainly seemed to be plenty of food and drink, Susanna stood to one side of the gallery watching three brown-robed Buddhist nuns conclude a ceremony. It had been as low-key and unobtrusive as Angie had promised, and Susanna found their sonorous chanting remarkably soothing.

'What's the ceremony, again?' she asked Angie quietly.

'It's partly about all the people in your drawings, and laying their suffering to rest,' said Ange. 'And also for an auspicious beginning for your exhibition, welcoming something new. You know, the eternal cycle of life. That's how I understand it, anyway.'

'Sounds good to me,' Susanna said. 'Finn seemed to like it, too.'

'It's wonderful how he's taken to the nuns,' Angie said. They were both watching the little boy sitting close to the brown-robed, shorn-haired women, quiet and relaxed, as he had been throughout their ceremony. 'He told me he wants them to keep living at our house. And as much as he hated Gabriel's singing, he loves their chanting. He says they're not doing it to show off or to make people like them, they're doing it to help people feel peaceful inside.'

'Does he? What a remarkable thing to say – and I agree with him. Thanks for arranging for them to come, Ange.'

'Susu,' said Angie, 'thank *you* for letting me.'

Susanna watched her sister go over and stand beside her son, one hand resting on his shoulder, as the nuns packed up their painted cloths and gong and the small statue they'd brought. *She's much more peaceful too. It's really easy to be around her, these days.*

Not long now till people started arriving. She had a last look around at what she and Lucy, with help from a couple of her students, had finished hanging the night before. Twenty-eight pairs:

twenty-eight graphic narratives in black and white, and their twenty-eight little paintings, bright and clear as gemstones. A photocopied stack of her artist's statement was ready for anyone who wanted more information about the things depicted – as much, at least, as was known. In most cases, such things as people's names were not.

Remember me.

The last pair on the wall of the gallery told the story of a woman, an ordinary Australian woman who worked hard all her life, looked after her husband and her two daughters, who loved, who did her best, and who, finally, died. In a car crash – that was the narrative's last image, after the slide into disaster. Chaos' still centre, and the car's four occupants, a few minutes after it had happened: *my mother, my son, my daughter, my nephew*. Leaning in at the driver's window, the head and shoulders of the young paramedic who'd witnessed her mother's last breaths. In the small acrylic painting, mounted above, she had painted her mother's left hand, old and delicately wrinkled, the prominent veins that had just carried their last freight of blood, at rest on the steering wheel. Her old-fashioned engagement ring and her simple gold wedding band, thin from fifty years of wear, gleamed eerily in the ambulance's blue light.

Susanna placed her own hand on the glass above her mother's painted hand. *Thank you, Mum*, she told her silently. *I love you. I love you so much. I always will.*

Then people were arriving, more and more of them. Vinnie and half the artists who had work spaces at Studio Lulu or did classes there. Belinda, her head of department, who had not only planted the seed of this show but turned bureaucracy inside out to support her this year, along with other people from the college. A touching number of Susanna's students, past as well as present. Lucy was introducing her to councillors, each of whom Susanna made a point of thanking warmly; many mentioned the *Arts Week* story with unequivocal pride.

The gallery was quite large, but it was starting to feel crowded, and the noise level was rising. Denise and Jo from the book group, and Andrea, the potter. Countless congratulatory kisses. *A buzz; there's a real buzz.* Wendy, from tennis, and Joe; *yes, you made it all the way to the outer 'burbs.* Andrew, his red hair gleaming way above most other people's heads. Susanna saw Seb greet him with a hug that didn't give anything away and a joining of their eyes that did, and she felt her heart swell a little more. *Be good to my boy*, she thought to Andrew, and an answer rose within her, *He will.*

There were nurses and doctors she'd got to know at the hospital, several of whom told her how they used to watch her drawing and had always been curious. But they seemed even more eager to see Stella-Jean, who was flitting about with Tessa, leaning on her friend's arm when she got tired or was in danger of being jostled. She had one of her extraordinary floral brooches pinned to a hairband around her still-short hair. *She looks well, she looks so well!*

Angie had taken Finn home with the Buddhist nuns, and returned herself just as the din was at its peak, having changed into a teal shantung sixties cocktail dress. Susanna was in black trousers and a top covered in tiny scraps of cloth individually stitched on, that Stella-Jean had made, and which, Susanna had been gratified to notice when she put it on earlier, made her look much slimmer. The sisters were standing side by side when Stella-Jean came up and gave her mother a congratulatory hug. 'This is fan*tas*tic, Mum,' she said. 'Can we go to Bali this Christmas?'

'Yes,' replied Susanna without a moment's hesitation.

Stella-Jean gave a heartfelt air-punch. '*Yesss!* I knew you'd say yes if I asked you now! Can Finn come too?' she asked Angie.

'Yes,' Angie said.

'All *right*. Can we stay for the whole holidays?'

'Can you not push your luck, for once in your life?' asked Susanna.

'You're the greatest, Mum,' her daughter said, and kissed her. She and Tessa chugged off again, into the throng.

The caterers were overwhelmed, and Susanna noticed that some of her students – Bianca, a couple of the Emilys – had stepped in to help, and Angelo and Tom were carrying empty bottles out to the recycle bins. She found a moment to thank them and Bianca told her that was cool, Susanna had made them famous, and did she know the show had been mentioned in about a hundred blogs already? And she herself could hardly keep up with the Twitter traffic.

'That's – awesome,' Susanna managed.

'Awesome!' Bianca giggled. 'It's so funny when you say it.'

Red stickers! The first time she saw Lucy's assistant put a red sticker beside one of the little paintings, she had the impulse to tell her, *No, don't, it's a mistake,* but then another went up, and another. 'Who's buying them?' she hissed at Lucy, who pointed several people out. The most amazing thing was, they were mostly people Susanna didn't even know. *People actually like them! They get it!* She felt like air-punching too.

She overheard Gerry, in a collarless shirt of periwinkle blue that perfectly complemented his eyes, skiting to people that the idea of *CENSORED* and the other stamps had been his. 'That's right, it was,' she said, stepping forward. 'And I don't know if I've ever thanked you for that, darling.' On tiptoes, she kissed his cheek, and he put his arm around her, smiling just like Robert Redford in his prime, and as the clutch of people around them stood back a little she realised that the council's photographer was there, lining them up. Susanna beamed, straight into the lens. *Savour this moment,* she told herself. *It doesn't get any better than this.*

THIRTY-NINE

'The one-way streets round here are a pain, Susanna; why don't you let me off at this corner?' Vinnie said. 'I can walk, it's not that cold.'

'Don't be silly, it's on the way,' said Susanna, threading her way expertly through the grey lanes of inner-city Richmond on a chilly winter's evening. 'I know this area like the back of my hand; Gerry and Marcus bought their office here way back when it was still mostly factories. Whose birthday is it you're going to, Vin?'

'Caroline, one of my old dyke buddies. Remember when *real* feminists used to change their family names to honour the matriarchy? So, she was Caroline Cora's-daughter. For ages. We told her it sounded like a dairy cow; we all used to go *moo* when she came into the room.' They both snickered. 'She's gone back to using Mitchell now.'

'Probably easier,' Susanna said.

'Big night out for you, eh? I mean, Circumflex? Woo hoo!' said Vinnie, making goo-goo eyes at her. 'I guess this is to celebrate this morning's article in the Oz, eh? You media *star*, you!'

Susanna ducked her head shyly. 'It's just one article. Not really that big a deal.'

'Yes it is, and you know it. Indisputably a big deal, and worth celebrating.'

'Gerry had already booked this. More to celebrate the exhibition itself, I guess.'

'Oh? Well, good for him! Um, Susanna – not that I'm the fashion guru but – do you really think those flats go with the outfit? I mean, they're cute as hell, but . . .'

Susanna flashed her an amused glance. 'I know, I've got high heels in my bag. I'll change before I meet Gerry, but these are *so* comfortable. My daughter gave them to me.'

'Don't think I've ever seen ballet flats with bunny-tail pompoms on the front before,' Vinnie commented.

Susanna took a peek down at her feet, smiling. 'She's made a range of them. *Frou-frou flats*, she calls them. Butterflies for the hippie chicks, rubber spiders for the goth girls – or is it the punks? Punk girls, maybe.'

'So cute. Just over here, Suzita, the place that's all lit up.' Susanna pulled over and Vinnie collected her things from the back seat, including a long tube wrapped in gold paper.

'Have a great party,' Susanna called, admiring Vinnie's dramatic appearance as she sauntered off: her floppy red pants and a piece of green fabric from somewhere exotic tossed insouciantly around her shoulders, her black hair lifting in the cold breeze.

'Count on that!' Vinnie called back, turning around to wave goodbye with her gold tube. It caught the party lights with a flash of brilliance. *The Pirate Queen*, Susanna thought, imagining her friend leaping between the decks of two sailing ships, brandishing her cutlass above her head, urging her trusty band onward with wild yells and her gap-toothed grin. *That's how I'll paint her. A fantasy portrait, the essence of our Vinnie.* For the remainder of the drive to the Visser Kanaley office, just a few minutes, Susanna's mind battened down the vivid image. It would be a big painting, almost life-size. A full-length portrait, bursting with Vinnie's *joie de vivre*.

This could be part of your next exhibition, a voice whispered in her head as she pulled up. *Portraits, of a different kind.* She felt goosebumps rise all up and down her arms.

Hold that thought, she told herself as she slipped the pompom flats into her bag and changed into the high heels, teetering momentarily on the kerb. Tricky things, heels, when you're not used to them. She put one hand on the roof of the car to steady herself, then clomped off cautiously down the footpath.

Dinner, just the two of them, at the recently anointed most fashionable restaurant in town. Susanna recognised an olive branch when she was offered one. Gerry had been the image of genial bonhomie at her exhibition opening, but had slumped afterward into brittle moodiness. Once, she would have done everything to jolly him out of it; now, she just let him be. But when he told her he'd made a booking at Circumflex, she'd been happily surprised. Under her slinky dress, she was wearing the Italian lingerie he'd bought her. Who knew what the night might bring?

The very first thing she saw once she'd heaved open Visser Kanaley's big metal front door was the article, clipped from the arts pages of that morning's national paper and pinned up smack in the middle of the vestibule noticeboard. She was a little surprised. Gerry hadn't rung her to comment; she didn't even know for sure, till then, that he'd read it. The interview, done on the phone, had been good: intelligent questions, which she felt she'd answered well. The paper had also sent a photographer to Studio Lulu, a guy with two impressive cameras who'd taken what seemed like hundreds of shots over two fastidious hours. She'd assumed they would be good, too, but on opening the paper this morning, she'd been chagrined to see that the photo they'd chosen was – well, terrible. Disappointing, but Susanna recognised that she had only herself to blame. The *Arts Week* people had given her full TV make-up, but left to her own devices for the newspaper shot, she hadn't bothered with more than her usual smear of lipstick. *And at my age, the camera is just not that forgiving.*

Ah, well. Susanna walked past the noticeboard, placing each foot carefully, wondering how on earth other women managed to walk gracefully in high heels. Marcus was waving to her from the fishbowl office at the far end of the huge space, and Gerry was standing there too, watching her advance. She tried to saunter, but without notable success.

'Susanna, my precious, *precious* girl,' said Marcus, putting down his empty beer and kissing her on both cheeks. 'Tell me, how does it feel to be a famous *artiste*?'

'Oh, I daresay I'll get used to it, eventually,' Susanna said with a giggle. She quite liked it when Marcus gushed.

'Oh, yes. Yes, yes, *yes*! And the opening was *fabulous*. Red stickers, did I not see *many* red stickers?'

'Some, as you know' she allowed, smiling. 'And a big thank you to you and John. I was so touched that you bought one of my little paintings.'

'But of *course* we did.'

'Cleansing ale, Suze?' asked Gerry over his shoulder, wrenching a stubbie of Coopers from its cardboard carry-pack. 'We were just having an end-of-week catch-up.'

'But now we're done,' said Marcus quickly. 'All catched up.'

Susanna waved the beer aside. 'No, thanks, not for me. I'll save it for the restaurant.' A quick scan of the empties suggested that this would be Gerry's third beer; she rather wished he'd waited to clink fizzing champagne flutes with her.

'Oh, the restaurant!' said Marcus, tapping her forearm. 'You've never been to Circumflex? You'll *love* it, believe me. And do *not* forget to have the lemon madeleines at the end – they are sublime. Proust would have wept.'

'I'll be sure and leave room,' Susanna promised, as a flash of intuition whispered that it was Marcus who was responsible for this occasion. He was the one who'd told Gerry he must take her somewhere special, who'd suggested the restaurant and even, possibly, made the booking. That's why he was hamming it up so much.

'I must go, before John starts calling me in a frenzy. Here's to your glamorous night.' Marcus kissed her again on both cheeks. 'Susanna, you look *gor*geous. You must wear heels, always!'

'Gorgeous,' Gerry murmured, and chuckled briefly.

'Bye-bye, Marcus,' said Susanna. 'Thank you!' They twinkled their fingers at each other as he left.

'You saw the clipping on the noticeboard?' Gerry asked her the minute they were alone.

'I did,' she said. 'Thanks for putting it up. I've already read it though.' He must know she would've read it. She looked at her watch. 'We should go soon.'

'Plenty of time. Oh, boy,' he said, taking another swig of his beer, 'as soon as we saw that photo we said, Susanna's gonna hate that.'

'The interview came out well,' she said, prickled.

'Not bad, but that photo. What a shocker!' Gerry shook his head. 'And in the national newspaper, too.'

'Lucky I looked good on national television, then, isn't it?' she returned tartly. 'Anyway, I'm not up for Miss Australia. At least, I didn't *think* I was.'

'Hey,' he said, opening his hands wide. 'No need to get upset about it. Just a shame, 'cause everyone looks at the pictures, they never read the text.'

'Gerry, could you not keep going on about that photo, please?'

'*Huh?* There was a photo. I mentioned it. One little photo – are you really that vain?'

'No,' she said. 'Actually, I'm not vain. I think it's *you* who'd be pissed off if you had a photo like that in the paper.' They stared at each other challengingly. 'How about we go and have dinner?' she said. 'I've been looking forward to it, you know.'

'Yeah, okay,' he agreed sulkily, taking one more swallow of beer and leaving the bottle on the table.

Susanna drove. They were both quiet, but once they got to the restaurant and had the attention of the staff, the glances of other patrons all curious to see who else had the taste and money to dine at Circumflex, Gerry's mood picked up. She asked him about his latest projects, in detail, feeding their conversation.

Not long after their main course arrived, Gerry asked her if the purchasers of her mother's unit had settled yet. Susanna's heart sank. *Oh no. Not now. But – I have to tell him.* She took a breath and screwed her courage to the sticking place. 'They have, yes,' she said. 'About a week ago, actually.'

He looked more puzzled than angry. 'You didn't tell me?'

She shook her head.

'So, why isn't the money in our account?'

'Because – I've opened a new account.' *This is terrible. I should have talked to him about this before, of course I should.* But she hadn't. She'd been too . . . scared. 'I thought I'd – because I – I haven't, ah, decided what to do with it.' She swallowed. 'The money.'

Gerry's face had gone very still. 'We've already decided what we're doing with it,' he said. 'We're extending the house, doing the renovations. Like we've always planned.'

'I don't want to extend the house,' she said. 'We don't need to, Gerry.'

'Is that so?' he asked in a low voice.

'Yes. The kids are growing up, they'll be wanting to move out on their own soon. Things are changing. I have my own studio now.'

'Things are changing, are they? What things, Susanna? Precisely?'

'My work,' Susanna said steadily, forcing her guilty feelings aside. They locked eyes. 'I want to paint, and use some of Mum's money to help me do that. It's my inheritance,' she finished defensively. She wished she'd done this differently, but it was too late now.

Gerry broke their gaze abruptly and didn't look at her for a good couple of minutes. He ate his meal with steely determination and then rested his cutlery deliberately on his plate. 'Get real, Susanna. You've had a lucky break with one show at a council gallery, and on the strength of that you think you can be a full-time artist?'

'Not full-time, I didn't say that.' Her heart was hammering. 'I'll keep working part-time at the college. But I *am* going to paint. I think that's what Mum would've wanted me to do with that money.'

'What complete and utter bullshit!' he exploded. At nearby tables, heads turned curiously. 'Your mother would have wanted you to treat that money as *ours*, and spend it on your family.'

She stared at her half-eaten meal, amazed that she had somehow managed to get this far through it, though she couldn't remember tasting a thing. 'No, I don't think that's true. I believe my mother wanted me to —' she swallowed hard '— to do what I'm going to do. Paint. Draw.'

Gerry's face was so hard with anger, he no longer looked handsome. 'I don't know what's happened to you,' he snarled, and pushed his plate away. 'You've turned into someone I don't know – some unreasonable, selfish bitch.' He pushed his chair back dramatically from the table and stood up. 'Call me when you've come to your senses.'

Susanna was still holding her cutlery. 'If you walk out of here now, Gerry,' she said quietly, 'I really don't know how we'll be able to put things back together.'

'Well, that's your problem, isn't it?' he said, and walked out.

It was like one part of her was watching another, or, rather, New Susanna, who was seated and still, was watching in her head a movie of what Old Susanna would have done. Old Susanna would never have let things come to such a pass, and if they had, she would have blamed herself for having so provoked her husband. Old Susanna, walked out on like this in a fancy restaurant, would have run after him, rent by guilt and humiliation, apologising, abject.

New Susanna did not.

Though her face was flaming, she calmly asked the waiter – who had not, bless him, hovered, but was there the moment she looked around for him – to clear both plates, and Gerry's place entirely. She asked him to bring her some tea, and also, if he would be so kind, some sheets of blank paper.

Once she'd finished the first sketch, she wrote *The Pirate Queen* in an unfurling banner at the top, and put that sheet aside.

On to the next. Stella-Jean: a multi-armed industrious goddess, with each hand busy making something different and clever and charming. And all around her, flowers, thick with bees collecting all the pollen. Golden pollen, powdering their little stripey legs.

A feeling rose deep inside Susanna, like a creature stirring, stretching: a quiet sensation, but thrillingly expansive.

Angie, as a pilgrim, a beautiful pilgrim with her cloak and her staff, setting out on the path. Susanna scrawled a note beside the drawing: *research pilgrim symbols/myths*. And on that path you can see rocks ahead, and a bridge, and a soft valley, and in the distance, mountains . . . Her road leads on further than the eye can see.

She remembered what Marcus had said about the lemon madeleines, and looked around again for the waiter. It was the first time she'd looked up since she started to draw. The madeleines were indeed delicious.

Her mother: whatever else was in Jean Greenfield's portrait, the background would be a page of shorthand, like giant faint calligraphy. Those few people who were able to read it would know that these were words of deep self-examination, and of forgiveness.

Seb: the sun would be in there. The red-gold sun of his lover's hair, the shining sun of his own sweet nature and delight.

And Gerry? Her – husband? Susanna smiled. A peacock, perhaps? Or one of his own works in progress: an interstice, awaiting connection.

Susanna paid the considerable bill with her own credit card. At some stage, she had kicked her high heels off under the table; now she took the ballet flats with their dear little silly bunny-tail pompoms from her bag, and slipped them on.

Alone, holding her new drawings in one hand, Susanna walked a course that just last year would have seemed impossible. A few diners watched her go; she smiled at them. Once, there had been a chasm facing her, and the person she might be on the other side of it was unimaginable. She had stepped from the brink, she was treading the ether; she was almost there. She could not quite see what awaited her, but it beckoned her on.

ACKNOWLEDGEMENTS

It's a privilege to acknowledge the unflagging support I have had from my agent, Fiona Inglis, and from the entire publishing team at Penguin, especially my esteemed editor Belinda Byrne, to whom Tigger owes his tinsel and I owe so much more.

In the US, I have had the backing and friendship of my agent Faye Bender, and editor Denise Roy at Plume.

Over the course of writing this novel, many knowledgeable people kindly answered my questions on subjects ranging from religious faith to shoulder dislocation. The fact that I subsequently played fast and loose with what they told me, subverting it for fictive purposes, is no reflection on the accuracy of their information. My grateful thanks to, among others: Michael Atkinson and Chris Kiral, Allie Buckner, Stuart Crichton, Marina Findlay, Ross Kennedy, Michio McMullen, Max Moon, Felix Pels, Susan Purdy, and the lively girls I met at Church by the Bridge.

First and last, from beginning to end, Phillip Frazer has been my sounding board and patient adviser, the steadying rock in the stream of my life. Thank you.

Also from Kate Veitch

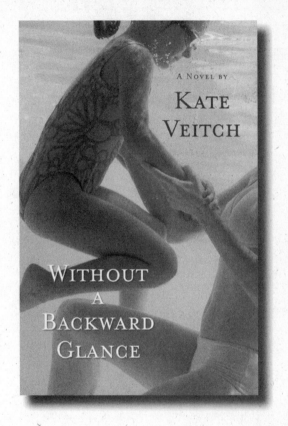

ISBN 978-0-452-28947-5

www.kateveitch.com

Available wherever books are sold.

Plume
A member of Penguin Group (USA) Inc.
www.penguin.com